"For pity's sake [illegible]

She did as he asked, [illegible] skirmish.

Pirates had nothing over women when it came to battle.

He tightened his arms around her and whispered in her ear. "Picture your intended. Picture his face. Can you see him in your mind?" He brushed his lips across her cheek, skimmed them softly over her mouth.

"Pretend these are his lips kissing you. Is this how he kissed you? You must be certain 'tis his face that you see." He touched his mouth to hers, soft, sweet.

A moan escaped her. Her eyelids fluttered.

"Shh, you must keep them closed. Picture Brett in your mind's eye. Do you see him?"

She whimpered.

"No?" Jack kept his voice neutral and smiled. Fiendish way to purge the man from her system. Deuced clever is what it was. His mouth moved over hers, conquering, devouring, burning his texture, his taste on her stubborn lips so his damned rival's name would never pass them again.

Praise for Jeri Black

Contests:
Historical Finalist "The Molly" Heart of Denver Romance Writers
Historical Honorable Mention "Put Your Heart in a Book" New Jersey Romance Writers
First Place Historical "Launching a Star" Space Coast Authors of Romance

The Dangers of Loving a Rogue

by

Jeri Black

This is a work of fiction. Names, characters, places, and incidents are either the product of the author's imagination or are used fictitiously, and any resemblance to actual persons living or dead, business establishments, events, or locales, is entirely coincidental.

The Dangers of Loving a Rogue

Contact Information: info@thewildrosepress.com

Cover Art by *The Wild Rose Press, Inc.*

The Wild Rose Press, Inc.
PO Box 708
Adams Basin, NY 14410-0708
Visit us at www.thewildrosepress.com

Publishing History
First Edition, 2022
Trade Paperback ISBN 978-1-5092-4632-8
Digital ISBN 978-1-5092-4633-5

Published in the United States of America

Dedication

For my husband, Delio. My love, my support, and my calm in every storm. I couldn't have done this without you. Thanks for letting me hash out my story problems even when you had no clue what I was talking about. And for being this book's biggest champion. You make all the difference in my worlds.

And to Mary Lou and Heather. My amazing critique partners and friends. I hit the lottery with you two.

Prologue

Falmouth, England
September 1751

Incessant screeching outside Celia Breckenridge's window proved to be a raucous squirrel and a strident crow, combatants for the same oak branch.

Ironically, the noise without, reflected the shambles within, where clothing, hats, cloaks, books, and other accoutrements for an extended trip populated every available surface of her bedchamber.

"Aye," she concluded. "'Tis all going to wreck." As her departure loomed, she became increasingly anxious. Papa grew grimmer by the day, Rianna resented being left behind, and Mama had taken to her bed, inconsolable that her eldest would soon leave her.

A crisp breeze rustled the brocade curtains, carrying the salty brine of the sea. She closed her eyes and took a bracing breath. "Don't stir coals, Celia," she chided herself.

Abandoning the window and the quarreling creatures, she faced the daunting task of packing. "God's bones, how shall I fit it all into two trunks?"

Four seasons of dresses took a prodigious amount of space. Indeed, the lot was stacked as high as her head, accompanied by stockings, slippers, chemises, and panniers. She kicked aside a stray shoe and spied her odious white gown.

"Mama's work, no doubt." Honestly, haircloth itched less. Intent on culling it from the herd, she yanked the white dress from beneath the others—using a bit too much force, it turned out, as the lot of them collapsed in her face.

She stumbled backward, tripped over her discarded shoe, and tumbled to the floor. An avalanche of dresses followed her down, after which shoes clomped to the carpet, and a tinkling of jewelry served as a finale.

All of it serenaded by a screeching bird and rodent.

"Bother." She blew a piece of lace from her mouth and sighed. Either the dress was the spawn of Satan or Providence was having her on. One seemed as likely as the other at present.

Minutes later, the door slammed against the wall and a short silence ensued—aside from the ill-tempered creatures outside.

"If this is an attempt to hide, 'tis an abysmal one. Mother will find you in a trice. Oh, look. What an adorable little squirrel."

Celia snorted. She should have known her sister would come running. 'Twas the curse of perceiving one another's thoughts and emotions. They could hide nothing from the other.

"Honestly, Celia. I *felt* you fall from the beach."

"Then you know I am perfectly fine."

"Nay, you are in a dither. Why are you still down there, you ninny?" The dresses shifted as Rianna waded in. "Come. I shall conquer your silks and save the day." Her face appeared above Celia's, wild spirals of blonde hair blown hither and yon. "Once I've rescued you from the marauding dress horde, you may help me repair my hair."

"Ha. Your true colors are shown to me now. 'Tisn't a knight come to my rescue, but a knave in want of my services." She shoved aside her clothing and Rianna hoisted her to her feet.

"You do know the clothes go *in* the trunk?"

"They preferred the floor." The sisters looked down at the mess. "Here." Celia thrust the vile white dress in Rianna's arms.

"What am I to do with it?"

"Burn it. Shred it. Cut it down to fit you. I care not. Just take it away."

Rianna blinked. *Aye, she sounded like a cuckoo.*

"Very well, I shall keep it. White does not favor your dark hair anywise." She held the gown against her. "Whereas I shall look quite fetching."

Celia rolled her eyes. Her fair-haired sister always looked fetching. Pity she had the temperament of a virago.

"Oh, I nearly forgot. You have a visitor."

"Bother." She hadn't the time or patience for guests. "Who is calling?"

"I do not know," Rianna confessed. "I was sneaking up the servant's stairs when Matthews spied me."

"I suppose I must go then." Celia waved at the dress horde. "I shall see to this later." She hurried down the curved staircase to dispense with her unwanted guest. Every delay seemed inordinately fraught, and she wondered whether her nerves or intuition were at play.

"*Don't* stir coals, Celia." She reached the parlor doors and halted abruptly, skirts still swaying as if her shock had created a breeze.

Before her stood Mr. Brett Kensington—her betrothed. Three days before she was set to embark. Three days with which to voice his objections to her father. Three days to deny her heart's desire.

"Brett." She threw herself into his arms and hugged him fiercely then pushed away to take him in. Tall and fit and impeccably dressed as always in an embroidered russet coat and waistcoat, his blond hair gleaming as brightly as his brass buttons. A sight to turn any maiden's head. She ought to be delighted to see him.

She was not. "What a lovely surprise."

"You are beautiful as ever, Celia." He took her hands in his gloved ones and squeezed, his pale blue gaze searching her face. "I am happy to see you, my dear, but Mother informs me I shall not have the pleasure for long?"

"Er, no. You shall not." Celia locked her knees together to starch up her crumbling spine. "I sail for Bermuda three days hence."

"Bermuda." He fell back a step as if her declaration had knocked him thus and shoved his fingers through his hair. "But…'tis so far." She had deliberately delayed writing to inform him, which was not well done of her at all. "Why such a risk does not bear consideration."

Bother. 'Twas exactly the reaction she'd feared. "I should like a walk," she said brightly and took his arm. "Would you accompany me, sir?"

Brett knew her nearly as well as Rianna and doubtless discerned her intent—to remove him before Mama appeared and cocked it up further. He searched her face and nodded.

Seaview sat high above the coastline, the stone

manor hidden from view of Falmouth Harbour by a rocky point, its granite cliffs having formed the paving stones they walked upon. Elm trees bordered the drive, their branches shading passersby as they strolled beneath their colorful leaves. Her intended remained silent, awaiting Celia's conversation. Any other time they would be chatting and laughing gaily, but in the moment her tongue felt awkward, her words difficult to form.

"Has your mother informed you of the circumstances prompting my voyage?"

"Nay, she simply said you are to leave soon, and I must make haste to see you. I gather you wish to visit your Aunt Margaret?"

"I did write you to explain," Celia informed him guiltily—and only just posted it. "Aunt Maggie is ill. A cancer. Her physician believes she has no more than a year left to live."

"I am sorry to hear it," Brett said gently, covering her hand where it rested on his arm. He knew Maggie of course. Their families had always been close. "She is very dear to you."

"So dear," Celia agreed. "Mama insists she must go to her, but Papa will not allow it. He fears she would not survive the voyage. Her *mal-de-mer*..." They both shuddered. For who could forget the disastrous rowboat incident some ten years past?

"I missed you, you know," Brett said after a moment. "Blackhurst is a grand estate and the villagers perfectly pleasant. But 'tis not Falmouth. 'Tis not home." He squeezed her hand. "My closest confidant is not there. Forsooth, I even missed your troublesome sister. No one ever quibbles with me. They are all too polite." His gaze cut to hers. "'Tis dreadfully dull."

"A dire situation indeed." Celia laughed. "I missed you as well," she said honestly. For how could she not? They'd seldom been apart growing up. Any lengthy separation felt an eternity. Which is how she knew he'd take the news of her voyage badly. "But you shall be earl someday. Of course, you must attend your uncle and learn the estates. And I must attend my aunt." She bumped his arm. "I have always wished to visit Bermuda, you know."

"I am aware." He grinned, calling forth memories of him teasing that a swashbuckler resided beneath her bonnets and skirts. "I distinctly recall a certain young miss hiding in her aunt's trunk. Alas, she was bitterly disappointed when the footman found her out."

Celia laughed. Not her finest moment to be sure, but a six-year-old's resources were limited. "If not for Mama's constitution, we should have sailed there ere now. And though the circumstances are dire, 'tis fortunate I am eager to take Mama's place."

"I comprehend your desire to do so Celia, but what of your safety? Is there no one there to see to your aunt?"

"Perhaps, but they are not family. How very awful that she should breathe her last without a loved one by her side." Indeed, it tore at her mother's heart.

Brett looked at her askance. "I find it hard to believe your father has sanctioned this."

"He can deny Celia nothing," Rianna said from behind them, hair restored, the wide pink bow of her bergère hat tied neatly under her chin. For now.

Brett stiffened at her sister's ill-timed arrival. The two were ever thrashing at one another like wind and rain. “Miss Rianna.” He bowed perfunctorily.

“Mr. Kensington.” She dipped a negligible curtsy. “Mama discovered you gone and sent me to accompany you,” she explained. “For propriety’s sake.” This was uttered with a healthy dose of irony as Rianna had proved a dismal student of the proprieties.

The three began walking again, Rianna trailing behind but close enough to hear their conversation. And comment when inspired.

“Papa has ensured my safety,” Celia informed her intended, her hands growing damp inside her blue kid gloves. “And I’m to have a companion, a Miss Crenshaw, who has indentured herself to a family there.”

“He’s hired an extra hand,” Rianna added. “A big, burly brute who’s to guard her like the Crown Jewels.”

“One man?” Brett rounded on Celia, his voice rising. “On a ship full of tars?”

“’Tis more than I should need,” Rianna opined.

“Captain Pierce assured Papa ’twas quite unnecessary,” Celia said, “but Papa insisted.”

“Unnecessary?” he spluttered, mouth falling open in shock. “To protect a woman?”

“Nay. ’Tis not what I meant.” Blast, she was mucking it up.

“Aye,” Rianna agreed with her sister’s silent appraisal and rolled her eyes. “Captain Pierce often takes passengers aboard the *Roundabout*,” she explained. “He’s assured us his crew is quite courteous. They sail for the West Indies but will stop in Bermuda to deliver Celia and Miss Crenshaw. And return for Celia next fall.”

Brett opened his mouth to speak, but Celia rushed

to add, "Papa has known Captain Pierce for years. He is much esteemed, else Papa would not allow me to sail with him. The 'guard' is excessive, and Captain Pierce told him so." She shrugged. "Papa would not relent."

Robert Breckenridge was a powerful man in commerce; a shrewd businessman, and well known to ship owners begging his custom. Although born the son of a blacksmith, he'd amassed a staggering fortune and managed to win the hand of an earl's daughter. He would stop at nothing to keep his wife and daughters safe. A fact Brett well knew.

They reached the road leading to town and retraced their steps up the lane.

"You do understand why I must go?" Celia implored him. She could not bear it if he tried to interfere. As her betrothed, he was well within his right to do so.

"I…Aye." He blew out a breath. "I cannot help but think I am partly to blame. We have never…that is, we're to marry someday. I had not given it a thought when I left for Blackhurst, but perhaps you have? Perhaps my neglect on the matter has prompted you to fly off to—"

"No." Celia put her hand on his arm, his tortured expression piercing her heart. Guilt stabbed at her anew. "No," she said again more gently. "'Tis naught to do with it, I promise. Faith, I'd not considered our nuptials either." *Or much at any rate.*

Aunt Maggie needed her, aye. But Celia needed Maggie too. She longed for an adventure outside her hum-drum existence. To be the leave-taker and not the one left behind. She and Brett had been close always, but the thought of marrying him without spreading her wings at least once…without one small taste of freedom… Her soul would surely wither and die.

"Daresay the two of you would have wed by now had you wished it," Rianna pointed out.

Her sister's comment startled them, and they shared a wide-eyed look before glancing away. Neither argued, for Rianna's words had merit. Their fathers had betrothed them on the occasion of Celia's birth when Brett was just three. As her seventeenth birthday had come and gone 'twas past time they saw to the matter of their nuptials—or so their mothers believed.

Brett cleared his throat, breaking the uncomfortable silence, and nodded to Rianna. "Who shall look after this termagant if not you?"

"Oh, Papa is sending me off as well. Apparently, I have much left to learn."

"Aye?" He lifted a brow, inviting Rianna to expound.

"Miss Amelia's School for the Edification of Young Ladies," Celia supplied and laughed at the cross-eyed face her sister made. "Papa paid Miss Amelia a king's ransom to take her back."

"Ah." Brett chuckled. "Then we shall both be the wiser upon your return."

"Lud, I hope not," Rianna grumbled. "I should hate to be as dull as you."

"How long do you stay?" Celia interrupted before the two could fill their sails. Odd that she'd been frightened to see Brett earlier but felt comforted by his presence now. Perhaps 'twas simply the familiar sound of he and Rianna harrying one another that set her at ease.

"A fortnight at most," he said. "I'm to join Uncle

Richard in London. He claims my mount is an embarrassment to the family and we must purchase a new one."

"Pity you," Rianna said dryly. "Daresay your horse shan't mind in the least."

He ignored her and turned Celia to face him, clasping her hands. "I shall speak with your father. You are so very precious to me, Celia. I would see you safe above all else."

Oh, she loved this man. She truly did.

Rianna looked away, her manner oddly subdued.

"You mustn't worry so." Celia threw her arms around him and hugged him tight. "When I return, we shall"—she swallowed—"we shall plan our nuptials."

Brett kissed her hands, her cheek, and her lips. "I shall hold you to your promise."

Chapter One

La Rochelle, France
July 1752

Boot heels striking the cobblestones disturbed the darkness. The stench of the waterfront beckoned, ensuring Jackson Beaumont's course would remain true. Such things were a constant, for no matter the port, they all smelled the same: salt and sea, rotting fish, and refuse. Heady stuff to a sailor, and a lure as potent as a woman's arms.

Light from a busy tavern spilled onto the narrow street. Drunken tars staggered in and out of the open doorway, their raucous shouts heralding an impending brawl. Jack quickened his pace. He'd no desire to engage the buffleheaded fools. But as he left the revelers behind, a faint groan reached his ears, barely audible over the din from the tavern. Wary, he scanned the area before squatting beside a rumpled form near the mouth of an alley. "Are ye well, mate?"

"The blighter stabbed me, 'e did. Got me in the back," the man croaked.

Jack inhaled sharply at the familiar voice and bent closer to peer at his face. "Travers?"

"Aye." He coughed. "Who be ye, sir?"

"'Tis Jack, of the *Bonny Lass*."

"Jack," the old voice trembled. "Saints be praised.

How come ye to be here?"

"A hold full of brandy. 'Tis a miracle I found ye, old man." He helped prop his former crewman to a sitting position. His groans of pain told Jack how much the effort cost him. As did the blood soaking his shirt. Rage lit his temper. "Who did this, Travers?"

"Bleedin' whoreson, Jean Pierre." Travers coughed and gasped, his voice threadbare and strained. "Son-of-a-gun was after me map."

"Map?" The fracas behind them swelled, reminding Jack the wharves were no place to linger. "I shan't leave you here alone, Travers. Have ye lodgings hereabouts?"

"Always thought I'd die at sea, with the wind in me face and a ship under me feet," Travers said mournfully. "Not in a stinkin' alley amid the filth and the rats." He clutched Jack's sleeve. "You'll not let the rats get me, will ye, Jack?"

Jack checked their surroundings, unease urging him to move. "The crew awaits my return to weigh anchor. Come old man, I'll take you out to sea."

A choked sound emerged, and the old tar's voice was thick with emotion. "Bless ye, boy."

Gently, so as not to cause further injury, Jack pulled him to his feet. Though only a short distance, the trek proved ponderous. They made frequent stops, the exertion causing Travers immeasurable pain. By the time they reached the ship, Jack was all but carrying him, and shaking with fury. Once aboard, he examined the wound and determined it was fatal.

The crew fashioned a pallet for their old shipmate on the foredeck, and Jack offered him a sip of water.

"Seamus?" Travers asked faintly. "Where be Cap'n

MacDonald, boy?"

"Seamus is gone," Jack said softly. It still pained him to speak of his loss. "Nigh on six years now. He left the *Lass* to me. I'm her captain now."

"Rest his soul." Travers' voice was thick with emotion. He would sail off this mortal coil shortly and join him. "Loved ye like a son, 'e did."

"Aye, he was a good man." Jack cleared his throat. "How shall I aid ye, Travers?"

"Me hat."

He smiled and flicked the man's cap with his finger. "'Tis restin' on yer nob, old man."

"Me hat," Travers repeated with effort. "Meant to search, but…war an' Spanish." He paused to cough, wheezing from the effort. "Bought it from a waterfront whore when me pockets was full—" Another cough. "—an' hers were let."

"Ye want the whore to have it?" Jack asked, confused.

"Nay," the tar croaked in alarm, grasping Jack's arm. "Me hat…must show ye…" His outburst cost him, and his hand flopped back to his chest. "You find."

"Aye, aye," Jack agreed to calm him. "I give ye my word. Rest yourself, old man. Look at the stars. Smell the sea. Taste the salt on your lips. 'Tis just like the old days, aye? When I was a lad learnin' the ropes from you crusty old tars."

The dying man's lips tipped up at Jack's words. He calmed and his labored breaths slowed. Jack kept a vigil until the old salt's soul ebbed from his body.

He crossed Travers' hands over his chest and lifted the cap from his head, peering inside. When he saw the extra panel stitched within, he smiled.

The first mate, John Smith, approached him. "Is he gone then, Cap'n?"

"Aye, Smitty."

"What have ye there?"

"His hat." After a few sharp tugs the panel ripped free, and a piece of wrinkled parchment fell out. Jack scanned the worn document's markings. "I'll be blowed."

"Aye?" Smitty peered over his arm.

Jack handed it over. "He said 'tis what Jean Pierre was after when he stabbed him."

"Filthy cur." Smitty spit over the railing. 'Twas hard to mention the Frenchman's name in any other fashion. "'Tis Spanish, the markings."

"Aye." Jack glanced over at his old shipmate. "He made me promise I'd look for it."

Smitty whistled through his teeth and passed the parchment back. "Heck Cap'n. Might have merit if the son-of-a-bitch killed 'im for it."

Jack refolded the page and tucked it inside his coat. "What say we find out?"

****

"I should not be here," Celia whispered in the darkness, voicing her unease with fatalistic clarity. She clutched the weathered railing and leaned out over the *Essex's* bulwark.

The prow of the ship cut through the shifting swells and forged ahead with alarming swiftness, bearing her inextricably away from the safety of Bermuda with every mile traversed.

"I should not be here," she repeated, her words snatched away by the strong summer gusts buffeting the ship. "Rianna." Though an ocean apart, her sister would sense her torment. "'Tis a mistake. I should not be here. Not now. Not *this* ship."

"Rings around the moon, disaster soon," a sailor singsonged to the helmsman, his mockery grating and unseemly given the portent swirling about them.

The helmsman shoved the fellow away and glanced uneasily at the night sky.

Celia's eyes slowly lifted, inexorably drawn by the gravity of the glowing orb. A pair of rings throbbed about the moon, haunting and pernicious in the black night.

The *Essex* bucked and pitched, spraying seawater in her face, the salt and tang invading her nose and mouth and clinging to her lashes. She choked and glanced wildly about, locking eyes with the helmsman. He flinched. Whatever he saw must have been alarming indeed, for he tore his gaze away and crossed himself. Celia nearly laughed at the absurdity but squelched the impulse as it would likely send the poor man diving over the rail to escape her. She looked a fright no doubt, especially to a superstitious sailor, with her dark hair blown loose from its pins and white face stark against the black of her mourning gown.

If only she had not been so impatient to leave. But Aunt Maggie was gone now and Rianna needed her, and it was months before Captain Pierce was due to collect her. Not even her impending marriage had deterred her from returning early. What would a few more months gain her? The outcome would still be the same.

Dark clouds slid across the ominous moon. Celia shivered. She could not explain this insidious presence, but it was tangible, like a separate being and it clung to her, suffocating, until she felt she could not breathe. Out there in the dark of night lurked evil—cloying, choking evil, and she cursed this comprehension, this *awareness* she and her sister were privy to, but which others were blissfully unaware.

She closed her eyes and breathed deep in an effort to gain control of her senses. A whiff of pungent tobacco assailed her nostrils. Her eyes popped open. Captain Abrams stood a short distance away, his lips clamped around the long, curved pipe cupped in his hand.

Lud, she was doomed.

When Mrs. Abrams learned she'd been alone on deck in the dead of night there'd be no end to the drubbing her ears would receive. The captain's wife sniffed out improprieties as relentlessly as a zealot descried sin. Celia could picture the woman's pinched lips and quivering chins as she delivered another scathing lecture on her unfortunate conduct. She'd been soundly chastised earlier in the day for speaking to a crewman. Such was the behavior of a harlot apparently, as the sailors inhabiting the ship were to be invisible to the women aboard.

The pall of Mrs. Abrams' disposition over the ship was as disquieting as this sense of foreboding that hovered like a specter in the night. She shot a furtive glance of apology to the captain for thinking uncharitable thoughts about his wife.

Unfortunately, he caught her look and strolled over to where she stood by the rail. His eyes scanned her face. Kind eyes, a soft brown framed with skin well weathered by wind, and sun, and sea. "Miss Breckenridge. How do ye fare this eve?"

Turn back! She screamed in her head. *Now. Please. Turn back!*

"I find myself a bit unsettled this evening, Captain," she managed and had to stifle the hysterical laughter threatening to erupt. Her grip tightened on the rail until her knuckles stood out like tiny white skulls.

"Aye, well, the start of a voyage is always the most difficult." He tapped his hand against his worn brown coat as if he'd stored a reservoir of knowledge there. Her heart gave a little squeeze. The gesture reminded her of her father, though Papa preferred to do his tapping against the arm of a chair. "Takes a bit to accustom oneself to the confines of a ship, doubly so in August when 'tis sweltering belowdecks."

"I imagine you are correct, sir." *Why could he not sense the danger?* It eddied all around.

Curse her for being the only one to know.

"Fresh air and a good long gander at the horizon will help." He held out his pipe. "Myself, I enjoy a nice smoke of the evening. I find it relaxes me."

Celia stared at the pipe with longing. "I don't suppose you'd care to share, Captain?"

Though his brows lowered, and his lips pursed, his eyes held a mischievous twinkle. "I felt certain ye'd met my wife, Miss Breckenridge. Buxom woman? About your height? Generous with her opinions? A rather, shall we say, stringent advocate of the proprieties."

How diplomatic of him. "Forgive me. I quite forgot myself."

"Quite," he agreed solemnly. "Fear not, I shall keep your secret."

"'Tis very kind of you, sir. Particularly since you

allowed me to sail with you."

"Aye, well, I confess 'tis happy I am to have ye aboard. After Mrs. Abrams' maid quit her post, I quite despaired. Now I've a companion to keep her occupied and out of my affairs." He chuckled. "Forsooth, madam, I came off with flying colors indeed. Ye paid for your passage."

Clearly, he would have paid *her* to suffer his wife's company. 'Twould require a staggering sum. Celia propped her elbow on the rail and rested her chin in the palm of her hand. "I fear I've missed an opportunity here, Captain. Perhaps we ought to negotiate a new contract."

He motioned with his pipe to the endless water surrounding them. "'Tis too late for it, miss. 'Twill have to serve as a lesson instead."

Too late. Celia felt those words more keenly than he would ever know.

"Duped," she lamented and did not need to feign the sorrow in her voice.

He chuckled again, unabashed, and nodded in farewell. "One makes the most of circumstance, Miss Breckenridge. I bid ye good evening."

Clouds continued to gather and blanket the night sky, the moon hidden behind a misty veil. Perhaps she'd overreacted. Likely her trepidation resulted from an understandable combination of guilt and nerves. She'd boarded a ship outside her father's protection. But her sister's despair had torn at Celia, and given her own grief, she could not bear to stay away any longer. Surely this was the source of her apprehension.

A drop of rain landed on her cheek then another. She took one last look at her surroundings and headed below.

****

Shouts of alarm startled Celia awake. Running feet pounded overhead. Her heart drummed out a warning before her eyes snapped open.

Boom! A loud crack rent the air.

She let out a frightened shriek and tumbled out of bed, dragging the bedding down with her. Outside her small porthole, a mast plunged into the sea. A tangle of sheets, braces, and fouled stays followed, the cables snapped free of their moorings.

Fear congealed in the pit of her stomach, leaching through her system like venom.

They were under attack!

Two more salvos thundered, one after the other. She scrambled to her feet and rummaged through her trunk just as another shot shook her.

An explosion belowdecks knocked her to her knees, causing the ship to shudder. Screams from injured men shot her to her feet again. She stood there, frozen, her mind unable to communicate with her limbs.

She had to think. *No.* She had to hide. But where? Where should she go? She thumped the sides of her head with her fists to urge a decision from it. The hold?

But what if the ship sank? Perhaps she ought to stay here in her cabin. Or the galley. The galley had knives. She'd never used one as a weapon. Still, survival might demand she try. Likely there'd be a barrel to hide in or—

Lud. Mrs. Abrams.

An image of the woman marching across the deck armed with a reticule or something equally threatening flashed in her mind. Celia chewed her lip.

Mrs. Abrams ought to have found *her* by now.

A hue went up. Feet scuffled in every direction. The clamor bolstered her limbs into action. She yanked on her clothes with violently shaking fingers then pressed her ear to the cabin door and opened it a crack to peer out. The din echoed eerily down the empty companionway: swords clanging, men shouting, the crack of a pistol shot.

Lord save her. A battle raged up there, and a short distance separated her from it all.

Celia poked her head out. Dust hovered in the air, accompanied by the acrid stench of spent gunpowder. Thin ribbons of smoke wafted down the narrow corridor. One slithered inside the cabin. She shrank away as though the thing might bite her and slammed the door closed. Tears, foreign and unwelcome, filled her eyes.

Why? Why hadn't she stayed in Bermuda? Last night. She'd known…she'd felt…she should have sensed the danger before she boarded. Or had she been too headstrong to notice? She raised her head and swiped at her eyes with her fingertips. She had to be strong.

And she had to find Mrs. Abrams.

Relief swamped her when she pulled the door open again and found the passage still empty. She located the captain's wife in her cabin, curled up on the bunk in her night-rail and sobbing hysterically. Celia bolted the door and rushed to the woman's side.

"Mrs. Abrams? Mrs. Abrams, are you hurt?"

"Pirates!" Mrs. Abrams shrieked. *"Bloodthirsty pirates! They shall kill us all!"* The sound of clashing steel punctuated her words.

"Dear God in heaven." Celia closed her eyes against the terror writ on the woman's face.

"Did you hear me?"

Her eyes blinked open. "What shall we do?"

"There's nothing to be done," the woman snapped and rose to her knees. Her graying hair hung about her shoulders in a tangle, her face pinched and splotched from crying. "You'd best pray Mr. Abrams routs those devils or we shall all die."

Celia's hand went to her breast, attempting to slow her racing heart by applying pressure. "Come, Mrs. Abrams." She grabbed the older woman's arm and tugged her from the bed. "We must get you clothed and hide."

She may as well have dressed a child for all the cooperation she received. Mrs. Abrams sat on a short bench while Celia pinned up her hair. Her splotched face and red eyes looked horrid against her copper gown, though the woman hardly cared for her appearance. She sat stiff and erect, lips pursed, gaze darting about the cabin like a felon looking for escape.

"'Tis all your fault," she burst out. "You've brought ill fortune to this ship. I don't know why my husband allowed you aboard."

Nasty old bird. "Daresay it had something to do with your lack of a companion."

"Hmph." The woman's lips pursed.

Beyond the window, smoke rolled across the water, allowing only wan light to filter through. How bizarre to be engaged in something so trivial as dressing hair while above their heads, sailors hacked one another to death. Celia plopped a mobcap over Mrs. Abrams' head.

The sounds of the swordfight came to an abrupt end. Only the hoarse moans of the wounded still carried to their ears. The two women shared an uneasy glance and fixed their attention on the cabin door. A familiar sense of foreboding filled the room. Celia's stomach roiled and her heart squeezed in fresh spasms of panic.

Mrs. Abrams felt it as well, for she latched onto Celia's arms and held her before her. "You must protect me," she hissed. "You are my companion. 'Tis your duty to protect me."

Celia struggled to pull free, but the woman's hands gripped her like a pair of shackles. Her patience fast reached its limits. "Mrs. Abrams, please. Get hold of yourself. You must let me go. We must hide ourselves immediately."

Pounding footsteps reached them from the companionway then stopped abruptly. Fists hammered against the portal. Celia's heart leapt into her mouth. She stopped struggling, her attention riveted to the door.

"Open up."

Neither woman uttered a sound.

The blows became more insistent. The door shuddered under the assault until the latch gave way and four brigands crashed into the cabin, swords drawn and ready. Mrs. Abrams shrieked and shoved Celia into the lead pirate. She slammed into him with a loud *oomph,* passing just a hairsbreadth from the tip of his blade.

The surprised man caught her against him with his free arm.

"Take her," Mrs. Abrams screamed. "Take that sluttish girl and go. Leave me be. Leave, I say."

Celia flinched at the woman's cruel words. A whimper choked past the tears clogging her throat. *"No..."*

The pirate, a dark-bearded scraggly cur, dressed in black, with a patch over one eye, peered down at her with a sickening one-sided smirk. "Aye, I'll be takin' 'er.

Her hand rose to cover her mouth.

His cohorts—one bald and one absurdly hairy—laughed from their position inside the doorway.

The bald one licked his lips. "Give 'er over, Jenkins. I'll have me a piece o' that."

"What are you swine doing?" A short, angry man wearing a brilliant azure coat shoved into the room, his words heavily accented in French. "Jenkins, release the wench."

Jenkins motioned to Mrs. Abrams. "The hag gave 'er to me, Cap'n."

"No," Celia burst out. "That is, she did not mean to. She...she is unwell. Otherwise, she would not have—"

"*Imbecile,"* the pirate captain raged, ignoring her. "I am surrounded by *imbeciles.* First you idiots destroy this ship then you shirk your duties." He stepped forward and yanked Celia away. "This piece is mine."

Hairy's face turned red—at least the parts not covered with hair. "That shot in the hull were an accident, Cap'n."

"Yours?" Jenkins bellowed at the same time. "We found 'er first."

The pirate captain's free hand shot out. A knife materialized in front of Jenkins' face. Celia ceased trying to break the Frenchman's hold and stared at the thing in shock. He pushed the tip of the blade beneath Jenkins' chin. The white of his lone eye doubled in size.

"I am the *capitaine*. You sail on *my* ship. Therefore, the *mademoiselle* belongs to me." The captain jerked his head toward Mrs. Abrams. "Take the crone. See if you can share her without killing her."

Neither man moved for several heartbeats. Jenkins finally broke the tension by taking a cautious step away from his captain's blade. With as wide a berth as possible in such close quarters, he approached Mrs. Abrams at the stern gallery.

Hairy and Baldy followed. The back of Baldy's head sported a skull and crossbones tattoo. At its base, a bright, pink ribbon tied off a narrow strip of braided hair, a garish counterpoint to his rough sailor's garb and bare feet.

"Stay away from me," Mrs. Abrams shrieked. "Stay away, I say." She shoved Jenkins into his fellows and ran out the door.

The pirates gave chase.

"Dear God, no." Celia turned to the Frenchman in horror. "You cannot let them hurt her."

"It is refreshing when they get along with one another, is it not?"

She stared at his soulless black eyes in horrid fascination—little pits of evil that surely led to perdition. He brushed a finger against her cheek.

"You are very beautiful, *ma petite*. We shall enjoy our time together."

She flinched and jerked away from his touch.

His eyes flared. "*Bon. Mademoiselle* possesses *l'esprit*. We French, we enjoy the sport, eh?" He swatted her behind. "Come along, *Mam'selle*. We must become better acquainted. You may call me Jean Pierre." He clamped a hand around her elbow and dragged her from the cabin. "Tell me what you are called."

Chapter Two

The carnage topside was beyond anything Celia could have imagined. None of the sailors from the *Essex* remained standing. To a man they'd all been cut down.

Mrs. Abrams knelt beside her torn and bloody husband whose sightless eyes stared beyond her to the heavens. Tears choked Celia's throat. She looked away. But her gaze only found more blood. More death. Or men crying for death. She felt her knees weaken, certain she would succumb with the others, the atrocity beyond what she could bear.

A thick, gray fog hovered around them—specters rising to claim the victims.

"Josiah. Curse you, Josiah, wake up." Mrs. Abrams shook her husband's body, determined to rouse him. "Do not leave me. Don't you dare leave me to these devils."

Her shrieks amused the pirates. Their vulgar laughter scraped across Celia's neck and shoulders like a twig studded with thorns. She tried to step forward, intent on bearing the woman away, but Jean Pierre held her fast.

"Do not concern yourself, *Mam'selle*. My men will see to her." She turned incredulous eyes on him. The villain laughed and swatted her bottom again. "And I shall see to you."

He put his fingers to his lips and let out a piercing whistle. "We have work to do *mes amis*. Transfer the women to the *Mirabelle*. You shall have the crone once this ship is sacked."

En masse, the pirates started toward Mrs. Abrams, forming a half circle as they approached. Rising slowly, her wary gaze flitted about as she backed against the bulwark. She wrapped her hand in the ratline and placed her foot next to a belaying pin, climbing to stand atop the rail.

The pirates snickered and elbowed one another, enjoying her futile attempt to escape.

"What are you idiots doing?" their captain shouted. "Get her down before she climbs the rigging."

Mrs. Abrams' head came up, and she looked to where Celia stood pinned to Jean Pierre's side, face blank, eyes empty, as though she'd already sent her soul to join her husband's.

"No." Celia's voice rose with her panic. "No, Mrs. Abrams, please. I beg you. Do not go. Oh, *please*, do not leave me."

Her entreaty galvanized the brigands forward, but they were too late. Mrs. Abrams disappeared over the side of the ship.

The faint sound of a splash marked her passing.

****

A shout roused Celia from her stupor. Her neck screamed in protest as she lifted her head.

The empty horizon stretched before her. An interminable desert of sea and sky.

Blue. Wretched, endless blue.

Her head lolled back against the main mast of the *Mirabelle*. Halfway to its zenith, the August sun climbed ever higher into the piercing blue void, a blazing ball of vicious fire searing her skin like a haunch of meat on a spit.

Trickles of sweat made the slow journey down the length of her spine. Though wisps of hair clung to her moist cheeks, her lips were dry, her mouth gritty and parched. Ironic really, to be so wet on the outside and arid within; her body slowly leaking out.

Small fires burned throughout the sinking *Essex*. Flaming debris littered the sea and floated about the two ships. The light westerly winds blew a majority of the smoke away. She glanced down at her tattered black gown and fiery red skin, thinking she might well begin smoldering herself.

Her gaze rose to her captors. Jean Pierre and a handful of his cutthroats took a reckoning of their plunder. Shares had to be split straightaway apparently, as there was not a man to be trusted among them. They salvaged anything that might bring a price, which included everything by Celia's estimation. Even their trunks of clothing had been transferred aboard.

A tug at her bindings caused the tight leather cords to bite into her wrists, which was when she realized she could no longer feel her hands. She wiggled her fingers. Tiny pinpricks stabbed clear to her elbows, a thousand little knives attacking her flesh. An agonized croak escaped. She clamped her lips together, fearful of attracting attention.

Jenkins sauntered over, still wearing his smirk. At his shoulder hovered a grim-faced corsair, his light blue shirt and striped, gray breeches spattered with blood. God above. She'd stepped through the pages of Robinson Crusoe. Only these men were horribly real.

Tendrils of icy cold fear slithered beneath the sweat soaking her torn gown, chilling her to the bone despite the wretched heat. Tears slid unbidden down her face to pool at her chin.

"What ails ye, ducks? Never beheld a one-eyed man before?" The pirate lifted his patch with the hilt of his sword, revealing a puckered seam of scarred red flesh. She willed herself not to flinch and averted her gaze. "We drew straws." Jenkins pointed a thumb at his cohorts. "I gets me share o' ye first once't Jean Pierre's had his."

Heart squeezing out fresh spasms of panic, Celia's teeth clenched against the roiling in her stomach.

"Haw," he chortled. "She thinks me a handsome devil, mates."

His fellows laughed.

The corsair remained impassive.

The pirate captain shoved through his men and yanked a fistful of her hair. "Do not touch her, swine." She caught a whiff of the man and gagged, the unbearable stench wafting from his brilliant coat an affront to its beautiful silver stitching.

"Only got one wench now." Jenkins reminded him. "Ye're obliged ta share."

Jean Pierre jerked his head toward the *Essex*. "You should not have let the crone jump."

Scrawled into Celia's brain like the markings on a tombstone were the images of tortured faces and mangled bodies. The noisome odors of sweat and blood and God only knew what else. Agonized moans and Mrs. Abrams' screams. She closed her eyes and said a prayer for the dead. And then she said a prayer for herself.

A low growl came from the corsair, much like a dog with its hackles raised. He shot her a malevolent glare and stormed off, the others following.

Jean Pierre brushed up against her and pinched her breast. She winced and clamped her lips together, his rank attentions sorely testing the limits of her blessedly empty stomach.

The Frenchman laughed uproariously at her revulsion.

As if his malodorous body were not enough of a strain, the fetid stench of his breath was nearly her stomach's undoing. She turned her face aside and coughed. He blinked and lifted his arm to take a suspicious sniff. His shoulders lifted in a Gallic shrug.

"Eh, you will get used to it." He headed for the companionway, yelling as he went. "Get to work. You three, follow me."

Celia's breath whooshed out, and she slumped against the mast in relief.

The remaining brigands split their time between taunting their captive and addressing themselves to the rum barrel. The more they drank, the worse their temperaments, and the rougher the manhandling—leering and groping until her clothing ripped—every inch of her skin had been abused. They staggered about, slurring their speech, and arguing over anything and nothing.

Perhaps they'd drink themselves to death.

A rumble of thunder rent the air then another and another. Relief washed over her. Sweet, merciful rain. She waited eagerly for the drops to—

The ship came in sight just as the rounds she'd fired blasted into the *Mirabelle.*

Shives of wood and metal flew into the air. Celia dropped her chin and closed her eyes against the cloud of debris raining over the deck. Dust flew into her nose. She sneezed and coughed and tried to hold her breath until it settled. Around her, men screamed, some in agony, others in alarm, as the ship erupted into chaos. She struggled violently against her tether. Shards of pain speared up her arms, but her swollen wrists refused to shift in the tight lacings.

Another broadside sailed across the distance. Her panicked gaze trained on the smoke coughing out of the ship's cannons. The round hit forward. Sails plummeted to the deck. Then one hit somewhere behind. More debris flew, and a fragment glanced off her elbow. She squeezed her eyes shut, unable to watch her own demise. A loud blast shook the deck beneath her feet, causing the *Mirabelle* to buck from the explosion. The familiar scent of burning gunpowder rose from the gun deck below. Her eyes flew open and slammed shut again as another cloud swirled into the air, searing her lungs.

A fit of violent coughing seized her. Hairy staggered past, screaming in agony at the bloody stump where his arm had been. One side of his face was blackened from shot, the other torn open and bleeding.

Bile burned a path to Celia's mouth. Her teeth clenched and frantic breaths panted through her nostrils. Frightened whimpers clawed their way up a throat as raw and tattered as her gown, until she realized the guns had ceased firing. As soon as the thought formed, metal grappling hooks struck the rail.

Her head pivoted slowly, cautiously, dreading what she would see. She gaped at a dozen men or more, all armed to the teeth, swinging onto the deck of the *Mirabelle*. Fear congealed in the pit of her stomach and leached through her system like venom.

Death or salvation had arrived.

A large—very large—and fierce looking man rushed toward her, sword in hand, his high black boots crunching over scattered debris. The loose sleeves of his white shirt billowed as he ran. An aura of danger surrounded him. The power of a warrior. His eyes looked everywhere but at Celia, which might have eased her trepidation somewhat had he not been bearing down upon her with alarming haste. Terror skittered down her spine as she imagined sharing the same fate as the crew of the *Essex*.

Why? Why hadn't she stayed in Bermuda?

The warrior's sharp eyes gave her a cursory inspection when he reached her. His chestnut hair was pulled back in a queue, the sharp bones of his swarthy face harsh and unforgiving.

"I shall cut you loose," he informed her, his voice deep and gruff. "Head for the companionway and hide until we have the ship secured." He stepped behind her and sliced the bindings away then moved between her and a pair of combatants.

Celia let out a choked whimper. Pain, raw and agonizing, tore through her hands as blood poured into them. Her legs melted beneath her, and she slid down the mast, landing on her bottom with a thud.

Her rescuer turned back, a scowl darkening his features. She sat with her elbows in her lap, hands held aloft while the excruciating circulation returned.

The man shrugged. "I haven't time for cajolery, Miss." He pulled a pistol from his belt. "Use this if there comes a need but have a care. 'Tis primed and ready, you'll note." He thrust the pistol into her swollen hand and pivoted to fend off a threatening blade.

The weight of the thing felled her arm and slammed her knuckles against the hard planks of the deck. The weapon jumped and discharged.

A man screamed.

Celia stared down at her useless hand in horror. Her eyes rose to find the pirate, Jenkins, jumping up and down on one foot while blood poured from the leg he held aloft.

An imprudent leap brought his foot down onto the narrow ledge of the open hatchway. A surprised squawk choked off his incessant howling as his sword sailed skyward and clattered to the deck. Arms flailing, he teetered back and forth until he managed to right himself.

Rage lit his un-patched eye when he noted the pistol in Celia's limp grasp. His hands rose as if he meant to wrap them around her throat and he took a few menacing hops toward her.

No! She kicked out to protect herself and caught his ankle.

The pirate's eye widened in panic. He lunged forward then reared back sharply to keep from falling over—which set him to hopping again. Celia watched in breath-held suspense as he neared the open hatch behind him then hobbled about just in time. He teetered back a few paces and his injured leg came down, eliciting a vile curse, but it helped him regain his balance.

Until another man tripped over his fallen sword and butted into him. With a shriek that could set a pack of wolves howling, Jenkins disappeared head-first into the hatch.

His opponent—a thin, leathery man with dull brown clothes and hair—stood rooted across the deck, his eyes locked on Celia and the spent pistol lying atop her useless hand. The man's jaw worked up and down. A reaction to her unfortunate marksmanship apparently.

The culprit who'd handed her the pistol came up beside her, his attention fixed on the open hatch. She glared up at him accusingly.

He blinked as though she'd pricked him and raised a brow. "Jenkins did not make a favorable impression, I take it? *Tsk*, madam. You frightened my man, Smitty, nigh to death."

She sniffed. Weapons aplenty were being brandished all over the ship. Why on earth had *she* caused such a stir? Of course, Papa always said the only thing more frightening than a pistol was a woman holding one. For the first time in her life, she felt the insult despite its veracity.

The man called Smitty had recovered sufficiently to engage the pirate, Baldy, whose braid now sported an entire row of colorful ribbons. Two of them belonged to her.

A bright spot of blue caught Celia's attention. Her stomach clenched reflexively.

Jean Pierre.

For a wild moment, she considered diving through the hatch—if only Jenkins were not there. She pressed her back more firmly against the mast and glanced about for a place to hide.

Crossing the deck with short, angry strides, Jean Pierre let out a bellow of rage when he noticed who stood next to her. Clearly this man inspired great emotion.

His amusement disappeared, and she saw again the fierce warrior who had breached the ship. While his stance remained relaxed, sword-arm held loose, tension rumbled off him like thunder at the edge of a storm. Only a fool would not feel threatened, and likely lose a limb if they came too close. Celia yanked her felled arm back, depositing the spent pistol onto the deck with a clank. Tucking her elbows to her waist, she drew her knees up in an effort to make herself as small and unobtrusive as possible until she could sneak away.

Jean Pierre came abreast of the hatch and paused. "Idiot," he shouted down to Jenkins and kicked the hatch cover closed.

The large man moved to stand in front of her, sword raised, legs braced apart. "Stay out of harm's way," he said over his shoulder. "Scream if there comes a need."

Scream? Dear God, she would have begun ages ago if she'd been able. Her throat was coated in dust and likely studded with splinters. She could not swallow, but perhaps 'twas a blessing.

The pirate leader paused a few feet away and genuflected, one hand resting negligently on his hip. He waved his sword in a gesture of welcome.

"*Capitaine Jacques*, what brings you to my 'umble abode?"

Jacques? Celia mouthed in surprise. Her eyes scanned the mountainous terrain of the man before her. He did not sound French—or look it either, if the vulgar pirate captain were any gauge.

"Johnny," Jacques greeted jovially. He gestured to

the burning debris surrounding them. "We saw the smoke and discovered you bilge-rats hovering nearby."

Celia grinned in spite of her predicament. *Bilge-rats* indeed.

Jean Pierre's lips twisted in a sneer. "Really, *Capitaine*, I think you stick your stinking English nose where it does not belong."

Stinking? Rather the pot calling the kettle black as she was an authority on the subject.

"'Tis been awhile since I've seen such destruction." Jacques pointed a thumb toward the *Essex*. "Nigh on three years. Port Royal, if memory serves. You were in the vicinity then, too."

The pirate shrugged. He and Jacques began to circle one another. "I confess I do not recall such an incident."

"Oh, now that is a surprise," Jacques' tone mocked. "To hear the word 'confess' cross your lips, Johnny." This amused the pirate captain. His face split into a broad smile.

Celia shuddered.

"Perhaps you'd care to unbosom yourself further," Jacques suggested. "Shall we discuss *La Rochelle?*"

"Ah. *Monsieur* Travers. He was a fellow shipmate, *oui*?"

"Was?" Jacques repeated. If words could turn lethal, this man's surely had. "An interesting choice of words, Johnny."

Jean Pierre shrugged. "I am, how do you say? Perceptive."

Aye, so was Celia. Fat lot of good it had done her.

The pirate took a stab at Jacque's shoulder with his sword.

Jacques smiled and batted it away. "A murdering bastard is what I would say."

The pirate captain *tsked*. "*Capitaine*, is this any way to speak? Travers, he had a choice, *n'est-ce pas*? Unfortunately, he chose to die."

Rage flashed in Jacques' eyes, though his tone remained light and conversational. "Ah, but not before he gave me what you sought, Johnny. A rather poetic revenge, wouldn't you say? Now here we are, and once again I find myself prepared to take what you tried to steal."

"Steal—?"

Celia could not make out the pirate's reply, they had moved too far away, but through the melee she heard Jacques' bark of laughter. Moments later they came near again, swords thrusting, bodies shifting in advance or retreat, a lethal dance that belied their jovial banter.

"I am a salvager," her captor said. "I find a wreck, and I profit from another's misfortune."

A loud snort escaped Celia. "Murdering bastard" was the more accurate depiction. Her eyes rose and caught Jacques' swift glance.

"For a thief, you are a terrible liar, Johnny."

"Ha, *Capitaine*, you wish to—"

A pair of feet shuffled close, startling Celia. Fighting surrounded her—swords hacked, knives slashed, a belaying pin wielded with deadly intent. She watched it all, a spectator caught in the midst of a battle—as though she'd taken a wrong turn inside the Colosseum and stumbled into the arena with the lions by mistake.

She scrambled to her knees, intent on crawling to

the capstan—the wheel-like structure would offer at least some protection if she huddled beneath it—but plopped back down, her momentum halted by a booted foot pinning her skirts to the deck. Her gaze trailed up the boot and mud-brown breeches. Jacques' back was pressed against the mast above her head, his sword locked in a test of strength with Jean Pierre's. The swords quivered dangerously, and for a moment she could not breathe, her lungs unable to cope with the sudden surge from her heart. Before panic completely owned her, Jacques turned the pirate's blade aside. He forced the brigand back and away from where she crouched.

The Frenchman made a sudden lunge. Jacques twisted sideways, the sword-tip just missing his ribs. The daft man smiled at his attacker, clearly enjoying himself.

"Have a care, Jean Pierre. This is my favorite shirt."

Jean Pierre smirked at the jest and saluted his opponent with his sword.

Celia felt sick.

Jacques began an aggressive assault, answering each of the pirate captain's responses with driving thrusts while he cheerfully baited the man.

"I must say your gunnery is sorely lacking."

"You wish me to compliment your gunners, *Capitaine*?" Jean Pierre waved an arm to indicate their surroundings. "They did very little damage to my ship." He wiped the sweat on his forehead with the sleeve of his coat.

Jacques glanced over his shoulder and waggled his brows at Celia. He gave the impression of a cat toying with a mouse. “Because I intend to take the *Mirabelle* as my prize. Rest assured, my men hit their marks with amazing accuracy.”

Jean Pierre’s nostrils flared and his eyes blazed fury. “I will kill you first, *Mon Amie*.”

The hatred in the man’s eyes stirred visions of the bloodshed on the *Essex*. Fear mauled Celia’s stomach. Jacques would do well to heed the pirate’s words. Winded or not, he was evil.

“You shall have to expend some effort then.” Jacques snorted. “These puny attempts will never do.”

A howl drew Celia’s attention to a tall man holding a sword to Hairy’s throat, forcing him backward over the rail. The pirate’s head disappeared from view then his feet followed his high-pitched squeals over the side.

She turned back to find Jean Pierre clutching the hilt of his sword with both hands, raising it high. He let out a bellow of rage as he swung the blade in an arc toward Jacques’ head.

Jacques dropped to his haunches. The swinging blade sliced through the air above him and he sprang forward, the force of his big body propelling his weapon up and into Jean Pierre’s thigh. Fluidly, as if performing some fencer’s ballet, he dropped back and pulled his sword free, bouncing on the balls of his feet.

Jean Pierre shrieked. Blood poured from the wound and down the leg of his breeches. Jacques raised his arm, circling his sword above his head, taunting the pirate captain with his own move. The pirate’s rapt attention followed the blade’s revolutions. Jacques’ arm hesitated. Jean Pierre let out a short scream and raised his arm in front of his face.

The sword came down.

Celia wrenched her gaze away. A clatter and a low thud followed.

Cautiously, she turned back, nearly swooning with relief at sight of Jean Pierre's motionless body. Jacques wiped his blade on the back of the dead man's coat. She felt compelled to congratulate him on his victory, which struck her as entirely inappropriate.

His gaze rose up the mast and down to where she sat against it. He tilted his head to the side as though puzzled she'd stayed precisely where she'd been tethered. Celia fought an eye roll.

Three long strides brought him to her, and she started, preferring distance to his towering presence. He sheathed his sword and knelt on one knee, which was hardly better as he was now far too close. She focused her attention over his shoulder, thinking to impose distance by avoiding his eyes.

And saw the corsair sneaking up behind him, scimitar poised to strike. She opened her mouth to scream, but a pitiful whimper was all that emerged.

It was enough.

Jacques snatched up the pistol he'd given her. *"Damn."*

She'd used the shot on Jenkins.

He spun about on his knee just as the corsair's sword arm began a trajectory downward and threw the pistol, catching the turbaned pirate between the eyes. She flinched at the loud *thwack* the weapon made when it connected with his face. He stumbled back and clapped a hand to his forehead.

Jacques surged to his feet and drew his sword.

The corsair's obsidian eyes flashed with hatred. The deadly scimitar rose once again. He let out a growl and advanced, his feral gaze flitting between Jacques and the deck behind him where she crouched. Jacques made a shooing motion at her behind his back.

A shot rang out.

The brigand's body jerked. Surprise lit his features as a crimson stain bloomed across the front of his shirt. His gazed dropped to his chest then back to Jacques as the echo from the shot faded away. Eyes rolling back in his head he crumpled, landing alongside Jean Pierre's body.

Behind the pirate, the sailor Jenkins had fought lowered his pistol.

"Smitty." Jacques sheathed his sword. "My good man. Excellent shot."

Smitty dipped his chin. "'T'weren't nothin' Cap'n."

Jacques turned to Celia and bowed. "Allow me to introduce myself, madam. Captain Jackson Beaumont of the *Bonny Lass* at your service."

Chapter Three

Ohhhh. Jackson. Celia felt ridiculously pleased. Jackson sounded ever so much better than Jacques.

She looked the man over. He really was enormous: tall, broad shouldered, deep chested. The breeze plastered his shirtsleeves against his muscular arms and ruffled loose strands of chestnut hair about his face. He was the most commanding figure she'd ever seen—and the most dangerous—though one would never know by gazing upon his face. His gray eyes were shot with twinkling sparks of silver, and he seemed ever amused. Likely he'd been born laughing.

It occurred to her then that his amusement stemmed from the fact that she'd baldly stared at him for several moments while he waited for her to introduce herself. But my, what a spectacular figure this Jackson Beaumont made.

His arm swept out, gesturing to their surroundings. "Rather odd circumstances in which to meet a lady, but we shall have to muddle through."

For heaven's sake, he behaved as though they'd just been introduced at tea. Next, he'd take a pinch of snuff and comment on the weather. He watched her closely and she knew he expected her to speak, but her throat was swollen and parched. One would think her pitiful attempt at a scream would have indicated a difficulty. She raised her hand to her throat, attempting to communicate the problem.

He raised a brow and his lips quirked. “Forgive me. ’Tis obvious my attempt to set you at ease has failed.”

And then he smiled.

Not one of those swift quirks of the lips she’d seen before. *Oh, no*. This was a full smile, with wide lips and white teeth, and eyes gone crinkly at the corners. Her entire being stirred and preened and fluttered helplessly beneath it.

Lud, a man could kill a woman with a smile like that. What on earth was it doing on a swarthy sea captain? Her gaze swept him from head to toe again. Dangerous he may be, but also, without question, the handsomest man she’d ever laid eyes upon.

An exaggerated sigh gusted from his lips. “What can one expect from a humble sailor who spends his days on a ship full of tars? Clearly, I am out of practice.”

Mm-hmm. Like as not the man “practiced” in every port he visited. And struck fear in the hearts of men unfortunate enough to displease him. Dangerous yes, and possibly daft. And really, even if she were able to speak, what on earth would she say to the handsome devil?

My, this stretch of ocean is rather congested this time of year, is it not?

He offered her a hand. “May I help you to rise?”

Celia frowned and shook her head. In no wise would she risk this giant touching her swollen hand. He might well rip it off.

Captain Beaumont sighed, feigning—she assumed—disappointment.

“Very well. I must attend to the business at hand.”

He gestured behind him to the skirmish still in progress, though most of the pirates had laid down their swords. “Fear not. I shall remove you to my ship. You will be safer there.” He pointed a thumb over his shoulder at the vessel tethered to the *Mirabelle* with grappling hooks.

“Spinnakers!” She cringed at the sheer volume the man produced. “Come over here, man, and see to the wen—” He winced and dropped his head. “Forgive me,” he said to Celia. “—lady. Take her to the *Lass*, and for pity’s sake, put her in the shade.”

With a short bow he took his leave, barking orders and disarming pirates as he went.

The man who’d dispensed with Hairy came running. He was as tall as his captain, but at least a score of years older and pole-thin, his long beard streaked with gray. Deep crevices carved his leathery cheeks. He spoke not a word. Just grabbed her arm, jerked her up, and tossed her over his shoulder. Her stomach slammed against his bony frame and the air whooshed out of her.

By the time she managed to catch her breath, he’d swung her over to the *Bonny Lass* via a dangling cable and dumped her onto a pile of cording near the helm. Thus relocated, he tugged a forelock in farewell and hurried back to the *Mirabelle*.

Celia slumped in her makeshift seat and gazed about the empty ship; her mind almost as vacant. The pungent stench of spent gunpowder hovered in the air here as well. Streamers of smoke drifted past. So much destruction. So much senseless death.

With her next breath she felt Rianna’s presence, as strong as if their hands were clasped together. Her heart lightened. The feeling lasted but a moment before reality clamped her breast once again. She was a woman alone on a ship full of dangerous men, her fate as yet undecided. Would Jackson Beaumont be her ruin or her savior?

Beyond weary, she closed her eyes and allowed her senses a short respite while the noise and confusion from the *Mirabelle* echoed in her ears.

****

Temporary repairs were made to the *Mirabelle*'s bowsprit and rigging. The dead consigned to the deep; decks swabbed; blood and filth washed away; supplies partitioned between the two ships. Fresh water replaced the rum barrel aboard the *Mirabelle*.

Celia listened to the captain's booming voice carry across the breeze. Beaumont divided his crew. Half would sail on the *Mirabelle*, half on the *Bonny Lass*. He split the pirates up as well. A wise move, for surely the brigands would be less trouble with their numbers reduced.

"Keep the knaves busy and out of mischief," he told his men. "They'll take your duties while you stand watch. Do not trust the dogs for any reason. Remain vigilant. Aye?"

"Aye!" His crew sounded only too happy to trade their roles as sailors for those of guards.

Men filed over to the *Bonny Lass,* preparing to weigh anchor. Like a flower attracting determined bees, the sailors swarmed around her, their buzz of conversation low and indistinct though no less threatening. She sat completely still, fearful of inciting the swarm, while her eyes darted about, seeking escape. Conversation around her ceased abruptly.

The captain had arrived.

He made his way to the scuttlebutt. Celia's gaze tracked the dipper of water as it rose to his lips. His head tilted back, and his throat worked as he swallowed. She felt her own throat constrict in tandem with his and knew a longing so intense it ached.

Beaumont lowered the dipper and stilled when he noticed her fixed attention. "Did no one offer you water?"

She shook her head.

The men surrounding her received a scathing glare and gave a series of noncommittal grunts in response.

"Please accept our apologies, madam. We've been remiss." He treated his crew to another scowl and motioned to a lanky young boy of about ten or twelve years. His son, perhaps?

"Give the lady some water, Andrew."

The boy took a dipper to her. She rose on shaky limbs and gulped the precious liquid down her greedy throat. *Heaven.* Nothing had ever tasted so exquisite. Young Andrew fetched another, then another, and she drank them down just as quickly as the first. He returned to the scuttlebutt a fourth time, but Captain Beaumont raised a hand to stay the boy.

An acute stab of loss pierced her, followed by a spark of anger at the man's cruelty.

He said nothing, just watched her with an expectant look on his face.

She shot him glare of reproach and opened her mouth to protest, but then her eyes widened as the water roared into her empty stomach with the force of a tidal wave. She immediately regretted her haste and wrapped her arms around her middle.

The captain quirked a brow, wearing a smug expression clearly meant to communicate if she weren't such a foolish twit she would not be suffering so. Her embarrassed gaze skittered away and clashed with the fixed attention of the sailors in her periphery. Their silent watchfulness unnerved her, like vultures waiting for their meal to succumb.

"N-No," she croaked and took a fearful step back. Her feet bumped against the pile of cording, halting her retreat. She raised her hands to ward them off.

Beaumont let out a curse and strode forward, dispersing her audience as he went. "The lot of you realize, do you not, that Jean Pierre's prize now belongs to me?"

As the pirates had sunk the *Essex*, Celia had an uncomfortable inkling *she* might be the prize.

He stood, arms akimbo, and marked each of the men with a warning stare. Those that were assigned to the *Mirabelle* stood at the ship's railing to watch the spectacle aboard the *Bonny Lass*, Smitty and Spinnakers among them.

Jenkins hobbled forward. "Fie, Beaumont, it appears ye're not as generous as Jean Pierre. He were goin' to give the wench to us once he'd had his share."

Blast. She was the prize.

Pirates nodded and voiced their agreement while Celia shook her head in vehement denial.

Beaumont gave Jenkins a pitying smile, the kind meant to convey one had to make allowances for those less intellectually endowed. "And you believed him? You are certain he meant to part with this comely bedmate?"

They shouted back an affirmative, including the

ones on the *Mirabelle*. Jenkins' smile turned superior.

Shame washed through Celia. Devil take them. They discussed her as if she were a strumpet to haggle over.

The captain folded his arms across his chest, his expression clearly skeptical. He glanced her way. She dropped her lashes lest her eyes betray her in some unintended fashion, though the heat of his gaze still burned. Sweat trickled down the side of her face.

"Then tell me this. How long would it have taken for him to 'have his share'?"

None volunteered an answer.

"Jean Pierre was a liar, as you all well know, but you may believe this: *I* shall not tire of her—" Celia's head snapped up and their gazes locked. "—ever."

Grumbles continued from the pirates bent on making mischief. Beaumont's men remained silent. She wanted to rail that she belonged to no one, least of all a pirate, but she was utterly alone on a ship full of men. Unwilling to plead her case before so many, she held her tongue.

Beaumont's eyes darkened and flashed like lightning. Celia felt the sizzle clear to her toes. His arm flung out and pointed to her, his words lashing with cold fury. "She belongs to me. Any man who cares to challenge me for her will die. Heed my warning. Keep your distance if you value your lives."

The menace in his voice caused her stomach to lurch. Her limbs began to shake. She was hot and sick and feared her skin may ignite at any moment. But her discomfort was nothing compared to the threat this man posed. She might have allowed herself to swoon if she weren't so frightened of what would happen to her while unconscious. Resignation settled like a lodestone on her heart. This man was her fate now and what he offered was *not* salvation.

"Ought'a at least have a go at winnin' her favor," one of his men grumbled.

"Oi've a fair reputation with the leidies meself," another complained.

Their captain shook his head and 'twas obvious, at least to Celia, that he was fast losing his patience. Not surprising, really. They appeared a thickheaded lot.

Before she realized his intent, Beaumont stepped close and snaked an arm around her waist, yanking her against his hard frame. Thoughts scattered as he bent her backward over his arm. For a heartbeat she stared into those commanding gray eyes looming over her. Eyes that told her to be still. Eyes that willed her to relax and allow him to—

She jerked her gaze away and struggled against his hold. "No," she choked. "Please, no."

Her captor smiled and raised a hand to brush the hair from her hot face. His husky voice sluiced over her, leaving a path of gooseflesh in its wake. "You're in luck, my sweet. I've saved you from that blackguard, Jean Pierre. I'm a far better man than he, I vow. And I've a fine reputation with the ladies." The raspy timbre washed along her nerve endings and smoothed away her resistance like silt in a streambed. Though his words were low and intimate, they carried across the deck.

One of his men snickered and called out, "Leidies, ye say? I expect ye mean old Nellie at Harry's tavern. An' here I thought I was gettin' me a whore. Perhaps ye don't know the difference, Cap'n."

The group surrounding them chuckled.

Beaumont turned his attention from her and gave the man a wicked smile. "You scurvies may not know the difference, but I surely do. Why, women fall at my feet. And do you forget, me hearties, that I dine with the governor on occasion?"

"Aye, well," the man closest to him opined, "'tis known ye go in the front door, but whether ye're dinin' with the gov'na or shinin' his boots, I can't rightly say."

Celia swallowed. Surely their captain would kill one of them. The fools were *laughing* at him. In her experience, this never boded well.

His smile disappeared.

She braced herself for his anger.

While still holding her in his clutches, he shifted his balance and thrust his booted foot into the heckler, knocking him into the man behind him, who likewise went into the next. The group fell over like ninepins until he'd not only sent the present antagonist to the deck, but the prior one as well. "How 'bout I shine me boots up yer arse?"

Laughter erupted on both ships.

The devil captain's attention swung back and latched onto Celia. Her stomach lurched. She shoved against his chest, though she may as well have been a flea trying to move a cannonball for all the good it did her.

An odd expression crossed his face. A curious mixture of humor and…pity? "That sunburn will be deuced uncomfortable in a few hours, little one." His eyes raked her face and shoulders. "'Tis a nasty burn, that. I suppose I ought to send you below and out of the sun."

She sagged against his arms in relief.

His gaze flicked to the side, and she followed his line of vision to the expectant looks of his men. She felt his sigh this time. As he took another breath, his arms constricted in concert with the expansion of his lungs, snuggling her tight and flattening her breasts against his hard chest.

"But before you take your leave," he continued, his voice huskier though somehow increasing in volume. "How about a little kiss to tide me over until I join you?"

He gave her no chance to reply. His hand cupped her head as his lips fused with hers.

Heat.

'Twas the first thought that popped into Celia's head. He smelled like…like heat and…oh, God. He tasted like spice and sin, and he would consume her if she didn't…she didn't…

She twisted against his embrace. He tightened his hold.

A sailor's amused voice slapped against her senses, forcing her awareness to their avid audience of tars and pirates. "P'r'aps ye're a might rusty, Cap'n. She ain't enjoyin' it."

The men chuckled.

Visions of Mrs. Abrams fleeing the lecherous pirates popped into her head. She panicked, terrified the others would join in the assault. Her hands flattened against Beaumont's chest and pushed.

He didn't budge.

Rampant fear breached her pores at every juncture where his body touched hers. She tried to turn her face away, but his hand cradled her head and held it immobile while his mouth continued to ravage hers.

The fear, the sun, and the water she drank all combined to set her stomach churning.

And then it heaved.

Beaumont's eyes widened in comprehension, and he wrenched his lips from hers. He made as if to thrust her away, but her sense of self-preservation rushed to the fore, and she latched onto the front of his shirt to prevent herself from falling. He lurched backwards just as she yanked herself upright and her stomach—unwilling to wait for this bit of repositioning—spewed forth like a bilge pump on a leaky frigate.

Down the front of his shirt.

The roar of laughter coming from the two ships was deafening. Celia spun about and ran to the rail where she continued to ignominiously retch over the side in full view of the men on the *Mirabelle*.

Exhausted, she laid her cheek against the rail and caught sight of a crewman wiping the grin from his mouth and pointing a thumb in her direction. "Gor, ye sure have a way wit' the leidies, Cap'n."

Another hooted, "Aye, when ye said ye had 'em fallin' at yer feet, I ne'er guessed it were their supper ye meant."

One aboard the *Mirabelle* shouted, "'At's a might messier than I likes meself, Cap'n. I expect ye ought'a court her over yon taffrail if ye wants ta keep yer bedclothes dry."

Pirates and crew alike dissolved into new fits of hilarity.

Celia seethed with indignation. *Disgusting cretins.*

Eventually her stomach finished its revolt. She turned and leaned her back against the rail, her limbs too weak to hold her up. She listed a bit, first to one side then the other. A slowly careening world felt normal, defining her somehow like a hair shirt on a sinner.

Her eyes rose to the captain's. His face bore an expression of righteous indignation, which pleased her under the circumstance. The scoundrel was patently responsible for his own undoing. She held his gaze across the short distance separating them, inconveniently wavering while she awaited her punishment.

With his eyes still locked on her face he took the bucket of water Andrew held out and dumped it down his shirt. Then stood there, dripping and scowling. The man looked angry enough to throw her overboard.

She glanced over her shoulder at the fathomless sea below and considered whether it might be a preferable fate. Mrs. Abrams had certainly thought so. Likely her skirts would drag her under before she managed to locate a piece of flotsam to hang onto, but compared to the retribution she'd suffer at the captain's hands, well…

His brow rose when she turned back to face him, apparently reading her thoughts. She responded by lifting her chin. Pitiful really, but it wasn't as if she could produce another pistol and shoot him in the leg too, no matter how lovely the sentiment.

He speared a glance at the snickering faces surrounding him, his jaw taught save for the muscle ticking there. His ego had clearly suffered a bruising.

Celia had no doubt she'd suffer dire consequences. She stiffened her spine, which corrected the listing a bit, and looked him defiantly in the eye.

"What is your name?" he demanded.

She tried to speak, but little more than a hoarse croak emerged. Lovely. The arrogant lout probably thought he'd rendered her speechless. She cleared her throat and tried again.

"C-Celia. M-Miss C-Celia Breck-enridge." Lud, was that her voice? She sounded as though she'd swallowed a bucket of sand.

"The wreck, she was the *Essex*?" So cold and impersonal he said it. As if an entire crew had not lost their lives defending that ship.

She nodded and blinked back tears.

"Where do you hail from, Celia Breckenridge?"

"Falmouth," she answered but when his arrogant brows rose with doubt she added, "recently from St. Georges."

"Ah." He nodded, as though her answers required his approval. "Welcome aboard the *Bonny Lass*, Miss Breckenridge."

Celia felt any number of things at present, but "welcome" was most assuredly not one of them. 'Twas rather like a chicken being welcomed to the stewpot.

He waited for her to reply then shrugged. "Come with me, Celia Breckenridge. Let us get you below before you collapse upon my deck."

Was he mad? She responded by hiking *her* brows up in a wide-eyed, incredulous stare.

The captain crossed his arms and waited.

Which made her nervous. Surely there were other alternatives. She glanced around and encountered a sea of eager faces staring back.

Perhaps not.

It appeared she had no choice but to follow the devil. Resignation leadened her feet. She took a short, tentative step in his direction.

Impatient, he strode forward and grasped her elbow, steering her toward the companionway. She stumbled, finding it difficult to walk in her weakened condition. Beaumont slid his arm about her waist as he propelled her forward, supporting her weight. She wondered if he resented having to touch her after she'd—

Well, she didn't really wish to ponder it.

"Andrew," the captain bellowed as they made their way below.

The boy scurried after them.

"Stay here," he ordered when they reached the door of his cabin. Andrew dropped to the floor and sat with his back against the wall.

Beaumont ushered her inside and led her to his bunk, gently seating her on it.

Her heart stumbled then resumed with punishing force, shattering the thin barrier of hope she'd erected.

God save her. The moment of her ravishment had arrived.

Chapter Four

Oblivious to Celia's inner panic, Captain Beaumont squatted at her feet, his gray eyes locked with hers as she sat rigidly on the edge of his bed.

"Had you family aboard the *Essex?*"

"No." She clasped her shaking hands in her lap, but her voice still trembled, and she hated him for it. "No one."

"The *Essex* was bound for England? You were sailing home?"

She closed her eyes against the pain the word "home" inflicted. "Yes."

"Why were you in Bermuda?"

"My aunt…she took ill, and I went to care for her. I stayed until…until she—"

Oh, she could not bear it, this anguish in her heart, in her soul. The loss, the grief; Aunt Maggie, Mrs. Abrams, Captain Abrams, the crew. So many. Too many. She did not want him to witness her suffering, to delve into her privacy, her life. Tears welled in her eyes and trailed a path down her cheeks.

The captain lifted his hand to cup her face, gently rubbing the dampness away with his thumb. Such a tender gesture. How he confused her.

"'Tis enough for now, lass." His voice was calm and soothing. Balm to her fraught nerves, as though she were a wounded animal he coaxed near. And she might have been lulled had he not spoken again. “Here, lie down.” With a hand to her shoulder, he pushed her backward on the bed, lifting her feet to pull off her slippers.

Her muscles tensed, her face and neck chilled and stiff. *He set me at ease so I would not resist his advances,* she realized bitterly. She crossed her ankles beneath her skirts and wrapped her arms protectively over her chest. He may be a large brute, but she’d not make it easy for him. Her hands were no longer bound. She would fight.

His fingers brushed the hair from her cheek, and she flinched. He drew his hand away and *tsked* his disappointment at her. She could swear she saw pity in his eyes.

Who was this man?

The one before her was so completely changed from the rogue who’d assaulted her only a short while ago, and even further removed from the devil warrior who’d bested the pirates.

“You may have difficulty believing this, but you are safe now.”

Ha. His actions made a liar of him, but under the circumstance, she thought it wise to hold her tongue.

“You are safe from *me*,” he added, his gaze boring into hers. “Appearances are important, even on a ship. I did what was necessary, and I shall not apologize. ’Twas done for your protection. The others will keep their distance now.” He glanced down at his damp shirt and his lips twitched. “You’ve had your revenge anywise.”

Celia peered into those eyes of smoke, hoping to discern a hint of this man’s character. She wanted desperately to believe him. She dared not.

"I shan't apologize to you either," she said, her voice steady and defiant.

That brought a smile to his lips.

"Then we are at an impasse." He stood and pitched his voice louder—for young Andrew's benefit, she assumed. "Rest if you are able. I must get these ships underway. Andrew will remain close. If you have a need he will see to it, else he'll fetch me."

Relief sighed through her limbs. He would not harm her. Not at present, leastways.

He took a clean shirt from his locker and pulled the soiled one over his head. She had to bite her lip to keep from gasping at his naked torso. She'd never seen the like. The sculpted muscles of his shoulders and back flexed and bunched with his every movement. 'Twas like watching a symphony.

Her gaze roved over him, the sunlight through the windows of the stern gallery obligingly illuminating. His snug breeches hugged his legs and hips as if loath to be separated from them. She suspected the width of both her thighs would not equal one of his. Indomitable was the first thought that came to mind, the man hewn by the forces of nature, like a Greek god or a Viking warrior.

The Romans would have made him a gladiator, she decided grudgingly. Or perhaps an Egyptian queen would choose him for her private slave. She liked that image better. He'd fan his queen while she sat on her throne and jump to do her bidding whenever she so much as—

Beaumont turned suddenly and caught her staring. Celia dropped her lashes, realizing belatedly she ought to have averted her eyes while he changed.

But heavens.

She'd no idea a flesh and blood man actually looked like that. Enlightening, to be sure, though no less embarrassing to be caught ogling him. She recalled shoving her hands against the solid wall of his chest. It did not look like a wall now. It appeared warm and dusky and firm. How would his bare skin feel beneath her fingertips?

Her eyes peeked back open. She continued her perusal, though she was careful to do so beneath the fan of her lashes. Except for a brief glance in her direction, he appeared not to notice.

He shook out his shirt. His biceps bulged and swelled as if attempting to escape the confines of his skin. The man probably didn't know what fat was. Doubtless all those manly muscles scared it away before it settled on that formidable frame.

Dangerous. His was a warrior's body with all the requisite nicks and scars to prove it. And for some reason she found this absurdly enticing, in the same way one is compelled to test a blade with their thumb knowing full well it will cut them. He donned the clean shirt, and she felt an acute stab of disappointment. Turning further away, he tucked his shirt into his breeches. A thin strip of white flashed on his hip where the sun obviously hadn't—

Oh, she really *ought* to close her eyes.

Appropriately covered now, he pulled the strip of leather from his nape and combed his fingers through his hair, clubbing it back more securely in its queue. Once restored, he faced her, his voice husky and…strained?

"Stay close, Celia Breckenridge. Do not go about my ship unaccompanied and allow no one else to escort you. You may trust Andrew, but he is too small to offer protection." With those parting words he left her alone in the cabin, taking all the air with him, or so it seemed. She took a deep breath just to prove to herself she could.

Alone.

Never had she felt more so. Not even when Aunt Maggie had passed. Her mind could not cope with the gruesome events of the past hours. It was as if her life had stopped yesterday morning when she stepped on the gangway in St. Georges and had only just resumed, as if the pendulum of her clock had finally been rewound.

Had she survived the pirates only to fall victim again? She prayed Jackson Beaumont was a man of honor.

Lethargy crept over her. Her mind screamed at her to remain alert, that she was not yet safe. But she was so very tired, and the bed was so very comfortable to her bruised body.

Her thoughts drifted to the image of Captain Beaumont's very large, very muscular, and very naked back as she surrendered to Morpheus.

****

A lecherous protector.

Jack gusted out a sigh so full of exasperation it could have filled a topsail. An admirable position to find oneself in. He'd saved Miss Breckenridge from hell and tossed himself into one.

He paced next to Crawley, the *Bonny Lass's* bosun and current helmsman, while his thoughts loitered belowdecks with his new cabin mate. Crawley carried on a lively conversation in which Jack's contribution consisted of an occasional grunt.

She was in his cabin. In his bed. What the deuce had he been thinking? *Had* he been thinking? Damned if he could recall. The woman had the body of a siren and the lips of—

He scowled darkly. Best not think of that vindictive little feature at present. He rubbed the sleeve of his dry shirt absently as if doing so would wipe the memory away. He could not recall ever being so angry with a woman. In spite of all she'd endured, she maintained an almost brazen façade of self-possession and stared him boldly in the eye. Jack admired such fortitude. Any other woman would have fallen into hysterics, assuming she hadn't fainted dead away.

But not Miss Celia Breckenridge. She faced his men with admirable fortitude. Stood her ground with calm defiance.

Watched while he changed his shirt.

Heat shot to his groin. The look on her face had been one of total fascination, as though she'd never seen a man before. Likely she hadn't. Bare leastways. That fixed attention of hers had been uncomfortable. The surge of lust catching him by surprise. He was sorely tempted to join her on that bunk, which would have rendered his promise of safety a damnable lie. Her interest was no doubt curiosity, yet blood had dispatched to his loins with vicious intensity.

Those eyes, green and turbulent as a storm-swept sea, had all but devoured him.

Jack rubbed his forehead.

The *Lass* caught the wind in her teeth, the prow

slicing clean through the waves with the *Mirabelle* standing a mile or so off. His gaze rose to a loose sail flapping aloft and the crewman climbing to tend it. Those poor, beautiful breasts burned scarlet by the sun. Likely she'd blister.

Bloody pirate bastards.

A familiar rage swept through him as he recalled Travers, stabbed and left to die in a filthy alley in La Rochelle. He flexed his hands and wished he'd wrapped them around the putrid little Frenchman's throat. Pity they had not come along sooner. They might have saved the *Essex*.

"Sally was her name," Crawley said. "Met 'er in Port Royal. She'd look right fine in emeralds, Cap'n, what with her pale skin and red hair."

'Twas all his men talked about since leaving France. Finding the fortune in emeralds and what each would do with his share. Jack confessed to a bit of fantasizing himself. He planned to purchase another ship once he returned to port. Gradually build up a small fleet and his fortunes along with it. Marry a penniless woman—one who'd be grateful to acquire an enterprising sea captain. Oh yes. He'd prove his mettle one day. To one man in particular.

Perhaps that day was nigh.

He considered his guest below. Miss Breckenridge would look fine in emeralds, too. A necklace of faceted stones, perhaps. They'd bring out the fire in her eyes and glisten like the clear, jade waters surrounding the Bahamas.

Ah. The Bahamas. Jack mentally slapped himself from his reverie and shot Crawley a repressive frown.

This morning he'd had a plan: Sail to the Bahamas.

Find the emeralds. Simple, really. But in the span of just a few hours he'd acquired a ship—the only bright spot in this miserable day—a band of bad-tempered pirates, and—here he couldn't help snorting again—a woman with a delicate constitution.

How was he to keep her in his cabin? And why the deuce could she not be old or ugly? He felt again those plump breasts pressed against his chest when he held her in his arms. Her small waist beneath his hand when he helped her below.

Those green eyes sliding over him like a caress.

"Cap'n," Andrew called, interrupting his thoughts. Which saved him from embarrassing himself in front of Crawley—a cock-stand would be difficult to explain with only the two of them present. He left the helm and went to where Andrew danced from foot to foot excitedly.

The boy sent a furtive glance about before whispering, "I think ye need ta go below and see ta the lady."

Jack considered this extremely unwise at present. "Why?"

"'Cause she's shiverin' all over, and she seems real sick-like ta me. She asked fer another blanket, but she wouldna wake up when I brung it to her. She don' look so good, Cap'n."

Damn and blast. Jack felt like a man saved from drowning only to be thrown to the sharks. He followed Andrew below and found Miss Breckenridge thrashing about on the bunk, her sable hair a wild tangle across his pillow. The tattered black gown framed skin turned a brilliant, ghastly red over her face, shoulders, and chest.

Shivers wracked her slight frame. He put his hand to her brow and cupped the back of her neck. "Poor lass. She's burning with fever. 'Twould appear Miss Breckenridge's trials are not yet over. Fetch a basin of water and a cloth, Andy." The boy scurried from the room. "Clean, mind you," Jack called after him.

He grabbed the blanket Andrew had thrown across a chair and covered her with it. When the boy returned with the water, Jack gently bathed her swollen skin. The water chilled her, and the trembling grew worse. She fought to escape his ministrations, her clothing chafing against her burns and causing her to whimper.

"This won't do." He placed a hand against her midriff to stay her. "Fetch a hammock lad. She'll rest easier if—"

Jack glanced up and realized Andrew had already gone. Apparently neither of them could bear a lady in distress. He continued to lave Miss Breckenridge's face and shoulders, cooling her fiery flesh.

Andrew arrived with the hammock and the two of them hung it from the rafters.

"Go and fetch my supper now, Andy," Jack instructed when they'd finished.

"Aye, sir." The boy fled the room again.

Once alone, Jack turned the unconscious woman to her side and unfastened the back of her tattered gown, pulling it gently from her body. Next came her panniers and stays, and he continued to remove clothing until only the thin, damp shift remained.

A sudden burst of rage shook him at the contrast of angry, swollen flesh against flawless white skin marred with blue and purple bruises.

The bleeding bastards.

Very little of her body was hidden from Jack's regard by the wet material as his gaze roamed the length of her. His breath halted. His lungs forgot how to breathe.

But she was doing a marvelous job of it.

Her full, ripe breasts rose and fell with her ragged breaths and so captured his attention he had to drag his gaze away. It trailed a path to her narrow waist, her slender hips, and her long, shapely legs. Carnal thoughts of them wrapped about his waist came to mind. Though badly burned at present, 'twas painfully obvious what an exquisite creature he beheld.

Jack pulled a sheet from his locker and spread it over the hammock to prevent the rough cording from abrading her tender skin. He wrapped his arms around her and lifted her gently. It felt…right somehow. He held her and felt her heart beat against his own. Felt her full breasts with each inhalation. Whispered soothing words in her ear.

He had to force himself to relinquish her to the hammock. She groaned and her eyes fluttered open, her gaze vague and distant. Reluctantly he laid the blanket over her, his voice soft and soothing as he brushed damp tendrils of hair from her crimson face. "*Shh,* Celia. You must rest now. Jack will take care of you. Go to sleep."

Her eyes surrendered and closed.

****

Rumors of Jack sleeping late circulated throughout the ship.

Ribald jokes and speculations as to the woman's current state of health followed. It was suggested Jack should feed her sparingly as washing his clothing daily might become a nuisance.

Buffleheaded sailors.

He stood near the quarterdeck and stretched, yawning loudly for the benefit of his audience, exhausted. Sadly, not for the reason they'd been led to believe. He'd spent the night bathing his patient's fevered skin.

"Ye appear ta be draggin' yer anchor, Cap'n," Rory, the *Bonny Lass's* sailmaker, observed. "Had a bit o' trouble sleepin', eh?"

Jack scratched his chest and forced another yawn. "*Mmm.* I value some things more dearly than sleep, Mr. Muldoon."

Crawley grinned and nudged Rory's elbow. "As long as ye've been abed," he motioned to the position of the sun, "a body would think ye'd be well rested by now."

Their captain treated them to a smug smile. "If my eyes had been closed, I expect I should." He winked. "You'll hear no complaints, mind."

Throughout the interminable day, Jack and Andrew looked after their patient. The crew watched over the unruly pirates, and curiously—or so it seemed to Jack—their captain. And the pirates amused themselves by creating mischief at every opportunity.

He felt like an actor in a horribly staged farce.

Crawley sidled up next to him. "Are ye keepin' the wench prisoner, Cap'n?"

Jack forced a chuckle and wagged his brows. "She's too worn out to leave the bunk." This earned him a puzzled look and a quirk of the lips that in no way resembled a smile.

He sighed. Perhaps he was a horrible actor in a

perfectly good farce.

****

Celia roused to sultry heat and the most pleasant aroma.

The scent of spice permeated the air, bringing to mind the kitchens at Seaview where cook baked the most delicious pastries in all of Cornwall. She pictured Rianna sitting next to her at the long block table in the kitchen with a glass of milk and a plate full of biscuits between them.

A quill scratching across parchment intruded into Celia's idyll, nudging her eyes open. A cabin, a fairly large one, came into view. Sunlight glinted off rippling blue waters through the windows.

To her left sat a square wooden table with four chairs. Her trunk sat in the corner. She stared at it curiously but could not reconcile her belongings with the room. The scratching came again, and she turned her head toward the sound.

Her gaze swept past a storage locker to a desk and halted on the scowling man poring over a ledger. His jaw worked slowly, chewing something.

He seemed familiar.

A harsh, striking face with sharp angles and a square jaw covered with what looked like a few days' growth of whiskers. Oddly, this made him even more attractive. He looked rugged and menacing. She frowned.

Quite menacing, actually.

Like a clap of thunder, the past events crashed into her awareness. Blood and bodies and flying debris collided with the sound of screaming and the smell of smoke.

Men laughing.

And the man who'd claimed her with a brazen kiss as bold and brash as if he were King George himself.

Her brows drew together, but only slightly. Her skin felt too tight. He'd told her to rest, but…what had happened after? She could not recall. She had no sense of time. The sunlight told her it was day.

But what day?

The captain's head snapped up as though her clamoring thoughts had disturbed him. Probing gray eyes held her hostage for several heartbeats. Frantic heartbeats—at least hers were. 'Twas debatable whether he employed such an organ.

He flipped the ledger closed and rose from the desk.

At once Celia felt vulnerable and trapped, as if unseen arms fastened her down. The man grew larger as he approached. And menacing. She shifted to rise. And swayed instead. She lurched to her side to find something to grab hold of while she gained her feet.

"Here now. You mustn't—"

She tipped upside-down, shrieked, and hung suspended for an instant before dropping to the floor on her hands and knees. Stunned, she flopped over onto her bottom and pressed her hands flat against the floorboards, assuring herself of its solid surface. Something resembling a fish net swung back and forth above her head, brushing against her hair like a makeshift scythe.

Her tormentor made a strangled sound and squatted down on his haunches to peer beneath the net, eyes gleaming silver. "I've noted you've a penchant for sitting on the floor, Miss Breckenridge. Are there no chairs in the south of England?"

Unsettled by his nearness, Celia swallowed and glanced behind her at the door. It appeared miles away at present. She turned back to discover his attention riveted to the floor and his face oddly flushed. She stared at his peculiar expression, confused by the abrupt change in his demeanor. Curious, she followed his gaze, and gasped.

She was naked.

Shift hiked up to the tops of her thighs and legs completely bare to the scoundrel's lewd gaze. God in heaven. *Where were her clothes?*

She let out another shriek, this one in indignation, and scrambled to her feet. The room spun dizzily, and she threw her hand out to catch herself, grasping hold of the net once again. It swung forward beneath her weight taking her arm and the rest of her torso with it. Her cry of alarm ended in a grunt when the captain's arm yanked her upright against his hard frame.

How had he moved so fast?

The spicy aroma wafted over her in a warm caress. She tilted her head back to see his face. He held her arms pinned to her sides and lifted a hand to her brow. The gesture felt warm and intimate. Familiar.

Memories stirred: a cloth to her face, a cup to her lips, a low voice coaxing her to drink.

"I've been ill," she told him.

"Aye, but your fever is gone now."

Her heart hammered against her chest. Surely, he could feel it thumping against his. She squirmed against his hold. "Please release me, sir."

He tilted his head to the side, his gaze roaming her features as if studying some rare species. "I fear I cannot. You are ill and a danger to yourself, 'twould seem." Though his voice was even and his expression solemn, his eyes shone with silver lights, clearly amused.

"I was merely startled and a bit clumsy."

He raised a doubtful brow.

Celia gritted her teeth. "'Tis insufferable you should presume I wish myself harm."

Those silver orbs started twinkling like merry little stars and he grinned, the effect devastating to her feminine senses. She mentally shied away.

"Perhaps not intentionally, but you do seem rather adept at disaster. 'Tis a natural talent, I'd warrant."

The cad. She refrained from pointing out he'd sparked her recent disasters. She had more urgent matters to discuss. "Where are my clothes, Captain?"

"In that trunk over there." He gestured with his chin.

She narrowed her eyes and pictured him hanging from the yardarm by his boots. "Why," she asked with galling patience, "are there none on my person?"

"Several reasons, actually." He proceeded to list them as though placing an order with the butcher. "You were fevered, your clothing chafed your burns, and your skirts prevented you from resting comfortably." He gave her a chiding look. "You flayed about quite a bit."

"Flayed," she repeated skeptically.

"Like a footloose jib, you were."

Mortified, she dropped her gaze to the lace at his throat.

"Was I…" She glanced up at his face then away. "Were you… Did anyone else…?"

His finger touched her chin to turn her gaze back to his.

"Of course not. I sent Andy away while I bathed you and made you comfortable. You were too ill to care for yourself, Celia. I give you my word, I comported myself as a gentleman."

In her limited experience, the definition of the word "gentleman" varied, not only between men, but also upon the situation. She'd discovered this at the age of sixteen on a moonlit terrace at her grandmother's birthday ball. Fortunately, her father had arrived to instruct the overly amorous young "gentleman" on comportment.

She searched the captain's face, looking for signs of deceit. Belatedly her mind digested his words. The impertinent cad had called her Celia. She ought to take him to task for—

"Bathed?" she choked.

Chapter Five

Captain Beaumont smiled sheepishly. Celia was overcome with the urge to slap him.

"My apologies. An unfortunate choice of words, that. I meant to say I kept your skin cooled by dampening it with water. I promise there was nothing untoward in my actions. Your skin is badly burned, Celia. You've begun to blister."

Blister. She touched her fingers to her sore mouth. Lud, she must look a fright. "Captain, have you a looking glass?"

For a long, disconcerting moment he stared at her, during which she grew lightheaded imagining the horrors he must see.

"Is it so terrible, then?"

"Aye," he answered honestly. "But there is nothing to be done for it. You must be patient and allow your skin time to heal."

Her legs began to shake, and she was suddenly thankful he held her up.

He noticed.

"You're trembling." His hand came up and felt her brow again. "How do you feel?"

"As if a pack of dogs mistook me for the fox."

A wide grin split his face. "Oh aye, they most assuredly did. Fortunately, my men and I snatched you from their snapping jaws."

Uncomfortable talking of the pirates, Celia glanced away and caught sight of the fiendish net. “Is that a hammock?”

“Aye.”

“I have always wanted to try one.”

“You’ve been *trying one* for two days.” He leaned down to whisper in her ear, “You’ve yet to complain.”

She fought the shiver his breath stirred. “Somehow I am not surprised.”

“The hammock sways when you are restless and has the benefit of air above and below to keep a body cool. When there is any air to be had,” he added ruefully. “’Tis deuced hot in here.”

Likely it would be cooler if one of them left. Perhaps she ought to suggest it.

“Would you like to sit at the table? Andrew is fetching our meal.”

“I…” she hesitated “…suppose I should like that.” What choice had she really?

“I found a robe in your trunk.” He reached for the garment lying across his bunk.

Were her cheeks as red as they felt? “How did you know the trunk was mine?”

He dipped his head to peer into her eyes. “’Twas not difficult to determine.”

“I suppose not,” she conceded, wishing he would not look at her so intently. “Mrs. Abrams and I were not of a size.”

“Not at all,” he agreed with a bit more authority than he ought.

She had to clutch at his shirt for balance while he guided her arms through the sleeves of her robe. The scent of spice wafting from him made her mouth water.

"Jean Pierre's men said Captain Abrams' wife jumped overboard. Do they speak the truth?"

"Aye, and they bound me to the mast to prevent me from doing the same."

He grunted. A response she found difficult to decipher. "Though I deplore their treatment of you, I am heartily glad you were unable to follow the woman."

Which reminded her of their disastrous kiss and how she'd considered jumping over the rail of his ship afterward.

His lips curved knowingly. "I would have fished you out."

Hmph. Doubtless he would have.

"Come." He helped her to the table and sat her to his left. Instead of taking his seat, he scowled at the door. "What the devil is keeping the lad?" He stalked over, yanked it open, and bellowed, "*Andrew.* A meal before the sun sets, if you please."

"Aye, Cap'n. Cracking on," the cabin boy called from a distance.

Apparently satisfied, the captain returned to the table and sat down.

The hard, wooden chair made it difficult for Celia to get comfortable. "I had thought you'd already eaten. The cabin smells so strongly of—"

"Cinnamon," he finished for her. "I've a fondness for the bark. Does it offend you?"

"Oh, no. Quite the contrary," she assured him. "I am fond of it myself. A rather costly indulgence, is it not?"

He shrugged. "I've a friend, a Dutchman, who's partial to French brandy. We accommodate one another through trade."

Mention of trade normally piqued Celia's interest—she was her father's daughter after all—the fact that it did not, told her she must be quite ill. She leaned her head back against her seat, weary of holding it up. Mama would be appalled at her posture. The irony amused her.

Andrew stumbled into the room beneath the weight of a large tray. He dropped his burden on the table and gaped at Celia in surprise. "Afternoon, miss. How ye feelin'?"

Celia attempted a smile for him, but her sore mouth hindered the effort to something of a sickly smirk.

The boy looked fascinated.

"I, ah, believe I feel a trifle better than I look."

"I expect so," the youngster nodded gravely.

She caught the captain's amused expression. "I must indeed look a fright."

"Oh, aye," Andrew agreed cheerfully. "Yer skin's all red an' blisterin' an' yer face is swollen an' it—"

"Andy," the captain interrupted, struggling not to laugh. "'Tisn't polite to tell a woman she looks poorly."

"It ain't?" the boy asked, perplexed.

"Nay."

Andrew pondered this for a moment. "What're ye s'posed ta say if'n they ask ye?"

Celia cleared her throat and waited expectantly for the captain's reply.

He winked at her. "Why, 'tis simple, lad. Ye must lie."

"Aaahhh," said an enlightened Andrew. "Too missish fer me. Best ta avoid 'em, I'm thinkin'."

Both Celia's hands came up to protect her sore

mouth and she coughed to prevent herself from laughing. The man was a devil, no doubt about it.

The captain chuckled. “Get ye gone scamp and leave us to our meal.”

“Aye, Cap’n. Miss.” The boy tipped his cap and scurried from the room.

“How did Andrew come to be on your ship?”

“His father was a sailor. Drowned at sea in a storm.” He picked up a knife and fork and began slicing ham from the tray. A bowl of peas, ship’s biscuit, and a bottle of wine rounded out their meal. Simple fare, but Celia’s stomach did not mind. It growled vocally.

“I took young Andrew on as my cabin boy to help his mother. ’Tis difficult for a woman alone to raise and feed a young boy.”

“’Twas very kind of you, Captain.”

“Jack,” he corrected. “Here, take a bite.” He forked up a small bite of the ham he’d cut and fed it to her. “You must call me Jack, Celia. We’re bound to this cabin together so we shall hardly be strangers.”

“Oh, we cannot possibly.” She was betrothed after all and this man—

Hmm. She’d no idea. “Captain, have you a wife?”

“No.” He seemed amused by the question. “Nor have I made any promises. You?”

“Yes, actually.”

“My condolences.” He set her plate in front of her.

“Thank you,” she replied before she caught herself. “That is—”

He waved a hand, indicating she need not bother explaining, and poured them both a glass of wine.

Guilt stabbed at her. “His name is Mr. Brett Kensington,” she said brightly. “He’s a wonderful man.

We've known one another always. Our fathers betrothed us after I was born. I postponed our wedding to sail to Bermuda. Brett is very understanding, you see." She sounded ridiculous, even to her own ears. Why she felt the need to defend him, she could not say.

"Brett is he? An unusual name. 'Twas my father's, though I met a man from Surrey called the same."

"How interesting. It is an unusual name." Though she doubted Brett would approve of her discussing it with him, or of her current residence. Nor would Papa. They both deserved better of her. "Of course, I cannot stay here in your cabin, though I do thank you for your care. Have you another space I might occupy?"

"No, but I would not allow you to move there, regardless. You're safer here with me."

Safe? Another distinction seemed in order here, though she supposed he meant from the pirates and his crew. She thought of his tanned back and his casual removal of her clothing and heat crept up her neck. She could not possibly remain in this cabin alone with him. "I most certainly will not. 'Tisn't proper."

"Propriety rowed away the moment those thieving bastards attacked your ship, madam. I'll not sacrifice your safety to social strictures. They matter naught to a pirate or a sailor in his cups. You'll remain here with me." He forked up another bite of ham and stuck it in her mouth when she opened it to argue.

She glared, though a tiny part of her felt relieved. She did feel safe with him, leastwise where the others were concerned. Regardless, she could not allow the arrogant lout to bully her.

"I'll not," she said, once she'd chewed and swallowed.

"You will, even if I have to tie you to the bunk."

Celia picked up her fork and contemplated stabbing him with it. Pity he was sitting down. She took a bite of her food. The ham tasted quite good, considering it had been prepared on a ship. Although it had been so long since she'd eaten, likely a strip of leather would satisfy.

The captain took her silence for acquiescence and nodded. "'Tis well met. You shall suffer my company for a week, ten days at most."

"Oh?" she replied, amused. "Do you intend to sprout wings and fly across the Atlantic?"

His words began to register then. She set her fork down and straightened in her chair, dread spiraling through her limbs.

"You…are bound for England, are you not?"

Jack blew out a breath and lifted his gaze to Celia's.

Her eyes widened. "I…naturally assumed. That is—"

The poor lass. Likely she thought her nightmare would never end. "Our course is not England, Celia. We're carrying the pirates home, before we continue. I've a hold full of that brandy I spoke of."

"Where is home?" she asked tentatively.

"The Carolinas. I live in Charles Town."

"The Colonies," she gasped, as incredulous as if he'd told her they sailed to the moon. "Sir, I cannot. Why, 'tis even farther from home than Bermuda."

"Have you ever been to the Colonies?"

"Of course not." Clearly, she thought it a godforsaken place, barbarous and full of heathens.

"Then you shall have a new adventure. Charles Town is a beautiful city. Your health should be greatly improved by the time we reach port."

"No." She fell back against her seat and crossed her arms beneath those lovely breasts in defiance. "I refuse. I will not go to the colonies."

Jack shrugged and remained silent, allowing her to consider her position. Or lack thereof.

It did not take long. "My father is very wealthy, sir. As am I, in my own right. Name your price to turn this ship around, and we shall gladly pay it."

Though she proposed a reasonable alternative, he would have to decline. He refused to return to England unless his pockets were lined with gold—or emeralds. Not to gain a pithy reward for a man's cosseted offspring.

"I am sorry to disappoint you, lass. But I've pirates to bring to justice, and another ship to see to now. 'Tisn't possible."

"B-but how shall I get home? I was not supposed to be on the *Essex*. My family will have no idea what has become of me." She squared her shoulders and treated him to a fierce glare. "'Tis completely unacceptable, Captain. You must change your course immediately."

He quirked a brow, amused at her highhandedness. "No."

She stiffened and turned her face away, refusing to look at him. Jack found himself looking forward to her next argument. Though she was not very good at making them, she did so with a passion he enjoyed. Her eyes closed, and she obligingly filled her lungs with air. He hoped she would not suffer any lasting damage. Such perfection did not deserve to be marred. She turned to him sharply, and for a moment he wondered if she'd guessed at his thoughts.

"You cannot abscond with me across the ocean, sir. My grandfather will hear of this." He poured himself another glass of wine, held the bottle up, and raised a brow in question. She rolled her eyes and shook her head no.

'Twould appear her entire family tree would be trotted out in her defense. Interesting, she hadn't threatened him with her betrothed yet. Jack would've guessed *Brett* to be the very first in her arsenal. "And your grandfather would be?"

"Burlington."

Jack stared at her blankly.

"As in, the Earl of— Surely, you've heard of him."

He thought about it. "I do not believe so, no."

This did not please her, judging by her gasp of outrage. She stood abruptly. "It hardly signifies whether you have or not. He is a powerful man. And you cannot abduct me against my will. 'Tis kidnapping."

"Kidnapping?" Jack snorted. The ungrateful chit.

"Aye," she huffed and grabbed the edge of the table for support, her fit of temper sapping her strength. Good. He had a strong inclination to render her backside as red as her face.

"You wished to remain on the *Essex* then? Or perhaps 'twas the accommodations aboard the *Mirabelle* you found satisfactory?"

She refused to meet his eyes, but he watched the fight drain out of her. She sank back down to her seat.

"I thought not." He pushed her plate closer, a subtle urge to eat.

"But Rianna needs me," she whispered softly. "She is my sister."

Ah. A sister now. And still no Mr. Kensington.

Her head lifted. Devil take her, her eyes glistened with tears. "Please, I beseech you Captain—Jack. Turn this ship around."

'Twas Jack's turn to look away. He shifted awkwardly in his chair. Like most men, he could not abide tears. He reached over and grasped her fingers, giving them a quick squeeze.

"Calm yourself, Celia. I cannot gad about the Atlantic with a group of pirates aboard. I must turn them over to the admiralty for a proper hanging. As the only survivor of the attack, they're certain to require your testimony. We shall find you transport to England. Charles Town is a very busy port."

She pulled away and clasped her hands together in her lap. A tear splashed to her thumb. Damn the woman. They'd been having such fun.

"And after you've dealt with the pirates. Have you a destination then?"

"Aye." But he would not be telling her about it. "We shall sail south to, ah, the Caribbean. I've an obligation there."

"Would you consider delaying your trip there to return me home? I will pay you handsomely, Jack. You've my word. And Papa will most assuredly wish to compensate you for my rescue. 'Twould mean a very large sum for you and your men."

Jack stared at her sun-ravaged face, damp now with tears. He should not care for her circumstances. He'd rescued her from the pirates and provided safe passage. Once they reached port, she was no longer his concern. But his heart could not reach an accord with his mind. 'Twas pity, of course. He was not an uncaring soul.

"You said you were not meant to be aboard the *Essex*. How were you to return home?"

"On the *Roundabout*. Her captain, Captain Pierce, is well known to my father."

"When is Captain Pierce due to collect you?"

"Not until the end of October at the earliest."

He mulled this over. "We've time to return you to Bermuda to meet his ship then. Fear not, Celia," he heard himself say, though he could hardly credit it. His fortunes awaited him in the Bahamas. "I shall see to it you are returned home. In some fashion or another."

She exhaled a gusty sigh. "It seems I've little choice in the matter."

"Eat madam," he ordered. "There's naught to be done about your present circumstances and little use in worrying over them." He picked up her fork and scooped up a bite of peas.

"I am not hungry."

Jack ignored her protests. "I'll not have you wasting away on my ship. You are too thin."

"I've always been thin."

"Eat," he commanded. "Or I shall force you to drink Scully's restorative tonic. He is our cook, and I promise you there is not a more vile tasting substance on earth."

"You, sir, are a tyrant." She turned her head away when he tried to feed her the peas.

"You flatter me, Miss Breckenridge. I am but a simple sailor." He tried again, and she put up her hand in protest.

"There is still ham left." Apparently, she did not favor peas. Pity. They were a ship's staple. Unlike fresh vegetables, they could be dried and stored in barrels.

"Very well." He forked up another bite of ham.

"I really am not hung—" Jack stuck the fork in her mouth. She crossed her arms mutinously, forgetting the burns on her chest, and winced. He took pity on her and pushed his chair back.

"If you will excuse me, I must see to my ship now. Let me help you back to the hammock."

Her face blanched. "I believe I should prefer the bunk for a spell. If you've no objection."

"None a'tall. Though I suspect you'll find the hammock more comfortable. You may try sleeping in it again tonight." He held out his arm to help her rise and smiled winningly. "I shall remain close by to catch you."

Chapter Six

One by one, Celia's blisters ruptured and dried.

Burned skin turned white and peeled, leaving the flesh beneath raw and pink. Her lips scabbed over, cracked, and bled. This occurred most often whenever she spoke, frowned, ate, yawned, or heaven forbid—laughed. Captain Beaumont gave her a salve that Scully the cook kept in the galley for burns, but it offered minimal relief.

Night became her solace and her freedom. She found the heat during the day unbearable, but the breeze turned cooler when the sky darkened, buffeting her tender flesh with blissful relief. She sat on a blanket near the uppermost deck, the forecastle or fo'c'sle as the sailors called it. The ship dipped and climbed the meandering waves under a dark night lit with millions of stars.

Rianna preyed on her mind. Plausible reasons for her distress tormented Celia. Given her sister's propensity for mischief, the possibilities were endless. Would that she could sense the reason behind the emotion. Unfortunately, it was not how her intuition worked. If so, she might have escaped her own folly.

Now she sailed in the wrong direction. Because Jack would not turn around.

They'd reached something of an accord whereby she stopped wishing him to the devil, and he stopped shoveling food into her mouth at every opportunity. She continued to plead with him to change course. He continued to stubbornly refuse.

They did manage to hold civil conversations with one another. As she suspected, Jackson Beaumont had a wicked sense of humor. He reveled in her laughter, though with her lips splitting constantly, she considered the man something of a curse.

As Jack had suggested, she found the hammock more comfortable to lie in. To her mortification, he had to help her climb in and out of the thing several times before she could do so without assistance, teasing her unmercifully as he did.

Her tormentor dropped down next to her and stretched out his long legs to gaze at the stars. "Quite an impressive tapestry nature weaves for us every night."

Drawing her legs up, she wrapped her arms around them and rested her cheek on her knees. "Do you ever tire of it?"

"Never. I suppose a sailor sees more of the stars than anyone. They're our constant on unpredictable seas."

They sat in silence, two strangers tossed together by circumstance. Her thoughts returned to Rianna. A vivacious creature, her sister, this desperation so out of character for her that Celia could not help but worry.

Jack finally spoke, though he kept his eyes fixed on the stars. "You've been quiet today, Celia. I comprehend you're disappointed about our destination, but…is aught amiss? Has someone caused you unease?"

A tear rolled down her cheek and dampened her skirt. "Nay Captain, I've been lost in my own musings

’tis all. I comprehend I’ve brought this misery upon myself, and I am uncomfortable with the truth of my actions.”

His head turned to her—his face shadowed in the dark. “And how, pray, have you done so?”

She’d become familiar with this man’s many moods and expressions and could easily mark his scowl from the sound of his voice. She leaned her head back to contemplate the night sky with him. Perhaps the answers to her life had been scried in the stars for the two of them to read.

“I became restless, you see. Frightened I would be married and settled without ever experiencing a true adventure. As I was already engaged, I did not require a season as my friends did. I felt cheated. Not by my betrothed,” she said quickly. “Rather the excitement of meeting someone new, the hope of making a match, of the unknown. I had missed it all.

“When we learned Aunt Maggie had taken ill, I begged my parents to allow me to sail to Bermuda and care for her. I am—was—fond of my aunt and thought it a grand adventure. Until I saw how very ill she was. When she passed, I was not content to wait for Captain Pierce to collect me.”

Jack shifted to face her. She felt those keen eyes in the darkness. They’d be the color of pewter, dark rimmed and piercing. “And because you wanted adventure and chose to return prematurely, you brought your attack upon yourself?”

“’Tis not quite so simple, but yes.”

The ship creaked in a long, slow sigh as he pondered this. A sail chafed at the sheets overhead. “Who would have gone to Bermuda to care for your aunt if you had not?"

Celia's lips curved in a tiny smile at the memory. "My mother was determined to go, but she becomes dreadfully ill when she travels. Papa would not permit it. 'Twas quite a pickle until I managed to convince them to allow me."

"Have you given any thought to what might have become of your mother had she been aboard the *Essex*?"

"No," Celia admitted. "But she would not have been. She'd have sailed home on the *Roundabout* with Captain Pierce as my father had arranged."

"What if she, too, had decided to return early? Would she not have been homesick for her husband and daughters?" He'd begun to sound like a barrister now, guiding his audience through the facts as he'd determined toward an inevitable conclusion.

"I do not know. I suppose she might have been."

"You may plague your conscience with what 'might have beens' for the rest of your days, Celia. The simple truth is this: 'Tis the past and cannot be changed. You must cease these recriminations. Set your mind at rest and allow your body to heal. Torturing yourself serves no purpose." He leaned toward her and spoke in a low rumble. "Torturing is a pirate's job, you see."

Celia smiled at his foolishness, which caused her blasted lip to split open. She dabbed at the spot with the heel of her hand. "Perhaps I should make a good pirate."

He stroked his chin as though seriously considering her pirate-worthiness. "'Tisn't possible. You've too soft a heart, lass. We pirates are a bloodthirsty lot. We've no compassion."

"How do you know I've a soft heart?"

"Your concern is for your family, not yourself. And you defend your betrothed even though you do not wish to marry him. There is obviously something disagreeable about the man."

Stars above. How had she maligned poor Brett so? "Oh, but Mr. Kensington is truly—"

He raised his hand to shush her. "Do not trouble yourself defending the man. I shall not believe you anywise." Laughter tinged his voice and Celia realized he teased her. Which meant his eyes had little silver sparks in them now.

"I daresay you must be a horrid pirate as well, Captain. My being aboard this ship and unmolested is proof."

"Ahem." He glanced over his shoulder. "We shouldn't wish that bit of information to become known. You shall raise hope where none should be raised." He sounded amused again. "I pray you keep the state of your virtue between the two of us."

"I shouldn't dream of ruining your reputation, sir. Particularly if doing so would imperil me. However, it does prove my claim, does it not?"

"Oh, I don't know. Likely there's a bit of a pirate's soul in all of us. Else we'd find life rather dull; I should think."

Celia's gaze roamed about the shadow-shrouded ship to the dark sea beyond the railing. She did not think the words "pirate" and "soul" belonged in the same vocabulary. She straightened, aligning her back with the fo'c'sle, and rested her hands on her knees. The gentle breeze tickled her neck and flirted with her hair.

"I cannot erase their images from my head," she said softly, forcing Jack to lean closer to hear. "At night, when I close my eyes, I see those men from the *Essex*. Lying there. Dying. Over and over again. I smell the smoke and hear the screams. And sometimes they're my own. I don't know if I shall ever be the same again." Tears streamed a path down her cheeks. "It has changed me. I am frightened. And I am angry. I am so damned angry, Jack."

She balled her hands into fists and struck them against her knees, a punctuation to her emotions.

Unable to help himself, Jack plucked Celia up and settled her onto his lap. He twined his fingers with hers and held her, offering his strength and comfort. He leaned his cheek atop her head and spoke against her hair.

"I've been all over the world. Experienced things you cannot begin to imagine. I've seen horrible acts of cruelty. Aye, there is evil in this world. And you've witnessed a bit. But I've also seen remarkable feats of heroism by the most unlikely of men. I've had the honor to call some of them friend."

"You killed a French pirate and rescued a…charred woman," she added.

He brushed his cheek alongside hers to whisper, "Only slightly charred. Most of her is still in good order." He squeezed her fingers. "I shouldn't throw her away just yet."

Her head fell back against his shoulder. "I am relieved to hear it." He snuggled her tighter against him and let out a sigh of his own, of contentment.

"My point is our experiences are simply fibers of

our character. They do not own us. They do not define us or our lives unless we allow them to. 'Tis a choice to live in fear. You cannot change the past, no matter how you might wish it. You have your life. You have hope. Those from the *Essex* do not. You are strong, and you've survived. You must honor the fallen by living."

Silence followed his words. The ship dipped, the sails snapped, and the timbers groaned. Jack pushed her windblown hair away from his face and stroked his fingers through the long, sable strands. She sighed, and he felt it against his body like a long, slow caress. He oughtn't have put her on his lap. But she felt so good in his arms, soft and gentle. She made him feel strong and protective. A balm to her bruised soul.

Her breath hitched, and her voice trembled. "Thank you."

He rubbed his cheek against her silky hair in reply.

"What will become of me once we reach Charles Town, Jack?"

"You shall bide with me until we find you passage home." His body making decisions again without his head's permission. He tugged on her hair. "You needn't be afraid anymore."

"I am relieved. I do feel…safe, with you," she admitted.

"Even as I abscond with you across the ocean?" He chuckled.

She peered up at him and her lips curved. Jack felt that tiny little smile glow inside him, enormously pleased he'd put it there. "Even so."

Jack pulled her head back down to his shoulder and leaned his cheek against hers. "I suppose 'tis chivalrous to make a lady feel safe. It shall have to do. I should prefer to chase you around the cabin and have my wicked way with you, mind."

Her fingers covered her lips, and she giggled. "Behave, sir."

Snuggling her closer, he slid his arms up beneath her breasts and lowered his voice to rasp in her ear. "Very well. Tell me about this poor, unfortunate Brett who's to be saddled with you."

****

Crawley and Jenkins stood toe to toe when Jack stepped on deck. Crawley's face was flushed with anger and Jenkins, well, with a patch covering one eye and the other blackened from the broken nose he'd suffered when he plunged into the hatch, 'twas difficult to determine which emotion currently rode the man.

Jack considered the two. "Have we a problem?"

"This son-of-a-gun thinks 'e don't hafta do no work," Crawley snarled. "Says 'e's feelin' poorly and canna pull his weight."

"Aye?" Jack looked Jenkins over and received a glare from the black eye. "He looks sound to me."

"Me leg's swelled and me nose is broke," Jenkins spat, his fury diminished somewhat by his comic tone of voice. The broken nose turned his speech into a whine. "Can't see out o' me eye."

Jack glanced at Crawley, who rubbed a hand over his mouth to cover his smile. "'Tis fortunate that swabbing decks does not require good eyesight, Jenkins."

Jenkins stiffened, and his hands fisted at his sides. "I ain't swabbin' this tub, Beaumont."

"If I had known you preferred scrubbing my other ship, I would have left you aboard her." Jack gestured across the blue horizon to the *Mirabelle*. "Howbeit, you are bound to the *Lass* until you reach port and a locked gaol."

Jenkins limped closer to Jack. "The *Mirabelle* is mine, ye bleedin' bastard. I'm next in command after Jean Pierre."

"Ah, but pirates above all understand the quirks of fate," Jack goaded. "I won the day, thus you forfeited the prize. The *Mirabelle* is mine."

"Ye've won naught. Be warned, Captain." Jenkins raised a fist. "I shall slit yer throat before I let ye have the *Mirabelle*. The end of yer days is nigh."

"Perhaps you ought to swim to port then," Jack suggested, unimpressed.

"Sod off, Beaumont."

The ship dipped over a swell just as Celia stepped up from the companionway. The abrupt shift caught her unawares, knocking her sideways into Jenkins, who was forced to use his injured leg to maintain his balance.

"Friggin' mutton," he swore and latched a hand onto her arm to right himself.

Fire singed Jack's eyes at the sight of the filthy sod touching her, and his temper ignited. He snatched her elbow from the bastard's clutches and pulled her to his side. His actions caused Jenkins to stumble forward on his injured leg.

The pirate grunted in pain and drew himself upright. His lip curled. "Per'aps if ye minded yer sails instead o' this bitch's skirts ye wouldn't—"

Jack's fist slammed into Jenkins' face.

The pirate flew backward and landed on the deck with a thud.

Feeling cheated, Jack dropped his hand to his side and shook it out. The reprisal was unconsciously done on his part, and he very much wanted to thrash the man while fully cognizant of his actions.

Celia grabbed his arm with both hands, sensing his thoughts perhaps.

He gave her hand a reassuring pat, but when he spoke his voice lashed with menace. "Touch her again and I'll keelhaul you, you filthy bastard."

Jenkins rolled from side to side, howling while blood spilled from his mouth and nose.

Andrew swung from the yardarm like a pair of breeches hung out to dry, his face brimming with excitement. Bloodthirsty little urchin. He ought to send the boy to the galley with Scully.

"Clap him in irons," Jack ordered.

"Done put Blue Tooth in 'em this mornin', Cap'n," Crawley said. "The curs enjoy them iron bracelets."

"Bugger off," Jenkins snarled, blood beginning to form a puddle beneath him.

"And give the bleeding lubber a holystone," Jack said to Crawley, his temper flaring at the bastard's insolence. "He'll clean his blood off my deck or feel the lash."

Celia flinched at his tone, and he wrapped an arm about her shoulders.

"You are unharmed?"

"Aye, Jackson. I do beg your forgiveness for causing a stir."

"You did nothing of the sort." Jack tucked her arm in his and led her away to the stern of the ship. "'Tis I who must apologize for allowing the man to touch you. It shan't happen again."

Crawley and Ollie hauled Jenkins to his feet. He spit out a mouthful of blood and his front tooth along with it.

"You would not truly keelhaul the man, would you Jack?" Celia asked, her expression troubled.

"Nay, though the blighter deserves his hide scraped from his body. The *Lass* is due for a careening. Plenty of barnacles down there to do the job."

She blanched at his words. "He appears to harbor a grudge against you."

Though gratified by the concern in her eyes, Jack did not wish her to fret. "There's little cause for worry. A few nights in the hold with the rats shall do wonders for his disposition."

****

One ought to manage going topside for air without an ornery sea captain dogging their heels. Celia was convinced Jackson Beaumont existed to bedevil her. Any topic would do. Today he'd chosen her unfortunate incident with his pistol.

"A body could spit a ball with truer aim."

Pity he was so big. It made it hard to ignore him. "'Tis impolite to slander my marksmanship, sir."

"'Tis a crime to call it marksmanship. I'm confident Jenkins would agree."

"As only his leg was injured, perhaps not."

"You may be correct," he conceded. "The man did have a leg to spare if he lost one."

She placed a hand against the wall of the narrow corridor as the ship rolled and allowed an image of Jack swinging from the halyard to bloom in her mind.

"You've the manners of a ruffian. Doubtless acquired from years at sea. And the Colonies," she added to goad him. Reaching the steps, she glanced over her shoulder to see his reaction.

Jack shook his head mournfully. “Your narrow-minded Englishness does you no credit.”

“I do not believe ‘Englishness’ is a word.”

“Oh? A governess, are you? Here to instruct me on my grammar?”

“Someone really ought to.”

His chuckle echoed in the companionway. “My tutor shall be offended by your slander.”

“One can imagine the stamp of instructor you were reduced to.” The chuckle turned into a laugh. “But then, one must also make allowances for the intellect he had to work with.”

“You wound me, Miss Breckenridge,” he said cheerfully.

They came topside. At the last step Jack reached out and slipped an arm around her waist to assist her. A simple grasp of the hand would’ve sufficed. A chiding look and a pointed glance where his arm yet lingered conveyed her exasperation with him.

His expression bore a ridiculous combination of confusion and innocence. He gave an exaggerated sigh and released her.

She supposed she ought to be flattered considering her appearance. Her mouth had mostly healed with only a small scab left on her upper lip, her complexion now a pinkish hue with scalloped edges of white where the skin had peeled away. Though she still itched, she no longer flaked, and it appeared she’d have no lasting damage. Except for the unfortunate color. Jack insisted it looked quite fetching.

Mama would weep.

The morning was fine, if a bit breezy, with high puffs of white clouds shifting across the brilliant blue sky overhead. The frisky winds snatched at her bonnet and tossed her dark skirts to and fro like a church bell calling the faithful. Strong winds meant a fast ship. Indeed, the *Bonny Lass* soared over the waves with every inch of canvas filled.

A sudden lurch of the ship caused Celia to stumble and throw her arms out. Doubtless she resembled a drunken tar trying to navigate his way on dry land. She straightened and managed to regain her balance but stumbled again at the arresting sight that greeted her.

She turned to Jack. "Is that land?"

"Land?" He looked to where she pointed over her shoulder and stroked his chin. "Why, yes, I believe it is."

His crewmen all wore foolish grins. Even the pirates were amused.

"Is…is it the Colonies?" she couldn't help asking, her voice emerging as if she'd asked him to confirm a horrible disease. Landing on a crude continent could hardly be better, she reasoned.

Pitying glances and disappointed shakes of the head answered her. Jack still looked amused. Celia couldn't determine which reaction she found more vexing.

He came forward and took her arm, steering her to the rail. "Aye, you see the Colonies, Celia, though we're far from port yet."

"Then why trim the sails?" She pointed to the men in the rigging. "You are slowing the ship, are you not?"

"The winds are unusually strong and blowing nor'east. 'Tis nigh impossible to enter port under such conditions. We shall allow Spinnakers to take the lead and follow the *Mirabelle* in if he's able." Far off in the distance the white spec of the *Mirabelle's* sails showed against the horizon. Jack leaned his elbow against the rail and caught the heel of his boot on the cording stacked beneath.

"You are unable to guide the ship yourself?" Frankly, this astonished Celia. 'Twas incomprehensible he would cede authority to another man or that he lacked a necessary skill. He seemed so competent.

He reached up and tugged on a lock of hair the wind had blown loose from her sturdy bonnet, twining it about his finger. "I'm capable enough. But I shan't allow pride to replace good sense. Spinnakers has been the *Bonny Lass's* navigator since long before I signed on. As he instructed me, I bow to his experience."

"You and your crew have sailed with one another a long time then, have you?" They seemed a family almost, the men aboard this ship. It showed in small, inconsequential ways, such as the way they all laughed together. "How did you come to own the *Bonny Lass*?"

"I inherited her from the former captain, Seamus McDonald. He and his wife, Rose, essentially adopted me when I signed on."

"How old were you?"

"Six."

"Six! Good heavens. What of your parents, Jack?"

"Dead." The word was short, clipped, his tone flat and emotionless. Clearly not a subject he cared to discuss.

"But you don't sound like a common tar. If you went to sea at such a young age, how did you come to be educated?"

A small smile played about his lips. His gaze roamed about the ship as if conjuring memories long stored in the places it touched. Celia followed his gaze, imagining him as a young boy growing up under the influence of tars.

"It so happened one of the crew was a schoolmaster. He took a voyage as a young man and decided he preferred the sea to spoiled aristocratic children. Captain McDonald insisted he tutor me and gave him a portion of my share as payment. I found this deuced unfair." He smiled, his eyes gone distant with memories. "I was a greater trial than any of his former pupils, I'll warrant."

Celia gave a soft snort. "Doubtless you still are. Is this man in your service now, or did he finally succumb?"

Jack looked off in the distance toward the *Mirabelle*. "He learned to tolerate me. Fortunate, as he is also my navigator. Spinnakers excels in mathematics. 'Tis one of the reasons he is so very good at what he does." He shook his head sadly. "He shall be devastated when he hears of your slander."

She smiled. "And were you a good student?"

"Abysmal, though instead of rapping my knuckles, he handed me a holystone." He glanced around the ship and shook his head ruefully. "I've sanded every inch of these decks a dozen times at least."

Her smile turned into a laugh. "Judging from your 'abysmal' behavior, 'twould appear you've much yet to learn."

He tugged on the lock of hair still twined in his finger, letting it slip free. "As I am eight and twenty now, he's quite given up on me."

"As old as that are you?" She looked him over skeptically. "One would never guess."

Another of those breath-halting smiles parted his lips, promising all manner of decadent delights. "I am well preserved."

"You are childish," she corrected. "And a rascal and a lecher." And so horribly attractive and undeniably male that fate must surely be punishing her.

"All of that, am I?" He reached for her hand. "Quite an interesting sort then, don't you agree?" He brought her fingers to his lips and held her gaze as he kissed them. "You shan't grow bored with me, I vow."

Precisely. Devil take him. Perhaps if she dangled a note that said "I am betrothed" from her hat so it hung before her eyes. A constant reminder seemed imperative in this man's company.

She straightened her spine. "I shan't grow anything with you, sir, as I am a betrothed woman. I'll thank you to remember it."

"Come now, Celia." His smile turned coaxing and adorable, like a little boy begging for a treat. He reached for her hand again. "Even promised women deserve a few enjoyments."

"Not," she snatched her hand out of his reach, "with you."

She bobbed a swift curtsy and walked away, stifling the urge to run.

Chapter Seven

On Tuesday, the first of September, twelve days after Celia's rescue, the *Bonny Lass* entered Charles Town Harbor on the heels of the *Mirabelle*.

A harrowing arrival to be sure.

The powerful gusts beat the ships back. Just as Jack declared they'd be stacked on Charles Town bar with the other vessels trying to make it into port, the winds calmed slightly. It seemed a portent to Celia, as if an invisible hand passed through the current of air long enough to lure them in.

Her misgivings were born out when, as soon as the ships began the treacherous entry across the pass from the Atlantic to the harbor, the gusts increased in earnest, nearly dashing them against the rocks. Only by the grace of God did both ships make it through. Jack and crew acknowledged the shaking fists from the ships caught on the bar with a jaunty wave and a bow. Celia clutched the rail as her legs had turned to pudding.

Her first glimpse of Charles Town revived her, filling her with awe.

Nestled between the Ashley and Cooper rivers, the town formed a small peninsula, the tip of which jutted out into a natural harbor. Charming buildings winked like jewels in the bright morning sunshine; warm, inviting, and blessedly solid. Nothing like the image of crudely built structures she'd embraced.

Veering northwest, the ships made their way to the mouth of the Cooper River. The *Bonny Lass* nudged into her berth at a dock Jack referred to as Pinckney's Bridge, while the *Mirabelle* anchored off her stern in the river.

"Mr. Oliver," Jack called. "Row to the *Mirabelle* and tell Mr. Smith to belay unloading his prisoners. I'll speak with the port officer and have this group transferred to the gaol first."

"Aye, Cap'n." Ollie and a couple of hands lowered the skiff into the water.

Jack turned to Celia.

Embarrassed, she wiped at her eyes with her gloved fingers and looked away. "You must think me very foolish, Captain, but when I was taken aboard the *Mirabelle*, I thought never to see land again. Even after you rescued me from the pirates, I would not permit myself to hope. I simply awaited whatever fate chose to grant me. But now we have arrived and…" Her gaze rose to meet his. His eyes had gone soft, his smile tender, and suddenly she wanted to throw herself in his arms and weep like a child.

She squared her shoulders and cleared her throat. "I am grateful to you."

Capturing her hand, he held it in his and bowed. "My sincere pleasure, madam. And now I beg you to collect yourself. As much as I would spare you this ordeal, we must visit the constable."

Celia sighed in resignation. Deliverance had its price. "I should much prefer anonymity to public testimony."

He placed his hands on her shoulders and touched his forehead to hers. "I shall spare you all I am able, but

I'll not allow these villains to escape justice."

"Aye." She lifted her hands to cover his. "I know."

"Once we've finished, I shall introduce you to my home."

"I've a lengthy voyage to Bermuda before me. I should enjoy the solid earth beneath my feet for a spell."

He gave her a repressive frown.

"Uh, Cap'n," Rory interrupted.

"What is it?" Jack asked, still scowling, though what she'd said to annoy him, she could not imagine.

"The weather's sort'a queer-like, ain't it?"

Celia followed Jack's gaze skyward. A chill pierced her spine.

The sailmaker scratched his head. "I'm thinkin' we're in fer a blow."

Jack's gaze dropped to Rory, who shifted uncomfortably beneath it. "Damn. I suspected as much. We've two ships, two cargos, and a load of pirates to see to. Is that not enough?"

Rory said nothing to this as he obviously had no control over the weather.

"Pirates, damsels, and now the bleeding weather." Jack clenched and unclenched his fists. "How the devil am I supposed to find anything when fate thwarts me at every turn?"

Find? It seemed a rather odd thing to say. Celia turned to Rory in question.

He shrugged.

"How bad?" Jack asked, his gaze flicking in a circuit between sea and sky and land.

"A real pisser, I expect." Rory pulled off his cap and wiped the sweat from his brow.

"No doubt the town's been praying for rain," Jack said. "If so, they've outdone themselves famously. 'Tis deuced hot. A day or two would you say?"

"Two, no more," Rory replied then nodded as though his head were confirming what his mouth had declared.

Jack ran his hand over his scalp, cupping his neck. "We shall divest the pirates and head back out to sea until it passes. Find Scully and tell him to buy provisions to last another week."

"Aye, Cap'n." Rory tipped his cap to Celia and beat a hasty retreat.

"Apprise the *Mirabelle* of our plans," Jack called and stared after him, his gaze distant and unfocused. His chest swelled and he blew out a breath. Then he turned back to Celia and his lips curved. "And you thought your life unexciting, Miss Breckenridge."

****

"Ho, Jackson B!"

Jack's head snapped up and his temples immediately took to throbbing. Surely the stress of the day had conjured that voice. His mind's way of saying, "Aye, it could be worse."

He abandoned the possibility when he caught the look of fascination on Celia's face, and turned, though every instinct screamed not to.

Elgin Ireland swaggered up the gangway in an outlandish scarlet coat replete with wide black cuffs and carved ivory buttons. The astounding number of ruffles on the man's shirt ought to be taxed. They billowed out in a mass exodus from his gold waistcoat and again from the cuffs of his coat sleeves, concealing his hands entirely.

"I need a drink." Jack clamped a hand over his aching skull.

"A friend of yours, I presume," Celia murmured from behind him.

He twisted enough to glare at her beneath his hand. "I ought to flog you for that."

"Ye scurvy dog. Come ta darken the shores o' Charles Town again, have ye?" Ireland's tricorn tilted jauntily forward atop a shoulder-length wig of fat white curls. Dyed-red plumes of some ill-fated bird poked through the crown of his hat and shuddered with each stride as if warning the masses to flee. A dark smudge near the corner of his left eye turned into a tattoo of a bird in flight as he drew near.

"This day has gone to hell," Jack said.

Ireland gave him a hearty slap on the arm. "What sort of greeting is that, me bucko?"

"Why the deuce are you here? I thought you in Curacao."

"Hell mate, that were five months ago." The volume of the man's response caused Jack to wince. No mean feat considering his own booming voice.

"Your crew mutinied?"

"Har. Ye're a lively one, Jocko," Ireland hooted. He leaned his head to the side to peer around Jack, his eyes flaring appreciatively as they roamed over Celia.

Jack ground his teeth together. Though she remained behind him, he felt her stiffen, momentarily distracting him. He doubted her Mr. Kensington was as attuned to her as he.

The bewigged annoyance before him shook back his coat tails and made a leg, displaying what had to be the longest pair of boots in existence. They stopped mid-thigh and folded into wide cuffs reaching to his knees.

"Begad Ireland," Jack choked. "How the devil do you walk in those hideous things?"

Ireland ignored him and nodded to Celia. "Introduce us."

"No." Jack jutted chin out and crossed his arms stubbornly.

"Why ye disagreeable whoreson," Ireland sputtered. "What's the matter? A'feared I'll take her from ye?"

Like as not the scoundrel would plague him all day if he did not. He let out a sigh of resignation. "I most humbly beg your pardon, Celia, but may I introduce Mr. Elgin Ireland?"

"*Captain* Elgin Ireland," the fop corrected and bowed so low his plumes brushed the deck.

"That is entirely a matter of opinion," Jack grumbled.

Ireland *tsked*, giving Celia his undivided attention. "And you are?" He reached for her hand but Jack's arm shot out, anchoring her to his side and out of Ireland's reach.

"This is Miss Breckenridge," he said with ill grace. Celia grinned up at him. He returned a warning frown lest she encourage the man to linger.

Ireland's brows rose clear to his wig. He glanced between the two of them, lips pursed and eyes narrowed in shrewd assessment. A sly smile spread across his face. Jack didn't like it. "Delighted to make your acquaintance, Miss Breckenridge." He bowed again.

"Captain Ireland," Celia responded with a polite nod when Jack's hold prevented her curtsy.

His smile widened. "Evanston's fit to be tied, Jocko."

"Which one?"

"Does it matter?" Ireland waved absently, rings glinting in the sun, his gaze fixed on Celia.

She smiled again. At Ireland.

The woman could not find the peacock charming. If so, Jack would be duty-bound to protect her from her deplorable judgment as well. He tightened his hold and grunted when she elbowed him in the ribs.

"I suppose not. They're both useless as pilots and nowhere to be seen when we arrived."

Ireland snorted. "Ye took 'em by surprise. They was at Pink's havin' a pint. How'd ye sail into port while the others are trapped off the bar?"

"We flew, didn't we, sweet?" Jack winked at Celia and gave her a squeeze.

Ireland snorted again, but then his eyes widened, and the snort turned into a fit of coughing. He rapped his chest with his fist, which caused the plumes in his hat to shake at them.

"What the deuce is Jenkins doin' aboard the *Lass*, Jocko? Come to that, why the devil is the *Mirabelle* at yer heels? Have ye taken up with Jean Pierre, then?"

"Hardly." Jack snorted. "Jenkins and the rest of the *Mirabelle's* crew are our guests until we find them a nice cell to reside in."

"Oh?" Ireland's eyes lit with intrigue. "'Tis a nasty eye he's got there."

"Aye." Jack glanced over and grinned. "Looks like a squid pissed in it."

"Or a rotted clam," his contemporary suggested. "And Jean Pierre? He allowed you to take over his ship and crew?"

"Of course not."

"Where is Jean Pierre?" Ireland stroked his pointy black beard. "Is he a 'guest' as well?"

Jack knew he would regret this. "I killed him."

"Did you now?" The other man's face lit and a broad smile spread across his face. "Do, do tell." He waved a be-ringed hand in the air. "I am enthralled. Spare me not. I should like all the gruesome details."

The limit of Jack's patience had been reached. 'Twas admirable he'd lasted this long. "I haven't time to blather with you now, Elgin. I must turn these pirates over to Constable Latham and head back out to sea. Rory says we're in for a blow."

"Does he now?" Ireland's face sobered.

"Aye. Now get yourself and that gaudy coat gone."

The peacock shook out his sleeves and fingered the ruffles at his throat. "Jealous of my fashion sense, he is," he said to Celia.

"Go," Jack shouted, startling a group of pelicans from their perch on the dock. They soared over the water's surface to where the *Mirabelle* lay at anchor and plopped down one-by-one next to it.

"Very well." Ireland laughed heartily. "I shall leave. A pleasure, Miss Breckenridge." He lifted his hat in farewell, but Celia halted him as he began walking away.

"Captain. Are you aware of any ships destined for England or perhaps Bermuda at present?"

Ireland tipped his head to the side. "As it so happens, the—"

"You'll not want to book passage yet," Jack interrupted. "Wait until this weather passes. You've business with the admiralty as well. You may have to return to testify otherwise."

Celia's face fell, and Jack felt like a bastard for disappointing her. "Oh. Yes. Yes, of course."

"I'm off." Ireland headed toward the gangway. "You owe me a pint, Jackson B," he called over his shoulder without looking back. "I'll have the tale, and I shan't give ye a moment's peace until I do."

Jack sighed. "The slack-jaw means it, too." At Celia's look of inquiry, he shrugged. "The man's a nuisance, but harmless. Fancies himself a Lothario, so unless you wish to suffer his company and my sour disposition, I beg you, do not encourage him."

She tugged a mock forelock. "I shall avoid attention, sir."

He let out a snort and released her. The woman was a siren with legs. Long, shapely legs. "Perhaps if we put a sack over you."

****

A portly man with drooping jowls, Constable Latham featured deep set eyes and a red bulbous nose, hinting at a love of spirits. Celia's suspicions were confirmed when he bent over her hand, and she caught a strong whiff of port on his breath.

She and Jack followed the gentleman to his parlor; a rather benign looking room befitting its somberly dressed owner and done in varying shades of beige and brown with a small, woefully inadequate window left open to encourage a breeze.

Once they took their seats, Jack launched into an accounting of piracy and murder on the high seas. Except for a point or two required for verification, Celia remained silent. Perhaps time and repeated telling of the tale would deaden her reaction to it, but for now each charge struck her like pebbles thrown at a window—she constantly flinched.

“As the one who discovered the crime and brought the pirates to heel, I’ve claimed the *Mirabelle* as my prize,” Jack finished.

Silence fell. The atmosphere of the room grew heavy, doubtless a result of an absent breeze coupled with the weighty thoughts of its occupants.

Latham shifted in his seat. “I hardly know what to make of these charges, Captain. Quite disturbing. Quite, quite disturbing.” His manner belied his tone, however, as his gaze flitted about the room and paused longingly on the door a few times. Perhaps the messy affair required more fortitude than the man possessed.

Jack had obviously been correct when he maintained the citizenry were tolerant of pirates. He leaned forward and trapped the constable beneath a hard stare. She recognized it as the one he used on his men. It caused them to squirm as if ants had colonized in their breeches.

Constable Latham was no exception. He appeared not to know what to do with his hands. He tapped them up and down on his knees, crossed them over his paunch, and dropped them to his sides on the settee. Then tapped them on his knees again.

“I comprehend the admiralty must be notified as the crime occurred at sea,” Jack pressed. “I only ask that you keep these men incarcerated until they are tried.”

“An entire crew?” the constable blustered. “I hardly think—”

“Miss Breckenridge’s life is in danger,” Jack

interrupted, "as she is the sole survivor from the *Essex*. You shouldn't wish to risk her safety, sir. I know her grandfather—the Earl of Burlington, by the bye—shall be grateful for your decisive action in this matter."

"Burlington?" The constable paled, his mouth opening and closing like a fish. At Jack's nod his face flushed to a sickly puce. Celia couldn't help but stare. Ghastly color, what with that big red nose of his.

She shot Jack an amused glance out of the corner of her eye. He'd not been impressed with her grandfather's title when she'd tried to exploit it, though he'd no compunction against doing so himself.

Their host twisted his pudgy hands together. "Well I… of course, of course, bring them along and we shall lock them up straightaway." He gazed out the window and said absently, "I do hope they all fit."

"We shall deliver the pirates directly and set sail shortly thereafter," Jack informed Latham. "I must round up extra hands for the *Mirabelle* first. We're in for a good blow, which we'll ride out at sea. You'll want to see to your own property, Constable."

The constable's eyes widened, and he flushed again. Perhaps he feared storms.

"Oh no, Captain. You shall remain here in port until this issue of piracy is settled. I'll not allow you to swoop in, dump the matter on my doorstep, then fly off again. No. No, no, no, no." He shook his head from side to side to punctuate his words, his jowls set aquiver.

"I am hardly 'dumping the matter on your doorstep' Constable. I simply wish to spare my ship and the *Mirabelle* damage. We shall return straightaway once the storm has passed, you've my word."

"Nevertheless." The constable remained firm. "If

you wish to press charges against those men, you'll remain in port to do so, and the admiralty shall decide the matter of your claim against their ship. Those are my terms."

Jack's face turned to stone. His eyes shot sparks while he stared at Latham, as if forging the man into someone more satisfactory.

Celia placed a hand on his arm. "Captain, you are absolutely certain of this storm?"

"Aye," he groused.

"Why not leave the pirates aboard until it has passed?" she suggested. "The constable may lock them up once you return."

"My dear woman," Latham sat forward, all puffed and ruffled like an angry goose. "The law is not a convenience to be employed whenever one suits. Either you are charging these men with piracy, or you are not."

"But, sir," Celia argued. "Surely our circumstances warrant—"

"Absolutely not." Latham sliced a hand through the air to cut her off. "Oh, I understand a woman of your station is quite used to pampering and indulgence, but this is a matter of law and a matter for men to decide."

For a moment Jack thought Celia had stopped breathing, until he realized fury held her immobile. All that contained anger arrested him. He imagined it unleashed in his bed.

Latham sat back and folded his hands on his over-fed waist, quite pleased with himself. The toe of his buckled black shoe twitched over the carpet. Jack wished to punch his smug gob. "Now, Captain, let us be done with this unfortunate business. Do you intend to remain in port and press charges against these men? Or will you take yourself off to sea?"

"You will do your duty and lock those men up," Jack responded, wiping the condescension from the constable's fleshy face.

Celia's gaze flew to his. "But, Jackson—"

"I'll not let the bastards get away with what they've done to you," he said, glaring at Latham. "Or those other unfortunate souls." Even if he did have to depend on this useless excuse for the law to guard them.

The constable tut-tutted at Jack's language.

"But what of your ship?" Celia bit her lip.

Jack watched her teeth nibble her plump flesh. Such a pretty mouth to be so abused.

Her eyes narrowed on his face as if she could read his thoughts.

"We'll unload the cargo and batten them down," he said, dragging his gaze from her mouth.

She clutched her hands together in her lap. "I shall never forgive myself if your property is damaged on my behalf."

He reached over and patted her gloved hand. "You are not to blame." His gaze locked with Latham's. "I hold this man entirely responsible."

The constable's face paled.

Jack stood and pulled Celia to her feet, unable to bear the useless ass's company any longer. "Send word where you wish the pirates delivered, Latham. I must see to the ships." He tugged on Celia's arm, interrupting her brief curtsy, and pulled her out the door.

Chapter Eight

Wagons lined the docks, horses stamped in their harnesses, and tails switched at flies in the oppressive Charles Town heat. Celia commiserated with the poor beasts. With the sun beating down on her black mourning garb she felt like a chunk of coal burning in a grate. Even the breeze felt scorched. She and Jack sidestepped two sailors hauling an oaken cask down the gangway. Three more passed them on their way back. Seagulls screeched overhead amid shouts between the ship and the docks.

"Where are they taking those barrels?" She asked as they stepped onto the ship. "Do you own a warehouse nearby?"

"Most of what I bring back is sold before I set sail. Those are the buyers' wagons collecting their goods." He leaned over to confide, "Charles Town is a cultured city, you understand. Loves its French brandy and Flanders lace." He lifted his tricorn and wiped his forehead against his sleeve. "I thought to try wallpaper as well. I've heard the French designs are all the rage. And paneling. Mahogany. Excellent price. Man was desperate to sell."

"Lace?" Celia separated the wheat from the chaff. "You did not mention lace to me, sir."

His mouth split into a devilish grin as he resettled his hat. She fought the urge to fan herself. He oughtn't smile like that in this heat.

"I wanted to save you from turning pirate. You did mention an aversion to keelhauling, if you'll recall."

"That was before I knew you had lace aboard." She eyed him shrewdly. "Flanders, you say? What sort of price does it fetch here in the Colonies? Do you sell directly or use a broker?"

And now Jack's gaze turned shrewd.

Blast. Perhaps she oughtn't have broached the subject of trade with him. Men universally found a woman's interest in business distasteful. But not Papa, who'd declared he'd be damned if he'd raise stupid daughters so their fool husbands might feel superior.

A bit revolutionary, Papa's attitudes.

"Merchant's daughter," she reminded him with a prim smile.

Jack shrugged and humored her. "I've four or five buyers who'll purchase the lot. The brandy is more lucrative, as war with France pops up with alarming regularity, thus thwarting the refined palates of colonial gentlemen."

"You've sold all of your brandy as well?"

"Nearly half thus far. I shall trade what remains for spices when we sail." Cinnamon. She stared at his mouth and flushed.

"Where will you keep the remainder of the cargo?" Lud, she really needed a fan.

"I've a friend who allows me the use of his plantation on occasion. He's several sturdy outbuildings I use for storage." He cast a weather eye about. "I plan to make use of them since we've two ships to unload."

Rory called up from the dock. Jack waved back. "If you will excuse me?"

"Of course."

She made her way abaft where she watched Smitty and Spinnakers prod the pirates on the *Mirabelle* into the waiting dories that had rowed out to collect them. She turned away, relieved the villains would be locked up and no longer a threat.

Her gaze sought out Jack. His powerful body bent and strained alongside his men, masculine and utterly compelling to her feminine senses. 'Twould be a disaster to tarry here overlong. Still, she would miss him. The contrary man had carved an unwelcome place inside her heart. One she feared would forever ache once she returned to her betrothed.

Shortly thereafter, Jack recruited her to record the cargo in the manifest, noting each item's destination as it left the ship. Grateful for the distraction, it saved her from pining over a man she had yet to leave.

****

The sun sat low on the horizon before the watch was set and the remainder of the crew given leave to seek their homes and amusements.

"I am thrilled to depart this ship, Jackson," Celia said tiredly when he came to collect her, though a bit nervous at another unknown. Still, the thought of peering into Jackson Beaumont's life intrigued her. "'Twill be lovely to sleep in a real bed tonight." She paused and eyed him suspiciously. "You do have a bed for me?"

"This may surprise you, madam," he drawled. "But my household is quite civilized. One might even call it staid."

"Never say so." She feigned a look of shock as they left the docks, her hand tucked in the crook of his elbow. Though still sweltering, the lowering sun meant a measure of relief from the heat. She lifted her face to the negligible breeze as they turned a corner from Bay Street to Tradd. Charming two-story homes lined both sides with the occasional single or three-story mixed in. The architecture was unique in that the narrow, gabled end of the buildings were only one room wide and faced the street. Most residences had iron fences opening onto a walkway, and Celia caught glimpses of beautiful gardens through the wrought iron gates.

Jack allowed her to make her impressions without comment.

"I've never seen homes like these, Jack." She paused to peek through one of the fences. "Lovely, but so narrow."

"They are designed for economy of space, though we've spread beyond the walls of the city. Most have a covered piazza along the side to shelter the house from the heat."

He stopped near a three-story home of weathered brick and the ubiquitous iron fence. The size of the house surprised her, as she'd seen few so large. The gate came open when Jack touched it, and he paused to inspect the latch before gesturing her through with a flourish. "Welcome, my lady."

She curtsied as she stepped onto the stone path and passed beneath a beautiful tree filled with fragrant white blossoms—magnolia grandiflora, Jack informed her. A wild abundance of ivy and fern covered the ground and colorful flowers bordered the walkway.

"Oh, Jack," Celia breathed when she reached the center of the garden. A grand old oak stood sentry, as broad as it was tall, its crooked arms spread wide to shade the garden and a large portion of the house. Strings of the southern gray moss she'd heard about hung from its branches and a great stone bench curved around the trunk. "'Tis lovely."

His home should not be inviting. She preferred a practical, masculine place, barely fit for a female. Her stay was not supposed to be enjoyable, but rather a necessity.

"It seems quite a large house for an unmarried sea captain." Indeed, the place was rife with opportunity for a fertile female. Celia hated her, whoever she turned out to be.

Jack shrugged. "I bought it from a cabinetmaker's widow. She took her children and moved back to York after her husband died. The family lived in the upper two stories and used the lower to display the pieces the man made. Smitty converted his workshop there into a small house." He pointed at a building the size of a carriage house with a small garden to one side. A short path led between the back of the main house and a block structure she assumed to be the kitchen, with another garden—vegetables this time—planted in-between.

They continued up the steps to the piazza that stretched the length of the house. A set of French doors opened farther down, and a wrought-iron table and chairs sat behind a rail overlooking the garden. He opened a green painted door and ushered her through it.

"Meagan. Where are you hiding, me love?" Jack called and tossed his tricorn on a hook.

Laughter reached them and shuffling footsteps followed. A middle-aged woman in a serviceable blue dress and white apron came into view.

"Aye, I'm here ye rascal. Come ta beg fer me favors again, have ye?" She swiped at her damp forehead with her apron, her apple cheeks flushed from her labors. Tendrils of white-blonde hair escaped her mobcap and clung to her face.

Jack wrapped her in his arms and twirled her about. "Have you come to your senses, love, and tossed that worthless scoundrel aside?"

"Jackie." She laughed. "Put me down before ye hurt yer back."

Jackie? Celia grinned. This man had more monikers than a thespian. Oh, but this one was adorable. She should have great fun with Jackie. Perhaps Captain Jackie or Jackie B.

He shot her a quelling glance, easily divining her thoughts. He gave Meagan a squeeze and planted a loud, smacking kiss on her cheek before setting her back to her feet.

"Allow me to introduce you to Smitty's wife, Meagan," he said to Celia. "Our fair Meagan is a most excellent cook and keeps the house with young Molly's help. When we're in port, Smitty divides his time between refitting the ship and whatever chores Meagan finds for him. Meagan, this is Miss Celia Breckenridge. She's to be our guest."

Celia smiled and took the woman's rough, reddened hand. "I am so pleased to make your acquaintance, Mrs. Smith."

"Oh, Meagan will do, dearie. We're an informal lot around here." She patted Celia's hand. "Welcome to Charles Town. My Johnny spoke of yer tribulations, and it breaks my heart, ye poor dear. We shall see ye nice and comfortable, and soon ye'll forget all about them nasty ol' boats."

Jack cleared his throat at the insult to his ship, but she ignored him.

"'Tis very kind of you, Meagan. I am certain my stay here will be lovely." Celia slid a glance to Jack. "I expect we shall become fast friends. We must if we've any hope of gaining the upper hand with this rogue."

"See here, madam," he objected hotly. "I'll not have you brewing mischief between me and my Meagan."

"Leave me wife be, ye rovin' sea dog." Smitty entered the room. "She's a smart woman, my Meagan. Too smart ta be takin' up with the likes of ye. Find yer own." He draped a possessive arm over his wife's shoulders.

Jack stroked his chin and turned speculative eyes upon Celia. Her heart thumped enthusiastically. *Traitor.* She threw her hands up to ward him off.

"Ill-mannered females," he grumbled.

Meagan chuckled and put her arm through Celia's, steering her into the hall. "I'll show ye to your room, miss, so ye can freshen up afore supper. Ye're probably starved nigh to death, bein' stuck on that boat all day long."

"Make that woman stop calling my ship a boat," Jack demanded of Smitty. Meagan's lips curved in a mischievous smile. 'Twould seem Jack wasn't the only rascal in the house. Celia liked Meagan already.

"Supper's nearly ready. Molly's keepin' an eye in the kitchen fer me. I'll send her up directly to help ye get settled."

"'Twould be lovely, Meagan, thank you." Celia smiled and lifted her skirts to keep from tripping on the narrow stairs. "The captain seems very fond of you."

"Aye." Meagan chuckled. "I've known him from a wee lad, though 'tis hard to believe the scamp ever was small."

"Jack and your husband have sailed together for a long time?"

"Oh, aye. We've all had a hand in raisin' him, ye see. Seamus and Rose, and John and me. Much of the crew as well."

Celia tried to picture Jack as a young boy, growing up under the influence of so many. She supposed it wasn't much different than an aristocratic upbringing. Servants and governesses had more of a hand in the raising of a child than their parents, though of late it had become popular for parents to take an interest in their offspring. Her mother thought it appalling to embrace child rearing as a fashion.

"How did he come to be with you?"

Meagan's head shook, her expression bemused. "I surely don't know. The *Lass* was docked in Southampton at the time. John said the boy just showed up one day, askin' Seamus to take him on. Refused to speak of his family, though Seamus tried to find them, for 'twas obvious from the lad's speech and manners he didna belong there on the docks. But Jackie, well, all he'd say was his parents were dead and he wanted to go to sea." She motioned to a pair of doors when they reached the landing. "Those are his rooms."

They headed up a second flight of steps, the close confines of the staircase overwarm as they climbed higher. "Well, ye never met a man with a softer heart than Seamus McDonald, and no mistake. He couldna leave the boy alone there, so Seamus took him on. He and Rose, they'd lost their daughter to a lung fever, ye see, and Jackie, well…Rose figured he was a gift from God sent to heal the hole in their hearts. John and I were never blessed with children, so Jackie became our little blessing too."

Tears stung the backs of Celia's eyes. How perfectly amazing that fate had brought them all together. Just as it had done her and Jack. She cleared her throat. "'Tis hard to imagine that scoundrel below as a lost little boy. I rather pictured him as a little terror."

"Oh, most assuredly and never ye doubt it." Meagan laughed as they reached the top of the stairs. "Rose and I, we shared the mothering of young Jackie when the men were in port." She rolled her eyes. "Ye can imagine the language they taught him."

They entered the bedchamber Celia was to use. Beautiful, carved oak furniture populated the space, including a trundle bed with a white, embroidered coverlet and a wardrobe with her trunks placed alongside it. Candle and flint sat on a small bedside table.

"You never learned of his family?"

"Never spoke of them. 'Twas years before we learned his surname. Sad, is it not?"

"He said Spinnakers educated him."

"Did he now?" Meagan's eyes widened in surprise. "He talks little of himself. I should consider it a compliment, miss."

"It seems only fair," Celia said wryly. "He's pried enough of my secrets loose."

"Oh aye, and he'll use them to bedevil ye," Meagan warned, smoothing down the coverlet.

"Aye, he does," Celia grumbled.

Across the room, a long window framed with frilly white curtains was open to catch the evening breeze, the old oak visible beyond. Her sister would love the gorgeous old tree. A smile creased her lips. Were Rianna here, Celia would compare the hanging moss to her hair. Perhaps she'd learned some bedeviling herself.

"'Tisn't the fanciest to be sure, but a step above where ye've been restin', I expect. Molly will sleep here in the trundle bed with ye so ye shan't be alone in the house with Jackie."

Celia's cheeks warmed and she wondered if Meagan knew of her sleeping quarters aboard ship. Since her husband had captained the *Mirabelle*, perhaps not.

"'Tis lovely Meagan, truly."

"I'll go see to yer meal," Meagan said and started back down the stairs. "Ye'll find fresh water and towels at the washstand."

"I shall make haste." Celia eyed the bed longingly as she removed her gloves, bonnet, and dress, having become an expert at managing her own clothing aboard ship. She used a small bar of lavender scented soap to scrub the dust from her face and neck. Unearthing her hairbrush from her trunk, she soon had pins piled neatly on the vanity.

A light rap came at the door as she worked the stiff brush through her long tresses. "'Tis Molly, miss." A lively young woman with light brown hair, soft blue eyes, and a smattering of freckles across her face entered and bobbed a curtsy.

Celia rose to greet her. "I am pleased to meet you, Molly, and I thank you for your assistance. I'm a bit weary after a long day on the docks."

"Think nothing of it," Molly replied cheerily, her smile bright and friendly. "Would ye like a fresh gown unpacked?"

"Please. You'll find one at the top of that first trunk."

Molly rummaged inside and pulled out her best black gown. "Ye poor dear. Mourning are ye? I'll just shake it out and lay it on the bed, shall I?"

Once her hair looked presentable, Molly helped her work the gown over the wide panniers at her hips and fasten the short row of buttons.

"There ye are, good as new."

Perhaps on the outside, Celia thought as she headed down to dinner. The inside longed for the bed she'd left behind. She wondered how many more of Jack's secrets she might uncover during her stay. Her flagging spirits lifted. Perhaps this detour to Charles Town would turn into the adventure Jack promised.

****

French doors stood open to the sultry evening, the yellow-papered walls of the dining room aglow in the light of the waning day. This room had been made just for her, Jack decided, this vibrant, green-eyed beauty who radiated her surroundings. Even the black shroud of her mourning garb could not dim her glow.

He sat her to his right and took his seat at the head of the table. It disturbed him how natural her presence here felt. A man could spring his own trap thinking such foolishness. Forget his purpose.

Ah, but not this man, for the woman was already promised.

Meagan bustled in after them. "'Tis simple fare

ye'll be having this eve, what with ye newly arrived and all." She placed a thick venison stew on the table in front of them with a basket of freshly baked bread. "I'll be stocking the larder now that ye're home."

A rather loud growl issued from Celia's stomach. She flushed and covered the offending organ with her hands. "Oh Meagan, it smells wonderful."

Jack chose to be a devil. "A pity you'll not be able to enjoy it."

Her gaze flew to his as if he'd uttered a blasphemy.

"Whyever not?" Meagan's brow wrinkled.

He ignored the question and gave Celia a meaningful look. "'Tis *stew*. The meat and vegetables are mixed together."

She widened her eyes in censure and kicked him under the table.

Meagan's hands went to her hips, gaze shifting back and forth between them.

"Miss Breckenridge is a very orderly person," he explained. "Eats each item on her plate one at a time. First her meat then her vegetables and so forth, never mixing a blessed thing, though I'm confident it all congregates together once it reaches its destination. 'Twas most piteous work, her meals aboard the *Bonny Lass*. You should have seen her fishing through Scully's lobscouse."

Celia snapped her napkin open and dropped it over her lap. "Those hard biscuits hid the…meat, I believe you called it? I was told there were vegetables."

"The stew here is contrary to her exacting palate," he continued.

"I shall soldier on." She sniffed. "Pay him no mind, Meagan. It so happens I adore stew, and this looks divine."

Meagan beamed at her. "I've a cake to serve ye fer dessert. Been rappin' me Johnny's knuckles to keep him out of it."

"You've likely bloodied them by now," Jack guessed.

"Nearly so." She laughed as she headed out of the room. "Ye'll want to eat quickly if ye've need of his hands on the morrow."

"'Tis odd to be dining at a table that is not moving." And in the *colonies,* no less. Her sister would be in a taking when she learned of it.

Jack ladled stew into their bowls. "Likely you'll not rest without being rocked to sleep."

"On the contrary, my body is so weary I shan't recall lying down." Celia took a bite of her meal and closed her eyes in appreciation. "Oh, this is delicious. And look, Jackson, the vegetables are cut into very large chunks."

They conversed little, as they were both hungry, and Meagan came in to clear the table just as they pushed their empty dishes away.

"Delicious, Meagan," Celia complimented her. "I must take care lest my clothing grow too tight whilst here."

"Ye need some meat on yer bones, Miss Celia. Ye're too thin."

Jack's gaze fastened on Celia's bosom. They looked perfectly proportioned to him, the soft mounds swelling above her dark gown plump and healthy. He turned his attention away from temptation and back to Meagan.

"Where is your husband, madam? I thought he'd be

threatening life and limb by now."

"Fussin' in the kitchen and calling ye foul names."

He shared a conspiratorial wink with Celia. "Perhaps we ought to have more stew."

Meagan grunted. "Ye may have avoided mutiny aboard yer ship all these years, but ye're about to suffer one in yer kitchen."

"I don't doubt it." He leaned back in his chair and stretched his legs out. "Bring him along with the cake then if you must."

Smitty trailed Meagan and their dessert into the dining room. Jack discussed his plans to unload the *Mirabelle* with him while Celia's eyes drooped to half-mast, and she listed to port.

"I should prefer our scribe again tomorrow." Jack startled her from her stupor. "Though I doubt we shall coax her anywhere near a ship."

Smitty shrugged and helped himself to seconds.

Celia's spine straightened. "On the contrary, sir. I believe I shall see this particular journey to its end. Which includes the unloading of that awful pirate ship."

"'Tisn't so bad," Smitty said around a mouthful of cake. "We set the picaroons to work on her. She's much improved, though she wants careening."

"There's a good girl." Jack patted her hand. "I should prefer to focus my energies on the cargo and not those tedious manifests." And, he was forced to admit, but only to himself, that he'd grown rather fond of having her around.

"Ye're aware the admiralty ain't in port?" Smitty said, changing the subject. Celia's fingers stiffened beneath Jack's hand. He gave her fingers a squeeze.

"They've a ship anchored in the bay."

"Aye. She'll be sent back to England for repairs, but she hasn't officers aboard. Tattle is, her replacement arrived a month past without a captain—the old buck took ill and died at sea. The officers took command of his ship and escorted a fleet of merchants to the Caribbean."

Celia's gaze flicked between Jack and Smitty worriedly. "When will they return?"

Jack stroked her delicate hand to soothe her, the feel of her soft skin soothing him as well. She might be forced to remain in port for a spell, perhaps until he returned if the admiralty were obliging. He balked at the satisfaction the thought produced.

She was not for him.

"Could'na say." Smitty reached for the cake. "They sailed some three weeks past."

"Leave off, man, before you take ill." Jack moved the plate a few inches away.

Smitty reached a hand out to stop him and scooped up another slice. "Never took ill from me wife's cake."

Chapter Nine

Provisions Scully ordered began arriving at the ship around midday. Provisions for a voyage they would no longer take. Jack was not pleased.

"Take an accounting of what they've brought," he said to Celia, "whilst I have a word with my cook." She gave him a jaunty salute and turned back to the barrel-laden wagon.

He found Scully in the hold, sweating profusely and hoisting a trunk with Crawley. Scully's hair, which normally consisted of a neat braid, hung tangled over his shoulders as if seaweed had populated his head. His deeply tanned face looked pale and strained, suggesting he might whip the cat at any moment. Jack kept a respectful distance. Physically anyway. His booming voice made up for it.

"Why the devil are provisions arriving when we're unloading this bleeding ship?"

The trunk thudded between the two men's feet. Scully blanched and put a fist to his mouth. His cheeks bulged out as though his fist were a bellows filling them. Jack took another step out of range, having no desire to wear the contents of another person's stomach.

"Uh, beggin' yer pardon, Cap'n, but ye said ta order sufficient fer a sennight. What wit' transportin' Jenkins and his lot and unloadin' the *Lass*, I plum forgot all about 'em."

Crawley snorted and scratched his chest. “All the elbow bendin’ ’e did at Pinks yester’eve fogged his noggin, more’s like.”

“Sock-head. Shut yer gob.” Scully’s sudden spurt of anger cost him. He put a hand up to squeeze his temples. Doubtless the dank smell of the hold provoked his condition.

Jack crossed his arms over his chest, his steely-eyed stare taking the wind out of their sails. Feet shuffled and their heads dropped with mumbled apologies.

“You’ll come topside now, Mr. Sullivan, and inform me what else is expected. I shall attempt to intercept the rest. You may join us, Mr. Crawley.”

Scully tugged a forelock and started up, wearing an appropriate hangdog expression. Time spent unloading the wagons in the blistering heat should serve as punishment for his oversight. Jack followed, Crawley at his heels. They joined Celia at the wagon where she conversed with the driver, nodding as he pointed to its various contents.

“Thomlinson’s,” Scully pronounced as he looked over the goods. “An’ a few chickens from the pock-faced woman what sells ’em at market.”

“Mr. Crawley, inform the woman we shan’t need the chickens. Miss Breckenridge and I will visit Mr. Thomlinson and cancel his delivery.” Jack stared at the wagonload of goods and considered what to do with them. “Remove all of this to my house, Mr. Sullivan. Tell Meagan you’re to store it in Molly’s room above the kitchen for now.”

The wagon departed with a chastened cook aboard.

Jack and Celia set off in the opposite direction.

Clouds continued to build overhead, stacking one overtop of the other. The strengthening breeze snatched away their fragmented laughter, as if gaiety detracted from the importance of what nature worked to create. He entertained her by peppering her with stories of Charles Town's more colorful inhabitants as they passed by their homes.

When he launched into an imitation of the starchy matron who lived on the corner, voice rising and trilling in a squeaky falsetto, Celia halted and clapped a hand over her mouth. "The woman does *not* sound like that."

"I should call on the old crow to prove my claim, but then I should have to answer for it by suffering her company." He shuddered for effect. "Running a gauntlet would pain me less."

"Less than passing through rows of men bent on beating you?" Celia scoffed. "Daresay the poor dear does not deserve such slander."

He latched onto her arm and held her against his side when a strong gust nearly took her down the street with it. Wind could be surprisingly accommodating. "Save your pity, madam. She's a snarling beast of a woman who would eat you for her breakfast. Calls to mind an old, gout-ridden aunt of mine."

"Oh?" An ocean of doubt imbued that one syllable. As if she thought it unlikely he'd come into being like most humans.

"Aunt Esther. Nasty old harridan. Used to thump the floorboards with her cane. Or one's ankles if you dared come within striking distance. Terrified the servants. Father always gave them an additional half-day off after one of her visits." He chuckled. "Once they mutinied and forced him to—"

Jack blinked and stared at Celia, gobsmacked by his loose tongue. He hadn't spoken of his family for over two decades. And suddenly, effortlessly, the words had tumbled from his mouth. Devil woman. All her bleeding talk of siblings and family had resurrected memories long buried.

An uncomfortable silence ensued.

"I've an odd aunt as well," Celia informed him, picking up the conversation. "Aunt Posy. Though I shouldn't describe her as a harridan, she's quite eccentric. Wears the grandest wigs you've ever seen. A tiny woman, Aunt Posy is, and the wigs nearly as tall as she. Has a fondness for bows, too. Stitches them on her gowns and all through her wigs. She must have twenty at a time tucked into her curls. Her poor maid is ever dusting the powder from them, for Posy's fond of her powder, too." She grinned. "Perfumes and powders make Rianna ill. Posy's quite put out when she has to forbear them, but she must if she wishes to visit with her niece."

Fighting hard to rebury his ghosts and restore his equilibrium, Jack cleared his throat. "Wigs and bows, eh? Sounds a heavy load to bear. Has she the neck of a dock hand, perchance?"

Celia laughed. "Hardly. A faint breeze would blow her feet from under her."

"Perhaps we could run her up the *Lass* then. Drop her from the yardarm. Doubtless she'd prove an excellent sail."

Two sets of gloved fingers rose to hold her lips together. A snort erupted from the pressure of holding her laughter in. Her eyes widened in surprise, cheeks flushing crimson, and she touched her fingers to her nose as if to confirm the sound had originated there.

Jack chuckled, delighted to have something new to tease her about.

"What will your neighbors think of us, laughing like simpletons in the street?"

He fingered the buttons of his coat and shrugged. "They will think we've come from Pinks."

"Pinks?"

"A tavern over on Chalmers Street. A bit of an oddity, as each of its three stories has only one room. Boasts a mammoth-size fireplace to cook in. Pretty place, Pinks is. Nice color."

"Pretty? A tavern?" Always a skeptic, this woman. "'Tis pink you say?"

"No, gray," he said, just to be contrary.

She rolled her eyes and walked faster, forcing him to catch up. "You should have been a barrister, Captain. You'd likely confuse the courts so thoroughly they'd forget why they'd gathered."

"A barrister?" He tugged his tricorn low against the wind. "I should be bored unto death. So difficult to find a worthy opponent, you see." He gave her a roguish leer. "I find beautiful women a much more agreeable diversion."

"Pity them."

Impertinent twit. Jack paused near a shop on King Street and steered her through the door. "Enjoy this," he warned. "'Twill likely be the only shop you shall visit for a time."

Chin high, spine straight, she sailed regally past him, prompting him to tug on her bonnet ribbon as she passed. As he'd hoped, a lock of hair plopped down to join its fellows, the bonnet no match against the strong gusts. He grinned like a naughty schoolboy and followed her in.

The proprietor, Mr. Thomlinson—tall and thin with a sparse thatch of sandy hair on his pate—waved to Jack by way of greeting as he tallied a customer's sale. The woman, buxom and formidable in an appalling shade of red, bent over the counter and stabbed a finger at her bill.

"I'll just go and interrupt that magpie, shall I?" he said to Celia. "She looks to have enough wind to blow Thomlinson to the Azores."

Celia touched his arm. "Why not wait until the woman has finished her business? Surely, she shan't be long." She stepped away from him toward a table piled with cloth.

He sighed and removed his hat. "I know what you are about, Miss Breckenridge."

She smiled over her shoulder while she strolled about the dim, candlelit shop, the sturdy shelves filled with bags, jars, and all manner of utilitarian items. Various barrels of goods lined the walls underneath. Skins and furs hung from hooks next to dried herbs and spices.

Jack had little interest in spices and other whatnot—unless he carried them on his ship. Making a profit always interested him. The olfactory barrage from the countless stores crammed inside the single room made his eyes water. He preferred good, clean sea air over this pungent tomb any day.

The argument between customer and proprietor continued and it soon became apparent the woman's grasp of mathematics was deficient. Thomlinson glanced up. Jack sent him a look of commiseration and received a nod of thanks in return. The bell over the door tinkled. A handsome woman wearing an enormous beribboned hat entered the store with a black female servant on her heels.

He smiled upon recognition and tipped his hat. "Mrs. Bedon."

"Why, Captain Beaumont." Mrs. Bedon smiled warmly. "I'd no idea you were home."

"I arrived only yesterday, ma'am." He motioned for Celia to join them. "May I introduce you to my guest? Miss Celia Breckenridge of Falmouth. Miss Breckenridge, this is Mrs. Bedon, one of Charles Town's most gracious hostesses. I believe I pointed her house on Church Street out to you." Actually, he'd demonstrated Mr. Bedon's duck walk for her.

"Oh, yes." Celia grinned and curtsied. "What a lovely home you have, Mrs. Bedon."

"Why, thank you, dear." Mrs. Bedon beamed. "Do let me welcome you to Charles Town."

The door opened again and another woman, this one dark, trim, and energetic entered, interrupting their conversation. "Captain Beaumont. How fortunate to see you here, sir. Father asked after you just the other day. Welcome home."

"Mrs. Pinckney." Jack bowed. "Delighted to see you again. Miss Breckenridge, may I present Mrs. Pinckney. Her husband, Charles, is our chief justice and her father owns the Stono River Plantation."

Celia's eyes lit with interest. "A plantation? Truly?"

"Aye. Mrs. Pinckney is quite popular with the local planters," Jack explained. "Solved a problem with the indigo. Many a planter's pocketbooks are plumper due to her ingenuity."

"Indigo? How marvelous." Celia grabbed Mrs. Pinckney's gloved hand. "Such a pleasure to make your acquaintance."

Jack's eyes narrowed. One would think she'd met a princess the way she gushed. Mrs. Pinckney appeared taken aback as well.

"My father is a merchant," Celia explained. "He invests in all manner of cargo and properties. We—he—should be very interested in your indigo."

Mrs. Pinckney's brows hiked at Celia's halting explanation. A look of understanding passed between the two women. Interesting. Jack would bet a sizable sum Celia participated in her father's endeavors. 'Twould appear Miss Breckenridge and Mrs. Pinckney were kindred spirits.

"Miss Breckenridge hails from Falmouth." As if it explained her abundant enthusiasm.

"I should be happy to show you about my father's plantation," Mrs. Pinkney offered, "should you care to visit Stono during your stay."

Celia glanced at Jack. "I should like that very much."

"'Tis settled then. Captain, send a note by the house whenever you wish to visit. I've no doubt Papa will enjoy a glass of port and a nice long chat with you."

"And I should be happy to indulge in your father's port," he assured her. The woman badgering Mr. Thomlinson finally departed. "If you will excuse us, I must speak with Mr. Thomlinson. Oh, and a word of warning, ladies. Dangerous weather approaches. Prepare yourselves and your properties." He bowed.

“Mrs. Bedon, Mrs. Pinckney.”

Celia curtsied. The women waved the two of them off and continued conversing.

Jack concluded his business quickly, much to his companion’s disappointment. The winds had gained strength during the short time they’d spent inside. She leaned her head back with her hand clapped to her bonnet to gaze at the scudding clouds.

“Doubtless those women are burning with curiosity about us.”

“Thankfully they are both too well bred to ask.”

“Pity the weather is turning up foul.” She sighed wistfully. “I might have enjoyed visiting more of your shops.”

He took her elbow and quickened their pace to the wharves. “I will bring you back.” He smiled down at her. “We shouldn’t like you to leave Charles Town with coin in your pockets. Much better if they’re to let.”

****

’Twas early evening, the sun hovering just above the horizon, when the *Mirabelle* slipped from her berth to moor in deeper water. She bobbed up and down in the bay, testing her chains like an exuberant colt fighting the bit.

Stripped of her sails, the *Bonny Lass* rode some distance away, her empty yardarms a stopping place for an exodus of birds fleeing the coming storm. The wind snagged the hair from Jack’s queue and whipped it in front of his face as he stared out over the churning bay at his skeleton of a ship. She, too, chafed at her anchor cables in the choppy water. She brought to mind the image of a slain Viking warrior, eager to embark on that final voyage to Valhalla. He fought the urge to raise a hand in farewell.

Celia stood quietly at his side, seeming to understand the emotions governing him at present. He could not decide if this annoyed or relieved him.

****

The southeasterly breeze died.

Jack and Smitty kept peering at the sky, their somber attitude not lost on Celia, who'd been around sailors enough to know their uneasiness boded ill. The men prepared the house for the coming storm: tiles nailed down, shutters firmly secured, loose items stored away. Spinnakers arrived to help and wait out the storm. He made his home on the ship and Jack had ordered him to leave it.

Meagan and Molly worked in the kitchen, the September heat sweltering as they prepared enough food to see them through several days.

"Where is Andrew?" Celia asked suddenly, abashed she'd only just noted his absence.

Spinnakers paused and wiped his brow. "He left with his mum for North Carolina shortly after we docked."

"In this dangerous weather?"

"They travel by river a fair piece inland and they've several stops along the way. I expect they shall be safe enough."

Shortly thereafter, the winds picked up, changing direction to a brisk, northeasterly. Trees bent and swayed in the gathering gusts. Debris scattered along the street and went soaring.

Darkness descended. The rain commenced in fits and spurts and gradually increased, lashing the windows as the wind howled mournfully through the eaves. Airborne missiles slammed against the house.

Those sheltering inside congregated in the downstairs parlor. Though lit with several lanterns, the heavy darkness outside permeated the light within. Celia sat with Molly on the floor while the younger woman peppered her with questions about the English court. She'd no idea why they were on the floor, but with the lot of them sprawled about the parlor, it did seem rather like a picnic.

The men began a card game and enticed Meagan to join them.

"Meagan shall partner me," Jack announced. Both Smitty and Spinnakers vehemently objected. "'Twill keep the game honest."

"Honest?" Smitty scoffed. "At cards? Captain Bluff here thinks us buffleheads."

"Did you hear the man?" Jack said to Spinnakers. "He called me a cheat."

"Ye are a cheat. And ye think with Meagan as your partner, we'll not object."

Smitty leaned across the table and treated Jack to a ferocious glare. "Snatch me wife from beneath me nose so's ye can steal me blunt, too?"

"Aye," Meagan agreed cheerfully. "I'll be fillin' me pockets with coin and no mistake."

"Ha." His expression turned smug. "I'll have me blunt back from me wife."

"Ye are a bufflehead ta think it," Meagan corrected her husband. "'Tis my own to spend and ye'll not touch a farthing."

Celia laughed at their antics. "Perhaps you'd care to visit the shops with me, Meagan. I've promised to leave my coin with the Charles Town merchants."

"Oh, I'll spend these fine gents' blunt, Miss Celia. I've my eye on a nice length of ribbon at Clark's on Bay Street. 'Tis a good place to purchase furbelows and the like."

"If it still remains," Spinnakers said under his breath, but they all heard him, and it was like a douse of cold water thrown on a cheery fire.

Everyone fell silent.

Meagan kicked him in the shin.

"Ow." He yelped and glared at Smitty, who smiled nastily back at him.

"We've had our share of foul weather in these parts, Miss Celia," Meagan soothed. "And a hurricane or two. Charles Town will clean up and move on as we always do. We shall spend our coin and no mistake."

"Aye, miss. Ye've naught to fear." Smitty picked up his cards and winced.

Chapter Ten

A violent fury unleashed upon the city. It shrieked and howled and lashed at the earth like a mortally wounded beast. Conversations began, sputtered out, and began again as the storm raged and tensions mounted. The winds increased in velocity, clawing the tiles from the roof and flinging them into the night.

Spinnakers raided Jack's study for a book. Molly remained on the floor, knitting a new blanket for the baby her brother and his wife were expecting.

Jack prowled the house. Testing doors, checking windows, familiarizing himself with the structure of each room as thoroughly as a soldier gathering intelligence. His gaze sought Celia's often. 'Twas unnecessary, of course. She'd already proved her mettle, though the noise was a bit unnerving. Perhaps he'd sit with her and hold her hand in his big, strong one.

Meagan stayed in constant motion, stacking jars, folding linens, polishing silver. Her husband followed her about, nodding from time to time at her continuous stream of chatter.

Near midnight, a large branch crashed through Jack's bedroom window. The men rushed upstairs to make temporary repairs. Meagan and Molly trudged up behind them with towels and mops. Meagan waved Celia away when she made as if to follow, leaving her to grumble alone in the parlor.

Suddenly, the tempest pealed above her head as if it had split from the heavens and severed the house in two. She snatched up a lighted taper and flew up the stairs.

"Miss Celia," Molly called from Jack's bedchamber. "Ye'd best not go up there."

The candle's flame sputtered out, but Celia continued her wild flight to the uppermost landing in the dark and rushed to her bedroom door.

A large, gaping maw in the ceiling exposed the room to the elements. Through it, a swirling black cauldron stirred in the sky. The wind whipped at her clothing and spit rain in her face. She tossed the taper aside and threw her body over the chest containing her aunt's keepsakes to shield it from the weather.

Spinnakers arrived with a lantern. He shook her shoulder and shouted over the shrieking winds. "Go back down. 'Tis too dangerous."

"My trunk," she yelled back. "My aunt's belongings are in here."

"I shall bring it down."

She moved to the end and grasped one of the rope handles. "I shall help."

A vise gripped her ribs, and the handle tore from her grasp. Jack marched her to the stairs with her feet dangling above the floor. He set her down on the landing and nudged her toward the steps. She turned back to argue, but his flinty-eyed stare stopped her.

"Go, you little fool."

The men emptied out her trunks and mattresses and stored them in Jack's sitting room, which was already cramped with furniture and items they'd moved for safekeeping.

"The tide will not crest until sometime after noon," Jack said later as they watched a torrent of water sweeping past the front window.

"What does that mean?" Although Celia feared she already knew.

"The house will flood." He moved away from the window and motioned to Smitty and Spinnakers. "We must prepare."

The three men ran out the back door to the kitchen. Spinnakers helped Jack haul the barrels of foodstuffs into the house, which they placed in the narrow hallway outside his room. Their supply was substantial—stores from the two ships combined with the provisions Scully had forgotten to cancel.

At least they would not starve.

Meagan emptied the cabinet outside Jack's room of linens and stowed jars of spices and crockery inside. Celia took the linens downstairs to stuff around the doors. Smitty carried armfuls of his and Meagan's clothing in and returned to collect Molly's.

All they could do now was wait.

****

Fierce winds and pelting rain continued to weaken the roof until most of the tiles and structure beneath were ripped away, leaving the entire upper story vulnerable.

Molly's knitting needles click-click-clicked in her lap while her eyes darted to and fro in time with the winds. A shriek howled through the eaves followed by a loud thump. Something large struck the wall of the house. Molly flinched and knitted faster.

"'Twill be the most expeditious blanket ever

made," Meagan said to Celia.

Molly dropped her needles and covered her ears as successive missiles assaulted the house.

Celia poured a small draught of sherry and pressed it into the poor girl's hand. She winced at a loud thump and gulped the contents down. Celia poured her another, which Molly obediently drank, and shortly thereafter, she stretched out on the rug and slept.

Jack urged Meagan and Smitty to retire to his room for a few hours' sleep. Spinnakers moved a chair into the dining room and read by the light of a lantern perched on the end of the table.

The tempest rose to a crescendo of depth and sound that trembled the earth. Celia closed her eyes against it, her nerves stretched taught by the storm's relentless beating. Jack dropped down next to her on the sofa, a snifter of brandy in each hand, and passed one to her.

"Drink." He wagged his brows suggestively. "I've a fondness for inebriated women."

Her lips twitched. "'Tis refreshing to learn your tastes run toward the refined. Heretofore I suspected they merely had to be breathing."

He chuckled and raised his glass to her. "I am most interested to learn where you rank yourself then, Miss Breckenridge, as I've fancied you from the very first."

"Beast." Her traitorous heart quickened.

"There's naught to fear, you know." He stretched his booted feet out, crossing his ankles. "I shan't allow any harm to befall you."

"'Tisn't fear so much as the persistence that wears upon me, Jackson. I shall survive."

Lines of weariness etched his face. He leaned his head back and closed his eyes. "You need something else to occupy your mind."

"Knitting is out of the question." She glanced down to where Molly lay sleeping.

His lips tipped up. "I don't suppose you'd care to mend my clothes?"

"I don't suppose."

"I should tell you a story."

"Should you?" She'd deliberately sounded skeptical though she thought it a marvelous idea.

"I've been known to spin a yarn or two." He settled back in the corner of the sofa. "What should you like to hear?"

She slipped off her shoes and tucked her feet up under her skirts, resting her cheek on her knees. "Anything of my choosing?"

"Anything. What shall it be? A tale of mermaids and sea monsters? Fierce Viking warriors? Perhaps a brave knight and fair damsel?"

"The tale of Jackson Beaumont."

"Jackson Beaumont?"

"*Mm-hmm.* The story of how a tender young lad came to be on a ship full of tars."

Eyes beaming suspicion, he sat up and scratched the stubble on his jaw. "Why the devil do you wish to hear that?" The wind whipped up at his words, in perfect accord with his sentiments.

Celia wagged a finger at him. "You have charged yourself with easing my trepidations, sir. Don't be tiresome. I wish to know about you." She tried to contain her excitement, though she felt certain he heard it in her voice. An overwhelming desire to hear his confessions assailed her. A longing to have an intimate knowledge no other person shared—a piece of Jack she could call her own.

He shifted and blew out a breath at the trap he'd set for himself. "You are certain you wish to hear my sordid story?"

"But of course." She gave him a bright smile. "Sordid stories are the very best kind."

His grunt indicated his thoughts on the matter. She waited, thrilled and expectant; less mindful of the hurricane now.

"Very well. When I was but six years old, my parents were robbed and murdered by highwaymen." *Oh, Lord. Perhaps she should have chosen the mermaids.* He stared at his brandy, his voice flat and emotionless. "My sister Em was fourteen, my older brother Kyle had just turned nineteen. 'Twas a difficult time for the three of us. Not only had we lost our parents, but we were all of an age that separated more than united us."

She reached to clasp his free hand in hers.

He regarded their joined hands. "Kyle was becoming his own man, preparing to someday fill Father's shoes as viscount, and Em was a silly young girl with a head full of dreams and a terrible crush on his friend, Charlie. As the youngest of the brood and a bit of a surprise to my parents when I came along, I was doted upon and spoiled outrageously by my parents and sister."

This explained a great deal, though Celia kept the thought to herself.

"I was an unruly boy, stubborn and headstrong. My true purpose in life, as I saw it, was to drive my elder brother to distraction. Kyle had no patience for me. He steadfastly avoided my company, which only encouraged me to dog his heels at every opportunity."

"'Twould appear you've something in common with my sister then," Celia laughed. "Rianna delights in tormenting me."

"'Tis the lot of the youngest, I suppose." He rubbed his thumb over the back of her hand absently. The warmth spread up her arm and nestled in her heart—a place it was not entirely welcome, as its extraction might prove painful. For now, he was big and strong and safe. Her port in the storm, she thought wryly.

"My sister did her best to fill the emptiness after our parents died. 'Twas daunting for a young girl her age. I became willful and belligerent, especially with my brother. Kyle was at a loss what to do with me. As we were never close, he sent me away to school, believing the headmasters were better equipped to handle my temperament. I was bitterly opposed to it, of course. They dragged me from home, screaming obscenities at him while my sister wept from the stoop."

"You poor boy." Celia squeezed his hand, flinching when a projectile crashed into the house.

He squeezed back. "School was a disaster, my rage at losing my parents and being torn from my home ever present. I missed my mother, and I missed my sister, but my brother was heir and had guardianship of me. Though Em pleaded with Kyle on my behalf, he would not relent.

"My only escape came from dreams of faraway places and exotic ports, of running away and never returning. For what was to become of me? My brother made it abundantly clear that as the second son, I was the 'useless spare' and therefore must live off his largess or join the church, unless I was fortunate enough to marry an heiress." He snorted. "Marriage. The last thing a young lad of six wants to contemplate is being leg-shackled to a girl."

"Ah." Celia laughed at the image. "So you shared young Andrew's attitude toward our sex at the time."

His lips quirked. "I've since changed my opinion."

As if she needed reminding. "This I had already gathered."

The smile turned into a boyish grin. "Well then. I was permitted a visit home for the Christmas season, though the bitterness between me and my brother made it a miserable one. I stayed long enough to celebrate Em's birthday in January. Against my desires, Kyle packed me off to school again.

"Thereafter, I regularly engaged in fisticuffs with the other boys at school. After several severe punishments by the headmasters, I ran away and made up my mind to never return. I ventured south by cajoling farmers and vendors to take me up on their carts until I reached Southampton. Once there, I signed myself on with a sea captain as his cabin boy."

A bittersweet expression crossed his face, his eyes distant with memory. "Captain Seamus McDonald became a father, a mentor, and a friend. He tried to discover where I hailed from, but I refused to tell, and no one in Southampton was searching for me. Eventually he stopped asking. Seamus knew, however, that I came from the upper classes and had me educated as such." He lifted his glass and swirled the brandy inside, watching it reflect the candlelight. "I traveled all over the world aboard the *Bonny Lass*. Seamus left the *Lass* to me when he died six years ago, two years after his Rose passed on."

A fortunate man, Jackson Beaumont. "But how did you come to settle here?"

"Jamestown was our home port, but it ceased being so after Rose passed. We'd spent a good deal of time in Charles Town. I decided to make my home here after I inherited the ship. Most of the crew came with me."

It occurred to Celia she still held hands with him. Of a sudden it felt far too intimate with the two of them alone. She gently placed his hand next to him on the sofa. "Have you never returned to find your family? To let your brother and sister know what became of you?"

"No." He looked down at his now empty hand. "I'd no wish to hear Kyle's censure and I knew he'd force me to stay. After I'd grown, well, too much time had passed, you see."

She nodded. "I cannot stop thinking of the agony my family shall suffer if I fail to return on the *Roundabout*. 'Tis truth we do not realize what we have until 'tis gone, Jackson. I daresay your brother has many regrets."

"I have given some thought to the matter of late, as your concern for your family has brought to mind my own. It has been over twenty years, though at times it seems like yesterday."

"Then 'tis high time you set things aright. And Jack," she laid her hand over his, "'twould be my pleasure to accompany you, if you wish it. You have done so very much for me. I should welcome the chance to return your kindness." Although her betrothed might have something to say on the matter.

His dark gaze roamed her face in the dim light. "I shall bear that in mind."

****

Dawn approached.

Hammering rains continued to batter the city. The rivers and bay forged through the streets. Everywhere was water. Everywhere more rushed in. The flood rose, swelling the garden and rising stealthily, one step after another until it topped the stoop and ran across the piazza. In less than an hour, the rags Celia had stuffed around the doors were saturated and drifting into the rooms with the oncoming surge.

The house's inhabitants retreated to the stairway. They watched in numb silence as the floodwaters progressed. Tradd Street became a raging torrent that swept past the house like an angry mob, dragging along anything that stood in its path. A barrel slammed into the front window, smashing the panes; the rushing water forked into the house.

"Lud, Jack." Celia jumped up from her seat on the stairs. "You've water pouring in from the sky and the sea. What shall we do?"

But he was already running down the steps, Spinnakers and Smitty at his heels.

"We shall die! We shall die! We shall all die!" Molly wailed.

The normally stalwart Meagan sat behind her. Fortunate, as the woman's tears would hardly be a boon to the girl's overwrought condition.

"There, there, Molly," Celia tried to comfort her. "We are not as easily defeated as that. You must have faith. I've not survived thus far only to be bested by a bad-tempered storm."

"Oh, but 'tis sore affrightened, I am, Miss. The house, 'tis blown away and the rivers encroach. I shall die and never marry." Molly fell into another fit of sobbing before collecting herself and sniffed. "I should have liked children."

Interesting, the regrets one has when they believe their life at end. Though she might be cursed for it, marriage had been the least of Celia's. She carefully avoided determining what they might be now. To feel regret was to give up hope and this she refused to do.

Molly gasped and turned to Meagan. "Do ye suppose me brother's house is a'floodin'? Lawks, I never gave it a consideration." She said to Celia, "'Tis a small cottage, Miss. He's no stairs to climb up."

A hammer pounding drew their attention. Jack and Spinnakers held a board over the broken window—no mean feat as they strained against the force of the water rushing in—while Smitty nailed it in place.

Meagan let out a snort, sarcasm tinged with hysteria. "They'd as well plug it with one o' me spoons as dam that swell."

"Ain't gonna hold long." Smitty dug another nail from his pocket and hammered the next into place.

Celia chewed her lip and watched them work in silence.

The men stepped back to view their handiwork. Water still leaked around the edges, but the geyser had been deflected.

Spinnakers shrugged. "'Tis somethin' I suppose."

"Aye." Jack glanced toward the foyer, where a few inches of water now stood. "It matters little, I expect, as the tide won't crest for hours yet."

Celia looked past them and out the window where the newly formed Tradd River flowed. An anchor settled in her chest. Jack let out a long sigh and turned back to the stairs, shoulders slumped, face taut. She longed to reach out to him, to stroke his face and neck and shoulders until the tension eased. Soothing him would soothe her.

He started up, his boots shedding water with each step. He noticed Molly sobbing and looked to Celia.

"She fears for her brother," Celia explained, waving a hand to indicate the deteriorated condition of their shelter.

Smitty passed by him to sit with Meagan, and Jack dropped down next to Molly, awkwardly patting her shoulder. "There, there, Mol. You've naught to worry over. This house is sturdily built. She'll hold. Your brother's property lies inland a fair piece. I doubt he's flooding such as this."

"Ye truly believe so, sir?" she asked earnestly.

"Aye, Mol. I suspect we've the worst of it here in the city next to the rivers and bay."

Although placated about her brother, the sight of all the water below did little to stem Molly's tears.

"Perhaps you ought to rest," he suggested

"'Tis an excellent idea, Molly. You slept little earlier. Have some wine and a bite of bread as well," Celia encouraged. "Come, I will take you." She pushed to her feet and pulled Molly up the steps past the others. Once she had the girl settled, she headed back down.

"Molly's on a blanket in the hall. The poor dear fell right to sleep after—" Her legs folded beneath her, and she sat down hard on the steps. "Dear God." She ran a shaky hand over her face. An endless pit of water greeted her, rising inexorably higher.

Charles Town Bay had relocated to Jack's foyer.

Her hand seemed permanently affixed to her

mouth, as if she could trap her emotions and prevent them from emptying her of courage. She felt Jack's gaze settle on her and she wanted to thrust it away. She could not be weak. Not when he needed her to be strong. The steps creaked. His strong arm engulfed her as he sat. She closed her eyes and allowed herself a moment to absorb his heat, his strength, the ever-present scent of spice. But only for a moment. 'Twas dangerous to allow her senses to wallow in him.

Jack leaned his cheek against the top of her head, his low voice adding to her heightened awareness. "I promise to keep you safe."

She reached up and squeezed the hand draped over her shoulder. "'Tis very gallant of you to say, sir, but if you have not yet noticed, your house is destroyed." Her eyes filled with tears at the enormity of his loss. "I'm so very sorry, Jackson. 'Tis such a lovely home."

"Aye." He rubbed his cheek against her hair, and they remained thus for a time, each digesting the impact. His world had shattered, but here he sat, holding her, and promising her safety. She had to resign herself to the possibility that she would not leave this place anytime soon. Wrapped within the security of his embrace, it hardly seemed as tragic as it ought.

He must have sensed something of her thoughts. "Here is the truth then." His lips brushed her temple when he spoke. "I only saved you from the pirates, so I'd have an extra wench about to clean up the mess."

Spinnakers overheard and chuckled.

Celia sniffed and wiped at her eyes. "How can you jest?"

His head leaned against hers. "Only think of the unfortunates who have no shelter. You may be certain the town is razed. Many souls lost. I am anxious for my crew and their families, but I am alive." He squeezed her shoulder and his voice cracked just a little from the effort of maintaining his aplomb. "And I've a comely wench in me arms. 'Tisn't doughty for a man to cry."

"You are absolutely fearless, are you not?" She smiled through her tears and patted his knee. "I've never met another like you, sir."

Jack grunted. "Nor are you likely to. The King threatened m'father with a gelding should he attempt to sire more offspring."

"Aye," Smitty chortled. "Rumor has it there's a price on his head if he tries ta mate."

He flashed a grin at Smitty and missed Celia's start of surprise. *Would he marry?* Sea captains were like as any to do so, her uncle Giles was proof.

How could a wife let him go? She would never be able to do so. To watch him sail away over and over and never know whether this time would be their last. The backs of her eyes stung. 'Twas a foolish notion and of no consequence. This man had no place in her future. Still, the thought of Jackson Beaumont raising a family with another woman disconcerted her greatly.

Chapter Eleven

Flood waters continued to rise up the stairway until half the treads were covered. Celia and the others removed to the second floor to stretch out amongst the furniture and supplies. The house groaned from the stress of water rising within and torrents raging without. Debris crashed into the windows and the French doors as the flood swelled and rushed through the streets with abandon.

By eleven in the morning, the water came perilously close to where Celia sat at the edge of the landing. She stared in horrid fascination at the devastating changes the night had wrought. What would become of them if the storm did not abate soon? Hours felt like days as the hurricane raged. They were all exhausted. How would they find the strength to save themselves?

Then the winds shifted and blew from the southwest. The tide turned back swiftly, as if nature had recalled her troops. Within a quarter of an hour, the waters had receded several feet. Although the ferocious winds and rain persisted, the flood continued to decline and for the first time in hours, the group holed up on Tradd Street breathed a sigh of relief. Those who had yet to sleep finally rested. When the hands of the clock reached three, the fury had finally spent.

Molly and Spinnakers still slept, but the others

were anxious to take stock of the house. Meagan paused at the landing and pulled the hem of her skirt between her legs, tucking it into her waistband.

Smitty stood arms akimbo, scowling at his wife. "What kind of woman raises her skirts in company?"

"The kind that wants to keep her hems dry." Meagan shrugged. "'Tis more than me kitchen clothes."

He rolled his eyes. "As if bein' half-naked in the kitchen is somethin' ta speak of."

"Aye?" Her hands went to her hips, and she fixed her husband with a gimlet glare. "When ye wish ta don a dress and have *your* skirts sashayin' in and out of a lit hearth, ye're welcome to it. Else I'll thank ye to mind your own affairs as I'm not of a mind to catch meself on fire." Thus said, she headed down the stairs.

This made perfect sense to Celia. Necessity had made her adaptable. She rucked her skirts up past her knees and found Jack's avid gaze fixed on her legs. Shivers of anticipation tensed the muscles of her abdomen. She ought to be offended, not thrilled, damn the man. She squared her shoulders and started down the steps behind Meagan.

Jack's hot eyes widened at her comically. "Miss Breckenridge. I am speechless. You would forsake propriety for your hems?"

"Hang propriety. I haven't the least inclination to soak my clothes in an effort to spare you the sight of my ankles. Do turn your head if I offend you."

His voice turned low and husky. "Why, I've no complaint whatsoever, little one. I should happily view anything you wish to show."

She rolled her eyes, ignoring the tremor that raced down her spine, and stomped after Meagan. The frigid water was well past her knees as she sloshed through it. Halfway through the foyer, her foot caught on a large chunk of debris. Losing her balance, she tipped to the side.

"Celia!" Jack shouted as she lunged in the opposite direction, attempting to right herself. Alas. 'Twas her undoing. She overcompensated, teetered, and toppled backward, dropping like a stone on her backside.

A geyser spewed into the air, splashing her face. Waves rippled across the water's surface in every direction. Her clothing quickly saturated, and she gasped at the icy chill to her skin. She spat and sputtered and blinked the droplets from her eyes.

Jack jumped into the water behind her.

A tiny head popped up in front of her, the serpent's beady black eyes reproached her for disturbing his swim. Celia's lungs constricted. A narrow, forked tongue slipped between its fangs, hissing a threat.

She screamed.

The snake swam for her then, its body swaying from side to side as it propelled itself through the water, fangs at the ready to strike.

Scrambling backward on her hands and feet like a beach crab, she came up against Jack's legs. He stepped wide to allow her through and snatched the serpent up out of the water when it followed. It struggled and coiled around his arm. Celia let out another yelp, fearing it would bite him, but Jack held the thing securely beneath its head. He trudged over to the broken window and threw the snake out. She lumbered to her feet and wrapped her arms about her waist as shivers of cold and fear wracked her body.

Seeing that the danger was past, Smitty sloshed

around them and chased after Meagan.

Jack turned from the window and eyed her so thoroughly she felt a blush start beneath the chill bumps on her skin, the sensation oddly painful. "'Tis a strange method you have of keeping your skirts dry, madam." He shook his head. "Hang propriety indeed."

He moved on through the house while Celia seethed and glowered at the bounder's retreating back. Until she heard another splash in the dining room and slogged after him.

****

Jack passed through the empty space where his garden gate once stood and across the broken path to the piazza. His foray through town had been dismal; the fortifications around the city destroyed, ships thrown ashore and broken apart, streets littered with all manner of debris. Swelling water had ravaged bridges, livestock, and crops; wind splintered trees and peeled away buildings. The docks had all been obliterated.

The storm blew the *Bonny Lass* onto the shoreline with two broken masts and a gaping hole in her hull. Jack had yet to locate the *Mirabelle.* 'Twas possible she rested at the bottom of the bay. When he'd sailed into port mere days ago, he'd gained a second ship, intended to buy a third, and the prospect of a fortune in emeralds awaited. Presently he hadn't a ship, and the funds required to repair his house and the *Lass* would likely beggar him.

In the moment, the emeralds seemed a cruel joke as they'd no way to retrieve them if they did exist. Damned Latham. He ought to be strung up on a yardarm. Pity none were available to accomplish the deed.

Several of Jack's men were left homeless, though thanks be praised, none of his crew or their family had been lost. A miracle and a blessing as so many poor souls had perished. They moved as a group from dwelling to dwelling, making temporary repairs or shelters to see their families through until more permanent restorations could be made. 'Twas the best they could do for now.

Ironic that Miss Breckenridge thought him fearless. If she knew how badly Jack wanted to howl his rage and beat his frustrations into something—anything—her esteem might not be so easily given. Of everything he'd lost, or may still lose, forfeiting her good opinion did not bear examination.

He found Smitty in the dining room on a ladder prying broken glass from the French doors. "Good news. I've located enough clay tiles to repair the roof."

"Aye?" Smitty climbed down with a pail of broken glass. "What did ye trade?"

"Ivory. Drayton's a thief, but with supplies scarce he has me over a barrel."

"The ivory will fetch a king's ransom if ye take it up north to sell." The older man pulled his handkerchief from his pocket to wipe his brow.

"The tile's fetching a king's ransom here and now. Not to mention the timber. Betwixt the house and the ship, I've need of a small forest." And a larger purse.

"Reckon so. How will ye get the tile here? Will Drayton deliver it?"

"Not bleeding likely." Jack snorted. "'Tis best accomplished by boat. The roads are impassible by wagon. I barely made it there and back on the poor nag I rented."

"Where will ye find a boat? Perhaps ye hadn't noticed, but the harbor's empty. What ain't at the bottom leastways. Most are restin' on the streets and in the shops. Heard a sloop sailed through Pinckney's stables and smashed inta the house. An' the mast is pokin' out his balcony door."

"Aye, 'tis." Jack grinned. "I had occasion to see it. We shall borrow Drayton's barge and move it ourselves. 'Tis the least he can do after robbing me of my ivory."

They turned when Celia—streaked with dirt from mobcap to hem—made her way down the stairs with a bucket in her arms. Wisps of dark hair slipped from beneath its covering and stuck to her damp face and neck. She looked like a servant and damned if she didn't heat Jack's blood.

He crossed his arms and treated her to a fierce scowl. "What are you about?"

"I am cleaning the muck off the stairway."

"Upon my word, you've more cheek than forecast, woman. I ordered you to—"

She cut off his words with the slash of a hand. "Scupper it, Captain." And out the door she went.

Jack turned to Smitty, who now bore a foolish grin. "Did you hear her?"

"Aye. She appears a mite vexed with ye."

Which perversely, he found even more stimulating. "Nonsense. She's charmed."

They set to work emptying the flood-damaged furniture from the carriage house, setting aside what could be saved and breaking the rest into firewood. Smitty and Meagan had moved into Molly's room above the kitchen until their home could be made habitable again. A space was made in Jack's sitting room and hammocks strung for Celia and Molly to sleep in.

When he passed the dining room, Jack caught sight of Celia on her knees like a supplicant, her taut little bum hiked in the air while she scraped wet sand with a fireplace shovel. He grinned like a naughty schoolboy and leaned against the doorframe to admire her arse swaying to the tune of her labors. His hips twitched, recognizing the refrain. If he positioned himself behind her just so…

"I suppose you'll want wages."

She pushed to her feet, cheeks flushed, bosom conveniently heaving from her exertions. Although the mobcap still covered her head, much of her hair had slipped its tether with random locks strung about her shoulders. Jack appreciated a good rebellion. Mud streaked her forehead and a large clump had attached itself to her bodice. He imagined dipping his hands into the sludge and squeezing those lovely breasts, leaving his handprints behind as a memento.

He'd ship the dress to Mr. Kensington with his compliments.

Celia pressed the back of her hand against her forehead. "I expect I look a fright."

Jack disagreed. They looked delightful. Lush and bountiful and—

Two little creases formed between her brows, head tilting to the side. Her foot tapped impatiently while she waited for…? Damn. Was there a question?

"No?" he guessed. Her gaze turned skeptical, compelling him to expound. "'Tis not so very different from when you had blisters." What was a little muck, anyway? "Can't be helped, really."

She gasped and her eyes darkened to the color of emeralds, fittingly, and flashed green sparks.

Clearly, he had muck for brains.

He opened his mouth then closed it, instinct and a healthy dose of caution silencing him. Her face turned scarlet, and her chest rose and fell in agitation.

God, she was stunning when she was angry.

His cock stirred. Quite brave of it, and woefully, woefully stupid. Clearly a body's survival instincts turned frighteningly lax in one's lower extremities. Perhaps nature feared the continuation of the species otherwise. Males were invariably angering females over something.

She crossed her arms, lifting her bosom so the clump of mud hung precariously above her wrist. He stared at the spot while her toe tapped out her ire. "The sight of me offends you?"

"No," he protested and stepped forward with his hands outstretched, though what the bleeding hell he meant to do with them, he'd no idea. "I only meant that—"

The shovel she'd used materialized in her hands. She brandished it at him like a club. "Do not touch me or I swear I shall—"

"Charming the ladies again are ye?" Spinnaker's voice froze them as he entered the room. "Quite the rakehell ye are, Captain."

Spinnakers was laughing at him, but Jack did not care. The interruption gave him such giddy relief he could hug him. His ever astute and timely helmsman acknowledged his grateful look with a nod.

Celia lowered her weapon a few inches, though the

air around her still sizzled with indignation.

"They've found the *Mirabelle*," Spinnakers continued, undaunted by the crackling female in the room. "Spurred up Vanderhorst Creek. Took off the corner of the Baptist church before she dropped anchor on Meeting Street. Bowsprit's broken off and the hull's full of holes. Starboard rails are missing."

"Aye? She'll be the Assembly's problem now," Jack said and meant it. "With Constable Latham's compliments."

"We foraged inside and found a few hammocks and a bit more sailcloth."

Jack took in the barren room. "We shall take whatever Providence supplies and be grateful." It rained every day. He and his men had covered the missing sections of roof with sailcloth in an effort to prevent further damage to the rooms beneath. Rory and a few of the crewmen who'd been rendered homeless bunked down there at night. They kept pails on hand to catch the leaking water. He didn't envy them. It was hot, dank, and humid.

"Aye. Providence." Spinnakers snorted. "Ye heard about the Bedons?" He shot a glance at Celia, who remained poised to strike.

"No. How have they fared?"

"Dead," the helmsman said, his voice flat. "Tried to escape the house during the flood, but the current swept them away. Mrs. Bedon, her three children, servants, and slaves. Drowned them all save for the master and one servant."

The shovel clattered to the floor. Celia's face turned white.

"But…I only just met her." Tears welled in her

eyes. “How can this be?”

Spinnakers shot Jack a look of apology and fled the room.

Twin rivers spilled down her cheeks. Jack closed the distance between them, unsure what to say. He fussed with her loose hair and straightened her mobcap.

“Many souls were lost in the hurricane, love. Too many.”

“But…she was so kind to me.”

Her shoulders began to shake and then she sobbed—great, mournful wails that wracked her body and pierced his soul. He pulled her into his arms.

“There, there, love,” he murmured, rubbing his hands up and down her back. Her arms slid under his open coat and clamped around his waist. God’s bones, he could not abide tears. He should rather be clubbed with her shovel than see her in pain. All for a woman she barely knew. But how like her. She never did a blessed thing he expected; defiant when she should be afraid, angry when she ought to be amused.

And now she wept all over his favorite linen waistcoat for a dead woman and her family. Simply because Mrs. Bedon had been pleasant. Jack held her tighter and rested his chin atop her head. It felt good to hold her—even while she ruined his clothes.

He glanced about his shell of a dining room, the French doors scratched and marred with broken panes, floors covered with the flood’s leavings, walls stained and dirty. The flood had loosened the tiles in the entryway and saturated the floorboards, warping the planks. All would need torn out and replaced. What were a few items of clothing then?

“Celia, love, hush now.” He pressed his lips to her

temple.

She rubbed her face against his chest, as if she found the motion soothing. It soothed him as well, but then touching her in any manner did.

"I apologize, Jackson," she managed between sobs. "I—I—" Another pitiful wail erupted. She would not be stopping any time soon.

"Come." Jack turned her to the door and wrapped his arm around her shaking shoulders. "I shall take you up to lie down."

"I've work to finish here," she protested, though her feet moved docilely alongside him.

"I promise to save it for you. I'll not let a soul near your muck."

Her lips creased at the corners in what he surmised to be a smile as he led her up the steps.

"They must have been so frightened, Jack. I cannot begin to imagine such terror. Her children ripped from her arms and swept away."

"Don't love. They're with God now." Steering her into his room, he stood her next to his bed then fished through his wardrobe for a handkerchief to mop up tears that had no end. After several futile attempts to stem the flow, he gave up and tucked the damp cloth in her hand.

"Why must so many people suffer, Jackson? The Bedons. Those poor sailors on the *Essex*. Mrs. Abrams and I, we heard their screams. I felt them suffer—inside of me—I felt their cries as if they were my own. It pierced my heart. I despaired of their agony while we remained unscathed."

Jack was not certain who she cried for now. She'd locked the horror of the bloodshed aboard the *Essex* away apparently, and this latest tragedy had sprung it all loose. He wrapped her in his arms and held her close.

"Mrs. Abrams went mad with fright. When she found her husband, she—" Celia's body convulsed and fresh torrents of tears ran down his chest, his waistcoat soaked through to his shirt now. "—she shouted at Mr. Abrams. Begged him not to leave her. His eyes…I shan't ever forget his eyes. Empty. So empty, Jack. Like his soul had hatched from his body."

She pushed away to look into his eyes, as if to reassure herself that his weren't empty too. "Perhaps 'tis the truth of life. That we mortals are born in the shell of our body, and we spend our lives striving to free ourselves of it. That death in reality is birth?"

Jack had nothing to say to that. He'd seen too many ugly deaths to agree.

Her head dropped and she shook it slowly from side to side.

"Shh," Jack crooned when she ran out of words. *"Shh,* Celia. She's gone. They're all gone now." He put a finger beneath her chin and raised her face to his. Placed a soft kiss on her lips. "Their deaths are not your fault, love."

"I know that, Jackson." She lowered her head and sniffed, wiping at her eyes with the damp handkerchief.

"No, you do not." He gentled his voice. "'Tis what torments you still. That you survived. 'Tis no more your fault you lived than it is that they died." He lifted her chin again. "You are not to blame."

"I am so very fortunate to have you, Jackson." She touched her palm to his cheek. "I shall never be able to express the depths of my gratitude."

He kissed her palm. “You needn’t.” His head lowered. Her hand slid to cup the back of his neck. Their lips touched while their gazes continued to hold one another.

Somewhere inside those shining green depths, Jack lost course.

Oh, what a heady feeling it was, to founder with this woman and never wish to surface. His lips brushed over hers, and her arms wrapped around his neck, drawing him closer. Their mouths dipped, parried, and fused. He tasted soft flesh and honeyed warmth and knew only hunger. Pulling her to him, he melded their bodies as well as their lips. They sank down to the mattress. Inside his brain a warning flashed: Dallying with this woman would be unwise. Irrevocable. But Jack cared little for rational thought. For any thought. Not when she felt so good, not when his body sang as though he’d finally arrived home.

His head lifted to gaze upon her precious face.

“Oh, Jack.” Her hand stroked his stubbled jaw.

The sound of his name on her lips sent flames licking up Jack’s spine. He pulled her beneath him and again experienced the sense that he’d found home. She moaned and dug her fingers into his hair, tugging his mouth to hers. Their bodies knew what was right and what they needed. His lips trailed along her throat while his hand slid up to caress her small waist, her ribs, her—

“There be plenty o’ buckets up here,” Rory called from the stairs.

They jerked apart and stared at one another, breaths labored, hearts hammering. Jack glanced over his shoulder. Thankfully, no one appeared at his door. They heard Spinnakers' low-voiced reply as the men trudged up the next flight of steps.

Jack sat up and pulled Celia with him. She looked away and stared out the window, her face flushed crimson. A bucket of rainwater would be welcome at present, though it felt as if they'd already been doused. He wondered if she was embarrassed or ashamed or—dare he hope—as disappointed as he that they'd been interrupted. His hungry gaze roamed over her.

This was torture. To taste the forbidden fruit only to have it cruelly snatched away. He dropped his head, and his lips twisted in a wry grin. The blotch of mud from her bodice was now smeared all over his waistcoat.

He touched his fingers to his brow, but when he glanced at her again, he saw the streak on her forehead still remained. 'Twas some comfort, at least. She'd not bathed herself entirely on him. His groin tightened at the image, and he closed his eyes against it.

If there was a God, then surely Celia suffered from thwarted desire, too. He opened his eyes to peer at her face.

Her gazed collided with his and she said in a small voice, "I forgot myself, Jackson."

Jack nearly laughed at the absurdity. He would *never* forget.

****

Avoid Jack.

Celia considered this objective imperative and not in the least cowardly. Given his large size and booming voice, 'twas easily managed. Eschewing his company resulted in her detachment from the rest of the household, allowing her ample time to reflect upon her deplorable lack of constraint.

How could she have forgotten herself so completely? Her, an engaged woman who genuinely esteemed her betrothed, though apparently not enough to recall she had one.

She'd fallen like a wanton onto Jack's bed—*his bed*—mindless with passion.

Ye gods, the man's mouth was delicious. She'd have to give up her favorite biscuits now. Cinnamon would forever bring to mind his kiss, those lips like a confection one constantly craves.

Devil take him.

And those big, rough hands. She wanted them to touch her everywhere—be everywhere—at once. It frightened her to think what might have happened had they not been interrupted as much as it maddened her that they were. He could not be irresistible to her.

She would not allow him to be.

Determined to exhaust her mind and body into submission, she scooped, scraped, scrubbed and hauled away buckets of grime from the floors.

Gentle butterfly wings of sensation interrupted her self-castigation, followed by the familiar prickling of ice at the base of her skull—her sister's ever-present disquiet traveling through the ether. Impressions flitted across her mind, troubled and frustrated.

What a pair the two of us make.

Rianna's conflicting emotions beat against Celia's own and somehow managed to sharpen her longing for Jack, a subtle battering, but as relentless as a hurricane. Stars above, she had to find a way home before she dishonored herself, her family, and most importantly, Brett.

The man she owed her fidelity to.

Chapter Twelve

Dawn's copper rays peered through the gap between the curtains when Celia woke in her hammock, exhausted and unsettled. She placed the blame on Jack. The burden of their peccant behavior still lay heavily on her conscience.

Boots pounding down the stairs confirmed the rest of the household was stirring. Molly had risen and gone. Dropping to the floor, she wended her way to her trunk, eager to join in the work. She dressed quickly and hurried downstairs and out the back door.

The kitchen resembled an army camp. A constant flow of humanity entered and left, accompanied by shouts and bangs as men went about their labors. Jack had invited his crew and their families to a daily meal prepared by Meagan, Molly, and in some small part, Celia. Her contribution tended more toward organization rather than the actual cooking of things, which was really best for all concerned. Those who cared to eat were expected to serve themselves from the meal set out on the scarred, wooden table.

"Good morning, miss," Meagan greeted cheerfully, her hands coated with flour while she kneaded dough. "Did ye sleep well?" Her eyes scanned Celia's face. "Ye look a might peaked."

Celia did not know how the woman survived roasting day after day in the sweltering kitchen, feeding scores of hungry mouths, her cheerfulness incongruent with the grueling labor she performed. She admired Meagan immensely.

"I was a bit restless last night," she said, annoyed evidence existed. To be fair, mourning could hardly be considered flattering to one's complexion. The dark smudges beneath her eyes likely complimented her shabby gown. She'd brought three mourning gowns to Bermuda in expectation of her aunt's passing. Two remained, both little better than rags at this point.

"Ye should avail yourself of Jackie's bed."

Heat infused her cheeks. Not after yesterday's passionate encounter. The spicy scent of him on the sheets would torture her the night through. She'd never get a moment's rest.

"'Twould be selfish of me to ask it. I've been nothing but a burden to him."

"Nonsense. He'll tell ye so himself."

"My conscience will not allow it."

Meagan turned mulish and tried another tack. "'Tisn't proper. Unmarried women at their rest near an unmarried man."

Far too late to worry about propriety. At least concerning sleeping quarters. Obviously, Meagan had not learned of her sharing Jack's cabin. Celia saw no reason to enlighten her, particularly after her recent transgressions. "There's little to be done about it." Meagan looked ready to argue further, so she added, "Molly is there. After everything that has happened these past weeks, I confess I feel safe knowing Jackson is near."

Her words had the desired effect. Meagan's features softened. She gave Celia a pitying glance. "I suppose with those other men in the house, 'tis best to have Jackie close by. As ye say, there's little to be done."

"I suspect I'll find passage to Bermuda soon, which should alleviate your concerns. I wish to send a letter off to my family, though I pray I will arrive before it."

"Ye'll find what ye need in the bureau at the end of the upstairs hall."

"When do you expect the next packet to arrive?"

Meagan shook her head. "We've no packets this far south. Riders take the post north. 'Tis handed off until it meets up in New York with the packets sailing to Falmouth. Elseways, sea captains carry the mail on their ships. Write yer letter, miss. I'll have John see it gets off."

****

Jack slammed through the door of Harry's Tavern, Smitty at his heels. Once his eyes adjusted to the darkened interior, he spotted Constable Latham at a table in the corner with one of the Evanston brothers. The Evanstons were charged with piloting ships entering Charles Town Harbor to their destination. A useless inconvenience, the Evanstons.

"Why Captain Beaumont," Bernie Evanston greeted him, his tone mocking. The constable's presence must have buoyed his confidence. Absurd, considering both men combined could not produce a full backbone. "I desire a word with ye, sir. Seems ye entered port without a pilot and failed to report to the pest house. Have ye been away so long ye've forgotten the law? Or mayhap the rules are subject to yer whimsies?"

Ah, yes. Ships were required to stop at the pest

house upon entering the harbor. Persons who arrived ill were quarantined to deter the spread of disease. Another useless inconvenience as the pest house had done naught to prevent sickness.

Jack flicked him a look of contempt. "Stubble it, Evanston." He turned his attention to the constable, whose expression grew increasingly alarmed the longer he stood there.

"Jean Pierre's crew is walking freely about town, Constable. Perhaps you'd care to explain why?"

The constable straightened and jutted his chin out, presumably for Evanston's benefit. Jack kept the man pinned beneath his gaze. Latham swallowed audibly. His hand rose to fuss with his lapels before dropping back to twitch nervously on his tankard. At least the damned fool had enough sense to be afraid.

"I do not answer to you, Beaumont," Latham blustered. "I'll thank you to remember it."

Jack grabbed a fistful of coat and hauled the man to his feet. "You are mistaken, sir." He enunciated each syllable with painstaking precision. "You will answer to me."

Latham's complexion turned purple, either from fear or the chokehold Jack had on his collar. "The gaol flooded." His bluster turned to sputtering. "The building is uninhabitable. They had to be moved."

Evanston stood, belatedly coming to the constable's aid. He addressed Smitty instead of Jack, however. "You stand aside while your captain molests an officer of the law, sir? Should you not intervene?"

Smitty searched his jacket for his pipe. "Cap'n don't need my help."

"Moved where?" Jack demanded. "And why the

deuce are they loose on the street?"

"To the workhouse." Latham tugged at his coat to free it from Jack's grasp. "And they are not 'loose on the streets,' Captain. They've been consigned to help clean the city. 'Tis a monstrous task we've before us. Everyone must work to restore order." Everyone but him, apparently.

Jack let out a disgusted snort. "The bastards are worthless. You'll not get a day's labor out of the lot."

"They've little choice in the matter, sir. And they are under supervision, so you've no reason to fear."

Deluded ass. *How long would that arrangement last with the constable's propensity for laziness?* He ought to throttle some sense into the man. "We had an agreement, Latham."

"Circumstances change, Captain."

Pressure built behind Jack's eyes until he feared they might explode. "My ship is wrecked, you bleeding bastard." He shoved Latham back into his seat. "The *Mirabelle* is lying broken in the street, all because you refused to jail those men if I sailed out to safety."

"Well, I—"

"Hear me well, Latham." He planted both fists on the table and leaned over him menacingly. "If any harm comes to Miss Breckenridge, if those roisters so much as cause her to break a fingernail, I will hunt you down and string you up from the yardarm of my broken ship."

Latham gasped in outrage, the spidery veins on his cheeks prominent against his mottled complexion. "How dare you threaten me, Beaumont."

"You are mistaken, sir." Jack's voice lowered to a threatening growl. "I state a fact." He turned on his heel and caught Harry's gaze from behind the bar. The pub owner nodded. Jack dipped his chin and stomped from the pub. Smitty joined him on the street.

"See to it a man remains outside the house at all times."

"Ye don't believe yer jiniper-lecture impressed the good constable then?"

"Nay. The bouncer would sooner consent than hear a noise. She's in danger now, Smitty. I should have taken the picaroons back out to sea and drowned the lot of them."

"Aye. Would'a spared us an inconvenience. Perhaps ye ought'a send her north and put her on the next packet outta New York. Get her far away from here."

"No." The word was vehement and final and somewhat of a shock as it all but flew from his mouth, startling Smitty. Hell, he'd startled himself.

"Have ye another ship ta mind then? We might take her overland south to Savannah or up north a ways. Perhaps the militia would help."

Was he mad? Give Celia over to a group of bored and lazy soldiers? "I shall see to her."

His friend and first mate said nothing for a moment, his gaze curious at first then far too knowing for Jack's comfort. "You…intend to keep her then?"

"For a time." The less said the better at the moment. Particularly as he had no idea what he intended. It seemed imperative Celia stay with him and so she would.

"We'll take her with us to the Bahamas?"

"God, no."

He'd no desire for her—a woman betrothed to an heir and a wealthy merchant for a father—to learn his entire future hinged on a phantom fortune in hidden treasure while he currently boasted a crumbling house, a broken ship, and rapidly dwindling funds. He felt worthless just thinking it.

"She is not to know of the emeralds. The less said the better, for everyone concerned."

Smitty shrugged, his expression suggesting he'd given up trying to decipher Jack's motives. He only wished he understood them himself.

****

Though warm, the fragrant kitchen was blessedly peaceful, aside from the sounds Meagan made as she hacked away at the old block table. The woman appeared to take undue pleasure in reducing the chicken to various parts.

"I tell ye, 'twill be a miracle if the tile ever arrives," Meagan grumbled. "Roads unfit to travel and ships and boats—or what's left of 'em—a layin' willy-nilly and cloggin' both rivers. We may as well resign us to sails for a roof."

"I had such hopes for those sails." Celia batted a fly away and sighed with dramatic flair. "I thought to sew skirts for the three of us. I've torn both of my black gowns until they're hardly fit to wear. Sailcloth is quite durable and would suit our needs splendidly."

"Oh, aye." Meagan chuckled and tossed some scraps in a bucket. "We shall start a new fashion in town. The Widow Price will hire a modiste straightaway."

"I'll have a shirt as well," Jack said from the doorway.

Celia stilled at the sound of his voice and looked away, unable to meet his eyes.

Sin had found her. She'd known she could not avoid him forever, just as she'd known she would not be able to face him in the wake of their passionate kiss.

"'Tis only fitting. As you seem to enjoy ruining mine." He sounded so grumpy she couldn't help but grin. When she looked up, his eyes gleamed with mischief, all sparkly and alive. Damned eyes.

"Honestly, Captain, how long will you cry over that shirt? How was I to know both baskets were not full of rags?"

He gave her an exasperated look. "Was one clean, perchance?"

"Both baskets had been washed."

"And you could not tell the difference between clean rags and clean clothes?"

"They were both rather gray, given the water Molly had to use. The ruined clothes were added to the rag pile. I failed to notice I had one of your shirts until I went to wring it out."

Jack crossed his arms and leaned against the doorjamb, raising his brow in query.

"I, er, noticed how large it was when I shook it out." She lifted her chin. "Really, Jackson, how was I to know you had not thrown the shirt into the rag bin?"

"'Tis the second shirt you've ruined. If this continues, you'll be stitching your way back to England."

"Second shirt?"

"You ought to recall the first one. You whipped the cat all over it."

"You brute." Celia's face heated at the reminder, along with her temper. "Had you not abused me, your clothes would have remained dry." She glanced at

Meagan, who had stopped chopping to listen.

"'Twas for your own good." Jack shot a glare at Meagan. She maintained her regard, lips pursed to contain her smile. *What did he expect? That she would suddenly become deaf for his convenience?*

"Nevertheless, I fail to understand why 'tis ruined."

"The smell." His lip curled in disgust. "'Twouldn't leave it."

She dropped her head and shook it from side to side, willing the words back into his mouth. But then the reminder of his ill treatment angered her anew.

"Beast of a man that you are, 'twould take an entire roof to garb you anyway."

"Mayhap we should all huddle beneath Jackie to stay dry," Meagan chortled.

Celia covered her mouth to hide a snicker.

He shoved off the doorjamb and went to the table to fill a plate. "I've suffered enough of your barbs tearing at my hide. I shall seek more tolerable company."

"Pity them." Meagan chuckled and started chopping again.

Rory came through the kitchen door and removed his cap. He held it loosely, turning it 'round and 'round in his hands. He bobbed his head to Celia and Meagan by way of greeting.

Jack straightened, jaw tense, eyes searching. Not surprising. Rory's manner did not bode well. "Well? 'Tis obvious you've something to say."

"Aye." Rory cleared his throat. "Well, uh, 'tis just that…" He twisted the poor cap in his fists. "We're in fer another blow, Cap'n. Ye'd best put off repairs and see 'bout tyin' down."

Celia's hand rose to her throat. It had taken only one of Rory's predictions to make a firm believer of her. They were still reeling from the proof.

"Odd rot it." Jack plunked his plate down on the table. "How bad of a blow? Surely not a hurricane?"

Rory nodded. Celia wanted to clamp his head in a vise to stop its movement. "A strong'un, I reckon. I thought me cracked at first, ye ken. Why, 'tis barely a fortnight since the last. But I'm sure o' it now and there's no use wishin' otherwise."

Jack turned to look out the doorway. Celia followed his gaze. The wind had definitely picked up some. "Damn and blast. Ladies," he turned back to Celia and Meagan. "You know what must be done. I shall send a couple of hands along to assist." He picked up his plate and strode out the door, shoveling food in his mouth in between shouting orders.

An invisible fist thumped against Celia's stomach. How was she to get home? She had a family. A betrothed, for pity's sake. Every passing day made it harder to remember.

Damn Jack with his towering strength and protective arms. His husky voice. Forever bent on making her feel safe. Alive. Like a woman. She must get away. Now. Before the Atlantic became a wall through which she could not pass.

****

Once again, the hapless city of Charles Town withstood nature's fury. Jack trudged up to the third floor to assess the latest damage, bemoaning wind, rain, and sea as they'd brought him naught but trouble of late. Fortunately—if one could find anything about a *second* hurricane fortunate—this one wasn't nearly as violent as the preceding one. The house hadn't flooded, though the winds had been fierce all the same.

He folded back his shirtsleeves, prepared to remove anything new the storm had blown in. He could ill afford a tear to his clothes as Celia seemed hell-bent on ruining them. He'd soon be swaggering about naked if she failed to cease her destructive ways. It wasn't as if he had the blunt to replace them. Perhaps he'd present her father with a bill.

The wind ruffled his hair when he reached the uppermost landing. A few stars winked behind the scudding clouds. He paused at the open doorway.

Celia stood in the center of the room; eyes closed, arms stretched wide, leaning back into the wind. A light sheen of mist dampened her face.

His lungs caught and he held his breath.

Water pooled on the floorboards at her feet. The makeshift roof of sailcloth had long since blown away, which left the walls reaching pitifully toward the heavens like a turtle stripped of its shell. Tree branches dipped and swayed gracefully around her. The rustle of leaves sighed in the dark. Fitful clouds hovered about the moon, intermittently spewing moisture. She looked content, as one with her universe.

Peace rayed from her to Jack.

There had never been a moment when he hadn't thought her beautiful. Even with her skin blistered and raw, that sense of innate beauty had shone through. But now, in this moment, with her dark hair whipping about her shoulders, she was positively spellbinding.

He started forward, caught in her orbit, and circled her with his hands on his hips. "Upon my word, have my eyes deceived me? Or has the *Bonny Lass's* figurehead come to life?"

Her eyes furled open and blinked up at him. "'Tis a bit pagan of me, I suppose, but 'tis so wonderfully free up here beneath the open sky. I feel as if I've broken my bonds with the earth and soared into the heavens." Her eyes closed again. "I should like to be a sorceress."

Jack smiled at the notion. He'd definitely fallen under her spell. "Believe me, love. You are most assuredly a witch."

"A witch, am I?" Up fluttered those long, long lashes. Tiny droplets clung to them, reflecting the moonlight. Her gaze focused on his face. He felt ridiculously honored. "Shall I test my powers on you, then?"

"Not if you've any mercy."

"Fie on you, sir." She tossed her head playfully, eyes sparkling like green gems. Portent swept over him, a veil fluttering before his destiny. A glimpse then gone before he'd had a chance to peek. "We witches find the very idea of mercy abhorrent."

Her shining face and impish smile coiled around him, binding him to her.

Witch indeed.

"A pagan sorceress, did you say?" He tilted his head and regarded her thoughtfully. "Such a vixen would surely flirt with scandal, would she not? Have a bit of fun?"

She dropped her arms as though the mention of scandal had awakened her—or brought her to her senses. *Damn.*

"Fun? What do you propose, sir?"

"Just a wee dance," he suggested, all innocence.

"What sort of dance?" She glanced about as if

noticing how alone the two of them were.

"I had occasion to visit Austria a few years past with a friend and fellow sailor. Whilst there, we visited several taverns where I learned a dance from the local peasants. Quite enjoyable, really, though as I mentioned, entirely scandalous."

Her brows rose slightly. "What is this dance? I fail to understand what could possibly be so scandalous."

"I cannot recall the name. Permit me to show you." He stepped forward and reached for her hand. She gave it up willingly.

Naïve girl. *Had she learned nothing?*

"To begin, you lay your hand on my shoulder." He placed it thus while his own settled on her waist.

"Goodness," she managed faintly. He could feel her breath quickening beneath his hand. His responded in kind.

He lightly grasped her free hand and held it aloft a short distance from her shoulder. "This hand rests in mine." Her eyes widened so he gave her his most charming smile, which unfortunately had the opposite effect he'd intended. Her hand tensed on his shoulder, and she looked away, refusing to meet his eyes.

Perhaps she had learned a few things.

"We move in steps of three."

"Perhaps we ought to go below." She glanced at the door. "'Tis unseemly for the two of us to be alone up here." Her voice quivered. Fear or arousal? Damned if he'd let her escape before he found out.

"We move in steps of three," he repeated. "Like so: One, two, three. One, two, three. One, two, three." He counted the steps off as he moved her about the open room.

She leaned away from him and dropped her head to watch the movement of their feet. *Could there possibly be another woman more adorable?*

"Tell me, do you always grace your partner with a view of the back of your head?"

Her head popped up and she grinned at him, abashed. "'Tis doubtless the pagan way."

"I should think a witch would know."

"I suppose I have never been properly trained. Mama detests the mere mention of witchcraft." An odd thing for her to say. She'd sounded in earnest.

"Aye?"

A hesitation then she shrugged again. "I believe I've mentioned my sister and I are close."

"Aye," he drawled out slowly, wondering what this had to do with witchcraft.

"In truth, we are far more strongly connected. We…feel things. Know things about one another or our surroundings. Without the need to speak of them."

Her confession surprised him. "You and your sister are witches?"

An odd, high-pitched giggle escaped her, and her toe stubbed against his boot. His hand tightened on her fingers, and he stroked her waist, giving it a reassuring squeeze. She was silent for a moment, contemplative, while the wind teased her hair and dried the moisture on her face.

"I haven't the slightest idea." She shrugged. "I've often wondered if we have Romany blood in our veins. The townsfolk maintain we are twins in truth, only Rianna waited two additional years to make her own grand entrance. Some think our odd connection passing strange."

A dangerous attitude to be sure. Ignorance and a fertile imagination could incite fear and all manner of violence.

"How do your parents respond?"

"Mama was frightened when we were little, for we hadn't the presence of mind to conceal it. She called us God's angels, his little messengers, though should you ever meet my sister, you'll find the notion laughable."

Her lips curved in memory. "If any dared blame us for some misfortune, Mama would correct them, quite sternly mind you, then she would pray and we would join her, asking God to forgive them for their sins against us. And then she'd tell our father." She grinned. "Mama is not to be trifled with, you see."

Jack chuckled at the picture she painted. "And what of your father?"

Oddly, this question made her uneasy. She bit her lip while she considered her answer. "I believe I mentioned Papa is a merchant?" At his nod she continued, "The populace is overfond of his purse strings. He's quite powerful, Papa is, and should you disparage his daughters, you cease to exist in his eyes. Persist, and he will ruin you."

"You are saying I must call you a witch in private?"

"Aye." She laughed. "Do not let Mama overhear."

He grinned. "I should love to make your mother's acquaintance. She sounds terrifying."

"But you should hardly believe it to look at her. My mother is the consummate lady—gentle, kind, compassionate. A halo would not look out of place on her golden head."

Jack smiled at the longing he heard in her voice.

"You must favor your father."

"Aye. I am dark while Rianna favors Mama. Which hardly seems fair as I've Mama's temperament. Rianna is our father incarnate. An absolute termagant. A halo would tarnish the instant it touched her head."

He could not help bedeviling her. "You mean to imply yours would not?"

"Certainly not." She swatted his shoulder.

"Mmm." He twirled her about in smooth, flowing circles as he hummed an Austrian tune.

"I miss them. My family. I really must find passage home straightaway." A wry smile curved her lips. "Perhaps between hurricanes, as they appear a regular occurrence here." She patted his shoulder. "I've realized what a burden I have placed on you, Jackson. You've much to worry over, what with a house and ship to repair. I shan't inconvenience you any longer. I shall find passage on my own."

Chapter Thirteen

Blister it. The woman was determined to cock it up.

"Nonsense. 'Tis no bother as I am near the wharf every day. I am happy to perform this small service for you."

"I thank you for your generosity, but I can no longer ask it of you. I should like to get out of doors regardless, though I daresay I shan't enjoy the sights such as they are now."

Odd rot her ill-timed independence. How the devil was he to protect her if she went gadding about the city? "Celia, I beg you, do not leave the house. Not unless I accompany you." Jack dipped his head and his gaze snared hers. "Please."

Her eyes narrowed. "Whyever not, Jackson?"

He pulled her closer. He did not wish to frighten her. "The streets are dangerous, love. Folks are destitute. They've lost everything. Left without a roof over their heads or food to eat. Those at the fringes of respectability have become criminals to survive. Desperation does that to men. And women." He cleared his throat. "Alas…the town wardens have put the pirates to work cleaning up the city. They are not always locked in the gaol." The mere idea of her coming into contact with one of them congealed Jack's blood.

She stiffened and missed a step. "When they are at work, they are guarded?"

"They are under the wardens' supervision, but I put little faith in their ability to control the brigands. You know well the threat they pose." She nodded but did not appear nearly as alarmed as she ought. "I must insist upon it, Celia." His voice was terse. "I will have your word."

"My word?" Celia stopped dancing, forcing Jack to halt as well, but he refused to relinquish his hold on her. Opportunities like this were rare, and he meant to make the most of it.

"Aye, your word. I'll have it now, if you please."

"You are a tyrant." She tugged on her hand, but he refused to release it.

"Aye," he agreed. "I will do what I must to keep you…safe." The pause was brief, but he felt certain she'd heard it.

Her gaze dropped. When it returned to his, the fight had gone out of her. "Forgive me. I don't know why I am behaving like a—"

"Witch?" Jack supplied helpfully.

"Aye, you rouse my best qualities, Jackson."

"Of course. Blame the innocent sea captain." He twirled her in circles across the room until she laughed and begged for mercy.

"A witch can smell a lie, you know," she told him sagely. "'Innocent sea captain' indeed."

"I haven't a thing to do with your sorcery, madam, therefore I am innocent." A ruddy load of balderdash, that.

"In absolutely no circumstance should you be considered innocent, sir. It goes against the laws of nature."

Aye, well, his attraction to her went against the laws of man. Not that he cared much about breaking them. "Now you are acting the shrew."

"I quite resent that." She laughed. "I am simply being sensible."

"Pity." He expelled a forlorn sigh. "I had thought pagans more… Oh, what is the word?"

"Gullible?" she asked sweetly.

Jack chuckled, delighted with her. "Why must you always malign—"

Boards popped beneath his feet and the floor started to give way. Celia latched onto his shirt and yanked.

The sound of lace tearing preceded his body toppling into hers. The two of them tumbled to the floor—she on her back and he on top of her. He held himself immobile—except for his heart, which thumped an enthusiastic hosanna. The gods were finally smiling upon him. Jack felt certain of it.

They remained thus while their bodies became horizontally acquainted.

She opened her mouth to speak, but he shushed her.

"Lie still, the boards beneath us might give way." He was fairly certain this wasn't true, but what sort of fortune-hunter would he be if he did not make the most of it? They stared into one another's eyes, breaths shallow.

Jack raised himself to his elbows, as if to test a shift in weight, and treated her to his most sultry tone. "I am flattered by your advances, love."

Celia choked on a laugh, her lungs hampered by

his weight. "You are wicked."

"Aye," he said silkily. He could not resist, his mouth lowered to hers while he spoke. "And you are a tempting little witch. Your poor mother, all of her hard work for naught. What is this spell you have cast over me?" His lips skimmed hers, soft and teasing. He breathed in her sigh as she tilted her head back, lifting her mouth to his.

Footsteps pounded up the stairs. She turned her head toward the sound. The intruder, obviously male, was a dead man.

"Uh, Cap'n, ye might want to move yerselves downstairs afore ye continue yer, ah…discussion," Rory suggested from the doorway. "If ye're not aware, ye're about ta fall through the bleedin' floor."

Celia's face flushed. She squirmed beneath him.

A wide grin split Jack's mouth. Perhaps he ought to thank Rory.

She shot him a repressive frown and lifted her head to peer over his shoulder. "An excellent suggestion, sir. One cannot dance from this position, after all."

Jack's gaze heated and bored into hers with enough intensity to singe her irises. Shivers wracked her body in response while his groaned in silent despair. He dropped his voice to a husky whisper for her ears alone. "I assure you, madam, we most certainly can—"

Her hand clamped over his mouth. "Cease. Immediately, you devil. And get off of me." He nipped at her fingers with his teeth. She yanked her hand away.

Sighing heavily, he did as she bade, pulling her to her feet. They stepped gingerly across the floor and followed Rory out.

"My poor mother should not concern you nearly so

much as my angry papa," Celia warned as they headed down the stairs. "Doubtless he will do you harm if he ever learns of this."

Jack waved a hand dismissively. "I shouldn't worry on that account. Only think, once he's recovered from the shock of us sharing a cabin and living here together, what harm is there in a little dance?"

Sparing him an ironic look over her shoulder, she said, "What harm? Why, he will do murder. Be warned, sir. A merchant he may be, but he is also the son of a blacksmith, his mettle forged from the hardships he suffered as a lad. He shall be your greatest enemy."

Rory stopped and turned to face them, though Celia and Jack continued on down. "I hope ye'll belay yer father's revenge, Miss Celia. Leastways until we find the *oof—*"

Jack elbowed him in the gut as he passed.

Celia paused and regarded him curiously. "Until you find what?"

Jack grasped her elbow and herded her on down the stairs. "Until we find the Dutchman we trade our brandy with. He enjoys several ports in the Caribbean and the, er, debauchery to be had there," he added, hoping to embarrass her and thwart further questions. "Daresay Rory has spent his share of the profits already, haven't you, sir?" He shot a meaningful glare at Mr. Loose-gums.

Rory rubbed his belly and followed at a discreet distance. "Aye." He coughed. "Spent."

****

"Bufflehead. Never saw a one what teetered on his pins like a bloody drunk."

"Ye're talkin' through yer arsehole ag'in, ye ninnyhammer."

Jack shook his head. The long-anticipated tile had arrived though his men might kill one another before they unloaded it all. He hoped the earth remained solid beneath its weight. After two hurricanes, he could not discount the possibility of an earthquake, as some divine being seemed annoyed with him at present.

Smitty paused next to him and wiped the sweat from the back of his neck with a handkerchief. "Need a damned breeze."

"I fear I must caution you, sir." Jack peered up at the sparse clouds and abundant sunshine. "Prayers concerning the weather have disastrous effects around here." Hurricanes were not uncommon in October or even November on occasion.

Smitty chuckled. "So they do."

"Ahoy Cap'n," Crawley called from the gate. "We've finished out at the widow Martin's. Young Andrew and his mum will hardly know a storm put upon the place when they return."

Jack thought that unlikely. "Molly promised to see to their garden. Have Scully accompany her. The man's useless with a hammer."

"The wife threatened to split him with a cleaver." Smitty chuckled and tucked the handkerchief in his coat pocket. "Ye'd best keep him out of her kitchen lest ye find yerself without a cook when we sail."

Crawley's eyes lit, doubtless picturing Meagan carving up their surly cook. "I'm ta tell ye Major Duncan begs a word when ye've a moment ta spare."

"I haven't a moment to spare." Jack had work to do. Setting his ship to rights was more dream than possibility these days.

Spinnakers joined them. “Came upon Blue Tooth at Harry’s Tavern yester’eve. Sluicing his gob with one of the workhouse wardens. Jenkins joined them.”

“Jenkins?” Jack turned on him. “The pirates and a warden? What the devil?”

“Aye, the devil.” Spinnakers tugged on his ear. “And his minions. The most vicious dog rules the pack.”

Smitty spit on the ground. “Seems queer like, don’t it? The scurvy dogs have yet to come near Miss Celia.”

“Of a certain the bastards are brewing mischief, but I’ll be jiggered if I know what.” Which made Jack uneasy but standing around jawing about it solved nothing. He headed for the gate. “See to those wagons. We shall start on the *Lass* immediately after we finish the roof.”

“Thank Christ,” Crawley said with feeling. “Them emeralds call to me in me sleep.”

Smitty chuckled. “Mayhap ye should ask ’em where they be hidin’ so’s we’ll find ’em sooner.”

****

Celia knelt on the floor before her trunks, unpacking and sorting her dresses. She’d had to give up mourning as her black gowns were no longer fit to wear. Aunt Maggie would forgive her breach of custom. She had detested mourning, maintaining life should be celebrated, not death.

A letter slipped from her clothing and fell to the floor. She recognized it at once, having received it shortly before Maggie died. A swell of emotion assailed her as she opened her correspondence, her past and present colliding.

My dearest Celia,

News of your aunt's decline deeply saddens me. Would that I might prevent your suffering. I am certain your heart weeps for her pain. Know that my thoughts are with you always. I shall not bore you with the trifles here, except to say difficulties at Silver Oaks abound.

I look forward to your return in November and mourn the interminable wait. Hurry home to us safe and whole, my Celia. I shall count the days until your return.

With warmest love and affection,

Brett

God above, what an awful punishment this man had been served to be saddled with one such as she—a feckless mate unable to control her shameful lusts. She was not worthy of him. Not when she desired Jack so. But Jack would soon sail out of her life. And take with him a heart that rightfully belonged to Brett.

She brushed at the wetness in her eyes. She would spend the rest of her days making amends to him. And pray it was enough.

****

Lumber arrived from Boston. Unfortunately, Jack had forgotten his purse when he left the house and needed to make haste before it all disappeared. He took the steps two at a time, but once he reached his room, he decided to change to a lighter coat as the day promised to be a warm one.

A familiar giggle floated through his open window, prompting him to move closer as he tugged off his waistcoat. Celia's voice reached him from the floor above.

"My, how bold you've become, sir. And to think you were shy when first we met." Another giggle assaulted his ears. “Ooh, that tickles.”

Jack’s vision dimmed and turned red around the edges. *The blackguard.* How dare the man enter his house and touch what was his? By damned, he’d kill the trespassing whoreson with his bare hands.

He stalked from his room and moved stealthily up the stairs. How could the faithless witch cuckold him in his own house? Never mind that she was promised to another. Everyone knew she belonged to him.

Her husky voice reached him as he gained the top step.

“Oh, you like that, do you?”

Pulse roaring in his ears, it took several moments before he’d calmed enough to peer into the room.

The floor had been ripped out with only the cross beams remaining but for a small patch near the window. Celia knelt there, dress bunched about her knees, stocking-clad legs crossed at the ankles behind her.

Jack gaped at her exposed calves and swallowed.

“Can I touch you there?”

Blood crashed through his ears all over again, his head as violent as the seas of Cape Horn. He leaned farther inside.

At last, her paramour came into view. She rubbed her finger over a furry little squirrel, cooing to him softly. Embarrassment warred with uproarious laughter. The woman would drive him mad one day. The furry rodent must have sensed his presence because he twitched his tail and scampered up the oak to safety.

“A fine fare-thee-well,” Celia called after him. “Ungrateful little beggar.” She continued to mutter under her breath as she backed carefully across the beams.

Jack watched her delightful little arse come toward him as she crawled. Then tiptoed out of the room to watch and wait.

Once she'd gained the doorway, she stood to dust off her skirts then spun about and bumped into him. She let out a shriek and lost her balance, clutching at him for support.

The sound of a rending tear followed.

His amusement turned to annoyance. He grasped her elbows to steady her and beheld the rent cloth.

"Damn and blast, woman. Why must you always attack my shirts?"

"Jackson Beaumont, you scared the life out of me." Celia shoved at his chest and stamped her foot.

"Aye? Why are you up here, madam? I distinctly recall telling you to stay away."

Her features blanked and her gaze skittered from his. "I, um, you see, there is this little fellow who visits me from time to time." She peeked back up at him. "He is usually hungry, so I bring him food."

"'Tis a damned squirrel."

"Yes, but just a little one. I think he might have lost his mother in the hurricane. He appears to be all alone."

Jack shook his head in disgust. "He is greedy and has no wish to share your largess with his fellows, more's the like."

"No, truly, I fear he hasn't anyone. I've only ever seen him alone."

"You are not to crawl around on this floor." He shook her arms in frustration.

"But he was hungry."

"He's a damned squirrel!" Jack roared, as if added volume might penetrate her stubborn skull.

"Oh, very well," she snapped. "But he is a hungry 'damned squirrel.'"

"I have had enough of your cheek," he snapped back, torn between the desire to thrash her tight little bum or mount it. He closed his eyes against the wave of heat sluicing over his body. He was mad, surely.

When he opened his eyes again, he pinned her with a glare. "The creature can climb if you had not noticed, you foolish twit. He lives in a bleeding tree. You can damned well feed him on the ground."

"Oh." Celia blinked. "Well, I had not thought of that. Of course he can. But he is so shy. Nothing like our bad-tempered squirrels back home." She gave him a brilliant smile that caused his gut to clench painfully. Surely this could not be healthy. "I shall coax him to the bench under the oak. Perhaps he will sit with me there. 'Twill be lovely."

She started past him for the stairs. Jack shook his head to clear it. She must think him daft if she thought the matter settled so easily.

He trotted along behind her. "You do not truly believe our discussion finished?"

"Of course not. If there is one thing I've learned about you, Captain, 'tis that you are quite troublesome. Unfortunate really."

"I beg your pardon?" He'd all but choked it. "You disobeyed my orders, madam."

"Yes, yes, I know." She waved her hand airily. "Do bludgeon the matter to death, sir. 'Tis the only way you shall be satisfied." She reached the second landing and started down.

He stayed behind since he had yet to don his coat. "Someone needs to turn you over their knee and blister your backside, woman. Which is precisely what I shall do if I catch you up there again," he shouted after her.

Her hand came up and she wiggled her fingers at him. "Such violent tendencies in a man cannot be healthful, Captain. Perhaps you should consult a physician."

"No need, as long as I've you to bludgeon." He turned to enter his room and came up short. Meagan stood in the doorway of his sitting room—the one Celia and Molly currently used—with a bundle of dirty linens in her arms. She glared daggers at him.

" 'Bludgeon' is it? Touch one hair on that girl's head and I shall take me fryin' pan to yer thick skull."

Jack threw up his hands in disgust. "Beset by harpies at every turn. Is it any wonder a man takes to the sea?" He stalked into his room.

"Ye'll mind your manners lest ye 'take to the sea' with an anchor chain wrapped about yer ankles," Meagan called after him.

He slammed his door.

Chapter Fourteen

A long sigh fluttered the wisps of hair framing Celia's face. She pushed her plate away and slumped back in her chair. This used to be a cheerful place, the yellow-papered dining room reflecting the sun's golden light. As twilight deepened, shadows ghosted over the scraped-bare walls, the erratic flicker of candlelight resembling a life slowly snuffing out.

Jack frowned at her plate. "You are not hungry this evening?"

"My family knows, Jackson. They are distraught and I cannot bear it. Papa will blame himself. Mama has surely taken to her bed. And my sister…my poor sister…"

Rianna's anguish beat at her constantly.

He lifted her hand from the table and clasped her fingers. "They shan't know you departed early for a month or better. 'Tis not unusual for a ship to arrive later than scheduled. Repairs or illness often force a captain to put into port before continuing on. Your family may learn the *Essex* is missing soon, but they cannot possibly know its fate. You've naught to worry over now."

Naught to worry. Would that it were true.

It was not.

"No." She shook her head wearily. "Something is amiss. I know. I sense it. They know. I must return to them posthaste, Jackson."

Jack lifted her chin and his gray gaze trapped hers. "Calm your fears, sweet. Guilt and worry are the source of your disquiet."

"I pray you are correct, Jackson," she said in a small voice. "I fear you are not."

"You need a diversion." He turned her hand over and traced the lines of her palm.

She should dearly love one. Being confined to the house day after day was slowly driving her mad. "I received a note from Mrs. Pinckney. She's invited us to join her at Stono this Thursday. I should enjoy the outing immensely if you've time to spare."

His expression told her he did not.

"I understand, Jackson." She said it quickly because her emotions were raw, and she could not bear the remorse in his eyes.

"We will visit Stono before you return to England, love. You've my word." He pushed his chair back and rose. "Come, let us adjourn to the study. I will allow you to beat me at chess."

"Allow?" Her eyes narrowed. "Your skills at comforting a woman are nearly as lacking as they are at chess."

"*Tsk* Miss Breckenridge." He pulled her from her chair and led her from the room. "'Tisn't at all sporting of you."

Celia's eyes lit with challenge, as Jack had intended. "Prepare to suffer a proper thrashing."

"Thrash away, little one," he whispered in her ear. She shivered against his arm, launching a wave of heat over his skin.

They removed to his study, and he held up a

decanter of sherry, raising a brow. At her nod, he poured a small draught and himself a brandy. They moved to the small table set up near the empty hearth, but neither took a seat yet.

She sipped her sherry. "I should not be drinking spirits as I shall need all my wits where you are concerned." She looked up when he remained silent. "Why are you staring at my mouth?"

A good question.

"Jack?"

'Twouldn't do to tell her he should like to sip some sherry too—from her lips or anyplace else she'd allow him to pour it. "You feared me when we first met."

"You gave me good reason."

"I?" Jack flattened a hand over his chest. "I risked my life for you."

"Spare me the knight in shining armor drivel. My rescue was not your purpose—though a benefit, to be sure."

"'Tis grossly unfair of you, madam. Do forgive me for arriving on a ship instead of a white charger—"

"A horse wouldn't have you, sir."

"—to rescue your pretty hide—"

"Then proceeded to accost me."

"—and kissed you for your own protection."

Scorn flashed in her eyes. He much preferred an angry Celia over a despondent one. This one was much more fun. "Protection? *Bah.* You stole the prize from under their noses and flaunted me before them."

"Would you rather I had left you?"

"No." 'Twas more of a reaction than a reply, rather like a grunt.

Fomenting her annoyance was unwise, but Jack

could not resist. He touched her elbow and lowered his voice to a sultry rumble. "Shall I kiss you again? A kiss befitting a gallant knight?"

She snorted. "I should rather kiss your horse."

He grinned. "He gave me leave to kiss you in his stead. Something about oats. Or a mare." He shrugged. "I really don't speak horse that well."

Celia's gaze met his and a wicked gleam entered her eyes. "'Tis understandable, as you speak *ass* so perfectly. Though the animals are of a similar species, I imagine the language is not at all the same. Rather like Spanish and Portuguese, wouldn't you say?"

Jack barked out a laugh, and she smiled, so obviously pleased to have forced it out of him. Gauntlet indeed, but at least she no longer fretted over her damned family.

"Upon my honor, Celia, you could drown a man gushing such pretty compliments. I am wounded." He attempted a soulful look but suspected a remnant twinkle of mirth still lingered in his eyes. "You should kiss me to make amends."

This prompted an insulting laugh. "I shan't be kissing you again, sir. My mother warned me of silver-tongued rogues and silver-eyed devils."

"Which one am I?"

"Both."

Jack liked her answer. Very much.

Her expression turned guarded. She looked pointedly at the hand still holding her arm. "Unhand me so I may trounce you at chess."

Fie. She desired his company—as long as he kept his distance. He looked down at his hand on her arm, then back to her face. "I think you are afraid to kiss me again."

"Don't be silly." She straightened her spine. "We've established you are not nearly as frightening as I once thought."

"Yet you are afraid." Her cowardly green eyes lowered, as if they longed to hide beneath her hems.

He touched his fingers to her chin and waited, patiently, until her gaze rose to his. "Perhaps you are afraid of yourself?"

She attempted a light laugh, but it sounded frantic. "Whatever can you mean, Jackson? Must I remind you that I am betrothed?"

"Ah yes, your Mr. Kensington. You wear the man like a chastity belt, did you know?"

A choked sound escaped her, and she tugged her arm free, cradling it as though he'd burned her. "This is utterly ridiculous, Jackson. What do you want of me?"

"He cannot make you feel," Jack persisted, determined to force her to see the truth. "He will never give you what you crave. What a woman needs from a man."

Angry color stained her cheeks. "How could you possibly know? I love him. I have loved him my entire life."

"I loved my sister too."

Her brows scrunched and she gave her head a shake. "What?"

"You speak fondly of the man, but never passionately. Never as a lover. You say you grew up together. He is your friend, yes?"

"Yeeeesss," she reluctantly agreed, dragging the word out as if she feared handing it to him all at once.

"He is your *brother,* Celia. At least where your

heart is concerned."

"Of all the—" she sputtered and took a step back.

"Has he kissed you?" Jack pressed and snorted when her eyes skittered from his.

Her chin came up. "Of course, he has kissed me."

"Like a brother?"

"How dare you, Jackson Beaumont. You make us sound so… so…" Words failed her. "He is my husband. Or shall be when I return."

Anger roiled in Jack's gut. He took a sharp breath, amazed when he didn't exhale fire. *Husband.* He wanted to spit the vile word at her feet and stomp on it.

"You want me."

"I do not," she huffed.

"You desire me."

"You are mad."

"And you are a liar. In my room. On my bed. You wanted me. Where was your damned betrothed then? Did you think of Brett while you kissed me?"

She gasped, eyes dark with scorn and shooting sparks, body trembling with fury, and skin flushed with high color. Christ, she was beautiful when she was angry.

"You kissed me. You kissed me and you enjoyed every single moment. Do not dare say otherwise."

Her mouth opened and closed, struck mute by his charge. She crossed her arms at her waist and clutched her elbows, closing herself off.

Coward.

Jack leaned forward and raised his brows. Her chin came up. The toe began tapping again, drumming her fury into the carpet. He sighed. This was not precisely what he'd planned. Hell, he hadn't a bleeding plan.

He pulled her to him, trapping her arms at her sides. She held herself rigid, like a damned mast, and refused to meet his gaze. He whispered in her ear, "I can prove my claims, you know."

Curiosity got the better of her. "How?"

"Close your eyes."

Her look told Jack he was daft.

"For pity's sake, Celia. Close your damned eyes." She did as he asked, and Jack felt like he'd won a major skirmish.

Pirates had nothing over women when it came to battle.

He tightened his arms around her and whispered in her ear, "Picture your intended. Picture his face. Can you see him in your mind?" He brushed his lips across her cheek, skimming them softly over her mouth.

"Pretend these are his lips kissing you. Is this how he kissed you? You must be certain 'tis his face that you see." He touched his mouth to hers, soft, sweet.

A moan escaped her. Her eyelids fluttered.

"*Shh,* you must keep them closed. Picture Brett in your mind's eye. Do you see him?"

She whimpered.

"No?" Jack kept his voice neutral and smiled. Fiendish way to purge the man from her system. Deuced clever is what it was. His mouth moved over hers, conquering, devouring, burning his texture and his taste on her stubborn lips so his damned rival's name would never pass them again.

"And now? Was it like this?" He gave her another slow, drugging kiss.

She shook her head. "No."

"What was it like then? This kiss your Brett gave

you?"

"It was perfunctory, I suppose. Like a farewell kiss."

"Perfunctory? One, say, like your father might give?"

Her brows puckered and her eyelids quivered.

"No peeking." He rubbed his cheek against her brow. "You must answer my question."

"I suppose it might have been." Her breath whispered over his neck. "I daresay it does not signify Jackson, as I've seen my father kiss my mother farewell in precisely the same manner."

Jack rubbed his cheek against her temple and ran a hand up and down her spine to soothe her. "I am not certain I'm able to give you a perfunctory kiss, but I shall try." He pressed his lips to hers, intending to make the contact hard and fast, but lingered a moment because his lips were not inclined to depart hers so soon.

"Was it similar to your Brett's? Did you feel him then?" He snuggled her closer in his arms.

"No. What is the purpose of this, Jack? Other than a shameless excuse to kiss me. What can you possibly hope to prove?"

"I wish to show you the difference between lovers and friends."

"With kisses?" She opened her eyes.

"Aye."

"Your nefarious plan failed. At no time could I picture Brett—either as a friend or a lover."

Jack quirked a brow. "Telling, is it not?"

Her expression changed, torn between anger and intrigue. She bit her bottom lip and damn, but he wanted those teeth to sink into him instead.

Anywhere would do.

He raised an unsteady hand to brush his knuckles over her cheek. "If he were a lover, shouldn't you imagine his arms holding you? His lips touching yours?"

She closed her eyes and swallowed. When they opened again, they were sharper, greener, and flashing with ire. "I suppose you are being a friend to point this truth out to me?"

" 'A friend?' " He tipped her jaw up, tilting her head back to touch his lips to hers. "Nay, Celia. You mistake my motive entirely. I mean to show you whose arms should hold you." He rubbed his forehead against hers and her eyelids closed against the force of his gaze. "Whose lips should claim yours. Which man will make love to your sweet body." His mouth trailed a path from brow, to temple, to ear. "I mean to be your lover."

"Jack," she whispered. Just Jack. Was his name a sanction or a plea? He cupped both sides of her head, burying his fingers in her thick, sable hair as his lips fused with hers.

This particular kiss had purpose: it was meant to surmount all she thought to deny him and teach her the power she alone possessed. He wanted to banish all memories of her life before him, because he wanted her life to be him.

He wanted to claim her soul.

Gratitude weakened his knees when she kissed him back, matching his ardor, and clutching his coat in her fists. Angling his head, he nipped at her bottom lip, teasing her with his tongue until she opened to him. He surged into her delicious mouth in triumph, ravaging and inciting her moans of pleasure.

Her hands skimmed over his chest to grasp his shoulders. Jack wrapped his arms around her, pulling her tight against his burgeoning cock, his body desperate now. He'd never wanted anything in his life like he wanted her. She quivered at his touch, tiny pulses that leapt beneath his fingertips as they trailed along the ridge of her spine.

A thousand fingers of need flexed beneath Jack's ardor, taunting, teasing, stoking his body with frustration. His hips ground against hers in agony. "Celia," he pleaded as his lips grazed her throat. "Be mine."

She pulled away and dropped her head to his chest, her breaths ragged.

"Be mine, sweetheart." Jack squeezed her waist and kissed her hair. "Let me be your lover."

"Jack, no," she whimpered, her voice shaking with passion. But when she pushed away, anguish showed on her face. "We cannot do this."

"Why? I know you want me." He hugged her to him. "Want this."

"Wanting does not excuse our actions. It does not permit us to behave dishonorably."

"Dishonorable?" He clasped her chin in his hand. "You think my feelings dishonorable? They are honest, Celia. Why should yours not be the same?" She flinched and he immediately regretted his words.

"Honesty, Jack?" Her stubborn chin came up and green fire scorched him. "Very well, let us be honest with one another. Yes, I desire you. There is little question of that. What if we give in to our desires? What then, Jack?"

What then? Likely he'd die from the ecstasy of finally making her his. From the rapture of writhing naked with her beneath him. From burying himself so deep—

'Twas not what she meant.

The toe tapped out a march on the rug again and damned if he wasn't being prodded up the scaffold to his own hanging.

"I will tell you," she answered for him. "We shall become…lovers." The word did not come easily to her. "Your ship will soon be repaired, but I shall be ruined, and you will be left with the dilemma of what to do with me."

Jack opened his mouth to argue, but then closed it again, struck with curiosity. He wanted to hear what her busy little mind had conjured as an outcome.

"Will you return me home and sail away, never to see me again? Surely, you'll have satisfied your lust by then. I should be easily discarded. No?" she said when she saw the anger on his face.

Damned impertinent witch. Her opinion of him deteriorated by the hour.

"You shall leave me here to pine for you while you sail in and out of my life? Or perhaps you will find my company so stimulating you will take me with you. Shall we sail the seas together, you and I?"

"People change." He pulled her back into his arms. "Desires change. I am not the same. Not since I met you."

She pushed away. "Then you are prepared to give up this mistress of yours, Jackson? To turn your back on the sea. To give up the *Bonnie Lass*?"

Give up the Bonnie Lass*? How could she ask such*

a thing?

He ran a frustrated hand through his hair. It had come out of its queue at some point during their embrace. When he'd all but devoured her. Heat roared up his spine and licked like flaming torches in his head. He shot her a glance hot enough to scorch her bodice and was rewarded by her startled gasp. Her hands skimmed the front of her gown as if assuring herself it still remained.

"How shall I keep you in pretty dresses if I give up my livelihood?" If he failed to find the emeralds.

"I have no need of your money."

"And I've no need of yours!" Well then. That had snapped from him like a sprung trap.

"I am already betrothed to a man who does not plan to leave me. Brotherly though he may be," she added scathingly.

Jack yanked her back to him and kissed her again, a kiss born of frustration. And fear. He liked her better when her mouth was busy, and she could not talk back.

"He isn't me," he told her when he broke the kiss.

She placed the flat of her hands against her waist and held herself rigid. "It matters little. If I do not marry Brett, I shall have no one. Unless you promise not to leave me."

Devil take her. The little shrew would rip his soul to shreds. His jaw threatened to buckle beneath his clenched teeth.

Her eyes scanned his face, reading him like a bleeding book, and her expression changed to disappointment. "I thought not." She whirled and fled the room.

Hell. What a bleeding mess. But what argument

should he have given? His funds were depleted. A house and a damaged ship were all he possessed—unless he found the gems.

’Twas the only way. He had to find the emeralds and he had to do so before Celia clapped eyes on her Mr. Kensington again. How the deuce he’d accomplish it, Jack wished he knew. But accomplish it, he would.

He had to.

Because he’d have to challenge the man for her otherwise.

Chapter Fifteen

"Poor girl," Rory mourned. "What travails she's suffered."

Red, the ship's master carpenter, ran a hand along the *Bonny Lass's* hull where she rested on her side near the shoreline. "Need our own sawmill to mend her up proper."

"And guards to keep the thieves at bay." Jack ducked under a protruding beam. "Now that the roof is finished and the floors ripped out, Smitty will oversee the last of the work at the house. Deeds, you'll serve as carpenter."

"Aye, Cap'n," his Egyptian apprentice mumbled, his face glum. Unhappy he'd be confined indoors most likely. Sailors preferred the open air, though the November weather was still overwarm.

"Captain Beaumont."

Jack wiped the sweat from his brow and spied Major Duncan approaching with Governor James Glen at his side. The crew scattered, leaving Jack alone to jaw with them.

"Imagine our good fortune. We've finally run you to ground." A robust man, the major. About the same height as Jack though a good twenty years his senior. The effects of long, hard days and endless calls to duty showed on his face, his deep-set eyes dark and gaunt against his bright red uniform.

"Good fortune you say, Major? 'Twould appear your society is sorely lacking." He nodded to the governor. "James."

The major chuckled. "It is indeed. And how have you fared, sir?"

"Better than many of these poor wretches, I vow." All along the riverbank, debris was piled helter-skelter. Jack had seen far too many empty gazes from those whose lives had blown away with the storms.

"Aye, 'tis certain we shall suffer ill effects for many months to come."

The governor gestured to the Major. "I've called upon the militia to maintain order. And restricted exports of food. We cannot afford to feed others when our city is starving, and the fields are submerged. Everyone wants for relief of some kind."

"Aye." Jack clasped his hands behind his back. "I should think the town will revolt soon."

Glen scowled at Jack's blasphemy. "Thank God for St. Phillips. These poor wretches' travails have been eased somewhat by the church wardens. They've doled out staggering amounts of food and clothing."

Red and Crawley yanked on a broken board. The loud crack drew everyone's notice.

"Aye, the wardens are veritable saints." Jack snorted. "Though I suspect the gates will be closed to them come judgment day."

The governor turned his attention back to Jack. "Rather philippic, Beaumont. I gather the wardens denied you?"

"Everyone receives aid, James. Including cutthroats and thieves."

A bead of sweat ran down the side of the

Governor's face. "What are you implying, sir?"

"That the pirates are receiving special favors from the wardens." Jack turned to Duncan. "I pray you maintain your vigilance, Major."

"Botheration." The major planted his hands on his hips and looked toward town in disgust. "The constable assured me the scoundrels were interned at the workhouse and the wardens had put them to useful work."

Governor Glen took out a handkerchief and dabbed at the beads of sweat dotting his brow, his tall, lean form doubtless sweltering beneath his bottle-green, velvet coat and excessive wig featuring precise, horizontal curls reaching well past his shoulders. Ireland would turn green with envy.

"Ah yes, pirates. I'd heard of your exploits, Beaumont. Rescued a fair damsel in the bargain, did you?"

Jack rolled his eyes. "Do not paint it up romantic, James. I rescued the only survivor and thereby the sole witness to their crimes. Now the blackguards are roaming the streets. Presumably *hauling away debris*."

"There is quite a bit of it," the governor murmured. "Have you shared your concerns with the constable?"

"Latham and I are not of the same mind."

"Oh, dear." The governor heaved a weary sigh. "Who is this woman? Has she any family?"

The last thing Jack needed was a nosy governor muddling into his affairs. "You do not wish to know."

"Get rid of her then. Straightaway. Surely there is a ship somewhere to take her home to…?"

"England." Jack thought it best to be vague. "She's to testify against the pirates when the admiralty arrives."

Major Duncan nixed that idea. "A proper investigation into your charges of piracy shall be delayed, Captain. The admiralty will not return for some time as there's an epidemic of some sort on the islands. The ships are all quarantined there."

"Demn. That may be weeks or even months away." Glen waved his handkerchief at Jack. "Take her up north. Likely the admiralty's in port somewhere up there."

Perhaps. But the emeralds were south. Jack pointed out the obvious. "I haven't a ship at present."

"Does no one have a vessel worth sailing?" Glen shook his head, lost in his miseries for a moment. "You do intend to repair it?"

Duncan clapped Jack on the back. "About those repairs. We wish to speak with you about the tub resting on Meeting Street. What say you to moving it?"

Red let out a snort, having come close enough to hear.

The major frowned at him. "Constable Latham says you claimed her."

Jack rocked back on his heels and crossed his arms. "I agree the *Mirabelle* ought to be moved, Major, but I've no inclination to do so. 'Tis true I tried to claim her, but the constable intervened until the admiralty could decide the matter."

Duncan looked unhappy; Jack was unmoved. "I understand you've ill feelings toward the man, Captain. However, I've been charged to return this city to some form of normalcy. To that end, the town has no use for ships in her streets."

"Had the constable not interfered and confined me

to port, she would not be lying there now," Jack pointed out. "Such is not the case, and I shan't suffer the inconvenience."

The major tilted his head in acknowledgment of his grievance. "Surely the ship may be repaired, Captain. Perhaps you've a mind to start a small fleet?"

"Before the storm? Aye. 'Twas my intent all along. Now?" He shrugged. "I haven't the time or the funds. I cannot help you, sir."

"Bah." Glen waved a hand in dismissal. "I've no use for you if you refuse to cooperate."

"Ah, but James, I have a use for you," Jack said softly.

The governor stiffened as though a sword had been pointed at him. "I do not care for your tone, sir."

Jack sighed. He'd have to work on that. He clamped a hand on Glen's shoulder. "Come now, James. 'Tis but a small favor I ask."

The governor's gaze raked him suspiciously. "What sort of favor?"

"What say you to a houseguest?"

****

Finally, the major and governor took their leave. Jack pulled a mock forelock at their retreating backs.

Ireland nodded a greeting as he passed the departing men, pausing to stare after the governor, doubtless admiring the wig. Sunlight glanced off his scarlet coat, stabbing Jack's eyes.

"God's teeth, Ireland. That damned coat nearly blinded me."

"Devil take ye, Beaumont." Ireland let out a booming laugh. "And here I meant to sneak up on ye." He lifted his feet daintily as he stepped onto the sand.

Jack shook his head in disgust. “Mincing fop.”

“Aye,” Ollie said from inside the hull.

“Why are you here?” Forsooth, Jack did not wish to know.

“Why, I’ve brought ye the name of me tailor, Jocko.”

“We shall mutiny,” Red warned.

“Your tailor should be shot. What the devil do you want?”

Ireland *tsked* at him. “I came ta offer me services, ye ill-mannered whoreson.”

Hands on his hips, Jack circled the dandy as if considering a mare for purchase. “I will allow ye’re a garish coxcomb, Elgin, but if ’tis a whore ye wish to be, ought’n ye apply to old Nell for a position?”

“Har.” Ireland slapped his knee. “The storm blew yer sense o’ humor out yer arsehole, did it?” He fingered the lace at his throat. “Haven’t a ship to sail at present. Figured I’d work for ye and save me coin. Can’t afford to scratch me arse at present.”

Jack gestured to his clothing. “And ruin your finery?”

“I shall take care not to muss it.” Ireland sniffed.

“I shall regret this.” But Jack needed the help, no matter how annoying.

“Ye need me, Jocko, as ye’ve a ship to make seaworthy. Heard tell she’s headed to the Bahamas. I’ve a mind to accompany ye there. Know of a man who might want a captain for his schooner.”

Eight pairs of eyes focused on Ireland in unison. The word “Bahamas” delivered a warning as clearly as a shot to their bow.

“Why do you believe we sail for the Bahamas?”

Jack fought to keep his hands at his sides instead of thrashing the answer from the man.

Ireland marked their intent faces and slipped his fingers beneath his wig to scratch behind his ear. "Heard it at the tavern."

"From?" Jack asked patiently, though his men were anything but. They crowded closer.

"Name o' Small. Used ta sail on the snow what sank in the last hurricane. Came off with flying colors, that one. Scurvy dog were so jiggered with drink he could'na stand on his pins. Captain refused him aboard. Be dead otherwise."

This was the first Jack had heard of it. "The *Ladybird* sank?" With the roads covered with fallen trees, the mail was being sent on available ships again.

"Aye. Up the coast aways."

Celia's letter had gone down with it, then. She would take the news poorly given her worry over her family.

"Why ye askin' 'bout Small, Jocko?"

"'Tis a surprise is all," he said smoothly. "I've some competition and did not wish my destination known. Change out of your finery, Elgin. Come back dressed to work. I vow I'll shoot you if you wear another hideous coat."

"Ye'll be pleased ta have me around, me bucko." Ireland laughed and slapped him on the back. "I shall liven up the place." He twisted the ends of his mustache and fluffed the curls of his powdered wig before sauntering off.

"The devil," Spinnakers spat when he was out of earshot.

"What magpie blowed upon us?" A rumble started,

hot gazes ricocheting between them.

Jack raised a hand. "Hold gentlemen. The pirates are searching for the gems as well."

"Someone flapped his gums," Ollie insisted.

"Likely so," Jack allowed.

Spinnakers stroked his beard thoughtfully. "Close quarters aboard ship. If any of ye conversed about the emeralds, the picaroons may've overheard."

Several heads dropped at that.

"Hold your tongues," Jack ordered, locking gazes with Spinnakers. They would have to be more circumspect in the days to come. "The day is wasting, gentlemen. Get to work."

****

Celia sipped a cup of broth in the kitchen and watched Meagan chop vegetables. Perhaps she'd go out to the garden later and watch bugs crawl. One should vary their amusements, after all.

With the floors completed, there was little to occupy her and nowhere to go since Jack had confined her to the house while he and his men worked on the ship.

Smitty sat beside her with his bandaged hand resting on the table. He'd crushed it two days ago—an incident involving a cat, a barrel, and a nervous horse—and spent his convalescence like a caged beast being poked with a stick. His mood did nothing to lighten Celia's own.

She'd yet to forgive Jack for kissing her witless last month. Her conscience reminded her she'd been stupid enough to participate in his silly game. *'Twas not my fault,* she argued back. Ten women combined did not possess enough fortitude to resist Jackson Beaumont.

’Twas all she thought about now—his lips, his arms, his voice in her ear. Sleep eluded her.

Her fingers drummed against the table while Smitty complained to his wife. She had become so bored with her thoughts she could no longer bear her own company. Haunting the kitchen was not much of an improvement save for the pleasant aroma of simmering chicken.

Meagan suffered their presence and went about her labors, her knife swift and efficient as it hacked up vegetables for the pot. If the British conscripted cooks to fight their wars, they’d be won in record time. The aristocracy would starve, of course, but sacrifices must be made.

“They’ve a ship now.”

“Who?” Meagan swiped at her damp forehead with the back of her hand. Tendrils of white-blond hair stuck to her temples below her mobcap.

“Jenkins and his dogs.” Smitty flicked a glance at Celia. “Cap’n believes they’ll follow when we sail.”

Celia swallowed and set her hand over the one drumming the table to still it. Her arms turned chill, as if the icy bay flowed through them. “Because of me?” She caught Meagan’s warning frown to her husband. “Please tell me.”

His gaze rested on his wife’s face, his ever-present scowl relaxing just a bit. “In part, I expect. They’ve lost everything, ye ken. Their ship, their cargo—”

“Their captain,” Celia supplied.

Smitty snorted, his words harsh. “Nay, the dogs hardly esteem one another. None mourned the loss of Jean Pierre. But they blame Jack for the loss of their ship. And their spoils—of which ye were a part.”

Spoils. How flattering. A girl dreams of being wildly popular, the toast of the season, inspiring men to vie for her hand. Something had gone horribly awry as Celia had achieved the status of "bone" for pirate-dogs to snarl over.

If any of Jack's men were hurt on her account…oh, she could not bear the thought. "I have put you all in danger."

"Nay," Smitty groused, impatient with her. "'Tis naught to do with ye, Celia. The cap'n has grievances and wants justice. The pirates have charges against him as well. They seek recompense. And revenge."

"John," Meagan admonished. "Ye needn't frighten the girl."

But Celia was already frightened. "My return to England will give them one less prize to fight over." She refused to call herself a spoil. "I should think my departure will ease all your minds. I shall sail on the first available ship whether the admiralty has arrived to take my testimony or not."

Another shared look between husband and wife. Neither commented. This must be how people felt around her and Rianna. They spoke volumes to one another without ever uttering a word. She found it extremely annoying to be the one left out of the conversation. Her fingers played out her agitation on the table.

"*My* mind will certainly be set at ease when I return." She thought of her family and sighed. "We do not realize how fortunate we are until we've lost that which we cherish most."

Which called Brett to mind. And the deplorable behavior she had to atone for.

Life was daunting, truly.

Meagan mumbled something beneath her breath that included "Jackie" and "discover." Her husband responded with a negative shake of his head. To Celia's surprise, he turned a glare on her. *Were the pirates her fault or not?* Clearly, he blamed her for something.

"What?" she finally snapped.

"Women." He slapped his palm against the table. "Trouble is what ye are."

His wife gave him a chiding look.

Smitty responded with a snort. He lifted his cup but paused before it reached his mouth. His face tightened as he stared pointedly at the table. Celia followed his gaze and stared at her hand in surprise. It had taken on a life of its own, pounding out a veritable symphony against the table's surface. "I'm tempted to fetch me hammer and nails."

Molly entered, untying her apron. "I've finished in the parlor, Meagan. I'll jus' fetch me cloak and head ta the market for ye now."

Meagan lifted her knife and pointed it at her husband. "John shall accompany ye."

"He will?" Molly glanced at Smitty.

His gaze slanted to his wife's. "Why?"

Meagan turned the knife over in her hand and said cheerfully, "'Tis necessary fer yer health, me love, for if I'm forced to abide yer bad temper much longer, I shall plunge this into yer arse."

Molly clapped a hand over her mouth, eyes dancing with mirth.

Celia felt no need to stifle her reaction. She laughed in Smitty's face.

"Damned rude women." He stood while Molly left

to fetch her cloak.

"I shall join you." Celia hopped to her feet. "I've a letter to post at the coffee house."

"Be damned if I shall—" Smitty began, only to be gainsaid by his wife.

"Ye will. The fresh air will do ye both good."

"Cap'n wants ye to stay inside," he said to Celia.

"You shall escort me," she pointed out.

Meagan slapped her knife on the table. "For heaven's sake, John. 'Tis a public market."

"Ye're sure in a haste to be rid of us."

"The good Lord knows I'm entitled to some blessed peace." Her brows lowered and her expression turned mulish. "Begone with ye."

****

A fine dust hovered over the congested street where workmen hammered alongside the makeshift market. Sights, scents, and sounds overwhelmed Celia—vendors hawking, wagons creaking, dogs barking. The smell of fresh and not so fresh fish mixed with limited offerings of produce, a few baked goods, and the pungent leavings of animals.

Meagan had promised a proper Christmas meal and to that end, Molly and Smitty bartered at the costermonger's stand while Celia waited nearby. She reveled in the sensory noise after Jack's imposed confinement, content to stand amid the hurly-burly activity and gawk.

A prickling along her neck and jaw unsettled her. The fine hairs at her nape bristled with awareness. She spun about, and her body honed in on the source of the disturbance.

Across the street, three slovenly dressed men with

lank, greasy hair loitered against a gray stone edifice. The one on the left nudged the one in the middle when he caught her watching, who in turn elbowed the third.

The sense of familiarity gave way to panic when she recognized them from the *Mirabelle*. Her hand rose to her throat, her pulse a violent throb against her fingertips. Belatedly, Jack's warning tolled like a funeral knell in her head.

Pleased by her reaction, the trio issued catcalls and made vulgar gestures. She took an involuntary step back and bumped into someone. Whirling about, she came face to face with Black Patch Jenkins.

"Afternoon wench," Jenkins greeted her with a smirk. He was still dressed completely in black—perhaps clothing rotted when it touched his skin. His un-patched eye roamed over her cloaked form. "Beaumont appears ta be treatin' ye well."

Every muscle in Celia's body tensed and she took a step away, choosing not to respond.

"Where be yer protector?" His eye gleamed hopefully. "Mayhap ye're alone?"

"No," she blurted. "I've companions." She gestured to the stand next to them.

"Pity. Me mates and I would'a performed a…service." His smile was polite, his voice solicitous. It made her skin crawl. "Else ye'd suffer a mishap."

"Sir." She unconsciously raised her hand to ward him off.

"Jenkins," Smitty appeared at her side and grasped her arm with his uninjured hand. "What the devil are ye about?"

The pirate's smile became a snicker. "Wench accosted me while I were goin' about me duties." He tugged a forelock and crossed the thoroughfare to join the others.

Smitty spat on the street behind him. “What did he want?”

Celia smoothed her shaking hands over her skirt. “Only to frighten me.”

He glared after the retreating pirate. “Cap’n ain’t gonna like this.”

Chapter Sixteen

The stairs were a cloud beneath Celia's feet. She floated down them filled with joy. Jack expected the *Bonny Lass* to be finished within a fortnight.

A fortnight.

Finally. They would sail to England. She would be home by March. She paused on a step and gripped the rail while her heart spread its wings and soared. *Mama. Papa. Rianna. I am sailing home.*

Not even last week's unfortunate encounter with Jenkins could dim her happiness. Jack vowed to kill the scoundrel when he found him. Smitty thought it unlikely, declaring cockroaches like Jenkins could slip through any crevice. It mattered little. Soon she would be far removed from the man's threat.

As if her thoughts had conjured him, Jack's voice beckoned when she reached the landing. She paused in the doorway of his room and discovered him tying up the laces of his shirt. He'd already donned his breeches, hose, and shoes. She could not determine whether she felt relief or disappointment at his state of dress.

She had not seen him in such a fashion since they'd shared a cabin together. At once an intense longing assailed her, nostalgia for the closeness between them without the burden of stronger feelings and guilt.

Time ever seemed her enemy.

The prospect of returning to her betrothed loomed

before her, transforming her nimbus of happiness into a cloud of gloom. She squared her shoulders. Jack had no right to make her feel sad. "Need help, do you?"

He turned to face her—arms akimbo, feet planted apart, hair loose about his shoulders—the very image of a dashing swashbuckler. Her pulse kicked and the curtains by the open window ruffled, the breeze carrying the scent of cinnamon to her. Her every pore breathed him in and sighed.

Silvery lights twinkled in his eyes. "I should have known you'd offer to help cover me rather than the pleasurable alternative."

If he only knew. Her face heated with an inconvenient blush. His lips spread in a slow, wicked smile. "I find it alarming you need help a'tall, Captain. One prefers to consider a man capable."

"You wound me, Celia." His rough voice scraped deliciously across her skin.

She leaned against the doorjamb, crossing her arms against a shiver. "What did you want of me?"

"Hmm?" He frowned, but then his face cleared. "Oh. I wished to inform you I may return late this evening. You needn't wait supper."

"Will you be dining out then?"

"Nay. I shall ask Meagan to keep me a plate."

Celia shrugged. "I do not particularly enjoy eating alone so I shall wait for your return. I should like to hear about the ship's progress. I grow impatient as the time to leave draws near."

He smiled, though in truth it resembled a grimace. His voice turned brisk, officious. "Very well. I shall conclude my business posthaste."

She tugged her lower lip with her teeth and

pondered his change in attitude. Perhaps he did not wish to dine with her? But that seemed silly. They always shared the evening meal together. She tried to search his eyes, but he looked to the bed. Two swords, a pistol, and a musket lay atop the brocade coverlet.

"What are these?" She stepped inside the room for a closer look.

"The weapons I keep on the *Lass*. Now that Spinnakers is staying aboard at night, I thought to return them."

Celia picked up a rapier, lighter and thinner than the cutlass lying alongside it. She swished it through the air experimentally. Jack batted the blade away when she pointed it at him. "I know how to use a sword. The crew on the *Roundabout* taught me when I sailed to Bermuda."

His brow wrinkled. "Why?"

"I was bored."

He fought an obvious eye roll as he scratched his back against the bedpost. "Skill takes years to master and common sailors are notoriously inept with a blade."

The man's arrogance rankled. She straightened her spine and assumed an en guard stance. "I learned enough to best my instructor in a mock duel."

Up winged a mocking brow. "Rather refines my point, does it not?"

Oh, what she wouldn't give for a rope and a razor right now. She'd tie him to a chair and shave that infuriating brow off. "I was quite good," she insisted. "A quick learner." She brandished the rapier before her, advancing and retreating in measured half steps. Once she had the rhythm of it, she increased her pace to three steps up, three steps back, swishing the blade in small figure eights with each advance. Odd, but the thing grew heavier. Her arm beginning to tell.

Jack regarded her display of swordsmanship dubiously. "I remain unconvinced."

"I am simply out of practice. Allow me a few moments and you shall see how easily I could—" Her feet caught and tangled in the rug, tripping her in the midst of a lunge. The momentum shot her forward and the blade straight into Jack.

A rending tear followed.

She landed hard on her knees, the rapier embedded in the mattress, her hand still wrapped around the hilt.

Eyes wide, face frozen, Jack stared. He might well have stopped breathing.

Celia scrambled to her feet, ignoring the pain in her abused knees.

"Jack! Dear Lord, I've stabbed you!" She groped at his waist and felt along his side where the sword had passed through. Although his shirt had a neat hole sliced through it, she failed to find any blood. "Where are you hurt?"

Frantic, she searched his face. 'Twas as if he'd turned to stone. He failed to even blink.

Panicked now, she spread the hole in his shirt wide and stuck her face in to peer inside—and discovered smooth, taut, perfect skin. Confused, she tugged his shirt from his breeches to have a better look.

He snapped out of his stupor and shackled her wrists. *"Damn and blast, woman!* This is the fifth shirt you've ruined. What, by all that is holy, do you have against my shirts?"

Relief nearly caused her to faint. If he could yell at her, he could not be hurt too badly. She yanked her hands free. "Do shut up about the shirts, Jack. Did I wound you or not?"

"Aye," he answered pithily. "You wounded my shirt."

She crossed her arms and tapped her foot in agitation. "I should apologize for my clumsiness, but clearly you do not deserve it."

"Oh?" He held the garment out and pointed to the hole. "I suppose you find it perfectly acceptable to stab a man's clothes."

Miffed, she pulled the rapier out of the mattress and gingerly laid it back on the bed. "A pity I missed your thick hide."

He tugged his shirt over his head and tossed it to her as he crossed to his wardrobe. "There. That should give you something to do while you await my presence this evening. See if you can wield a needle and thread without killing it."

She caught the shirt and her breath along with it at the sight of his naked torso. At how those huge muscles bunched and relaxed with fluid grace.

Monstrously unfair. To be pummeled witless with lust over such a beast. He turned with a fresh shirt in his hands, and she gasped. God help her. She had to clutch the bedpost to keep from throwing herself at him.

Jack's head shot up. His intense gray gaze focused on her.

Taking a deep breath, she offered up her best glare, hoping the heat in her cheeks would be construed as anger. "What I shall do while awaiting your august presence is rip this," she shook the discarded shirt at him, "into shreds."

He sighed heavily and donned his shirt and

waistcoat. “I fear I must reassess your competency with a sword. ’Tis likely you’d run a man or two through in your clumsiness. A rather crude technique but if it accomplishes the goal, well then…” He shrugged.

Celia stuck her nose in the air, stomped out of the room, and went down to the kitchen to beg a cup of tea from Meagan.

Meagan smiled when she entered and pointed to the kettle of water she kept hot. Celia nodded.

“Just take a minute.” She rested her spoon across the rim of the pot she’d been stirring and went to the cupboard to fetch the tea. “What have ye there in yer hands?”

Celia shook out the shirt and held it up for inspection.

The woman’s eyes bulged. “Stars above, how did Jackie’s shirt get such a big tear?”

“I ran a sword through it,” she grumbled.

Meagan blinked. “Whyever would ye do that?”

“He was in it.”

****

A week after she’d vanquished his shirt, Celia loitered at the table while Jack finished his breakfast. It occurred to her she had not purchased a single gift to take home. She’d not ventured far enough through town on her outing with Smitty to know whether any of the shops had survived the hurricane.

“When shall we leave?” she asked him, deciding an afternoon of investigation was in order. Surely a few vendors had rebuilt.

Jack went peculiarly still. He glanced up from his plate and swallowed.

Warning fires lit in Celia’s belly. She searched his

face for the cause.

Those eyes. All smoke and mist. But his face was carefully blank. “I shall leave within the week.”

She frowned. He’d said, *“I”* singular.

“But we sail for England, do we not?”

He shifted, squirmed actually, and cleared his throat. “Soon. I promise.”

A funeral march thumped in her chest. She laid her hands flat on the table and leaned close to search his features. “What are you saying, Jack?”

“I am sailing to the Caribbean.” His tone was defiant.

“But…why?” Confusion warred with hurt at his belligerent attitude.

Jack shoved his plate aside. “I must sail to Barbados before we cross the Atlantic.”

“Why?” she repeated, her voice gone shrill.

“I’ve business that has long been neglected. ’Tis where we were bound, you’ll recall, when we came upon the *Mirabelle*. I was to meet my friend, the Dutchman, in September to exchange goods: my brandy, his spices. He will have left my spices in care of a factor.”

She did not understand.

“My funds are depleted, Celia,” he said, exasperated with her. “I must pay my men. ’Twill only be a short delay. I promise. A month, perhaps a bit longer. You shall spend the Easter festival with your family.”

“Easter? Easter is three months away.” Her composure crumbled. “I have been missing for months. My family… You truly expect them to wait longer?”

“Surely you of all people understand the monopoly

the Dutch have on spices. Were it not for our friendship, I should never be able to procure such a valuable commodity. I cannot forgo the income."

"But…I've been waiting so long, Jack—" Her words tumbled to a halt at the closed expression on his face.

He responded with silence.

"Am I to understand you do not wish me to accompany you?" She was proud at how even her voice sounded while despair raged within.

His eyes flashed with silver sparks of irritation. Good, because he had thoroughly irritated her. "Jenkins and his men are sure to follow. I'll not place you in danger."

"Danger? They've done naught since we've arrived. But even so, you intend to leave me behind while you and your men sail away. You do not scent even a whiff of danger in that prospect, Jackson? Why have I been kept under lock and key these months? What is the point if you plan to leave me alone?" She smacked the table with the flat of her hand. "Why could you not find me transport on a different ship?"

"The docks have yet to be replaced. Few ships venture forth." Jack covered her hand with his, pinning it against the table. "I have a plan to keep you safe while I am gone. We shall sail for England immediately upon my return."

"You make no sense. If you must travel to the Caribbean, I shall go with you and—"

"Nay. I'll not take you with me. I am sorry, Celia, truly, for I know how anxious you are to return to your family. Please believe I would not ask this of you were there any other way, but this I must do first. I beg your patience."

"My patience?" she choked. "How can you ask such a thing of me?" She gave him a defiant look. "I shall find passage on my own once you leave."

He pinched the bridge of his nose and sighed. "'Tisn't possible. They will follow whatever ship you board. Would you endanger the lives of an entire crew?"

"Fie on you, Jackson. You said they would follow you."

"Aye. My aim is to convince them you sail with me, but I cannot be certain they will all follow. 'Tisn't as if the picaroons share an allegiance. Until the admiralty tries them, you are a threat. You must stay, Celia, and remain out of sight. 'Tis the only way."

"Jack, I shall forever be in your debt, for my very life as well as your hospitality, but I cannot wait. Do not ask it of me. Name your price. Whatever you hope to earn in the Caribbean, my father will double it. As will I," she added and gave him a smile of encouragement. "There. Now you've no reason to go. Take me home and your profits shall be fourfold what you should have earned in Barbados. 'Tis the least we can do to repay you. And we shall purchase your brandy as well."

Jack stood so abruptly his chair crashed to the floor. He towered over her, eyes flashing like lightning over dark and angry skies. "You," he spit the word out and jabbed a finger at her, "are not in my debt. Never insult me by saying so again. And *never* offer me payment. Do you comprehend me? Never."

Unable to find the necessary words to further her petition, Celia beseeched him with her eyes.

"'Tis done. My course is set." He snatched his tricorn from the table and quit the room, slamming the door behind him as he left the house.

Stunned and confused, she sat very still while the enormity of what transpired settled over her. She tipped her head forward until it rested on the tablecloth.

Devastation swallowed her.

"Oh, Rianna," she whispered miserably. "Whatever will become of me?"

****

By the time Jack returned to the house, the first stars winked in the early twilight, and the moon almost full with a ring circling it like a halo. He recalled something about moon rings…some sort of omen?

A good one, he hoped. He headed straight for the kitchen where Smitty and Rory sipped ale at the large, well-worn table.

Rory winced when he caught sight of him. "I don' know how I lets meself git talked inta yer schemes, Cap'n. I shall be the laughin'stock o' the whole crew."

Jack commiserated. Although he would not be telling Rory. He crossed his arms and fixed a frown of displeasure on him. "You are assuring Miss Celia's safety."

"Aye, but why me?"

"Because you are the smallest, aside from Andrew," he said patiently. "And he is not tall enough."

"Ain't 'cause ye're the comeliest dandyprat," Smitty said, looking him over.

Meagan entered with a skirt over her arm. She shook it out in front of Rory. "Try this one."

Rory's face scrunched and he took it from her gingerly, as though it were snarling at him.

Smitty chuckled into his mug.

Jack rolled his eyes. "I shall return momentarily." He sent Meagan a pleading look. "You will manage without me?"

"Leave him to me." Meagan shooed Jack off. "He'll be beatin' the gents off with a parasol, and no mistake."

He gave her a grateful kiss on the cheek and slipped out of the kitchen. Nodding to Deeds, who stood guard outside, he entered the house and took the stairs two at a time, but when he turned to start up the next flight, Celia was coming down.

"Ah. There you are." It occurred to him that he'd no idea what to say. He only knew he would not see her for weeks and the very idea of their separation caused him intense pain.

"I thought I heard you return, Jackson." Her light tone sounded forced. "Are you ready then?"

"Almost. We leave with the tide."

"Oh."

Not exactly witty repartee. Like him, Jack suspected she had everything and nothing to say at this point; her thoughts unwilling to evolve into words. "I wished a private moment to bid you farewell." He squeezed her arm. "Come, I've a gift for you."

She followed him into his room.

Odd, how barren the chamber looked now that his trunk had been removed to the ship. He'd never noticed before. A hunter green cloak lined with satin and adorned with a gold braided clasp lay across his bed.

"'Tis beautiful," Celia breathed, running her hand over the garment.

"Aye." Jack's gaze roamed her features, slowly

sketching each line and shadow to tuck away and savor during the long, lonely nights ahead. "'Twill compliment your green eyes."

An adorable blush washed over her features. Her gaze skittered away from his. "Well, I—" Her brow puckered in confusion. "Whyever did you buy me a new cloak, Jackson?"

"I need your blue wrap for Rory." He stroked her cheek. "Will you fetch it for me, love?"

"Of course." She rushed back out and up the stairs. She must have taken all of the air in the room with her. Either that or his lungs had mutinied. Deuced woman. Weighing anchor was a thrill, not a bleeding tragedy, for pity's sake.

Celia hurried back to his room and handed him her cloak. His hand actually trembled when he took it from her. They stood and simply gazed at one another. The silence grew pronounced and uncomfortable, prodding him on his way. Jack balked against it. Leaving her proved harder than he'd imagined. "I should go."

Her teeth sank into her lower lip, and she nodded. He stared at her mouth and his feet refused to move. "You must promise to have a care, Jackson."

"Do not fret, love." He smiled and cupped her cheek. He had to touch her or die. "I will return before you know I've gone, and then I shall whisk you off to England straightaway."

"Swear it to me, Jack." Her words emerged a strained whisper.

Sweet, merciful God, he could not bear this. "I swear," he whispered back.

She swallowed. Her eyes narrowed and her voice turned fierce. "Be warned, sir. I shall hold you to your word."

Jack stroked her soft cheek and placed a kiss on the top of her head. He cleared his throat. "Perhaps you'd care to give me a wee kiss goodbye?"

Celia's lips parted and she blinked several times, as if absorbing the import of what he'd asked. He held his breath, unable to read the emotions flitting across her face.

But then she stepped forward, her skirts brushing over his boots, and her hands came up to frame his face. For a spell-binding moment, her witch's eyes searched his. Then she pulled his head down and touched her mouth to his.

Jack let out a groan and clutched her to him, holding her so tight he wondered that she could breathe as he feasted on her soft, sweet mouth. She tasted like honey and smelled like heaven, and devil take him, how he wanted to spoil her with sin. His body shook with it.

Kissing her now, just as he was about to sail was unthinkably stupid, but denying himself this pleasure would have surely ended him.

Celia's arms slid up over his shoulders and wrapped around his neck. She let out a soft little moan and tightened her hold. He shoved her against the wall by the door and pinned her between his arms while his lips trailed a path along her jaw and down her neck. She gasped when his teeth nipped at the taut cord of her throat, the puff of breath a sensual rush in his ear.

She shoved him away.

The loss was severe and unbelievably wrenching, but probably for the best, as Jack was nearly mindless with lust and close to tearing off her clothes and throwing her atop that green cloak on his bed.

They stared at one another; panting, wary, before she let out a cry and launched herself into his arms again. Her mouth stroked over and over his, pausing at intervals to nip at his bottom lip with her teeth. Erratic tremors communicated to his groin with each little bite.

He buried his fist in her hair. It spilled free of its pins and cascaded over his arm as his tongue plunged inside her mouth to ravish hers. Her hands slid up the front of his coat and latched onto his shoulders.

Sanity reared its ugly head. Jack's body howled against it. He had to leave her before he could claim her. He broke the kiss and held her locked against him, gasping and struggling against his desire, but could not resist touching his lips to hers once then twice and again, brushing over and over until finally he managed to stop and release her.

The loss of support caused her to stumble back against the wall. One hand rose to cover her mouth, the other her stomach.

Jack stiffened. "Do not tell me you are ill."

Her eyes widened and her brows scrunched in confusion. "What? *No*." An embarrassed giggle escaped. "Not—not ill. 'Tis just so very lively in there." Her fingers tapped nervously against her lips. "An excess of emotion I should imagine."

"Desire," he corrected smugly, because he wanted her to know exactly what she felt for him.

She looked away, refusing to acknowledge or deny his claim. He closed the short distance between them and grasped her chin, gently turning her face up to meet his eyes.

"You and I, Celia, we must speak when I return. There is much to settle between us." Specifically, a foppish heir that would find himself short one bride when she returned home.

"Aye, Jackson." Her chin dipped against his palm. "We shall settle the matter."

He smiled then, a tender smile meant to soften any trepidation she might feel. He stroked her cheek and leaned down to press his lips to hers, sealing the bargain. Her hands clutched the sides of his coat.

"I must go," he said when their lips finally parted. "I will have your word, madam." He swiped the blue cloak up from the floor where he'd dropped it and tossed it over his arm. "Promise you will remain indoors and under the governor's protection." He straightened and pinned her with a threatening scowl. "I should be very annoyed to come home and discover Jenkins had absconded with you."

"I should be annoyed as well." She laughed. "You've my promise, sir. You have no cause to worry on my account. I shall not leave the governor's care."

"Thank you." He hugged her to him, relieved by her pledge.

"Please, Jack." She wrapped her arms around his waist. "Please come back to me."

Chapter Seventeen

Jack's heart soared while at the same time his conscience pricked at the plea in Celia's voice. He had to go. This voyage was their future.

"You may depend upon it, love." He kissed her hand. "Where is your trunk?"

"The men set it by the front door."

She repaired her hair before they descended the steps and went out to the kitchen. Smitty still sat where Jack left him, wearing a gleeful grin. Meagan had joined him at the table. She held a mug between her hands and wore much the same expression. Rory stood in the middle of the room dressed in Meagan's skirt, a ferocious glower beetling his brows, his breeches clutched in his hand like a club.

Celia clapped a hand over her mouth and turned to Jack, eyes dancing. His lips twitched. He squeezed her hand on his arm and sent Rory a harassed look.

"Here." He handed over the blue cloak. "This will hide your ugly face."

Rory snorted and took the garment from him.

The lot of them made their way from the kitchen to the foyer inside the house, Rory suffering much heckling from Smitty and Meagan.

Jack and Smitty hefted Celia's trunk and carried it out to the wagon. If his ruse succeeded, the pirates would believe she was aboard the *Bonny Lass* when they sailed. Ultimately, his success would depend on how well they executed the plan and duped the pirates. Rory—disguised as Celia—and her trunk would board the ship. The trunk would then be crated up to disguise it, placed in the wagon once again, and transferred to the governor's residence. Later, he'd slip back to the house for Celia, who would be disguised as Molly, and transport her to the governor's where she would remain until he returned.

They had five hours to accomplish their tasks and sail with the tide.

Once the trunk was loaded, the two men stomped back to the house to say their farewells. Jack took Celia's hands. "We do not want Jenkins' men to become suspicious. I shall wait until assured no one is following; perhaps two, three hours or more."

Her voice emerged whisper soft. "Be safe, Jackson."

Some beast must be ripping his heart from his chest. The pain was excruciating. "Aye, sweet witch." He lifted her hands and placed a kiss in each palm, trapping her tearful gaze with his. "Remember your promise to me."

She squeezed his fingers. "And yours to me." He released her hand and ushered Rory outside.

Smitty hugged his wife and closed the door behind them.

They strolled down the walk with Rory's arm wrapped loosely over Jack's while Smitty trailed behind.

"'Tis too much to hope you'll walk like a lady, Rory," Jack said, sotto voce. "Adjust your gait. Take small steps to hide your swagger."

"'Aven't a swagger." The hood of Celia's cloak muffled Rory's surly voice.

"Ye do," Smitty argued. "'Tis a wee one, mind, what with those pint-sized pins, but a swagger all the same."

Rory let out a snarl. "Sod off, ye barmy tongue-pad."

"*Tsk* Miss Breckenridge, your language," Jack chided softly. "You sound nothing a'tall like a beautiful young heiress."

"Thank the Lord fer that." Rory grunted.

Jack handed him up into the wagon then climbed in to take the reins. Smitty jumped up on the other side. They made their way to Pinckney's flat-bottomed boat. 'Twas a tricky business without docks, but they'd managed to load the *Bonny Lass* with the brandy and provisions. Aside from the five who'd been together at the house, only Spinnakers knew of Jack's ruse. The rest of the crew had been informed Celia would sail with them. They tugged a forelock respectfully as the cloaked figure passed. Indignation beamed off of the little man inside it.

Jack passed a hand over his mouth to hide a grin and escorted him below. Moments later he appeared on deck and joined Spinnakers near the helm. He clasped his hands behind his back and surreptitiously searched the waterfront for probing eyes.

****

Blue Tooth slinked away from the window and into the shadows as Beaumont and his men left the house. "Sits the wind in that quarter, does it?" He smirked as he skulked along the hedgerow. "An' with only one guard ta boot."

Footsteps crunched against the broken cobbles on the other side of the house. Stones scattered. An *oomph* and a curse followed. The pirate flattened against the wall until the sentry's clumsy footfalls faded away.

He slipped between a loose section of fence. Suspicion niggled at him. The wily bastard had dressed up his man as the wench. Plannin' ta make gooseberry's o' the lot of them. He smiled and made his way through the shadows.

"Methinks the good captain erred."

****

Celia donned her best lavender dress to meet the governor, though the prospect depressed her. The darkness outside the window spread to her heart. She picked up her new cloak and caught a faint whiff of cinnamon. Her eyes closed and she felt his nearness—the low rasp of his voice, those blazing silver eyes when moved by some strong emotion. Aye, she missed him already.

Dear Lord, she ached with want. How would she survive his absence?

Her agitation set her to pacing. Dread gained momentum, tolling a knell in her brain. She turned on her heel and faltered. Pain sliced from the base of her skull to the tip of her spine, a spear of ice splintering her back. Gasping, she braced herself against the wall, her breath shallow and knees weak.

Of a sudden the pain left her, almost as if it had never been, leaving only portent in its wake. *Jack.* Had the pirates caught them unawares? She pushed away from the wall and threw open the door—startling the three men on the other side.

Baldy's mouth curved. "Thoughtful o' ye ta greet

us, wench."

"No." Fear licked down her spine. Jack was not due back for hours.

Blue Tooth and their cohort snickered—she recognized him from the market that day. "Ye'll come wit' us now. Cap'n Jenkins wishes ye ta pay 'im a call."

She whirled away and screamed. Baldy yanked her hard against him and slapped a hand over her mouth, cutting her off. "Gag 'er and tie her hands," he said to Blue Tooth. "Fetch that wrap. Quick like."

The brigands hurried to do his bidding then carried her, whimpering, down the stairs.

Baldy took the opportunity to pinch her backside. "Thought ye'd escaped yer fate when Beaumont claimed ye, eh? And now ye'll pay a price. Jenkins gits ye first then I gits me a turn."

Celia paid him no heed. She was too busy figuring out how to escape them. She could run. Her legs were unbound. Aye, as soon as he set her down she would fly.

Once they reached the bottom landing, they dropped her to her feet. Baldy tossed her cloak around her shoulders and pulled the hood tight over her head while the others stood at her back. He pulled a knife and waved it in front of her face. "One noise, bitch, 'twill be yer last." She stumbled when he pushed her out the door, the frigid January air failing to penetrate her feverish thoughts.

Blue Tooth rushed down the garden path to the gate, peered up and down the street, and motioned for the rest to follow. Baldy shoved her, hustling Celia away from her sanctuary. Away from her future. Away from Jack.

Their destination was a scarred old building with a crumbling façade. She tripped over loose bricks and mortar littering the perimeter, her vision severely limited by the darkness and the cloak hiding her face.

Stone steps led up to the back entrance and more steps down to the cellar. Baldy ushered her through a warped, wooden door. His henchmen followed, kicking it closed behind them.

Total blackness surrounded Celia, the cellar dank and musty with age. Icy fists of terror clamped her ribs, squeezing, squeezing, punishing her lungs. She greedily sucked in air, convinced there was not enough. The taste of rot and decay assailed her mouth and she whirled, frantic to flee the suffocating pit, but a hand clamped her arm.

"Think ye'll escape, do ye?" Baldy's voice rasped in her ear.

Flint struck and meager light flickered in the room.

To Celia it was the sun.

Sanity returned with her vision. The floor above had rotted through in several places. Doubtless a result of the hurricane. Water glistened on a slimy wall next to them.

Baldy spun her about, propelling her across the garbage strewn floor through another door. A barred cell with filthy cots ran the length of the room. Meager moonlight filtered down from a small, grimy window built high in the wall. He cut her bindings and stepped back.

A much abused desk sat near a wall, the legs in front longer than those in the rear so it tipped backward, as if the weary thing had plopped down on its haunches. Behind the desk sat a man in shadow. He stood. The icy fists gave her lungs another hard squeeze.

Jenkins stepped forward. His mouth quirked up and the cheek beneath his eye-patch creased into three deep furrows—a smile of welcome, albeit a sinister one. He spread his arms wide. "An' 'ere ye be luv, come ta enjoy our 'ospitality once't again." He reached for her hand. Celia shoved both behind her back to avoid his touch.

"What do you want?"

He hooked a dirty hand on the lapel of his wrinkled, buttonless coat. "Why, since yer lover means ta leave ye behind, I thought ta offer ye me protection."

Impressive sincerity from the devil's minion. "I must decline your offer," Celia replied in a remarkably haughty tone.

Jenkins *tsked* and his mouth twisted in that hideous, lopsided smirk. "I must insist."

"What do you hope to gain by my abduction?" Conversation would be the least abhorrent interaction with the man and hopefully distract him.

"Ye shall serve as barter betwixt me and yer captain."

Bait, in other words. Likely he wanted to exact revenge on Jack for the loss of his ship. "You are despicable."

His lips twisted in either a sneer or a smile, with Jenkins 'twas difficult to tell. "Ye do turn a pretty phrase, ducks."

Hardly. She'd never said anything remotely pretty to him.

"Shall I take yer wrap?"

She shook her head and hugged the cloak as if it were armor Jack had given her. Baldy stepped from behind and snatched it from her shoulders. The loss devastated her, and she cried out as if they'd torn Jack away from her instead.

Baldy grinned and dangled it from his outstretched hand, taunting her with it.

"Beast." She stomped her foot. "Give it back."

Laughing fiendishly, her tormentor rubbed the garment between his legs then lifted it to his nose and sniffed.

"Enough," Jenkins snarled. "Leave us."

Alarm displaced Celia's bravado. His vulgar gaze flicked from her to the cot pointedly.

"Lookin' forward ta that meself," Baldy said cheerily. He offered her a lewd wink and tossed the cloak over his shoulder, sauntering from the room.

She ought to feel relieved only one man remained to contend with; alas, he frightened her more. Better to have two dogs snapping over a bone rather than one chomping on it—if you were the bone.

"M-my father is a merchant. A wealthy one. He will compensate you handsomely for my safe return."

Jenkins' eye lit and the cheek creased up in amusement. "Will he, now? Per'aps he'll offer us diamonds then?" He laughed at whatever joke he'd made and looked her over.

Appalled and exposed—even covered from bodice to wrists to boots—she wrapped her arms around her waist. The pirate snickered at her protective posture and took a step forward.

Celia took a step back.

They moved thus until she came up against the damp stone wall. Shying away from his penetrating stare and the smirk on his lips, she threw her hands out in front of her as a shield.

His nostrils flared. He yanked her to him and twisted her arm behind her back then snatched a fistful of hair and jerked her head backward. Pain tore at her scalp.

Ale-soured breath fanned her face.

"I shall enjoy this, ducks. I been waitin' a long time ta frig Beaumont's whore."

Her legs shook. Bile rose to her throat.

Where was Jack? He swore he'd keep her safe.

"Aye, he spoilt ye with a soft bed and clean linens. Ye'll learn to live without. If ye live." His mouth quirked at her look of loathing.

"Now Beaumont, he be a selfish bastard, keepin' ye all to hisself. Me, I share the spoils with me mates." He let go of her hair and ran a dirty finger along her cheek, and lower. It was as if he directed an ice floe beneath her skin. She held her breath, and her vision darkened. She was losing consciousness and welcomed the escape.

But her instincts to protect herself were stronger.

Bucking furiously, her body squirmed against his hold, turning toward the arm that held her pinned in an effort to twist loose. Which thrust her breast into his wandering hand.

"'At's it, luvvy," he hissed in her ear, clawing and pinching her tender flesh. "I likes a bit o' fire."

Celia whimpered and struggled until she'd freed her arm. She shoved his hand off.

Laughter hissed through his broken teeth as he clamped his dirty paws onto the panniers at her hips and gripped them like a pair of handles. He thrust his breeding organs against the juncture of her thighs, grinding her abused posterior into the course stone wall at her back.

"St-stop," she choked, barely able to speak.

The glint in Jenkins' gaze turned feral. "Eh? Why, we've only begun, luv. Allow me ta straighten yer dress." He let go of her mangled panniers and moved his hands to her bodice.

"No." She brought her arms up to block him and shoved, terror giving her strength.

He stumbled backward. Surprise blanked his features.

Panting from a mixture of fear and revulsion, Celia crossed her arms over her chest and clutched her shoulders. *Dear God, take me now before he touches me again.*

Jenkins' eye flared and he staggered back a few more paces. "Rebuffed!" he crowed. His paws clutched at his heart. "Ye wound me, luvvy." His hips continued to twitch as if molesting her still. Or gathering momentum. Teeth bared, he started forward to continue his fiendish enterprises. "But me cock'll be friggin' ye all the same."

Panic spiked Celia's gut. She cringed at his expression, his curling lip, his hands rising to abuse her again. Her vision dimmed until all she saw was black—black beard; black patch; the enlarged black pupil of his eye.

Blood roared like a tidal wave in her ears. A primitive instinct for survival overcame her limbs. She lifted her left leg and stomped down hard, so hard that as her foot hit the ground, it added impetus to the right one kicking out. The toe of her boot struck Jenkins' groin with considerable force. A grunt wheezed from him, the kind of sound that comes straight from the gut. His body convulsed.

Momentum from her kick knocked both of Celia's feet out from under her. She landed on her back on the hard, earthen floor. All her air whooshed out.

Jenkins teetered on his toes for a long, suspended moment then dropped to his knees with a keening moan and toppled over.

Wild-eyed panic gripped Celia until she finally managed to suck a breath of musty air into the void of her lungs. She rolled over onto her hands and knees and pushed to her feet. Stumbling back against the wall, she willed it to swallow her up while her assailant writhed on the floor.

He flopped to his side and vomited.

"You…bitch," he hissed between clenched teeth.

Celia watched him, dispassionate but wary, as he twisted in pain. She said nothing, which incensed him all the more.

"I—will—slit—yer—friggin' throat." He vomited again.

The door banged open. Baldy poked his head in, prompting Celia to inch further away.

"Eh, what 'appened?" Baldy laughed when he spied Jenkins on the floor.

"Slut—kicked—me—cods," Jenkins croaked.

"'Oy!" Baldy called laughingly to his fellows. "The wench ain't fond o' the cap'n. 'Twould appear she's done with 'im. You roisters stay there." He pulled the door closed behind him and stepped into the room, hitching up his breeches.

"Ye'll not—touch 'er—ye cur. Not—'til I teach—the bitch—a lesson. Savvy?"

Baldy considered Jenkins. Celia slinked a few more inches away. The pirate leader was in no condition to enforce his mandate, but some dire warning must have passed between the two men, because Baldy finally nodded.

Tears of relief flooded her eyes.

"Ye'd best not kill 'er, ye bastard, or I'll cut off them cods and feed 'em to the fish."

"Lock 'er up," Jenkins gasped, unimpressed. "'elp me—to the chair."

Baldy apprehended her and shoved her into the cell. She collided with the stone wall and hit her head. Pain exploded in her skull and a bright flash sparked behind her eyes. He twisted the key in the rusted lock and removed it. Then hauled his captain to his feet and helped him to the chair behind the desk, watching in amusement as he gingerly sat.

"Give me the key."

The pirate hesitated then snarled and dropped it into Jenkins' outstretched hand.

"Whiskey," he snapped. His minion saluted, but before he left to fetch the whiskey, he sent Celia a malevolent glare.

Never would she have thought being locked behind bars would feel safe. It would not last, of course, but for the time being, the bars kept the animals at bay.

****

Once he'd delivered Celia's trunk to the governor's house, Jack made his way back to the ship. 'Twas quiet. Too quiet. The only noise had come from James, jawing on and on about losing sleep. Charles Town's esteemed governor had become quite vocal with his displeasure of late. Jack rather pitied Celia.

He joined Smitty and Spinnakers on the foredeck. "Did anyone follow when I left?"

Smitty tapped his pipe against the rail. "Nay, though we put the cloak back on Rory and paraded him around the deck for good measure. Haven't seen hide nor hair o' the blighters."

Spinnakers stroked his beard and peered out over the railing. "Worrisome, is it not, when the sea dogs go to ground?"

Jack paced. *Where the devil were they?* One was always around the docks or watching his house. Hadn't they seen him put Celia aboard?

Talons of unease gripped his gut. Something was afoot.

"Belay sternwaying the ship into the harbor. Keep her anchored here until I return."

"Ye want me to follow ye, Cap'n?"

"Aye, Smitty. But keep your distance and a watchful eye. If the picaroons trail me and Celia to the governor's house, we'll know we've failed to convince them she's aboard the *Lass*."

He clapped Spinnakers on the shoulder, let out a booming laugh to keep up their ruse, then he and Smitty shimmied down the rope ladder to the skiff below. Spinnakers chuckled after them, their false merriment spurring Jack on. Thespians, they were not.

****

Celia clasped her hands beneath her chin, attempting to quell the shivers wracking her body. She dared not move about lest she draw unwanted attention to herself. Absurdly, her shivers kept time with the serenade of snores coming from Jenkins. The man gave her jimjams—he slept with his head lying on the desk, fist wrapped around a jug, mouth slack and dripping drool onto the wood surface. A grotesque sight, but preferable to his vile curses and grim threats.

Raucous laughter reached her ears from the outer room. Her eyes darted to the door. Jenkins jerked upright mid-snore, grunting from the discomfort the sudden movement must have caused. Tossing a glare at her, he stood with exaggerated care and made his way from the room so slowly a turtle could have run circles around his feet.

A wellspring of relief surged through Celia. She jumped to her feet and paced back and forth in her damp cell to get warm. *Where was Jack? Had he discovered her missing? Was he searching for her yet?*

Nearly an hour later, the door jerked open, and Jenkins staggered into the room, bits and pieces of a meal clinging to his filthy black beard. She stopped pacing and turned to face him, her posture stiff.

His lip curled. "I'm pissin' blood and me pouch is swelled ta the size of a coconut." An exaggeration, surely, though she refused to look for evidence of his claim. He bent slightly forward, bracing his hands on his thighs. Perhaps standing erect created a strain. "I might jus' slit yer throat an' toss yer carcass ta the sharks." Likely he'd gotten the idea from Baldy as that had been the plan for his "cods."

"You meant me harm. I only wished to defend myself." She eased backwards to the corner of her cell, though with him holding the key it was hardly safer.

"Harm? Bah! 'Twas but a bit o' sport I was lookin' fer. Same as ye give that bastard, Beaumont."

Celia gave him a pointed look. He'd clearly meant her to suffer, inflicting pain that had resulted in her kicking him.

He straightened to a slight stoop and shrugged a shoulder. "'Tis a mite rougher than ye're used ta, but ye wouldna been much the worse fer it."

Liar.

His continued discomfort came as a relief. The longer he suffered the less capable of rape he'd be. And the more time Jack would have to find her. His eye popped back open, and he spat on the dirt floor. "Ye made yer bed, wench. Ye'll be screamin' and beggin' fer mercy when I ride ye. I'll make ye wish ye were dead."

She wrapped her arms around her waist and shook her head. "I already do."

Spittle limned the corners of his mouth when he smiled—probably venom. "Oh no, bitch. Ye'll not die 'til ye've suffered at me hands." He jerked his chin toward the door. "And theirs."

Her flinch caused him to chuckle, cackle really, as the shaking of his body made the sound an octave or two higher than the norm.

A slow smile spread across her face, buoyed by false bravado. "And when Jack learns what you've done to me, he shall make you wish *you* were dead."

"Whore." He pulled a knife from his pocket. "Ye'll wear me marks the rest of yer life, short though it may be." He grew tired of baiting her and left, breathing heavily from the simple exertion of walking.

Celia dropped to the filthy cot and covered her face with her hands. Tears trickled down her cheeks, running through her fingers and snaking around her wrists. "Save me Jack."

Chapter Eighteen

Pirates visited Celia sporadically like vultures awaiting their next meal. They arrived in various stages of inebriation to ogle and taunt and swipe at her through the bars.

She held her hands fisted together at her waist and used the wall to hold her upright. Ugly, demented faces leered at her through the bars. They picked at the lock, the scritch-scritching raked across her nerves until she feared she'd go mad from suspense. Threats, dire and progressively creative, were hurled at her each time the scalawags tried and failed to breach her prison. They jerked on the bars in frustration and made lewd gestures.

One bold scoundrel pulled his manhood from his breeches and wagged it at her.

Exhausted to the point of numbness, the sight was more shocking than Celia could bear in her diminished state. Mad laughter burbled out of her like a cauldron venting steam.

The waggler's face flushed crimson and his mouth flattened to a thin, ugly line. He lunged at the bars. Her amusement offended his fellows as well, whose bent was to frighten, not entertain. Promises of retribution trailed in their wake as they staggered from the room and back to their jugs of rum.

Early dawn light shaded the dark room to charcoal

gray. The blackguards would soon take turns defiling her, her virginity forfeit to their sinister revenge. If Jack did not find her soon, this dawn might well be her last.

If only she'd been bold enough to confess her feelings to him. She relived the kiss they'd shared just hours ago, remembered the thrilling sensation of trembling in his arms. Her one true regret that she had not shared his bed.

She would never know his body now.

Much good chastity was, she thought morosely. Instead of losing it in a bridal bed she would forfeit it on her deathbed. The vile image vaulted her from the cot.

Tears spilled over. "Oh, Jack," she whispered hoarsely. "I wish with all my heart I had told you I loved you."

****

Jack slipped inside the gate and paused halfway up the path.

Deeds rushed down the steps from the piazza.

"What?" But Jack already knew.

"Cap'n." Deeds clutched his cap in one hand, a sheet of foolscap in the other. "She's gone."

The blood drained from Jack's face. He knew this because he actually felt it siphon away. He stumbled on the path and grabbed the fence to anchor himself.

"Who?" he asked stupidly because God help him, he wanted it to be anyone but her.

"Miss Celia. Jenkins nabbed her." Deeds held out the page in his hand. "I found this on her bed."

The wench for the map.

Jack stared at it, paralyzed, while his entire world sank beneath his feet.

"How?" Single words seemed his only means of communication.

"Hit me from behind." Deeds rubbed his hand over the back of his head and winced. In the bright moonlight Jack spied the blood when he pulled it away. "When I roused, I run through the house lookin' for her. I was on my way ta the ship jus' now."

"How did they know?" This was the crux of the issue. He'd planned so carefully but somehow, they'd figured it out.

"On my sammy-say-so, I don' know, Cap'n. Miss Celia stayed inside, just like ye asked. Mrs. Smith is worrit somethin' fierce."

"Where is Meagan?"

"She run to get some bandages fer me head. But I had ta find ye straightaway."

He'd turned to ice. His heart and mind frozen. Deeds' words bounced off the hard shell of Jack's new reality. He could not absorb them. Could feel nothing.

Meagan came running from the kitchens. *"Jackie."*

"See to him. Find me when she's through," he said to Deeds as he rushed to the street and intercepted Smitty.

They ran the few blocks to the waterfront and Smitty rowed them back to the ship. Spinnakers' eyes widened when he saw Jack, likely at his bloodless pallor. He felt cold, alarmingly so, as if his heart had stopped pumping to his extremities. His navigator clamped a hand on his arm. "What's happened?"

"The devils have Celia." Jack's voice shook with fury. "I left her there, ripe for the plucking, and now the bloody bastards have her."

Spinnakers' face blanched—they'd be a ship full of

ghosts by the time everyone learned of it. “Shiver my soul.”

The chill enveloping Jack’s emotions began to thaw. Behind it boiled a hot, black rage, intense and virulent. It came from the toes of his boots to the tips of his fingers. He raised his clenched fists to his head and howled his fury.

“Goddam,” Smitty choked and ran a shaking hand over his face.

Jack’s crew reacted as if he’d let out a war cry. They surrounded him within moments.

“Jenkins took Miss Celia.”

Silence greeted his statement. The men glanced at one another in confusion. None of them appeared eager to speak. Finally, Crawley took the bit between his teeth and stepped forward.

“Uh, Cap’n. Miss Celia, she’s here on the ship, ain’t she? Ye brung her aboard yerself.”

“Nay.” Smitty spat over the rail. “’Twas a ruse, not Miss Celia.”

Crawley scratched his head but remained silent when Smitty failed to expound. None could dispute the menace spewing off their captain.

Jack smacked his fist into his palm and paced, urgency riding his shoulders. “Arm yourselves. Pair off and fan out. Cover every inch of this city until you find her. Send a man back to alert the others when you spot her or one of Jenkins’ men. Spinnakers will remain near the ship. Return on occasion and advise him where you’ve searched.” Finally, he stood still. His voice burnt to a hoarse whisper. “Hurry.”

****

As soon as the door began to open, Celia

scrambled off the cot, unwilling to hasten her defilement by lying on the rack.

"Tonight, ye bleedin' whoremongers. Ye'll get the wench tonight," Jenkins snarled.

"See 'at we do." Baldy's voice.

The door slammed shut. Jenkins crossed the room to her cell, his eye bloodshot and leering. "Ah, there ye be, ducks. Waitin' on me pleasure like a good li'l trull." He grasped the iron bars of the cell and pressed his face between them. "Ye'll be spreadin' them legs shortly. Soon as the laudanum that whore Nell give me wears off. The boys are gettin' restless, ye see. Might be a bit rough with ye, seein' as they's had ta wait a spell."

She dragged her gaze away from Jenkins and his unholy smirk and stared at the far wall, willing her heart to slow, her breathing to calm. If only she could shut off her ears.

"We all have our partialities. Some coves likes ta bite, some beat on their whores a bit. Gits a man excited, ye see. Baldy, he ties them up with his ribbons." He flashed his blade at her. "I likes to carve me a bit of flesh here and there."

Fear slithered up her spine and an anvil settled on her chest.

Jenkins shuffled to the desk, his gait still hampered, and settled into his chair. Minutes later, his snores filled the room.

Fighting despair, she bent her head and tried to pray.

But the prayers would not come.

****

The day wore on with no sign of Celia or her abductors.

Jack harassed every official in the city: governor, major, the watch, and even the constable. Everyone had been alerted to her plight. 'Twas as if the pirates had disappeared. Or set sail. They checked with the port official to confirm no ships had come or gone.

How could he have been so bleeding careless? How had he failed?

If she were not dead yet, she surely would be soon.

The molten ball of the sun sank behind the rooftops. Dusk settled over the city. Deeds caught up with Jack at the ship.

"Cap'n. Me an' Artie saw some o' Jenkins' dogs go inta Pink House."

Blood surged into Jack's dead heart, reviving it. "Is Jenkins with them?"

"Nay, Cap'n, but mayhap they'll lead us to Miss Celia when they leave."

He stared off in the direction of Pink House. "How many?"

"Four, mayhap five. One we ain't sure of."

"You men. Follow me," Jack said to four of the crew who'd just arrived. "Smitty," he called across the street. "Come, we've got pirates to chase." Smitty left Spinnakers' side and hurried to catch up. The crew made their way to the tavern constructed of the pink-hued stone that had given it its name. Raucous laughter reached their ears as they approached the place. Artie motioned to them from the shadows in the alley.

"Cap'n." His voice was grave, and Jack heard a heart full of sorrow in that one word.

"Artie. Have any left?"

"Nay, Cap'n."

"Any in need of a piss yet?"

"Aye." Artie nodded. "One come out ta pump ship."

"Did he see you?"

"Nay."

Jack turned the corner and sidled up to the window to have a look. The pub was packed elbow to elbow, without an empty chair to be had. Several tars had provided their laps for the tavern wenches to sit on. Smoke filtered through the room, gathering in a nimbus about their ale-sodden heads.

Baldy and three of his contemporaries sat at a table swigging ale and shouting at a busty tavern wench with a beam broad enough to support a roof. Apparently, none of the revelers were drunk enough to offer her a lap. A man loitered against the wall, watching but not participating with the pirates. Likely another of Jenkins' cutthroats. Five then. But how many more?

Rage took another swipe at Jack. He stood for a long moment staring at the vermin, knowing what they'd likely done to Celia, and let the fury have its way. His hands twitched at his sides, and he fought to keep his feet planted where they were, to not storm inside and wrap his hands around Baldy's throat. He threw himself away from the window, clenched and unclenched his fists, and forced himself to breathe.

He was useless to her like this.

"We should drag the son-a'-bitches out o' there and beat 'em 'til they tell us where she is," Ollie was saying when Jack returned.

"Nay," Artie countered. "What if they keep their gobs shut? 'Tis best to follow 'em like Deeds said."

Jack nodded. "I agree with Artie. Beating would be the most pleasurable choice, but 'tisn't the wisest, for the game is called then.” He leaned against the wall outside the tavern and crossed his arms, considering, while the debate raged on around him. He hadn’t the patience to wait for the scum to stagger home. Not when God only knew what Jenkins was doing to her. Icicles formed in Jack’s veins when he considered the possibilities.

She needed him.

Now.

“One might do,” he mused aloud.

“Eh, Cap’n?” Deeds stood at Jack’s shoulder. “One might do what?”

Jack straightened from the wall. “What say we cull one from the herd? Take him for a stroll. Ask a few questions. Politely of course.” This last was met with so many feral smiles they resembled a pack of snarling wolves in the darkness. “His friends will likely think he’s found a whore to bed or staggered off somewhere to sleep.”

“Aye.” Ollie rubbed his hands together. “One gone missin’ ought’n ring any bells.”

“Deeds, Ollie, and I will take him with us. The rest of you stay here. If the others decide to leave, follow them. Discreetly.”

“How we gonna nab ’im, Cap’n?” Ollie asked.

“We shall wait ’til one comes out to pump ship. Not the Slive-Andrew against the wall,” Jack warned. “He may not be with them. The four at the table are the ones we want.”

“Aye, Cap’n.” Artie slipped around the corner to watch at the window.

“The rest of you keep to the shadows. Remain close enough for Artie’s signal. And keep a watch out for Jenkins. Do *not* allow him to see you. If that should happen, take him. Quickly."

The crew began to move but froze when Artie poked a head around the side.

"The scrawny one's leavin'."

The men faded into the shadows. The "scrawny one" staggered out of Pink House and walked a few paces into the alley. The sound of him pissing followed, accompanied by a few verses of a bawdy sailor's tune Jack rather enjoyed.

Their quarry made sufficient noise for Jack to approach unawares. When he hitched up his breeches and turned around, the toes of his shoes met Jack's.

The buck's head snapped up. His eyes widened and his mouth dropped open, jaw flapping up and down like a shutter with a broken hinge. Jack smiled. And waited for that moment when surprise turns to fear. When realization dawns that life and limb are imminently at risk.

His prey lifted a foot to flee.

Jack's fist shot out.

The momentum of the punch spun the man in a circle. He faced Jack again and crumpled forward. Deeds and Ollie appeared at his flanks, each hauling on an arm to hold him upright. Ollie pushed a long, wicked blade against his side. The man let out a grunt. Straw-thin hair fell over his eyes and a trickle of blood ran from the corner of his mouth into his scraggly beard. He glared at Jack.

"Where is she?"

He clamped his lips together, defiant even with a knife threatening him. He speared a furtive glance at the door of the tavern.

"What is your name?" Jack tried.

"Sylvester," he answered when the blade flashed in front of his face.

"Where is she, Sylvester? I ask again because I assume you want to live. If I am mistaken, then…" He shrugged and Ollie sliced the man's coat open from armpit to hem. He pushed the tip of the blade through the gap he'd made and pricked the buck's ribs.

Sylvester flinched and said bravely, "I ain't afraid o' ye, ye mutton monger."

Jack sighed. Obviously, the man considered Jenkins and his lot the greater threat. Come to that, so would he. But they had Celia and he had no time for this.

"Death it shall be, Sylvester. But not until you've told me what I wish to know. Come." He motioned to Deeds and Ollie to follow. Smitty took a place next to Jack and they walked on, his men dragging a cursing Sylvester in his wake.

"I'll not tell ye a bleedin' thing," the pirate snarled.

"Of course, you shall." Jack glanced over his shoulder. "Ollie—the gentleman holding the knife—will carve you into pieces until you do. Where should we throw your carcass? To the vultures or the fishes?"

"Bastards." Sylvester let out a whimper.

They came to the skeletal remains of a warehouse that had burned before the flood. The area eerily silent, void of any activity or persons who might come running at the sound of a man's screams. Deeds and Ollie shoved Sylvester across the debris littering the ground and inside the charred interior. Moonlight illuminated half the space and cast the rest in shadow.

"Now, Sylvester, I've four more men to torture

after you. One is bound to talk. You might as well spare yourself the agony."

"Ye may well get the bitch back, Beaumont. After the boys is done swivin' 'er. But Jenkins, he'll have that map from ye first."

Jack's fist shot out again. This time the blow felled his opponent, who stayed on his hands and knees spitting out blood. Deeds yanked him to his feet. "Shall we try again?"

"Jam it out yer porthole, Beaumont," the pirate snarled.

Ollie yanked on Sylvester's ear and jerked his head to the side. Moonlight flashed off the blade piercing the man's exposed throat. "Mind yer manners, Sylvia."

"Sylvester, ye bleedin' prat."

Ollie grinned evilly in the dark and even Jack's hackles rose. "'Twill be Sylvia soon as we cut yer ballocks loose, luv."

Deeds chuckled.

Their captive whimpered.

Jack turned to Smitty in disgust. He hadn't the patience for this. "Come. We'll take one of the others out to the ship to interrogate while Ollie finishes this one off."

"Ye can't leave me here wi' this devil," Sylvester screamed.

"Snivelin' cur." Smitty spat at his feet.

"Break his bones before you carve him up, Ollie," Jack ordered. "I've heard Jean Pierre's lot broke more than one man on the wheel. Show Sylvia here how it feels.

Sylvester's tortured screams followed them out.

"Coward," Smitty said in disgust. "Doubt Ollie's

touched him yet."

"Good. The more frightened he is, the sooner he'll talk."

They hadn't gone a block when Deeds called out, "We know where she is. Ollie snapped his little finger and he blathered like a baby."

Relief swamped Jack so thoroughly he clamped Smitty's shoulder to steady himself. "Thank God."

The three men ran for the tavern, leaving Ollie to manage their prisoner. When they neared Pink's, they saw the remaining pirates walking away and Jack's crew hugging the shadows in their wake. Jack, Smitty, and Deeds fell in behind.

And headed in the same direction.

Chapter Nineteen

A loud bang startled Celia awake. She bolted upright and placed a hand to her chest to bolster the spot her heart slammed against. Howls and scuffling came from the next room.

The clamor awakened Jenkins, who roused, stretched, and winced. He threw her a baleful glare and fondled his cods.

She averted her gaze.

The door burst open, and Baldy ran inside, arms waving. "He's here."

"Who?" Jenkins sneered.

"Beaumont."

A surge of grateful tears ran down Celia's face.

"Bastards." Jenkins levered himself up from the desk. "Ye led 'im here. Damn yer hides."

"Howbeit," Baldy snarled, gaze darting toward the high, dingy window. "Ain't no escape."

"Grab his whore." Jenkins pulled the key from his pocket and threw it to him. "The bastard willn't do aught while we have 'er."

Celia ran to her cell door and held on with every ounce of strength she possessed in an effort to thwart them from using her against Jack.

Baldy stuck the key in the lock and yanked so hard, the door opened with her attached. He caught her arm and shoved her back inside. She clawed at him until he clamped an arm around her and squeezed painfully. "Hold, bitch, or I'll crack yer ribs," he spit in her ear.

Jenkins lowered himself to his seat, cocked his pistol, and positioned it beneath the desk out of sight.

The door flew open, bounced off the wall, and almost slammed shut. Jack kicked it again and ran inside, Smitty at his heels.

Cold metal pressed against Celia's temple and the menacing cock of the pistol pierced her ear. She flinched, but her gaze had latched onto Jack.

Powerful, formidable, magnificent Jack stood mere feet away from her. He looked haggard, mouth pressed in a grim line, face seething with anger. But his eyes, oh his beautiful eyes, were centered on her and her alone. Her heart leapt from her chest and flew to him.

His attention fixed first on the pistol at her temple then on the arm around her waist. Lightning flashed in his eyes and thunder pulsed all around him.

"Visitors." Jenkins' lips curved in a nasty smile though he visibly shook in his seat, which Celia took immense pleasure in. "What a pleasant surprise."

Jack ignored him.

Baldy snickered and slid the arm at her waist over her breasts and around her throat. He hauled her back until they came up against the wall. Celia worried that Jack would disregard Jenkins and the hidden threat he posed.

Seeking to allay his concern, she smiled.

He flinched. Not at all the reaction she'd expected. For the first time she noticed the pistols he held in each hand. The left one rose and leveled on Jenkins.

"Filthy cur. I've come to send your black soul to hell."

"Have a care, Captain—" Jenkins sat forward, positioning his weapon so it pointed at Jack. "—lest ye see yer whore come ta harm." Baldy tightened his grip around Celia's throat, choking her. She clawed at his arm, frantic to warn Jack.

Smitty moved closer and raised his pistol as well. "Ye'll beg the devil to come and take ye if she does."

The pirate leader was unimpressed. "Perhaps we'll affect a trade."

Celia's distress snagged Jack's attention. She stopped fighting Baldy's hold and flashed her gaze from the desk to him and back again. He focused on her and flicked only a single glance in Jenkins' direction.

Frustrated tears filled her eyes. She blinked furiously and tried again to communicate the threat to no avail. She stamped her foot in frustration. Baldy took it as a sign of resistance and tightened his hold, cutting off her air.

Jack let out a savage snarl.

Dash it. She did not want Jack fixed on her. He had to concentrate on Jenkins.

"Cease, bitch," Baldy growled in her ear, his hold shifting barely enough to allow her to suck air into her deprived lungs.

"'Tis your own safety you should consider." Jack stepped back and raised his right arm, training the pistol in that hand toward Celia and Baldy. Jenkins shifted to realign his pistol with Jack's new position. Rather telling of him. Jack must have thought so too because he trained his gaze on the pirate leader.

He jumped back another step an instant before Jenkins' shoulder twitched. Two shots fired simultaneously. Pieces of brick exploded from the wall behind Jack.

Jenkins missed.

Celia's knees buckled in relief. Her silent scream was still trapped in her throat. The arm clamped around her neck held her upright, causing her to gag. Her eyes sought Jack's. He stood still, too still. Menace pulsed in the air around him.

Quiet settled over the room. The force of Jack's shot threw Jenkins' chair against the wall. It rocked forward and came down on all fours with a thud. Blood spread over the front of the pirate's coat.

Smitty went to the desk and yanked his head up. "Still alive."

"My mistake." Jack's eyes locked on Baldy. "Release her and I will let you live."

The barrel of the gun trembled against Celia's temple. She closed her eyes.

"Son-of-a-bitch, I'll kill her."

"Ye've only one shot, ye sock-head." Smitty snorted in disgust. "Give over."

Baldy let out a nervous giggle and tightened his arm around Celia's throat. "I shall take her to hell with me, Beaumont. Ye'll never ride yer whore again."

"How do you—" Jack's eyes widened, and his brows dipped in a ferocious scowl. "Deuce take it, Celia. This is no time for one of your swoons. I'll have none of your theatrics, now."

Theatrics? Celia stiffened in indignation. She had a pirate wrapped around her throat, for pity's sake. How could it be otherwise? She blazed annoyance at him. Why, she'd never swooned in her life.

Which gave her pause. Her eyes narrowed.

Jack watched her face closely, his focus so intent

she realized he *wanted* her to swoon. She blinked once, very slowly, to let him know she understood. Then she wobbled against Baldy.

"Celia," Jack shouted. "Damn you, woman, you've a bleeding pistol to your head."

All her concentration centered on the mechanics of swooning, having witnessed the act enough to know one's entire body went limp. She dropped her shoulders, dangled her arms, and willed every muscle in her body to relax.

A grunt issued from Baldy as she started to slide, and he grabbed for her, but her head slipped through his arm, gravity claiming her. He stared at her prostrate form, eyes frantic, having suddenly lost his shield. She might have felt triumphant if he hadn't a weapon.

His hand rose with the pistol.

"Freeze or die." The threat in Jack's voice stayed him.

The pirate's gaze dropped to her again. His lips turned up as the pistol lowered.

Jack fired.

Smitty fired.

Baldy flew back between two cots and slammed against the cell wall. Then his body slid down the grimy stone, leaving a streak of blood in its wake. The pistol dropped to the floor still wrapped in his dead hand.

And pointed at Celia.

"Christ." Jack threw his weapon down and covered his face with a shaking hand, terror for her still shredding his innards.

"She's sound, Jack." Smitty clapped him on the shoulder. "Ye're sound, ain't ye, Celia?"

Jack swallowed the egg-sized lump of fear in his

throat, uncertain whether *he* was.

She pushed herself up and scrambled to her feet, backing away until she bumped into the bars of the cell and whirled, her gaze colliding with Jack's.

One hand rose to clutch a bar of the cell door. Then the next. Her lavender gown was smudged and dirty, dark hair tangled. She gaped at him through the bars. Utterly beautiful.

"Celia," Jack whispered. In the moment it was all he could manage. She let out a sound, something between a sob and scream, threw back the iron door, and ran.

He opened his arms, and she launched herself at him, but then kept going, shimmying up his body like a bleeding monkey. Jack grasped her waist and tugged her back down, but she kept moving; hands fisting in his coat, foot slipping off his knee as she dug for a foothold.

"Celia." He lifted her up, turning in circles. "Stop. I have you now. I have you. *Shh.*"

Gradually her struggles ceased. She locked her arms and legs around him and held on. "Oh, Jack," she sobbed against his neck over and over.

Smitty tucked his pistol in his coat and patted her back awkwardly. "Ye like ta shriveled me old heart, missy. I'm too old fer such hullabaloo." She pulled away from Jack enough to reach an arm around Smitty's neck and press her damp cheek to his. "There now." He patted her again and stepped away. "Ye'll hafta come out shortly and let the others have a gander at ye. Deeds aged nigh on fifty years since ye last saw 'im."

Jack snorted. Deeds had aged? *What about him?*

Surely, he looked ready for a crypt.

Celia let go of Smitty and curled back around him. Smitty left them alone save for two dead pirates—Jenkins reposed in his chair, eyes wide and still now that death had claimed him.

"Are you hurt?" Jack set her to her feet and ran a thumb over her precious cheek.

She shook her head, unshed tears plummeting down her cheeks, and offered him a crooked smile. It pierced his chest. How could she smile? How could she smile *at him*?

"Those men, they…" he choked on the words, "…they forced you to—"

"Nay, Jackson." She placed her fingers over his lips. "They did not touch me. I was not put upon by them."

His legs nearly buckled with relief, though reason assured him she lied. He disliked pressing her, but he had to know what she'd suffered. "You've been here an entire day. Do you mean to say they left you untouched?"

A blush stained her cheeks. "They meant to exercise their manly humors on me. But when he"—she waved a hand in Jenkins' direction—"tried, I, er, kicked him. Rather hard," she added proudly. "He locked me up and promised dire retribution once he had recovered. He meant to try again tonight."

Jack gaped at her in awe. "You injured Jenkins? Again?" The scoundrel must have been livid after she'd shot him on the *Mirabelle* and caused him to break his nose. "Where did you—?" A dawning smile spread across his face. "You kicked him in the ballocks?"

Her teeth sank into her lip, and she nodded.

"It must have been a mighty kick." He chuckled. She was fortunate Jenkins had not killed her.

"I knocked myself to the ground," she said with relish.

"And the other men," Jack persisted. "How did you avoid them?"

"Jenkins would not let them near me. Not until he…" She cast her eyes down and shook her head. "He locked me in the cell and kept the key. I think he feared they would kill me before he'd had his revenge on me."

A tear slipped down her cheek.

Christ.

Jack pulled her into his arms, overcome with relief that she was safe and unmolested. He'd seen the sort of revenge these dogs were capable of. His gaze shifted to Jenkins' body. The bastard would have carved her up and tortured her until—

He thrust her away from him. "How did they know you remained at home?"

Her hands came up to cover his where they gripped her shoulders. A gentling touch meant to calm him. He growled at her. He would not be distracted.

"I do not know, Jackson. They did not say."

Fury clawed to escape. He shook her. "How the devil did they find out? How, Celia?"

She took him in, head to boots, and her expression changed. "I am well and whole. Because of you. Thank you for my life again." Damned tears ran freely down her checks.

Jack closed his eyes, appalled at his behavior. *What the devil was he about?* Abusing her since the pirates no longer could, apparently. Bleeding fool. He was mad, and she knew it.

"I'm an ass." He sighed and pulled her back into his arms, resting his chin atop her head.

"Aye. But you cannot help it."

"So good of you to understand." God knows he did not deserve it. He tightened his arms around her and rubbed his cheek against her hair. "I failed you."

"You saved me."

"They would have—"

" 'You may plague your conscience with what might have been for the rest of your days,' " she said, quoting him again. "You are here and that is all that matters."

"Celia…" He touched her cheek, overwhelmed with too many emotions to name.

"Take me home, Jackson."

****

Alone in the parlor, Jack nursed a glass of brandy and cursed the women in his household. First, he'd had to stand aside and watch jealously as one by one Celia clasped hands with his crew and thanked each for coming to her rescue.

He finally managed to extract her only to lose her to Meagan and Molly's clutches once they returned home. The women shoved him aside like a street beggar and sent him on his way. She'd been bathed, fed, and summarily packed off to bed.

Perhaps she needed their nurturing care more than him, but Jack needed to hold her in his arms. To feel her sweet breath on his face and the beat of her heart against his chest and know she was safe and whole.

What a failure he'd become. He'd yet to find the emeralds. The pirates had threatened her again. Doubtless she'd hie herself home to her Mr. Kensington on the next ship to port. Without the stones, how was he to woo her away from her damned beau?

"Beggin' yer pardon, sir."

He glanced up. Molly stood in the doorway, twisting her apron in her hands, brown wisps of hair poking beneath her mobcap.

"'Tis Miss Celia, sir. She ain't stopped a'cryin' since ye brung her home. Wept all through her bath. Meagan fixed her a tray, but she won't eat."

An unworthy feeling of triumph stole over Jack. "Did she say why?"

"Well, I said she'd been waitin' and waitin' ta go home ta her family. Doubtless she thought she'd never set eyes upon 'em again. She looked at me real queer-like and started a'cryin'."

"Where is she now?"

"In her room. Standin' at her window, tears a'runnin' down her face. I shouldn't think it good fer a body, all that weepin'. Shall I fetch Meagan?"

"No." Jack slammed his brandy on the table and jumped to his feet, startling the girl. "That is, I shall see to her myself."

****

Jack took the stairs two at a time and gave Celia's door a single sharp rap before breaching the room. She leaned against the window in her nightclothes, face splotched and awash in tears, hair still damp from her bath. He crossed the room and took her in his arms.

"Celia, love, what pains you so?" His presence prompted fresh torrents from her. He rocked her gently, his voice soft and soothing. "There, there, love."

"Jack," she cried miserably against his chest. Molly stood in the doorway, watching anxiously.

"Molly, will you fetch the brandy? And bring some bread and cheese with it."

"Aye, sir, straightaway." The girl bobbed a curtsy and hurried off.

Guiding Celia to a chair in front of the hearth, he sat and pulled her down on his lap, dangling her legs over the chair's arm. He smoothed her hair away from her face and rested his cheek atop her head. Her hair smelled like tropical flowers on a sultry night, warm and heady. Perversely, this comforted him while she suffered torments.

"Tell me what distresses you, love."

"I am the most horrid person, Jackson." She mopped at her face with a handkerchief clutched in her fist. "I cannot bear it."

Flummoxed, he leaned back and lifted her chin. Her poor, beautiful face, swollen and red from all that weeping. "Why would you say such a thing?"

The fireplace threw shadows and darkened her eyes. They glistened like gems beneath the well of tears spilling down her cheeks. "I forgot them. I forgot all about my family while the pirates held me captive. My mother, my father, Brett—they never entered my mind. Not once. I even blocked out Rianna. The one person who has been with me always. Comforted me," she laid a hand over her chest, "in my heart and soul."

Jack took umbrage at that. It bleeding well wasn't her sister who'd fought the pirates. And whose arms she was in now.

"It has been an age since I've seen them, and though I might never have laid eyes upon them again, I spared my beloved family not a moment's regret. How could I forget them, Jack? How could I do such a thing?"

Jack was wont to praise her for it as he'd heard enough of her bleeding family to last a lifetime. But he'd say what she needed to hear. He pulled her head to his shoulder and stroked his fingers through her dark, silken hair. "Ah, love. You could never forget them. You were simply trying to survive."

"No." She scrubbed at her damp face. "My thoughts were focused entirely on you. I prayed you would come for me before it was too late. I contemplated all the things I wish I had said—and done. I spared naught for them."

The tears turned to great, wracking sobs that soaked his shirt through. Though her agony wrenched his heart, her confession delighted him.

"*Shh,* love, shush now." He rubbed circles over her back and murmured words of comfort in her ear.

Molly knocked softly on the door and entered. Her eyes widened when she saw Celia sprawled on his lap. He frowned at her and shook his head. "Just set the tray there," he said, indicating the table next to them.

"I brung a pitcher of cool water and a cloth for Miss Celia's eyes."

An excellent idea. "Thank you, Molly."

"Be there anythin' else I can do fer ye, sir?" Molly dipped the cloth in the water and handed it to Jack.

"Nay, Molly. She'll recover after a time. You may retire now. Sleep in your room above the kitchen. I shall stay here and watch over her."

Molly looked to Celia uncertainly and twisted her apron in her hands. He wondered whether concern for Celia or fear of his intentions made her hesitate. "If ye're certain ye won't need me."

Celia lifted her head and reached out to clasp Molly's hand. "Please, Molly. Do go on to bed. I apologize for causing you worry." Her head fell back to Jack's shoulder, and she rubbed her damp cheek against it.

"Oh, no, miss," Molly said quickly. "Do not fret on my account. I hate ta see ye feelin' so poorly, is all. I'll take me leave now. Ye'll let me know if ye need anythin', won't ye?"

"We shall, Molly," Jack said, eager to be rid of her. "Goodnight."

"Goodnight, then." She closed the door softly behind her, leaving them blessedly alone.

He poured a draught of brandy and held it to Celia's lips. "Drink. 'Twill help calm you."

She wrinkled her nose and placed a hand over her stomach. "I am unable."

"I shan't take no for an answer. Be a good girl and drink."

It took her several minutes to get all of the brandy down. Once she'd finished, Jack poured another for himself.

"Lie back." He nudged her over his arm and dipped the cloth in the cool water to lay over her eyes. "Methinks you've not considered your circumstances clearly."

"My 'circumstances'?" She lifted the cloth from her eyes to peer up at him.

He popped a piece of bread in her mouth. "You lived in Bermuda for nearly a year. Since then, you've resided here in Charles Town. 'Tis a long time for an unwed woman to be separated from her family. Almost as though you'd moved away to begin a new life."

With me, he wanted to add. "You've seen me clash with the pirates. I rescued you from them. Charles Town is my home, Celia. Of course, you'd think of me and hope I'd save you." He fed her a bite of cheese. "If you'd been abducted in England, you would have prayed for your…father to rescue you."

Jack refused to mention the name of his nemesis. "Your instincts were focused on survival." Dropping his hand to her shoulder, he stroked the length of her arm to her fingertips, clasping them loosely. "You've condemned yourself unfairly."

"I haven't. Regardless of what you say, 'tis no excuse to forget them completely." She sat up and scowled at the bread he held. He realized he'd alternated it with the cheese. Terribly un-Celia-like.

"You've had an uncommonly trying day, love." He dipped his chin to peer into her eyes. "What say you rest now and wait until the morrow to punish yourself?"

She took a deep breath and nodded as she blew it out. He tried to nudge her back down, but she clutched her robe and fanned it. "'Tis rather warm in here, is it not?"

Chapter Twenty

To be honest, Jack's temperature had little to do with the fire and everything to do with the woman on his lap.

"'Tis the brandy. And the fire making you warm." He lifted the hair from her nape and blew on a damp spot to cool her. She shivered.

A pointed look at her lap conveyed her doubt. "My proximity to you is not helping."

"I am not finished comforting you." To that end, he untied the sash at her waist and tugged her robe off her shoulders while she watched, a perplexed frown on her face. He silently praised the relaxing effects of brandy and brushed his lips against her ear. She quivered. "Since you do not need a robe, a fire, and me, we shall dispense with the robe."

Lifting her up with one arm, he whisked the garment out from under her and tossed it over the adjacent chair, eliciting an indignant squeal. Before she could balk, he pulled her head back down to his shoulder and anchored her in his arms.

They were silent for a time.

His hand used the opportunity to wander over her hip and stroke her firm thigh through the cloth of her gown, allowing his fingers to trail over her knee and along the smooth, rigid path of her shin.

She sat up and toyed with the ties of his shirt. "I

was not only thinking of you in terms of my rescue."

"You speak as if it were a crime," he said, dropping his forehead to hers.

"Arrogant man." Her lips tipped up. "My thoughts should be entirely of you, I suppose."

"Precisely." It seemed only fair, as his thoughts were all of her. "I considered you from time to time as well."

"Aye?" She leaned away from him.

"A few times," he said as if confessing some strange malady. "Awake, searching," he dipped his head to brush his lips over her cheek, "breathing."

"So many regrets." She touched her fingers to his jaw. "The words I wished to say forever silenced. But then you burst through that door." Her brow wrinkled. "How did you find me?"

Jack squirmed beneath her. Her tight little bum felt delicious rubbing over his cock, prompting him to squirm a little more. At the moment he seemed to be the only one enjoying himself. "We followed the pirates from Pinks. The fools led us to you."

Heat pricked his loins. He'd be stiff as a pike soon, while Celia remained utterly unaffected, which began to irritate him. His hand flexed on her thigh. He did not wish to talk so he cupped the back of her neck and touched his lips to hers, mouth slanting, teasing, tasting, drawing her in.

She sighed against his lips and wrapped her arms around his neck, giving herself over to his kiss. "I am so happy you found me."

"Aye, little witch. I'm happy I found you, too." Employing lips and teeth and tongue, he skimmed beneath her jaw and down the column of her throat, prompting her to clutch his head and hold his mouth prisoner while she squirmed deliciously on his lap. Jack groaned and shoved his cock against her bottom. Venturing lower, he found himself thwarted by the neck of her gown. His hands took over, smoothing up her sides and skimming the curves of her breasts.

Beneath his lips, he felt her swallow. He thought she meant to stop him, but she gripped his biceps and held on while his fingers plucked at the ties of her gown. It fell open, revealing the delicate skin of her collarbone. His mouth lowered.

"The things they meant to do to me—"

Damn. Jack tore his gaze from his objective and met her eyes.

"—cruel and brutal things."

Like a bucket of icy water, her words doused him back to sanity. *What, by all that's holy, was he doing?*

"Defiled without ever knowing—" Her voice broke.

He was in hell. 'Twas where he deserved to be, clearly.

"*Shh,* love." He pressed his cheek to hers.

But she was determined to have her say. "The most precious gift a woman has to offer, and those filthy beasts meant to—" Her words choked off.

Her pain echoed in Jack's soul. Would that he could kill the bastards again for her. "You mustn't dwell upon it, love. 'Tis over now." The pirates they had not killed had been turned over to Major Duncan for a belated hanging. This time they would not go free.

"Aye." She laid the flat of her hand against his face. "By the grace of God, I am precisely where I dreamed of being—in your arms."

Jack's soul howled and his mouth swooped down to claim hers, an incendiary melding of desire and purpose. Of vindication. She looped her arms around his neck and returned his ardor with an exuberance that stole the breath from him. *Mine, mine, mine,* his body crowed in triumph. He tore his lips from hers and stared into her eyes, demanding a response.

The fire crackled. A waft of air blew in from the window he hadn't realized was partially open. He ought to leave.

"Jack." Her eyes lifted, his name a sigh on her lips. Her fingers speared his hair, raking his scalp to his nape and loosing the strip of leather binding his queue. Then she tugged his head down and, God save him, planted her sweet lips against his throat. Tremors rippled beneath his flesh when her tongue darted out, tasting him. Tongue and teeth grazed an unbelievably erotic path to his jaw, discovering the same terrain he'd explored on her.

"Celia," he gasped, shocked and utterly thrilled at her boldness. Her hands returned to his face, caging him until her mouth joined his. He tried to pull her close to still her—fool that he was—but she pushed his arms away and ran her palms down his chest to his waist, scoring his abdomen with her fingertips before gliding back up to tease over his flat nipples.

Jesus.

All these months of denying him and suddenly she's a tigress in his arms. His annoying conscience offered this as proof she was not in control of her senses and needed time to recover.

She grasped a handful of his shirt and pulled it from his breeches.

His conscience could go to the devil.

Yet he broke the kiss and wrapped her in his arms to stay her. "Celia." No other words would come, his brain clearly unwilling to defy the objectives of his body.

"I want to touch you, Jack." Beneath the admittedly loose cage of his arms, she continued to tug at his shirt. "I want my hands on your skin." Her breath fanned down the vee of his shirt, each exhale teasing his flesh as she pulled the last of it free.

Lust roared through him.

Those busy hands slipped under his shirt and trailed over his ribs, fingers twining through the crisp hair of his chest. He groaned. This had to stop. It would kill him when it did.

"Take it off, Jack." She pulled the hem of his shirt up over his stomach and raised her lips to his ear. "Please."

He yanked it over his head and threw it to the floor. His mind screamed *no* a second later. But her lips were already there, trailing sweet fire over his shoulders while her fingernails scored his flesh.

"Celia," Jack choked. God help him, he wanted to weep. "We must stop. You…you are distressed and—"

She stopped.

Agony tore through him. He closed his eyes, leaned his head back against the chair, and breathed. One breath. Two. Surely, he could conquer this. He was stronger than she.

"Jack?" His name trembled from her lips, and though his mind pleaded with him not to, he opened his eyes. He watched warily as her hands rose and came to rest over his chest. His heart banged enthusiastically.

He swallowed and gazed helplessly at her face.

"Jack," she whispered, his name both a sigh and an entreaty. "Make love to me, Jack."

Jack went still—save for the muscle twitching in his jaw—his eyes fierce with whatever emotion held him in its grip. Anger perhaps?

Celia brushed her fingers over his cheek. "I know you want me, Jack. And I want you." Though want seemed a feeble word for this ravenous hunger.

"Not tonight." His gaze cut to the fire as if she'd chased it away, his voice strained. "You shall regret—"

Oh lud. Chivalry? Now? She placed a finger over his lips. "My only regret is waiting too long. Delaying what is meant to be."

He pulled her finger from his lips and turned her palm up to place a kiss there. The heat in his eyes when they lifted to hers sent shards of terrible, agonizing desire through her belly. He dropped her hand as if it burned his lips. Flung his head back against the chair and closed his eyes. "After the violence you've suffered, you cannot be thinking clearly."

Undeterred, she lifted his hand and cupped it over her breast; over her throbbing heart. Placed her palm over his chest and felt it drum a warning. But she was not afraid.

His eyes opened. His fierce gaze bored into hers like a viper ready to strike.

Celia sucked in a breath. Perhaps a *little* afraid.

"Feel my heart beating for you, Jackson." She pushed her breast into his palm. "Only you. Hear my soul calling to yours."

A growl burst from his throat, the rumble of some untamed beast, dangerous and frightening and thrilling.

He lurched from the chair and strode to the bed with her clutched in his arms.

Triumph sang in Celia's soul.

Jack stood her on her feet and fisted his hands in her night-rail. The cloth slid over her quivering thighs. His forehead dropped to hers. "If you lament this come morning, I swear I will beat you."

In response, she lifted her arms so he could pull the gown over her head. Dropped her hands to his beautiful, hard chest, and touched her lips to the underside of his chin. "*Mm,* so hot."

"Witch." He lifted her naked body, fusing his mouth with hers.

Oh, she wanted this—his strength, his heat, overpowering and conquering. He swung her legs up and dropped her in the middle of the bed. His gaze traveled the length of her and back, burning her flesh where it touched. His throat worked up and down in a swallow.

Then he lunged.

She let out a squeak as his arms enfolded her and his lips dove to capture hers, drugging her with the taste of spice and brandy. He stole her breath and she found herself breathing through him, disorienting and thankfully brief, as his mouth relinquished hers to conquer other vistas.

While his lips traveled over her face and neck, and lower, his hands were everywhere, learning her, claiming her. She scraped her fingertips over his scalp, burying them in his thick, chestnut hair, and felt his pleasure through her hands.

"I love when you touch me," he whispered. The words skimmed over her body, brushing her naked skin.

"My hands exist purely to pleasure you." His head dipped and his lips claimed her breast, circling her nipple before he drew it into the haven of his mouth. Shivers rippled through her belly as he laved it with his wondrous tongue. "My mouth to taste you."

"Jack," she gasped, panting. His large, calloused hand abraded the aching peak of her other breast until unending currents of pleasure ran a path from skin to womb.

Moans rasped her throat. Her arms clutched his head to her greedy bosom, determined to keep his marvelous mouth imprisoned there. Foolish—to think she could control him.

She was his to conquer.

Her hands roamed over his massive shoulders and traced the muscles of his arms, exhilarating in the power leashed within. Her lips wanted at him too, but he kept exploring the terrain of her body, denying her.

When his fingers slid between the join of her legs, she jerked, and her hands tightened on his shoulders. Instinctively, she closed them against the threat of intrusion. Jack shifted and rose higher, wedging his knee between her thighs.

He lifted his head.

Smoke dark eyes smoldered above her. She stilled, held by his gaze, caught in the power of his will. His eyes held her pinned while his fingers, glorious masterful intruders, delved between her legs. They gentled over her aching flesh, so infinitely tender her body wept with pleasure. She wanted to wrap the two of them in darkness so the night would never end. He slipped a finger inside her, and she felt the drenching wetness when he removed it.

Flames ignited in his eyes. Their heat scorched her. In and out he played, the warmth increasing as fires kindled in her womb.

"Do you like that?" His voice rumbled as he nibbled on her ear.

Shivers wracked her. She hadn't the words to reply, and he did not compel her to answer. His thumb brushed a sensitive spot, and she bucked against his hand, moaning his name.

His head jerked up as if snagged by her voice. He rose above her, and Celia wanted to cry out from the loss of him, but he pushed her legs wide and settled between them, nudging back and forth against where she ached.

"*Ohhh,* Jack," she purred, wrapping her arms and legs around him to hold him there. He let out an oath and tore himself from her grasp.

Dear God, he shall kill me. Celia closed her eyes against the torment.

She ached everywhere.

Wanted everywhere.

The bed jerked beneath her. She lifted her eyelids to see Jack violently divesting himself of the rest of his clothing. Her lips curved.

He flung his breeches to the floor and turned. *Heavens! It was...that was...oh my.* He brought his beautiful, magnificent body down to cover her, the wiry hair on his legs tickling her calves. His knees spread her wide, and she felt the tip of his sex slide against her wetness.

Terrified suddenly, her heart lunged and tried to bolt free of her chest.

The fall of his hair as he bent over her cast his face

in shadow. Save for those smoldering eyes. “You belong to me and no other.” His voice was shredded and dangerous. “Say it, Celia. Say the words.”

This is what she wanted. What she’d longed for. To be claimed by this beautiful, fierce warrior. She lifted her knees to straddle his hips in supplication and clasped his face between her hands. “I love you, Jack,” she whispered against his lips.

Thunderbolts sparked in his eyes. A rumble echoed deep in his throat and his hips thrust.

Pain seared her. She cried out and clamped her legs to stay his movements, but he pulled back and thrust again. Then he lay still, panting heavily and trembling in her arms.

“Forgive me, sweetheart,” he managed, but she could tell the words threatened his control.

“I’m sorry,” she whispered, uncertain and uncomfortable. “I was not prepared for…”

But she needn’t explain it to him.

He kissed her neck, her jaw, her cheek. His hand stroked her breast and lightly pinched her nipple. The sensation cracked like lightning. Her hips jerked in response, and he groaned.

“S-sorry,” she said again, abashed.

Bracing himself on one elbow, he touched his lips to hers. “You mustn’t apologize for giving me pleasure, love.” He withdrew an inch or two and slid back in slowly. His eyes closed on a blissful sigh.

Celia’s legs tensed on his hips instinctively. A dilemma—that his pleasure should cause her pain, though the worst had eased somewhat.

“We will go slowly, love.” He nibbled on her ear, sending shivers rippling down her neck. “I promise 'twill get better." When he kissed her again, he mated his tongue with hers. A carnal kiss while he moved inside her in slow, even strokes. Though it burned, it was not entirely unpleasant.

Jack's breathing indicated he was enjoying it a great deal more than her. He paused and pulled away enough to graze her nipple with his teeth.

Her hips shot up, and her hands dug into his scalp, clutching his head to her. "Dear god, Jackson." He blew against the peak and nipped it with his teeth then flexed his hips, pushing gently inside her. Sensation sizzled over her belly, and her legs opened wider for him. She did not understand her body's reaction because she wanted him to do it again.

"Yes, sweetheart," he whispered hoarsely.

Pleasure and discomfort violated her equally. Celia whimpered in confusion, cleaved between the desire to draw him in and likewise push him away. Why had her body desired such torment? And why did he not suffer as well?

His rough hands anchored her thighs as his thrusts increased. Ripples of excitement washed away her discomfort. Her hips rose to meet him without her control. He cupped his hands beneath her bottom, positioning her so that each stroke of his sex struck like a flint against hers. Her hands splayed across his back, reveling in the hard muscles moving beneath them.

Face flushed, he loomed over her as a storm gathered in his eyes.

His tempest built inside her. She'd given herself over to him and now he controlled her every breath, every touch, every reaction.

"Please," she whimpered, because she sensed he

was keeping something from her that she wanted desperately.

"Let it take you, sweetheart," Jack urged.

She stared at his face, harsh and determined. A warrior's face. A conqueror. His eyes were almost black now. She moaned, and they flared, igniting her skin.

"Come now, sweetheart." His voice turned raw, urgent. "Come for me, now." He clutched her bottom tighter and his hips drummed faster, harder, relentless.

Shards of pleasure sliced through the incinerating heat. Celia's head fell back, and a scream ripped from her throat as she convulsed around him. Her fingers dug into his backside and pulled him deeper while spasms from her sex pulsed through her belly.

Jack crushed her to him with one last hard shove before collapsing on top of her. They lay unmoving, all tangled limbs, panting breaths, and glistening sweat.

Celia's eyes drifted closed. "Are we dead then?"

"Aye." His response was an echo rumbling from deep inside his chest.

"Aye." She sighed, content.

****

"Damn and blast."

The toe of Jack's boot caught the leg of the governor's ornate, overstuffed chair. He glared at the wealth of carved, painted scrollwork inside the newly decorated and ostentatious drawing room and continued pacing. Above his head hung a huge chandelier with filigreed arms, dripping a host of multifaceted crystals. It reminded him of an octopus he'd caught near Port Royal.

He ran his hand over the top of his head.

What the devil was taking James so long? The sun had risen an hour ago. He worried Celia might wake before he returned and discover him gone. He did not wish her to feel abandoned, or worse, regret over last night.

Footsteps clicked down the hall.

"Damn you, Beaumont," the governor groused as he entered the drawing room wearing a banyan over his breeches. "Can't a man break his fast in peace?" He rang for a footman to fetch tea and sprawled into a gaudy red chair, glowering at Jack.

"'Tis rude to keep your guests waiting, James."

"Why are you here?" Glen fixed him with a gimlet glare. "Though I should hardly be surprised. One hears you left a mess for the Watch to clean up last night."

"If they had done their job, I should not have had to do it for them."

The governor waved a hand. "Yes, yes. You warned us of the brigands' evil pursuits and so forth. Have you come to gloat?"

"Heaven forfend. I've come for a special license." The tea arrived and Jack took a seat. Neither man spoke until the footman served them and took his leave.

Glen lifted his cup to his lips. "What sort of license do you need?"

Were all politicians thickheaded, or was the man deliberately obtuse? "A marriage license."

The governor choked and tea spewed out of his mouth while Jack looked on with amusement. Thickheaded, apparently. It took several moments of coughing and wheezing before he was able to speak.

"'Tis a hanging offense to kill the governor, you horse's arse." He mopped at the tears streaming down his face with a napkin.

"Aye, but you spit my weapon all over the floor," Jack countered. "They shall never find it."

Glen shot him a sour look. "Perhaps I will kill *you.*"

"I shouldn't advise it. I am esteemed in this society. They'd hang you for sport, I fear."

"You do not actually intend to marry, do you?"

"Yes. Now be a good governor and get me that license."

"Who the devil are you marrying?"

"Miss Breckenridge."

The man's gaze turned shrewd. "You've said precious little about her and naught of her family."

"Oh no, James. 'Tis far too late for inquiries. She's lived with me for months now. I'll have that license, if you please."

"Gad, Beaumont. Are you mad?" He pinched the bridge of his nose. "Who is this girl?"

"Her father is a merchant in Falmouth."

Glen paused a strategic moment, but when Jack said no more, he took a sip of his tea and sighed in relief. "Thank heavens for that at least."

"Her maternal grandfather is Burlington."

The governor's jaw dropped. He slammed his cup back in its saucer. Jack winced, amazed the delicate china hadn't shattered.

"Burlington? The Earl?"

"Aye, that's the chap. Are you acquainted with him? No. Do not answer." Jack stood. "I haven't the time. Come along, James. I've a woman to marry, so let's be about our business."

Though he did so reluctantly, the governor rose to

his feet. "I should never have canceled my trip to North Carolina. Does she at least want to marry you?"

"Of course." Jack slapped him on the back. "She's mad for me."

"Lord bless her, that explains it," Glen said with feeling as Jack ushered him from his own drawing room. "Am I still keeping her?"

"Aye. I'll send word when we're ready to weigh anchor. Mind you, have the militia guard her."

"I fail to understand why you must leave her. Where do you intend to go?" Jack opened his mouth to speak but the governor raised his hand. "Nay. Say no more. I beg of you. I do not want to know. You must take that girl back home, Beaumont. Posthaste."

"Best hurry along with that license then, Governor."

Chapter Twenty-One

"Good morning, Molly," Jack said politely when he entered the house and found her sweeping the foyer. *Why were servants always about when one least wanted them?*

The girl paused in her labors to bob a curtsy. "Good morning, sir. Meagan is keepin' your breakfast warm."

He headed for the stairs. "I shall check on Miss Breckenridge first."

"Poor dear." Molly leaned on her broom and shook her head sadly. "I imagine ye left her plum worn-out yester'eve."

"She certainly was." Jack grinned, thankful his back was to her.

"But, sir," Molly called after him. "Miss is still abed."

"I shall knock."

As promised, he gave the door two soft raps before entering. Celia was indeed still abed, dreamy-eyed and rumpled, her bare arms holding the covers over her naked breasts. He pulled the license out of his pocket and launched himself onto the bed with her.

"Why, good morning, sir." She giggled and stroked his cheek.

"You look pensive." He leaned on his elbow and ran a finger along her puckered brow then kissed the spot. Her lips turned up in a smile, her face soft and radiant. Jack's pulse leaped and he considered the wisdom of diving beneath the covers with her.

"Last night you told me I'd breathed my last, but this morning I feel so wondrously, gloriously alive. 'Tis quite perplexing."

"My apologies." He tossed the document on the pillow next to her and nibbled on her ear. "I shall apply myself with more diligence next time."

"I'll not survive a next time." She giggled and pushed his head away. "I am quite certain a girl may only have her virtue stolen once."

"Stolen? Perhaps you've simply misplaced it." He pulled the covers lower and kissed the top of her breast. "Did you look under here?"

"Wicked man." She tugged on his hair, pulling his head up to peer into his eyes. "What if Meagan or Molly should come in?"

His mouth lowered to hers. "We shall ask them to leave." Her lips were like velvet and cream, soft and dewy and luscious and edible. He could feast on them for days.

Sighing, she opened her mouth to his and dug her lovely fingers into his hair, gently scraping her nails against his scalp. He broke the kiss and arched his neck, nudging his head more firmly into her hands.

"Fond of that, are you?" she purred in his ear.

"I desire your hands anywhere on my body."

"I'd no idea they were so valuable." She held them out to study them. "Perhaps I ought to consider these hands an investment. Sell shares and whatnot."

"You cannot." He grabbed the license lying next to her head and handed it to her. "You no longer own them."

"What is this?" She unrolled the document to scan its contents.

Jack plucked it from her fingers. "A special license from South Carolina's esteemed governor. We shall summon the parson. You will be my wife in a few hours. Therefore these—" He tossed the document aside and twined his fingers with hers, holding them prisoner on either side of her head. "—belong to me."

When he kissed her this time, it was with the confidence of a man who'd won. Months of fighting an invisible foe, of teasing, prodding, and seducing had finally come to fruition. His lips claimed hers not only as a man, but as her mate. One who would gladly die for her.

Celia broke their kiss and turned her head away. Apparently, his mate was not yet reconciled to being conquered. "Is this how you propose to a woman?"

He leaned back to peer at her face. "You do not approve?"

"Not particularly, no."

"Let me try again." He released her hands and wrapped his arms around her shoulders, kissing her ardently, and with considerable skill, even if he said so himself.

She moaned and wrapped her arms around his neck, obviously reconciled to being seduced. His lips wandered down the column of her throat to the crook of her neck. He nibbled, and she squirmed until she exploded into helpless giggles.

"Ticklish, are you?" Jack grinned and nipped at her shoulder.

"Hungry, are you?"

"Aye, wench," he growled. "And I shall make a meal of—"

The atmosphere of the room changed. Something in the air, perhaps. Whatever, it felt grim and disturbing.

His head popped up.

Meagan hovered at the door, hand to her chest, face florid and eyes shooting daggers at him.

Celia craned her neck to see and gasped when she saw the woman standing there. She turned an angry, accusing glare on Jack.

"What do ye think ye're doin, ye bounder?" Meagan's voice shook with anger.

"I am proposing." He kissed the tip of Celia's nose.

The woman's eyes bulged, and her mobcap slid over her forehead.

Jack choked on a laugh.

"Proposin'," she sputtered. "With her barely covered and ye on top of her?"

"'Twould appear it's a bit more complicated than I thought, isn't it, love?" He grinned down at Celia. "She requires a bit more persuading."

Her face turned scarlet. She clamped her lips together mutinously and refused to answer.

"Oh, now, see what you've done, Meagan?" Jack accused, giving Celia a wicked smile. "Now I shall have to start anew."

She coughed, her face flushed from the effort of holding her laughter in.

Meagan's jaw dropped. "Start anew? Are ye daft, man? Come away from that girl, immediately. Ye may speak with her below stairs when she's properly clothed."

"Oh, no." He grinned at his disheveled soon-to-be wife. "I'll not leave her until she agrees." Then added with a roguish wink, "I fear this might take a while, Meagan. Be a dear and leave me to my wooing."

The woman opened her mouth to give him what was certain to be a blistering scold. Jack stretched his leg out and kicked the door shut. A stream of curses filtered through it.

He gaped at the door in surprise. "I'd no idea she knew such words."

"I fear she is not pleased with you, Jackson." Celia managed, choking on her laughter.

Jack turned his attention back to his beautiful, naked objective. "I'd rather please you, love," he murmured and lowered his mouth to her breast.

****

A surly sea captain dogged Celia's heels when she entered the kitchen and found Meagan at the counter, chopping vegetables with such brutal force she wondered the poor things did not scream.

"I should like to apologize for our deplorable behavior, Meagan. We most humbly beg your forgiveness, don't we, Jackson?" She glanced over her shoulder at him and tilted her head in Meagan's direction.

He grunted.

She rolled her eyes and turned her back on him. "Might I have something to eat? I am absolutely famished."

"Of course, ye may." Meagan's voice was terse. "After all ye've been through," she sent Jack a scalding glare, "'twill likely take a few days for ye to recover."

"She's recovered," he snapped.

Celia sent him a quelling look. Honestly, the man pouted like a child.

Meagan's dispassionate gaze roamed over him. "What's stuck a burr in his bum?"

"He is angry because I will not marry him."

"What?" The woman's face turned the same mottled shade as Jack's. If this continued, the town would be convinced they'd a fever raging in the household. Celia folded her arms together, girding herself for the next skirmish.

"But he was in yer room and ye were—" Meagan waved a hand to indicate Celia's dress, or previous lack. "And he was—" Another wave at Jack and presumably what he'd been doing with her unclad person. "Ye must marry him."

"Not without my family present." Celia lifted her chin. "And not before I speak with Mr. Kensington. 'Twouldn't be honorable."

"Honor?" Jack snorted. "Am I to assume you were honorable last night?"

The bounder. How dare he say such a thing when he'd been the devil leading her to temptation all these months.

Meagan rounded on him, arms akimbo. "Apparently ye're not very persuasive."

"Apparently you mean for us to starve." They looked like two angry bulls ready to charge. "She's stubborn."

"Aye." Celia tossed her head. "And you are selfish. I'll not marry without my family."

"'Tis what ye deserve, ye wicked man," Meagan snarled at him. "Mayhap you should have proposed on yer feet like a gentleman."

"I thought I was supposed to propose on my knee." Trust Jack to be contrary.

"Howbeit, ye do not propose to a gently bred woman while lyin' atop her, ye rattlepate!"

Celia took pity on him. He would never have been caught in her bed this morning if she hadn't thrown herself at him last night. She wondered if her actions qualified as a seduction. The idea, though entirely inappropriate, thrilled her. "It matters not how he proposed. The result would be the same. My engagement must be broken first."

"You broke it last night." Jack received such a look of venom from Meagan that Celia felt compelled to protect him.

"But Brett is unaware of our attachment, Jackson, and he deserves better than you would have me do. I shan't treat him so shabbily." She raised her hand when he opened his mouth to speak. "Please. Do not ask me to marry without my family. I want…" She took a sustaining breath. "I want you to ask Papa for my hand. I want his blessing and—" Damn tears. She knuckled them away from her eyes. She'd never wept so much in her life as she had since meeting this man.

He was there immediately, pulling her into his arms. "*Shh*, love. Do not cry." She buried her face in his coat and breathed in his warm, spicy scent. "I cannot bear it when you cry, Celia." He kissed the top of her head. "Shush now."

The door opened and Smitty entered, doffing his cap. He took in the tableau in the center of the room and turned to his wife, brows raised in question.

She pointed her knife at them. "He proposed to her."

"Ah, lass," Smitty soothed. "'Tisn't as bad as all that. Ye don't have to take him. And ye needn't worry about yer reputation. We shall tell folks whatever story ye like."

Meagan snorted and laughed silently, her smile so wide her eyes nearly disappeared. Celia looked to Smitty and caught the twinkle in his eyes.

Laughter burbled out of her.

Jack stiffened. "You find that amusing, do you?" He walked her backward until she came up against the kitchen table. "Perhaps I should tell them what really happened last night," he whispered for her ears alone. "About the temptress that lured me into her bed."

"Perhaps you should."

"Or perhaps I should beat you as I promised."

She toyed with the lace of his shirt and sighed. "You cannot."

"Why?"

"Because I do not lament making love with you." Her eyes rose to his. "I will marry you, Jackson, but I insist on celebrating our union in sight of God and family. I want the entire world to know I pledge my troth to you. Only you."

His eyes sparked like a hammer striking an anvil. He wrapped her in his arms and claimed her mouth.

The fiery passion in his kiss shot a roar of heat to Celia's toes. She moaned and wrapped her arms around his waist, pulling him closer, wanting his hard body pressed against every inch of hers.

Distantly, Smitty's strangled cough came to her.

Jack groaned and broke their kiss. His forehead rested against hers, his breath unsteady.

"Perhaps ye ought'a feed 'em," Smitty suggested

to his wife. "They look hungry."

****

Molly snored softly in the trundle bed. Meagan had charged the girl with guarding Celia's virtue. Such as it was. She donned her robe and stole from the bedchamber.

Jack answered immediately when she knocked, surprising her, though it oughtn't. They'd both been terribly unhappy these last few days, which hardly encouraged sleep.

She slipped inside his room and pulled the door shut behind her without a sound. He sat on the side of his bed, clothed only in his breeches, his face shadowed in the wan moonlight filtering into the room.

"Celia." His voice was flat as she crossed to his bed. "You should be abed. I had not planned to rouse you for a few more hours yet."

Oh, she hated that voice. The disappointment. The resignation. Her own stubbornness and determination thrown back at her.

His soul spoke so clearly to hers.

In the shadows she stood before him with her hands clasped together, memorizing his beloved face. He was leaving her. She'd been stunned when he told her and furious when he refused to take her with him, spouting some drivel about possible pirates and Spanish treasure fleets from Cuba this time of year. Worse, he still expected her to stay with the governor. A man she'd never met. Coupled with his anger at her refusal to marry him, the chasm between them had stretched wider with each passing hour.

Tonight, she'd been struck again with what their separation would mean: weeks apart from one another.

Weeks to lament their angry words. She might never see him again. Anything could happen. Such were the vicissitudes of life at sea. This she knew first-hand.

Her heart became a leaden ball in her chest.

He waited for her to speak. His expression remained guarded. It shamed her the way she'd been punishing him. She loved him from the depths of her soul, and she'd given him naught but unpleasant memories to carry on his journey.

"What did you want of me?" he asked finally. The ache in his voice lodged in her breast.

Celia dropped to her knees and took his big, rough hand in hers. "I do not want you to leave this way." She lifted his hand to her lips.

"You've every right to feel the way you do." He tucked her hair behind her ear and cupped her cheek. "I've been unfair and for that, I beg your forgiveness."

A weight lifted from her chest. She closed her eyes and rubbed her cheek against the back of his hand. "May I stay here with you for awhile?"

He expelled a long, unsteady breath and lifted her onto his lap, his lips touching her brow. "I would have you for a lifetime and more, my sweet Celia. My heart is yours."

She lifted her face and kissed his mouth. "I love you, Jackson."

They fell across the bed. Those wondrous hands of his explored her body, memorizing every hollow as she tried to memorize his. Their coupling was swift and frantic and as necessary as light was to day.

He held her in his arms until the first tinges of pink glowed on the horizon.

****

At the easternmost tip of the island of Santa Maria de la Concepción, the *Bonny Lass* rode anchor. Wisps of white clouds painted the azure sky beneath a blindingly bright sun. Mottled shades of aqua and sapphire surrounded this tiny island near the southern end of the Bahamas chain, owing to the deep, hospitable reefs welcoming ships to her shores.

The few inhabitants of the small island showed little interest in the newly arrived invaders to their waters. Doubtless they suspected Jack and his crew of being pirates and preferred to turn a blind eye to whatever nefarious business they were about.

This worked in their favor.

According to the map, a tavern had once thrived here, a convenient stopping place for pirates sailing between the Turks and New Providence. Any sign of the building had been removed, either by the violent storms known to visit the islands or scavengers dismantling it bit by bit. All that remained were a few cottages belonging to local fishermen.

Eight men combed the empty spit of land marked by an "X" on Travers' map while their shipmates observed from the rail of the *Bonny Lass*. Others sat high up in the rigging and kept watch for sails on the horizon. An unlikely event, but Jack had no intention of being caught unawares.

He and Smitty walked some three feet apart in a parallel line with the others, swatting at the thick undergrowth with their swords.

"How many hurricanes do ye suppose have blown over this island over a score of years?"

"Enough." Jack grunted. "We ought to bring the rest of the crew out and comb the area quicker. Get cracking and get gone."

"This is all we've talked about for months. Every one of these men's dreams rest on this island, including yours," Smitty reminded him.

"Dreams change. People change."

"Ye still need yer share of the gems, don't ye?"

"I thought so." Jack stopped and stared out to where his ship lay anchored. "Perhaps I made a mistake."

"How can finding a fortune in emeralds be a mistake?" Smitty said to him, incredulous. "Ye've a right to, ye know. We was headin' to look for 'em before ye laid eyes on her."

"Maybe so, but she's what matters to me now and I disappointed her. Again."

"'Tisn't likely to change so ye may as well resign yerself to it."

"A cynic, is what ye are." Jack turned a glare on him.

"Aye. May as well resign yerself to that, too."

Ollie and Deeds tramped to their west, voices raised in a heated exchange. Rory and Crawley to the east of them were silent as church mice. The rest trudged further inland.

Jack started walking again. "I've an obligation to my men. 'Tis what kept me heading south when all I wanted to do was turn back."

"We thank ye, then." Smitty snorted, unimpressed with what Jack was certain he considered lovesick drivel. "Ye staved off a mutiny most likely."

Ollie kicked at a bush as he passed and tripped. He hopped to keep from falling and the unmistakable sound of splintering wood cracked the air. He yelped and dove to the side. Deeds dropped to his knees, and the two men clawed at the vegetation.

"Looks ta be a floor, Cap'n," Deeds shouted and the others came running.

A cheer went up on the ship when Ollie waved to them.

Jack and Smitty joined the men and began tearing back the overgrowth. It was indeed a rotted-out floor. But from what? A cottage, a storehouse, a tavern? A few feet from Ollie, Rory uncovered a metal hinge.

Smitty lifted a brow. "Trapdoor?"

Jack nodded. "'Twould be my guess."

"Hard to believe there's a cellar so close to shore," Smitty mused, scanning the distance to the beach.

"These islands are riddled with caverns. Likely this cellar, if it is one, is nothing more than a small cave. Regardless, we need tools. Rory, you and Crawly row back to the ship and fetch shovels, rope, and some grappling hooks to pry these roots away. And bring more men." Jack turned to Smitty. "We need to keep searching. This may not be the tavern."

"Aye." His first mate rubbed his hands together, his eyes brimming with excitement. "And quickly. I don't fancy givin' my share to any who happen along."

"We'll not be around to squabble about it. Let's shake a leg and find those barrels."

Chapter Twenty-Two

Although Celia found Governor Glen's society tolerable, she abhorred residing in his home. The place was close and cramped, each room piled full of every type of chair, screen, painting, sculpture, and carpet known to man.

A daily constitutional was required to escape it.

Fortunately, the governor had recruited his sister, Margaret, to come to town and serve as companion to his guest. She'd recently wed and lived on one of the large plantations upriver on the Ashley. Though Celia felt a twinge of conscience for separating the new Mrs. Drayton from her husband, she was too grateful for the woman's company to reject it.

Lifting her face to the wan February sun, she basked in its warm, gentle rays while the cool breeze played with her hems. Mrs. Drayton had deigned to join her on her walk today. As usual, their small contingent garnered more attention than either woman preferred.

Although the pirates had been vanquished, she was not permitted to leave the house unescorted. Governor Glen had been very strict on this point. Whether due to an abiding friendship with Jack or fear of him, she'd yet to determine. Regardless, at least two large guards accompanied her each time she ventured out along with a maid unless Mrs. Drayton joined her.

Her companion chattered about fashions, her

favorite subject, while Celia breathed in the tang of salt air and enviously watched a fishing boat bob on the bay. She longed for the freedom of a ship, the sea, and a fair wind to propel her over it.

"I think the blue silk, the pale one, like those little flowers in my brother's carpet. Do you recall? And an ivory lace stomacher and petticoat. What say you?"

"Pink." Celia shielded her eyes with her hand to watch a group of seagulls circling overhead.

"Pink? Truly? Well, I hadn't thought of it. *Hmm.* Why pink?"

"'Twill enhance your complexion." Celia turned to the woman, whose face was obscured by the large brim of her hat. "You've the loveliest skin. The ivory lace sounds nice."

She returned her attention to the gulls while her companion pondered a different color, tracking them over two ships moored nearby. She loved walking along Bay Street. The harbor made her feel closer to Jack. Although he'd only been gone a little over a week, she could not prevent herself from searching for the *Bonny Lass*. Of course, the ship was not there. A wave of disappointment crashed over her, and she chastised herself for her foolishness.

"'Twould look lovely on you as well."

"Perhaps." Celia hadn't the slightest interest in fashions. Now ships, well, she could discuss ships and their cargos for hours.

"Miss Breckenridge, if you will permit me to ask. What was it about Stono Plantation that interested you so? You seemed so very intrigued with the indigo crop, and I am curious as to why. Pray, of what significance is it to you?"

Celia sent Mrs. Drayton a sideways glance. She supposed it would not be unseemly to say. A different mindset existed here in the colonies, enterprise touted and respected in the manner of rank and privilege back home.

"My father is a merchant. My sister and I would never leave him in peace. He doted on us, and we spent so much time with him that we learned his business. We enjoy it immensely and have amassed quite a sum in our own right."

"No sons, *hmm?*" Mrs. Drayton guessed.

"Not a one," Celia laughed.

"Well, I applaud his attitude. Heaven only knows how many women marry reprobates who spend their dowries and leave them destitute. Or die without leaving enough for their wife's maintenance."

"Precisely." Papa had said as much on many an occasion.

"Your father must find it all amusing."

"Vastly." She smiled.

"Have you discovered many opportunities in Charles Town then?"

Celia turned to look at the sparse ships dotting the harbor. Without docks, few dallied here overlong. "Perhaps the indigo, someday." She refrained from pointing out the desultory prospects the hurricane left in its wake. 'Twould take years likely, before the town and the surrounding plantations recovered. A fact all the inhabitants knew too well.

"What about a husband?" Margaret Drayton gave her a sly look. "According to my brother, Captain Beaumont is besotted with you."

"I fear a sailor's first love will always be the sea."

Celia sighed. She understood this far better than she cared to. She'd left Brett behind for much the same reason. Excitement. Adventure. "How does a woman compete?"

"Oh, I doubt very much he finds a lonely ocean more attractive than you." Mrs. Drayton laughed and patted her arm affectionately.

"I fear his actions prove you wrong as he's gone to sea and left me."

"That will all change once the two of you are wed. You mustn't despair, Miss Breckenridge. Men are simple creatures. It often takes a while before they understand what they truly desire."

Celia doubted this applied to Jack. He always seemed to know precisely what he wanted. She knew he wanted her, which is what made his departure so difficult to bear.

"I trust you are correct, for I shan't like competing." Her gaze caught on the ship anchored close to where a dock was being built. Its hull was painted a dull gray with a great black bird in flight on the escutcheon. A puff of chill air blew over her neck. She squinted but could not make out its name.

It could not be.

The merits of blue silk versus pink occupied her companion again. Celia listened with half an ear, having no more to offer on the subject. Her gaze drifted back to the ship. Surely, she was mistaken.

"Mrs. Drayton." She interrupted what promised to be a soliloquy on bodice lace. "Are you able to read the name of that ship over there? The gray one?"

She squinted in the direction Celia indicated. "Oh yes. It says *Nighthawk.* Lovely name. Sounds dashing and romantic, does it not?"

"Nighthawk," Celia breathed. She turned a radiant smile on her companion. "Come, I am acquainted with her captain." She latched onto the woman's arm and marched her swiftly along the wharf.

"You are?" Mrs. Drayton trilled, dragging her feet against Celia's momentum. "Is he a friend of your Captain Beaumont's then?" She motioned for their escort to keep up.

Celia turned a beatific smile on her. "Oh no, he is my Uncle Giles."

****

Water lapped against the ship's hull, the sound as soothing as a lullaby. Celia stood at the stern gallery windows and drank in the sight she thought to never see again.

Falmouth Harbor.

Her former world was the same, and yet it felt different. She wept a little inside that the town had gone on without her permission. Apprehension at how her loved ones may have changed in her absence warred with the thrill of returning to the bosom of her family. And she worried that she may have transformed too much to fit within it now.

Voices filtered down the companionway.

"I tell ye Robert, ye want to see this cargo," Uncle Giles said.

"And you could not have summoned me *after* you'd unloaded it? You know I detest these leaky crates."

Joy burst through her chest at the sound of her father's voice. She turned slowly, uncertain whether her shaking limbs would hold her aloft.

A sharp rap on the door. “He is here.” And then Uncle Giles pushed it open, stepping aside so her father could precede him in.

“Papa.”

Robert Breckenridge had taken only three steps when Celia’s voice brought him up short. A lash would not have created a more visceral response. Color drained from his face. He stood motionless until she worried she’d overtaxed his heart.

“Celia,” he finally croaked. “Celia child, is it really you?”

“Aye Papa.” She rushed to embrace him. “I am home. I am finally home.”

“Did I not tell ye, Robert?” Captain Taylor’s hoarse voice chided. “Ye never listen, ye stubborn old goat.”

Her father clutched her to him. “Where did you find her?” He seemed smaller somehow, not precisely frail, but neither the robust man Celia had left behind. But then compared to Jack’s hulking size, all men seemed small.

“The Colonies.”

“*The Colonies.* Celia, how the devil did you get there?”

She stood back and brushed at her wet cheeks, mindful of mussing her father’s coat. Then laughed and brushed the tears from his face as well. “’Tis a long story, Papa.”

He gathered her in his arms again and hugged her tight. “Then it shall wait. I should rather hold you.” It felt unreal to Celia, her father’s familiar embrace. At length he let go, his voice gruff. “Enough of this foolishness. We must get you home to your mother and sister. Banes took the carriage to the smithy to have the horses re-shod. I expect he is still there."

"Stay with your girl, Robert," Giles instructed. "I shall have him summoned to the dock."

****

Celia's first sight of Seaview caused an upwelling of emotion so intense she shook with it. Home had become a feeling, a place where her memories were stored. And now this yellow stone manor perched on the cliffs of Cornwall became an agony wrapped in joy. 'Twas all rushing back to her. The trees leafing out for spring, the hedges, the granite-paved drive. Even as she gazed upon her beloved Seaview, she ached for the home on Tradd Street she'd left behind, and most especially, Jack. 'Twas as if her world had turned "on its beam ends" as the sailors liked to say. Her new life had become her old.

Beyond the house, the tide crashed against the rocks, sending geysers of salt spray into the air. She leaned her head out the window of the carriage and let the wind blow mist in her face.

The familiar taste of brine in the air confirmed it. She was home.

Her father threw open the front door and bellowed for her mother the moment he crossed the threshold. "*Marlena.* Marlena, come at once."

"Robert," Mama's wondrous voice called from the direction of the kitchen. "What is wrong? What has happened?" She came running down the hall, their butler Matthews and maid Annie at her heels. Papa stepped aside, revealing Celia to her. She skidded to a halt.

Her abrupt pause nearly caused Matthews to

trample her. Annie was not so fortunate. She let out an *oof* when she plowed into Matthews' back, causing the butler to lurch forward. The maid grabbed a helpful handful of coat and pulled Matthews back on his heels.

"Celia." Her mother's hands rose to her chalk-white cheeks, her horrid black gown a remembrance of pirates and death. "My baby." Red-rimmed eyes looked to her father for confirmation. Papa nodded, his eyes damp again. Mama opened her arms and rushed forward, her feet gathering momentum with each step.

"Mama," Celia whispered, too overcome with emotion to move. Her mother wrapped her in an achingly familiar embrace and rocked her from side to side. She stood back to hold Celia's face in her hands. "My prayers have been answered." She hugged her again. "Oh, Celia, we thought you dead."

"I am so sorry, Mama." Beyond her mother's shoulder, Matthews and Annie wiped at their eyes. The entire household would soon be awash in tears.

"My darling girl, where were you?" Her mother held her face again to peer into her eyes, but then her own widened. "Good heavens! *We had a funeral.* Robert,"—she turned frantic eyes on her husband—"the headstone in the cemetery. We must—"

"Do not fret, my dear," he said as he pulled a handkerchief from his pocket to wipe his face. "'Twill be destroyed immediately."

A headstone? Well, if that didn't give one the jimjams, Celia did not know what would. She'd seen enough death to know she did not wish to participate, even symbolically. She wondered that they had done such a thing when Rianna knew perfectly well she was alive. She pulled the lace handkerchief from her mother's pocket to dab at her cheeks.

"Where is Rianna?"

"Good heavens, Rianna." Her mother fretted as though she'd forgotten she had born a second daughter. "She is on the beach. Matthews, you must fetch—"

"I shall fetch her, Mama." She tucked her mother's handkerchief back inside her pocket. "The beach is our place. 'Tis only fitting I should find her there."

Marlena looked stricken at the idea of letting her daughter out of her sight.

Her father solved the dilemma. "We shall all fetch your sister. Come along." He held open the door and she and her mother passed through it.

Celia turned at the threshold to blow Matthews and Annie a kiss. A substitute for the greeting they should have received.

Annie dabbed at her eyes with her apron and elbowed Matthews in the ribs. "The master's so addled, he's doin' yer job fer ye. Think he'll dust the parlor for me?"

"Not bloody likely," her father said over his shoulder, causing Celia to giggle. He left the door open for Matthews to close and the three of them walked the path along the side of the house toward the sound of the waves.

****

A worn, stone path led down to the beach where Rianna stood tossing pebbles in the surf. Celia paused several feet away to take in her first sight of her sister in well over a year. Rianna's bonnet had blown from her head and hung down her back, her wild blond hair loosed and whipped about by the wind.

She looked so small standing there with her white

dress plastered to her legs in the misty breeze, a heavy, white shawl clutched about her shoulders; thin, weary, her posture diminished. *Where had her spirited sister gone?*

Rianna's head came up and her arms dropped to her sides. She spun about and faced Celia. The sisters gazed at one another, probing without the cumbrance of words. Rianna's shoulders went back, and *ah*, there was the tempest they all knew and loved. She closed the distance between them, eyes flashing, fists clenched.

"They think me mad, you know. The town. Them." She waved a hand at the bluff where their parents waited without looking up.

"I've long suspected the same," Celia said calmly, her heart flinging hosanna's against her ribs.

"If I am, 'tis your bleeding fault."

Celia *tsked* at her language.

"I learned to curse from my friend Penny. *At school*," she added with relish, because she'd objected to being sent there. "She's three older brothers."

"Ah." Celia nodded in understanding. All men knew how to swear. She imagined they learned it from the cradle. "Well, I hardly think it fair to blame me for your bloody madness. You've been a looby since the day you were born."

Rianna grinned.

Celia grinned back.

And ran into one another's arms.

****

Afternoon light rayed through the windows of the Breckenridge drawing room, turning its verdant shades of green into a sun-dappled glen. The women within, one dark, one fair, lounged side by side on the settee, giggling like schoolgirls. Celia had missed this, missed her sister's vivaciousness, missed this piece of her that had always made her whole.

Yet, she was still not complete as her heart had sailed off to the Bahamas.

"You have never seen so many turnips piled on a plate in your life." Rianna chuckled, the affection in her voice unmistakable. "The children could barely contain themselves. They had such fun, the little devils."

Celia raised her teacup to her lips. "You are the only person in Cornwall who would dare call the parson's children 'devils'."

"Aye." Rianna propped her feet on their mother's table next to Celia's. "As I am their instructor, I would know."

"I shall never grow accustomed to that."

"Nor I, to be sure." She plucked the biscuit from Celia's hand and took a bite. "I've discovered 'tis far more agreeable to appoint the work than perform it."

"They are doomed if they're to depend on your competence with either."

"Very well. Come with me on the morrow and judge my 'competence' for yourself. The children will be thrilled to have you, and you shall enjoy the outing immensely. You have barely left the house since your return."

"I…perhaps another time. I am not yet accustomed to being home. I should rather stay until I am." Celia could not bear the constant stares from the townspeople. Seeing them cross the street when they spied her coming. And the whispers. As if she'd been raised from the dead rather than stranded by a hurricane. Rianna's vehement insistence that Celia had not perished on the *Essex* had only served to renew the town's suspicion of their preternatural abilities once she arrived hale and whole as Rianna had promised.

Her sister had been fighting them for so long, she hardly cared for their opinions, but Celia was too raw at present. She sorely missed Jack's strength bolstering her. And his big, warm body keeping her safe.

She snatched her biscuit back from Rianna. "Do you suppose Pamela might bake more of these?" Since she'd returned home, she craved cinnamon: cinnamon biscuits, cinnamon cake, cinnamon custard. She'd even filched a piece of cinnamon bark to hide in her pillow. It helped her to sleep at night.

"If *you* ask it of her, she will bake an entire pantry full of biscuits." Rianna lifted her teacup in the air. "The prodigal returneth and all that. You've been home, what? A month now? And the servants still fall all over themselves to do your bidding."

"Nonsense. They simply like me better than you."

"Only because they have not yet heard of your swashbuckling ways. When they learn you've become a…what did you call them? Picaroon? I shall be their favorite."

"I am *not* a picaroon. I did kick one in the cods, however." Celia enjoyed being able to impress her sister with a term like "cods." 'Twas the first time she had mentioned any details of her abduction. Her family had been distressed by the accounting of her travails, thus she'd blunted the story as much as possible.

"You lie." Rianna jolted in her seat, gaping at her as if she'd sprouted a parrot on her shoulder. Odd that she sounded distressed. Very little shocked her sister.

"They swelled up like a coconut." Celia giggled,

amazed she could laugh about Jenkins.

Rianna sat back again, suspicious of her sister committing violence.

She grinned. "Jack punched him in the face and knocked his tooth out. Then made him scrub his blood off the deck."

A squawk burst out of Rianna, something between a squeal and a howl. Celia laughed out loud and toasted her with her tea. She rather enjoyed being the outrageous sibling for a change.

"Fie on you," Rianna scolded. "What manner of beast have you been consorting with?"

"A big, brutish, silver-eyed devil," Celia said smugly. "One who makes pirates quake in their boots and pray for mercy." She slanted her sister a look. "And is so devilishly handsome he makes my body hot and my blood sing."

"Argh." Rianna waved a hand in front of her face. "We should have asked for something cool to drink. 'Tis growing rather warm in here."

They giggled and shared another biscuit.

Growing pensive, Rianna toyed with the handle of her cup. "You've spent precious little time with Brett since your return. Don't you think you ought?

"I will *not* marry him." This had to be the hundredth time Celia had said so since her return.

"How can you know your heart so soon?" Her sister's sapphire eyes turned pleading, confounding her. "Does Brett not deserve every consideration? Forsooth, you may never clap eyes on your brute again."

"For heaven's sake, Rianna, why are you so determined to force us together? Before I left for Bermuda, you railed at the idea of my marrying him."

"Only because I did not want him to take you away from me. I've, er, come to know him since you were gone. He is much more agreeable than one might assume."

"Then you marry him." Her sister blushed, and Celia realized 'twas not the first time she'd done so when discussing her former betrothed.

"You hadn't the opportunity to come to know one another. The two of you would be married now if not for Maggie's illness."

"What nonsense. We grew up together. I daresay I know him as well as anyone. Is he the reason for your misery while I was away? You've yet to explain yourself." Rianna set her cup down and Celia could tell straight off she meant to distract her. "And none of that poppycock you've been feeding me. I well know—"

Voices reached them from the hall. Male. One outraged, yet dignified; the other low and threatening. Celia sat up, her heart banging against its cage to get out.

The door to the parlor opened and Matthews filled the doorway, but then a large brute shouldered him aside.

A very large, very angry brute.

Chapter Twenty-Three

Celia lurched to her feet.

"What is it, dearest?" Rianna stood as well. "You've gone white as a clout." She turned to the object of Celia's distress. "You, sir. What is your business here?"

Celia clutched her sister's arm. "Thank you for showing him in, Matthews."

Matthews hesitated. She gave him a nod of encouragement. The sound of the door clicking shut signaled a lengthy silence.

Jack towered over the room, face ashen. A muscle twitched in his jaw—a telltale sign of his anger. It vibrated from him, disturbing their former lighthearted atmosphere. His gaze burned into Celia's and, *dear lord*, his eyes were like embers, hot and smoldering and ringed with the charred remains of emotions spent.

Desire flared in her womb. He appeared unable to speak at present. Or likely didn't trust himself to. He fascinated Rianna. Celia could hear her sister's mind whirling as clearly as if she spoke aloud. She found the prospect of a new adversary thrilling but was somewhat disgusted with Celia's reaction to him.

He hasn't been sleeping, she thought tenderly. His fists clenched and unclenched, reminding her of all the lovely things he could do with those big, gifted hands.

Rianna snorted.

Celia pinched her and gave him a tremulous smile. He stiffened.

Words spewed out of him as if her smile were the quake that caused his emotions to erupt. "How could you, woman? How could you leave me like that? Do you have any idea how terrified I've been?"

Her eyes misted over. He loved her still. He could not be so angry otherwise. Not that the bounder deserved his anger. The thought made her smile wider.

Rianna frowned at her.

"Jack. You are here," she said stupidly, ignoring her sibling.

"Devil take you, woman." He advanced on her then, the look in his eyes dangerous and thrilling. "I swear I shall beat you as promised."

A gasp issued from Rianna and Celia wondered whether she was shocked that this angry, threatening man aroused her or whether she was merely thrilled with the "devil take you" and meant to share it with her friends.

"Are you certain you would not rather make love to me?"

"Celia," Rianna squawked.

She wished she could savor her sister's reaction, but Jack was there, standing before her, and he required all her concentration. He grabbed her upper arms and gave her a shake.

"Damn you, witch," he choked. "You gave me an apoplexy."

"I missed you, too."

"Neither of you are discussing the same topic, I fear," Rianna murmured aloud. "I feel as though I am eavesdropping on two entirely different conversations.

'Tis quite annoying."

Tears spiked Celia's lashes. She touched her palm to Jack's cheek. "I am so happy you are here, Jackson."

"No tears. I forbid them," he growled, and his hands tightened on her arms.

She laughed and they spilled over.

He crushed her to him and buried his face in her hair, those wondrous hands rubbing over her arms, her waist, her back, as if checking to make certain she was complete.

Starved for the heat of his big body pressed against hers, she wrapped her arms around his neck and cuddled closer.

Cupping her face in his hands, he tipped her head back, fusing their lips together. His kiss was ravenous, fraught with fear and need.

"No wonder you are so thin," Rianna said dryly. "This brute's been eating you."

Celia giggled against Jack's lips. He broke their kiss and sent her sister a quelling look. He had much to learn about Rianna.

"Why did you not wait for me? I vowed to bring you home before Eastertide, did I not?"

"I explained everything in my letter. Did you receive it?"

"Aye, Meagan gave it to me."

"Then there is nothing more to say. You know why I left. And before you berate me, do recall you chose to leave me behind. You could have been the one to bring me home instead of Uncle Giles."

"Damned headstrong witch." He clapped his hands on her shoulders and shook her again. "You'd no right to leave."

"We are *not* witches," Rianna huffed. "I vow I don't know what you see in this man, Ce. I find him insufferable."

Jack's gaze flicked over her, rather like a horse swatting a fly with its tail. "Who is this troublesome creature?"

Rianna's lips curved.

"My sister."

"Of course, she is." He snorted. "I might have known she'd be a shrew."

Oh, dear.

Venom oozed from Rianna's eyes. "Why you—"

"Celia." The parlor door burst open.

The floor dropped from under Celia's feet. *Not now.* Please God. *Not now.*

"My parents have finally returned. Come, we must surprise—Oh, I do beg your pardon."

"Brett," Rianna sang. "How nice of you to call."

"Is it?" His brows furrowed, and he rubbed a hand over his blond head, confused by Rianna's greeting and the scene he'd interrupted.

Violence raged in Jack's eyes. His jaw clenched, and he wheeled about to face Brett, who wore a puzzled but otherwise passive expression. But then the poor man was ignorant of the fury about to be unleashed upon him.

Celia clutched at Jack's coat—if she could just get between them—but he proved as easy to budge as the cliffs out yon window.

"I should like to make introductions," Rianna explained to Brett. "But I haven't been introduced."

"No?" Brett stepped forward to remedy the situation. He crossed his arm over his waist to bow.

"Mr. Brett—"

Jack grabbed him by the throat.

Brett's eyes bulged and his hands clawed at Jack's fingers.

"She's mine, you bleeding bastard," Jack roared. "Keep your distance or I'll gut you from stem to stern." He shook Brett in his fist. "Mine."

"Jack," Celia shouted, appalled at his behavior. "Release him at once."

"I'll not." Though Brett was certainly not a small man, Jack had the advantage over him in surprise. And rage. And sheer brute strength. "What is he doing here? Did you not tell him?"

"Of course, I told him." She yanked on his arm. "Let him be."

"Do control your beast, Celia." Rianna said to Brett, "What shall I do? Shall I kick him for you?"

Brett widened his eyes at her, to which Rianna responded in kind, their behavior more than passing strange. The two had seldom been in charity with one another, and now they communicated privately?

Jack stuck his face in Brett's. "You mean to steal her back, do you?"

"St-steal?" Brett wheezed. "W-Wouldn't insult—"

"There, you see?" Celia interrupted. "At least one of you is a gentleman." Jack's face darkened. Brett shot her an aggrieved look.

"You are behaving like a barmy fool, Jackson. Release him this instant." She stamped her foot. "Release him I say."

He stared at her while she tapped her foot and snapped impatience at him. His eyes dropped. She could tell he was wavering, though he clearly enjoyed having his hand wrapped around Brett's throat, the brute.

The door burst open again, and Mrs. Kensington ran into the room. Her aqua gown was markedly wrinkled from her travels, and haphazard wisps of chestnut hair floated about her nape.

"I cannot believe the news. Is she—" Her hand rose, shaking, to cover her mouth. "'Tis true," she breathed. "You are returned to us. Oh, Celia. We prayed for this day for ever so—"

Her eyes widened as she took in the rest of the room's occupants, and she noticed Brett dangling from Jack's fist. Angry color blazed in her cheeks. "Here now. Unhand him at once."

"Mrs. Kensington. How lovely to…" Celia's words trailed off as the woman marched to Jack and smacked him on the shoulder with the flat of her hand.

"What is the meaning of this outrage? Unhand him, I say." She punctuated her demand with another sound whack.

Good heavens, Celia had never seen such a fierce expression on Mrs. Kensington's face. Her flaming cheeks and hostile glare promised Jack death or dismemberment at any moment.

Unfortunately, he was little impressed with the woman accosting him. He glowered at her and she at him while Brett remained attached to his hand.

"Jackson Beaumont," Celia shouted to gain his attention. Lud, the man was in a lather. "You are frightening Mrs. Kensington. Release Brett. At once."

Mrs. Kensington let out a cry of distress and stumbled backward. Her hands rose to cover her mouth, her countenance so astonished Celia feared she might swoon.

Brett stopped struggling and gaped at Jack.

What on earth?

"Jackson?" Mrs. Kensington whispered. "Jackson Beaumont? *My* Jackson Beaumont?"

His brow furrowed, and he rubbed the back of his hand over his chin.

Celia's heart plummeted. This could not possibly bode well for her. Clearly the woman had some form of claim over Jack.

Rianna squeezed her hand in sisterly solidarity.

"Jack-a-dandy?" Mrs. Kensington laughed.

Jack's face leached of color. "Em?" His gaze flicked to Celia. He thrust his arm to the side—with Brett still attached—and inspected Emily Kensington from head to foot.

Realization dawned. "My word," Celia gasped and sank to the cushions.

"What?" Rianna snapped, as she was the only one still left in the dark.

Jack had gone so still he looked as if he'd turned to stone. His eyes sought Celia's again, clouded and uncertain. She smiled encouragingly. His gaze met Mrs. Kensington's again.

"Em, is it truly you?"

"Oh, Jackson." Her voice was thick with tears. She threw her arms around him. Jack locked his free arm about her waist and gave her a fierce hug.

"What. Is. Happening?" Rianna demanded of the room at large. "Here, sir," she rounded on Jack. "Unhand her. She is a married woman. Honestly, Celia. This man is a cad. First he accosts you, then Brett, and now Mrs. Kensington."

Celia shot her sister a repressive frown.

"I cannot believe my eyes. After all these years." Emily leaned away from Jack as she spoke, cupping his face in her hands. "You've come home to us and—" Her gaze followed the line from his shoulder to where his hand still clutched Brett's throat. "Jackson. What on earth are you doing? Release my son at once."

Jack gave a start. "Your son? This," he shook Brett, "is your son?"

Brett offered him a snide smile and pried Jack's fingers one by one from his throat. He coughed. "Pleased to make your acquaintance, *Uncle* Jack."

****

"Jack." Celia stumbled and he hauled her back against him into the library, closing the door. She turned within the circle of his arms. "Why, sir, this is entirely scandalous."

"Good." His lips skimmed her jaw. "'Twill aid my suit with your father."

"Scoundrel. You have compromised me quite thoroughly, I fear." She arched her neck as he nibbled a path to her ear.

"I disagree." He breathed against her skin. "The business requires constant application."

"Mmm." She slid her hands over his shoulders to toy with the ribbon at his nape. "While I applaud your intent, I fear we shall not accomplish much 'application' today. My father does not trust you, and your sister shall surely come looking for you."

He sighed against her ear, sending delightful little shivers down her neck. "I had to escape them. It shames me to say so, but I could not bear the attention any longer."

Celia brushed her lips over his. "'Tis overwhelming, my darling, to have a family appear in your life so suddenly. I am so very sorry about your brother. To harbor resentment all these years only to discover he's been dead every one of them."

Jack dropped his head to her shoulder and held her tight. His chest swelled against her with each breath. "I left Em all alone. I shall never forgive myself."

"You were a boy of six, for heaven's sake. What could you have done when your brother passed on? Faith, I cannot imagine the agony your sister must have suffered, losing her entire family mere months apart. She is fortunate she did not catch the typhus as well. Who can know? Had you been there, you might have taken ill also."

"No. Kyle had sent me away to school. And possibly saved my life."

"Oh, Jack." She touched her lips to his cheek. "You must be thankful your Em had Charles Kensington to marry. You were just a little boy."

"I would have been there for her. She would not have lost both of her brothers."

"It is tragic you were not. Shall I tell you what a wise man once told me? He said, 'you may plague your conscience with—' "

"Enough." Jack squeezed her ribs to stem her words.

"Flagellating yourself will solve nothing."

He searched her face and his expression changed. Silver lights flickered in his eyes, and his lips curved in a slow smile. "Perhaps you'd care to flagellate me instead." He lifted her higher, tasting her lips, gently at first, but as their mouths relearned one another their passions grew. “I need to be alone with you,” he whispered against her cheek.

The door opened and bumped into Jack, conspiring against them. He moved out of the way and pushed her behind him to face their intruder.

Celia’s heart wrenched for him. In his overwrought state ’twas unsurprising he’d overreact. She put her hands on his waist and leaned her forehead against his back. “Jack,” she said softly. “This is my home. There is no threat here.”

Jack said nothing.

Confused by his silence, she peeked around him. *“Papa.”*

Her father stood at the threshold, staring at her hands where they clutched Jack’s body familiarly, his expression cold and hard. She made as if to move to Jack’s side, but he held her behind him. Her father barked a short, sardonic laugh.

“She was mine long before you clapped eyes on her, sir. *My* daughter. *My* little girl. Never forget it.”

The two remained silent for a space. Though Jack blocked Celia’s view, she suspected they communicated steely-eyed threats and the silent, though no less overbearing, ripostes men performed so effortlessly. Like a pair of wolves circling one another without the growls. Which went to show how formidable a man Papa could be. He was several inches shorter than Jack, though robust in health and certainly demeanor.

She could not blame her father for not trusting him. What with Rianna’s vivid accounting and the bruises on Brett’s throat, his introduction to her parents had not been smooth. Thank goodness for Mrs. Kensington.

She'd loyally championed her brother and would hear no criticism of him—unless it came from her.

Jack tipped his head to her father, though she'd no idea what he'd just acknowledged. She stepped from behind him. He allowed it but caught her arm and pulled it through his.

Papa's shoulders went back, and he arched a dubious brow.

"I wish to take her to my ship," Jack informed him. Both Celia and her father looked at him in surprise.

"Why?" Her father's eyes narrowed and his lips thinned to an angry white line. "To abscond with her?"

"Of course not. She'd never forgive me." Meaning he would do so otherwise. Although it did nothing to endear Jack to her father, it was an effective way to assure him he would do nothing against her will. Papa detested platitudes.

"Why then?"

"My crew, they've grown fond of her. They deserve to see she is well. I was not myself when I discovered her gone. My fear became theirs."

"Oh, Papa, of course I must go." She'd given no thought to the crew. "You've nothing to fear, I promise. They are the very best of men."

Her father considered Jack's request—he hadn't actually asked—and a shrewd light entered his eyes. "I expect your sister might like to meet them as well. You recall how disappointed she was when she could not sail with you. Take her along. Oh, and your nephew as well," he said to Jack. "I imagine you'd like to become better acquainted with him."

A cunning man, her father. 'Tis what made him a successful trader.

"Of course," Jack said smoothly. "They are welcome to join us, aren't they, sweet?"

Celia wanted to bang her head against the wall. Jack was determined to prove his possession, with or without her father's approval. Instead of asking for her hand, the blasted man was slapping Papa's face with it.

She tried for diplomacy. "I am certain they would both enjoy a visit to your ship."

"Speaking of a visit, sir. You and I should schedule one, should we not? Would tomorrow morning be agreeable?"

"Aye." Her father looked pained. "The sooner the better, I should think."

Jack inclined his head and ushered Celia past her fuming parent. She paused to place an affectionate kiss on his cheek. "You are too much alike, I fear."

He wrapped his arm around her waist, giving her a quick squeeze. "I shall beat you for that, daughter."

"Fie. All the men in my life wish to beat me." She laughed as she sailed from the room on her lover's arm.

Banes drove their party to the wharf in the Breckenridge carriage. Once they'd alighted, Jack suggested he return for them in three hours' time. The carriage pulled away as the four of them headed for the dock where Jack's skiff was tied.

When they neared it, he turned with Celia on his arm. "Go away," he said to Rianna and Brett.

Rianna's brows dove in annoyance. She paused with one foot slightly forward of the other, like a pugilist preparing to throw a punch. Rather like David confronting Goliath given her diminutive size. "I beg your pardon?"

"Go occupy yourselves for a few hours while Celia

and I go aboard."

"Why can we not come?"

He rolled his eyes. "Because we've much to discuss without you lot underfoot."

"'Tis a large ship," Rianna argued. "Surely—"

"Come, Rianna." Brett tugged on her arm, in accord with Jack's suggestion. "We are not welcome."

She looked to Celia with an odd expression. Celia watched her curiously, puzzled by the apprehension she saw on her face.

Rianna turned her head and a wall went up between them. Apparently, Celia was not yet to learn what troubled her. Hardly fair as her sister's distress had been the impetus for her leaving Bermuda prematurely.

"Very well." Rianna allowed Brett to draw her away. "But you owe me a debt now Mr. Beaumont, and I shan't allow you to forget it," she called over her shoulder.

"I may not like that man," Jack said as he handed Celia into the skiff and jumped in behind her, "but even I feel a twinge of guilt for saddling him with your sister."

"I wonder." Celia thought about their parting. "There is something odd there. Some strong undercurrent of emotion between them."

"Your sister and my nephew?" Jack chuckled. "I cannot think of a more deserving pair."

"You are not a nice man," Celia chided.

He winked at her as he rowed away from the dock. "Love, I promise you shall soon think me very nice, indeed."

Chapter Twenty-Four

Only a few members of the crew remained aboard and still, Celia wasted precious time thanking each until Jack was able to pry her away. He ushered her into his cabin and closed the door.

Visions of her father rowing out and bursting in on them prompted him to latch it. The man would hardly approve of his plans as they involved a dearth of clothing and an abundance of pleasure.

A small smile played about her lips as her gaze roamed the space. By nature, Jack was a tidy man. He kept his things stowed away and his desk clear. Utter chaos reigned now—charts and mugs littered the desk, clothes strewn about the floor, bed untidy. Her fault, of course. He'd been too distracted to care for his things properly.

"I forgot what a mess I'd left behind. I ought to have tidied up."

"We shall tidy up before we leave." Her shawl slid off her shoulders as she wrapped her arms around his neck. "I missed you, Jackson."

Missed? What a colorless word to describe the oppressing ache in his soul since their parting. An ache that could only be assuaged by holding her, touching her, owning her. Unable to resist, he speared his hands in her hair, dislodging her pins.

"If you insist upon ruining my coiffure, you shall

have to repair it, or Papa will show up with pistols at dawn."

"I am repairing it," Jack said against her lips. "I prefer it loose." He plundered her mouth defiantly, relieved to have her to himself without her annoying family to intrude. Her hands dove into his hair in retaliation, tearing it loose from its queue.

"Ouch." His lips made free with the delicate skin under her jaw while his hands conquered the terrain of her spine to cup her arse. "I'd no idea you'd become such a savage."

"Mmm," she purred, plucking at the buttons of his coat. "I shall bite if provoked."

"God, how I love you," he choked.

"You ardently declare yourself when I threaten you with pain? You are depraved, sir." She shoved his coat from his shoulders as if it offended her. "Take this off. I want my hands on your skin."

His coat sailed in the general vicinity of his desk, rustling the charts. She laughed at his eagerness and started on his waistcoat. He'd dreamed of her ceaselessly, melding memories with fantasies, but this…this, his mind had not conjured. His beautiful, delicate, honorable Celia, stripping him of his clothes. Her hands slid over him, lingering on the muscles of his chest, eliciting a feral response beneath his breastbone. He yanked off his boots and stockings then divested himself of stock and shirt.

Impatience, and a healthy dose of eagerness, rent the seam. She grinned. "'Twould appear I am not the only one responsible for ruining your shoddy clothing."

"I shall do without."

"I rather wish you would." Her lovely hands

returned to coast over his skin, fingers sifting through his chest hair and, thanks be praised, her lips followed. She wrapped them around the hard nub of his nipple and nipped with her teeth.

Jack's cock pulsed and for a short, fraught moment he feared their interlude had ended. *Vixen.* He'd shame himself before his damn breeches came off. He lifted her up, gave her a hot, searing kiss, then dropped her to her feet to work the contingent of buttons at the back of her gown free.

"Remember my father." She kicked off her slippers. "Do not tear my gown."

"'Twould serve you right after the legion of shirts you massacred." He dispensed with her dress, panniers, stays, and finally her blasted chemise and tossed her, gloriously naked, onto his bunk, shedding his breeches as he followed her down.

Her hungry gaze fondled his naked body from head to toe as thoroughly as if she'd used her hands. Heat scored Jack's flesh. He dropped his head to her shoulder and imagined frigid seas and blinding snow.

Using the respite productively, Celia raised first one leg then the other to yank off her stockings and garters. He closed his eyes, refusing to watch what would surely be his undoing.

"Jack." She wrapped her arms around his shoulders and tugged him closer. "I cannot wait any longer."

He lifted his head. Sunlight bathed the cabin, but here in the privacy of their bed, shadows played over her face, whispering of mystery and hidden secrets. The kind a man was helpless to resist exploring. She'd enchanted him from the very instant he'd seen her tied to the mast. Every moment, every breath since had been for her. No man had ever been more easily bewitched. Her nails raked over his chest and the muscles of his stomach tightened in response.

She could not have been this beautiful before. Surely if she had he would not be suffering this blow to his senses now. He ran a shaking hand from cheek to shoulder then breast to hip to knee. He wanted to explore her for hours, but the demands of his raging lust would not allow it.

He rose over her.

Celia spread her legs and reached between them to guide him. *Sweet christ.* At the sound of his indrawn breath, she smiled—a wanton, wicked smile—and wrapped him tight in her fist.

Gombey drums pounded out the vicious throbbing of his blood.

"I've dreamed of this," she whispered, the silken web of her voice floating over him. Jack swallowed and beat back the ripples of pleasure her touch evoked as she brushed his cock against where she was luscious and wet. She moaned at the contact.

Currents of fire raced along his spine. He drove his hips forward and buried himself in her snug, clenching heat then pulled back and plunged again. His vision darkened from the sheer, carnal bliss of breaching her again. He tried to pull out once more, but she gasped and clamped his hips to keep him inside.

Breaths ragged, body twitching, Jack paused, desperate to thrust again.

But that was not her agenda.

Holding his hips immobile, she moved against him unrestrained, grinding herself on his cock-stand. God save him. He'd not survive the assault. Oblivious to his turmoil and his need, she labored on, unmindful of him entirely.

"Celia," he begged. She could not possibly miss the desperation in his voice.

"Yes, Jack, yes. *Ohhh,* please, yes. Like that." She raised her knees to press her feet into the mattress and impaled herself on him with unbridled abandon. Shamelessly gratifying herself as if he were a bleeding tool for her pleasure.

Jack stared down at her, shocked momentarily from his own urgent need. She threw her head back, her face flushed and damp. He felt her muscles constrict around him and she cried out—screamed—as her pleasure shook her.

Blood roared through his ears. His hips broke her hold and pounded into her as if the devil himself drove them, riding his own release and shouting her name as he spent inside her.

****

Celia lay wrapped in a cozy, somnolent peace, content to simply "be" with him. Her fingers played in Jack's hair as he lay panting atop her, until he lifted his head.

A wicked smile creased his lips. "Wanton."

Her cheeks flamed. She raised her hands to cover her face, too mortified to look at him.

"I am appalled, madam." He pulled her hands away to peer at her face, silver lights shimmering in his eyes. "You used me shamelessly."

"You do not sound appalled," she observed. "You sound smug."

"Nay, you are mistaken." He snuggled her closer. "I am most assuredly appalled."

"Pray, turn me loose then if you find me so appalling."

"I cannot." He nipped at her jaw. "I've discovered I've a penchant for appalling women. Perhaps you'd care to violate me again?"

"Perhaps not." She pushed against his chest.

He shifted to the side and gathered her in his arms. "I have never experienced anything so thrilling as making love with you," he whispered in her ear. His hot breath made her shiver. "I am your most ardent servant."

"Perhaps I do not wish a servant." She sniffed.

"You did a moment ago." He chuckled. She squirmed to get away, but he squeezed her until she stilled. "When can we marry, love?" He lowered his voice and skimmed a hand over her belly, raising gooseflesh in its wake. "Your servant wishes to attend you every night."

Oh, that husky voice. She could deny him nothing when he used it against her. She ran her finger over his lips. "You still wish to marry?"

"Don't be coy." He bit her finger. "If not for your stubbornness, we'd have wed in Charles Town."

"I shall discuss it with Mama and Rianna while you speak with Papa tomorrow. That is what you mean to discuss with him, is it not?"

"Aye, though I expect he shall be difficult. The man is not in charity with me."

She rubbed her cheek against his chest. "I cannot imagine why." Seeing Jack through her family's eyes made her realize it would take them a while to come to love him. He hadn't rescued any of them from pirates. Or kissed them witless.

"Alas, I am taking his daughter away." He stroked her hair, always happiest when his hands were tangled in it.

"Fie, Jackson. You were horrid today. No one could have approved of you." She drew circles on his stomach with her finger and smiled when his muscles jumped.

"If you thought me horrid today, you should pity those fools in Charles Town when I discovered you gone." He gave her hair a tug. "I expect the governor's ears are still ringing."

"The poor man. He had naught to do with it. What would you have had me do? Send Uncle Giles home with the news that I am alive and safe but not disposed to return yet?" She frowned when she saw him considering it. "Perhaps they should have been told I awaited my lover's pleasure and would return whenever he desired."

"I do like the sound of that." Jack pulled her atop him and kissed her.

"I thought you were my servant. What about what I desire?"

His smile turned wolfish. "You took what you desired. I've the bruises on my arse to prove it." His gaze turned calculating. "Perhaps I will show them to your father. We shall be wed on the morrow for certain."

"Beast." She scrambled off him. "I desire you to behave."

"No." He trapped her against his side and brought her fingers to his lips. "I do not believe you do."

No, she sighed, she did not. Instead of arguing, she changed the subject. "Did you complete your business in the Caribbean?"

His body tensed. She lifted her head to search his face. It lay in shadow, which suddenly felt significant. "Jack?"

"Aye, we did." A rather mild response considering how determined he'd been to go.

"Will you tell me about it?"

"Now?"

Celia grew suspicious at his reluctance. "Aye, now."

"Very well." He looked away and took a deep breath. Unease crept up her spine. "We sailed to the Bahamas. To Santa Maria de la Concepción. We had reason to believe a fortune was to be found there if one knew where to look."

"A fortune?" She leaned away from him. "Truly?"

"Aye."

"But I thought you sailed to Barbados. Your friend—" She paused when he shook his head. "Perhaps you'd best explain." One ought to be able to wind a clock backward when they found themselves at the precipice of unpleasantness. She had the overwhelming desire to clap her hand over his mouth and release his confessions in digestible bits.

Jack sat up and leaned against the wall behind them. Celia scooted up to join him there, pulling the sheet up to cover her breasts. He sighed heavily. "The man Jean Pierre killed in La Rochelle, Douglas Travers. Do you recall my speaking of him?"

"Aye. He was a former shipmate of yours."

"Before he died, he told me about a fortune in emeralds hidden on the island. 'Tis what the pirates were after when they killed him."

"Emeralds? You cannot be serious, Jack. You said you had an obligation to see to before you could take me home."

"And so I did." He lifted her hand and traced the outline of her fingers. "I swore an oath to Travers to search for the gems. And I had an obligation to my crew. They had a right to their share."

"But…" The happiness that had buoyed Celia slowly dissipated. "What about me? You would leave me and my family to suffer on a whim?"

"Not a whim. I had to see to their futures. And ours." Though his voice remained calm, color rode high on his cheeks. "Travers did not lie."

"You found them." Her voice was flat, funereal nearly.

"We found them," he confirmed and offered her a crooked smile. "I shall support us in fine style into our dotage and beyond."

"The emeralds were all you set out to accomplish then? Were you not there to trade your brandy?"

His smile vanished. "I had little left to trade. Much of it paid for supplies after the hurricanes. There was no need once we found the emeralds."

The weight of his words fractured her heart. "And you…you actually went *hunting* for treasure instead of returning me home?"

He stopped toying with her hand and clasped it tightly. "'Twas our aim from the start, to search for the emeralds after we exchanged the brandy for spices. But then we came upon the *Mirabelle*."

"But why did you leave me in Charles Town, Jack?"

"I could not take you with me. The pirates knew

we meant to find the gems. They took up with a man named Jedidiah Small, who helped them procure a ship. Small set sail the day before we planned to leave. I feared he meant to lay in wait and pursue us if Jenkins failed to take the map from me. I could not risk your safety."

"You should have returned me home first. Then you could search to your heart's content."

Jack sighed. "We surmised they would follow no matter what direction we took."

"They did not?"

"No, but I had no idea what awaited us in the Bahamas. Pirates are rife in the Caribbean, sacking towns and attacking Spanish trading ships before they gather in Havana."

It all sounded so very reasonable. Celia suspected reason had little to do with it. "Why not sneak me aboard another ship before you left?" she persisted. "Why keep me in Charles Town?"

"You know why." He launched off the bed and snatched his breeches up from the floor.

Celia sat up as well. "I want you to tell me."

"In no wise would I allow you to go haring off to that ruddy bastard you were betrothed to."

"That 'ruddy bastard' is your nephew."

"He wasn't then," Jack snarled.

Plague take ridiculous men. Celia jumped to her feet and located her chemise amid the tangled clothing. "Jealousy then." She snatched it over her head. "'Twas your true motivation, was it not?"

"No." A rasp of a syllable, that. And crowded with emotion. "What hope had I? A poor sea captain competing with a wealthy heir."

"Poor?" She threw her hands up in exasperation. *Were all men such idiots?* "You hardly live on the streets."

"Compared to your Brett, I do."

"For heaven's sake, will you leave Brett out of this?" She was tempted to kick him. "My family suffered torments over me, Jackson. And I over them. They had no idea what had become of me. *My parents carved me a headstone.* You knew what they suffered because you'd left family here, too. Family who had no idea what had become of you. How could you let them suffer? How could you let *me* suffer?"

"Damnation, Celia." Jack paced an uncluttered patch of floor and ran his hands through his hair. "'Tis not as simple as you would make it. I could not face them without the emeralds. You were meant to marry an heir. Your father is wealthy. Deuced take it, you are wealthy."

A fat lot of good wealth had done her. "I mean to marry a person, not his fortune."

"'Tis a pretty thought m'dear." He paused to face her with his hands on his hips. "But you've never had to do without, have you?"

"As I am an heiress, you will not have to do without either."

He turned away from her to gaze out the stern gallery windows. "I've no intention of touching your dowry."

She looked up in surprise. "Whyever not?"

"My brother."

"I beg your pardon?" Anger and confusion warred for dominance. She settled for glaring at his back.

" 'Worthless spares' must live off their wife's

family. I vowed I would never do so." He scooped the clutter off a chair and dropped into it. "I dreamed of returning one day. A man of wealth. A man of my own design. I'd look my brother in the eye and he would know I'd proved him wrong. Proved I wasn't," his voice lowered to a whisper, "worthless." His laugh was short, bitter. "You had to be an heiress. Doubtless your father believes me a fortune hunter."

"Of course not," she snapped, incensed by his selfishness. "My father is more discerning than that, sir. He thinks you an ass by your own merits."

Jack leveled his gaze with hers. "I did not expect you to understand."

"Oh, I understand you perfectly, Jackson." She paced the room in his stead, kicking the clutter out of her way as she went. "'Tis your pride you value above all else."

"By damned, Celia." He vaulted from the chair. "You mean more to me than my life."

"A bit of a contradiction, that. Oh, I've no doubt you would sacrifice yours to save mine," she said when his eyes flashed lightning. "But when it comes to placing my needs above your own, well, 'tis an entirely different kettle of fish, is it not?"

He bowed his head and stared at the floor. "Everything I've done since we've met has been for you."

Her mouth dropped open. "How can you say that?"

"You were determined to go through with your betrothal. I had to keep you with me until I'd won you over. I could not let him have you." His eyes smoldered a warning at her. "Do not dare say you wanted to marry him."

"I was not aware you wanted me. You made it clear the sea would always be your life."

"I had some pride. You with your wealth and your heir. How could I possibly be anything but a disappointment to you? A scupper draining all your shillings away."

"My God, I'd no idea you were so fanatical about money." She flung her hands in the air. "You seemed so sensible."

"I am sensible. Except where you are concerned." He clamped his hands on her arms and pulled her against him. "I desired you more than anything I had ever known. But you spoke so highly of your Mr. Kensington. I knew I should never come up to scratch. I hadn't that sort of—" He released her arms and turned away to the window and the water beyond. "—of character. What good was I to you? I can wield a sword, aye, but how often would you need my protection here?"

Good heavens. Where to begin? "I would not have married him, Jackson. Not after you. I thought I had no place in your life beyond Charles Town. I resisted you because I feared you would sail out of my life, never to return."

He turned to face her then, his expression bleak. Celia's heart cracked open a little more. She mentally slapped herself back to her senses. "I did not realize your affections had changed until I prepared to sail."

"It does not justify keeping me there. You had no right to manipulate my life."

"I wanted to be worthy of you." He traipsed the confines of the room, grinding his fist into the palm of his hand as he spoke. "To be worth what you had to give up at the very least. I did not want you to regret choosing me."

"Jack," she said helplessly, because she could not make him understand. "You and Brett are two entirely different men. I love you both." She winced. What a stupendously stupid thing to say. He whirled on her, eyes flashing, and she raised a hand to forestall him. "He is my friend. He is family to me. Can you not see? Our marriage would have worked because we are comfortable with one another. We know and respect one another."

"Then you already regret—"

"You cannot compare because there is nothing to compare. I fell in love with you, Jack. You. Passionately. I've never experienced the like. I would not have felt the same for Brett. I am fond of him, just as you pointed out in Charles Town. Do you see? My feelings have nothing to do with riches."

"You say that now, but you can't know how you would have felt later. You made it clear I had to give up sailing. How was I to care for you? The sea was my only option, but the thought of leaving you was more than I could bear. I had to find those damned emeralds so I would never have to leave you again."

"That is not precisely true, is it? Your brother died without issue, leaving you the rightful heir. You are a viscount and have been most of your life. You would not have had to leave me."

He put his hands on his hips, face flushed with exasperation. "How the devil was I to know that?"

"If you'd behaved honorably, you would have learned it soon enough."

"Hell." He turned away from her, muttering

beneath his breath.

Although she did not wish to, she had to ask. "What if you had not found the emeralds? What then? Would you have given me to Brett?"

"No." He swung back to her, eyes blazing with fire and smoke and fury. "I shall never give you up."

"Then what would you have done? Kept me prisoner until—" A sudden thought struck. "Where did they come from? The emeralds. Are they stolen?"

"Aye, they are from the mines in New Granada. Taken at least twenty years ago while we were at war with Spain, so you needn't worry over legalities."

"Your friend Travers stole them from the Spanish?"

"I've no idea who stole them. Travers bought the map from a…" He hesitated. "Prostitute." She rolled her eyes. After all she'd been through, he thought *that* would put her in a swoon?

It all sounded so farcical to her. Another chapter of Robinson Crusoe. "How very auspicious for you to come upon a dying man and appropriate his wealth."

Jack stiffened. "Fortunate?" His voice was raw. "To discover my friend bleeding to death in an alley? I knew nothing of emeralds when I found him and took him out to sea to die as he wished. He informed me while his life slipped away on the deck of the *Lass*. How little you must esteem me, Celia, to think I rejoiced in his passing."

His words stung as sharply as if he'd slapped her with them. God above, what had made her say such a horrible thing? Her voice shook with contrition. "I beg you forgive me, Jackson." She placed a hand on his chest. "'Twas my temper speaking. I did not mean it."

He pulled her into his arms. She buried her face against his chest and breathed him in, his essence warm and safe and comfortable. A contradiction to the bitter emotions roiling inside her.

"'Tis just that I am so angry. And hurt. I cannot reconcile my emotions. 'Tis ugly inside me." Nor could Celia understand how in spite of her anger, she still wanted to climb back into the bunk with him.

Perhaps she was a wanton.

"I am to meet with your father tomorrow." His chest rumbled against her cheek. "May I still speak with him?"

She stepped out of his arms. "'Tisn't as if we can change what has occurred between us." His jaw clenched. He did not like her answer.

"You sound as if you are settling now."

"I am simply speaking the truth." Though it hurt, she turned away from him. In part because she could not bear the wounded look on his face, but mostly because she felt like throwing herself into his arms and weeping like a child.

Blasted man.

"I should like to return to the dock now. We have kept Rianna and Brett waiting long enough." She picked up her stays. "Papa will likely come searching for me soon."

He grasped her arm. "We must resolve this matter between us."

She shrugged him off. "I've much to think on and little else to say at present. Take me home."

"Celia…" He dug his fingers in his hair, his frustration with her evident.

"Do keep in mind I can swim to the dock, Jack. You can no longer control my life."

Chapter Twenty-Five

Robert Breckenridge's office chairs were surprisingly comfortable, doubtless designed to set a man at ease whilst his pockets were let. The space contained dark, somber colors; heavy furniture; and thick carpets. No fancy scrollwork or gilding for this man of commerce. The room bespoke his wealth and personality more for what it lacked than what it flaunted.

From the windows, the view stretched beyond the buildings on the street to the waterfront beyond, allowing Midas to observe his domain. Jack cared little for the man's wealth.

He'd come to take his daughter.

They assessed one another in silence. Though shorter in stature, Celia's father was solidly built, the blacksmith's son evident in his stature. He wore costly clothing, dark and staid like his office. Clearly the man disdained frivolity, which Jack found refreshing if somewhat surprising, considering his humble beginnings. Like Jack, he forbore a peruke and wore his thin, dark hair clubbed in a queue.

Breckenridge's demeanor gave little of his thoughts away—doubtless why he was successful in trade. The ruthless ones never did.

Ensconced in the enemy's territory, Jack felt a great longing for the comfort of his sword. He'd left it behind, surmising Celia would consider him arriving armed in the same light as strangling her betrothed.

Unreasonable creatures, women.

By nature, he was not a patient man, but vowed to be in this instance as his future happiness rested on the outcome of this meeting. His father-in-law-to-be leaned back in his chair and rested his hands on the arms, his cool gaze the same shade of blue as his youngest daughter.

Ah. The eyes invariably betrayed one's emotions. Jack felt more at ease already.

"Though I shall forever be in your debt for rescuing my daughter at sea, I find your behavior thereafter deplorable, and shall not forgive your keeping her from her family." Jack was curious which particular behavior the man found deplorable. As this was Celia's father, a host of crimes could be laid at his doorstep.

He thought it best not to ask.

"I suspect you would like an apology from me, sir, but as I am not a hypocrite nor in the least sorry, I shall have to disappoint you. In fact, given the same circumstances, there is little I would change."

Breckenridge's face froze, likely because his eyes had frosted over. Jack admired his control and soldiered on, determined to deal with Celia's father in a forthright manner, though it would hardly endear him to the man.

"I was unable to give her up, even to her family." He felt his lips curve. "She became my life, you see. I could not bring her home until I was certain I had won her. Even then, I feared she'd see her Mr. Kensington and change her mind."

"Then you do not know my daughter very well,

Captain." Her father spat the word "captain" as if it were an expletive. All in all, Jack thought they were starting out swimmingly. "If you did, you would understand she's a steadfast sort. Knows her own mind. I daresay if she pledged her troth to you, she meant it. Her loyalties are not easily swayed." Here the man bristled with challenge. "Unless warranted."

"She changed her mind about Kensington," Jack pointed out.

"Bah." Breckenridge waved a dismissive hand. "I am the one who pledged her to young Brett, or rather his father and I did. Charles and I have long suspected they might choose otherwise. They are far too similar in temperament."

"Would that you had told them," Jack groused. "I have hated that man from the very moment she uttered his name. When I think of the number of times I wanted to sail across the Atlantic and call the bounder out. What a twisted piece of irony to find myself related to him. My own nephew."

"Aye." Her father chuckled. "Charles and I've had a good laugh over that." He appeared to recall he did not care for Jack and sobered. "You needn't worry over Brett. He's hopelessly in love with Rianna, who is doing her very best to make the boy miserable. Unlike her elder sister, my youngest hasn't the vaguest idea what she wants."

"I pray after all that has come to pass you will consent to our wedding."

He shrugged. "'Tis not my consent you require. My daughter is terribly unhappy at present. I lay the blame at your feet, sir. She is the one who must tolerate you, not I. Therefore, the decision is hers."

Jack blew out a breath. “I feared you would say that. As independent as you’ve made your daughters with their investments, I expected no less. Nevertheless, Celia insisted I petition you for her hand.”

“She told you about her funds?” Her father’s gaze hardened with suspicion. Bleeding fool. What did the man think? Jack had tortured the information from her? A delightful vision of Celia bound and naked popped into his head. He prayed her preternatural abilities hadn’t come from her father. The man might have a pistol hidden somewhere.

“Aye, she told me, which is another reason why I had to seek my own fortune. As a result, she’s angry with me. I ask you, what man wishes to come groveling to his intended’s family when he hasn’t sixpence left to scratch with?”

Breckenridge’s brows shot up his forehead. “Surely you do not expect me to answer that.”

“No.” Jack slumped in his seat. “Damn it all, Robert, I do not want her money or yours. Don’t you see? If I hadn’t funds of my own, how would either of you know for certain ’twas not her purse I was after? I’ve my pride—an excess of it according to your daughter—but I love her more than life. She is my beating heart.” He looked away and swallowed. Be damned if he’d lay the organ out for this man to dissect.

“All I want is her. Keep the dowry. Add it to her sister’s.” Jack snorted. “You shall need every advantage to marry that one off.” He leaned forward and pinned her father with a look of forged steel. “Be warned. Celia is mine now. I fought for her, and I won her, and I will never give her up.”

Her father fell back in his chair as if he’d been

shot. *Oh, now I've done it. He'll hie Celia off to a convent the moment we part company.*

"Given the circumstances, I should think you'd want us to wed quickly." Jack cleared his throat. "Her reputation must be in tatters."

"Oh aye, she's ruined, *Jack*." Apparently the man had not appreciated Jack using his given name. "Between you, the pirates, and that damned Abrams harpy, she has seldom left the house since she returned."

"Abrams? The captain's wife? The woman who drowned herself when the pirates took the *Essex*?"

"Nay, she did not drown," Breckenridge sneered. "More's the pity. Was discovered bobbing on the ocean. 'Tis shocking the ship's captain did not throw the bitch back once he discovered what he'd netted."

"Doubtless she recounted the attack to all and sundry," Jack guessed.

"And embellished what she did not know until my daughter was either vilely assaulted and her dead body discarded into the sea, or sold as a slave to the damn Turks for their pleasure." Robert's mouth curved in a grim little smile. "Rianna called the woman out."

"Did she?" Jack felt his temperature rise at the injustice done to Celia. "You did not allow it?"

"Her mother would not. Said she'd only paint the woman's claims up fine and sully her sister's memory further. Likely she was correct. Still. One desires satisfaction."

How Celia had suffered at the hands of others. Jack's blood hissed for retribution. "I shall handle the matter. No one slanders my Celia and escapes unscathed. I care not that the bleeding viper is a woman."

A gleam entered Robert's eyes. Regardless of Jack's own vengeful thoughts, it made him uneasy. "If you thought my daughter angry with you before, what do you suppose her reaction will be when she learns of your plans?"

An excellent point, damn the man. "Perhaps you would consider keeping the matter between the two of us?"

"Oh, no." Her father laughed. "You'll not involve me in your schemes, sir. I should suffer my wife's censure as well as my daughter's. But you needn't concern yourself. The woman has been taken care of." He drummed his fingers on the arm of his chair and smiled that little half-smile again. "I suspect her sister is to blame."

"Aye?" Jack was growing rather fond of his new sister-in-law, though he shouldn't care to admit it.

"Shortly after we met the woman in London, a rumor circulated about town. Marlena and I had returned home by then, but Rianna stayed on with her aunt and uncle for a time to visit friends. Someone put it about that Mrs. Abrams suffered a disease of the mind and her husband feared she might do herself harm if left alone. Word had it he planned to intern her at Bethlehem Hospital when he returned to port."

Jack's lips curved. "Diabolical. Celia says Rianna is her father's daughter." Robert acknowledged his offhand compliment with a nod. "Where is the woman now?"

"No one knows. Seems she has disappeared. Apparently she has a daughter, but fears the story may be true and thus the daughter will carry out her father's wishes."

"Nevertheless, we ought to marry to dispel any rumors that might surface now that Celia is returned. I've a special license from Governor Glen." Jack raised a brow. "You will give your approval, will you not? Your daughter requires it before we wed."

"She said as much?"

"Aye, she did. We'd already be married if she had not been so stubborn on the matter."

"I'll not stand in your way, but we shall have to enquire whether the license is valid here."

Jack was beginning to understand how salmon felt when swimming upstream. " 'Not stand in my way' can hardly be construed as an endorsement."

Breckenridge shrugged. "I do not know you, sir, and as I've grievances against you, I'll not commit to more. I suggest we speak with your brother-in-law. Charles' brother, Earl Blackhurst, is an acquaintance of Bishop Sherlock. The man's a zealot, but I suspect Blackhurst will enlist his aid."

Bloody hell, he did not wish to delay. "We should marry immediately. If questions arise later, we shall ask this bishop to intervene then."

"Why such urgency?" Robert's face mottled, and his eyes snapped blue fire, surprising Jack. He had sailed across the bleeding Atlantic to retrieve Celia. Of course he wanted to wed immediately. The man well knew of their attraction. It was not as if he could confess he desperately wanted her in his bed.

"Is she with child?"

Jack blinked. "Child?"

Blimey. He'd not given any thought to the consequences of their actions. He'd been so intent on the act—the intensely pleasurable act—itself. "A baby," he murmured and as the idea took hold, his heart swelled with delight. "Imagine, Robert, a darling little Celia with big green eyes and mink tresses. I should be in love from the very moment I hold her in my arms. We shall fill the nursery with them."

Robert shook his head. Clearly he thought Jack a bleeding fool. Aye, they were definitely bonding. "Do you intend to give her a choice in the matter?"

"Certainly, I—" His euphoria evaporated. "She's rather angry with me at present. I imagine she will—" He stood. They wasted time debating the matter. Celia would suffer much finger counting and censure if a child arrived too early. Jack could not let that happen. "Come. We will speak with my brother-in-law about the license." He thought of his beautiful, petulant bride-to-be. "And we had best be quick about it before I do something else to anger her."

Robert followed him out the door, chuckling. "I vow we shan't die of boredom around here."

****

With the sun hugging the horizon, the tree-lined road was peaceful, almost idyllic, were it not for the tempest thundering along at Jack's side. This wrath of Celia's could wear on a man. How many times could one exhaust the same old arguments?

"Neither of the letters I wrote to my family reached them." *Ah.* A new dispute.

"Aye?" He thought it wise to conserve his words.

Celia turned to him and studied his face. She knew him too well, this prickly woman. "Were you, by chance, aware of this fact?"

"Aware?" he asked, prolonging the inevitable in

the same way one delayed having a tooth drawn. She turned her gaze away from him, as if she could not bear to watch him answer. He blew out a breath. "Aye, I knew."

Her spine stiffened and her gait changed. Short, angry strides propelled her forward.

Jack followed in silence and watched birds flit, squirrels chatter, Celia fume. They rounded a bend and Seaview sat off in the distance. He wished it and the rest of Cornwall to the devil.

She whipped about to face him. "*Why* did my letters not reach my family?"

He stopped and said patiently, "The first one you sent went down on a two-masted snow called the *Ladybird*. It sank in the second hurricane." 'Twas how he thought of them: the devastating first and the preposterous second. She crossed her arms and tapped her foot, waiting for him to elaborate. He grew weary of her attitude.

"Why did you not tell me?"

"What would it have served?" He spread his arms wide in frustration. "The entire city was in a shambles and you'd taken the news of the Bedon's deaths badly. I knew you would write again, so why burden you with another tragedy? All hands were lost on that snow, 'twas more death and destruction to contemplate."

"And the other? What did you do with it?"

Anger ignited a low flame in Jack's belly. Deuce take the woman. He bloody well resented her accusations. He kept his voice low, dangerous. A warning. "Nothing."

Unmindful and reckless, she persisted, "If that is so, then why did it not arrive? And how did you know it had not?"

"Smitty found it in Jenkins' desk," he answered, his voice curt. "We assume he intercepted it from the mail rider, though we've no way of knowing for certain."

Color flooded Celia's cheeks and she looked away. Did she feel shame for accusing him?

By God, she ought to. He grabbed her elbows, compelling her to look at him. "I had no idea the letter had been stolen. I suspect Jenkins hoped to find mention of the emeralds in your correspondence. 'Tis the only explanation that makes sense."

Her gaze dropped and she stared at the buttons of his coat. "Jenkins did say I turned a pretty phrase. It confused me, but I thought he referred to my speech. Which was not at all pretty in the moment, but as the observation came from him, I did not ponder the matter." Her gaze returned to his. "Still, you did not tell me."

"No, I did not." An idiotic response but temper would not allow "a pretty phrase" from Jack either. Where had the woman he'd fallen in love with gone? He sorely missed her.

"For heaven's sake, are you going to tell me why?"

He closed his eyes and blew out a long breath before he answered, letting out a little steam. "To what end? You were angry with me for leaving you. I had no control over what became of your letter. What was done was done."

"What you are saying is you feared I should become more determined to return home rather than wait for you to finish your treasure hunting. Therefore, you let me believe my family had received it. Is that not so?"

The little witch. How bleeding self-righteous she'd become. "You knew they had not. Do not dare tell me otherwise. You and your damned intuition. I am not to blame for your woes, Celia."

She pulled her arms free and stalked off. They reached the drive to Seaview and she started up it.

"Damned if you'll keep avoiding me, madam." Jack caught up with her, as angry now as she. "Running off whenever the discussion is not to your liking solves nothing."

"All this *bleeding* deceit, Jack." She spun around to face him, voice shaking with fury. Oh, she was in a fine temper now. "You manipulate me and treat me like a child in order to shape me to your liking. I wished to come home. But you prevented me. You lied and kept secrets to force me to stay." She tossed her head, color high, hands balled into fists. "Your arrogance and jealousy have ruined my life."

Shock rooted Jack's feet to the lane. She could not have said what he'd heard. Not his Celia. The woman he loved beyond all else. Rage simmered below his skin and hissed through his pores. "I ruined your life?"

"Aye." Twin chips of green ice flashed at him. "They all went on without me because they thought me dead. But then I arrived, hale and whole, to a different world than when I left." She swallowed and continued in barely a whisper. "I do not belong here anymore."

He wanted to shake her. "You spent nearly a year in Bermuda before we met, if you will recall. Did you truly expect everyone's lives to simply halt while you were away? How utterly conceited of you, Celia."

"Conceited," she choked.

"Aye, and selfish. I had a life as well. Men depending on me. Men who had a right to their share of the gems. Was I to make them all wait? An entire crew? For one woman?"

Her face turned away from him. "Perhaps I wanted to be first. To mean more to you than your men. Was that too much to ask?" She faced him again, her tone reproachful. "Why did I not matter?"

Bitter gall burned Jack's throat, searing the back of his tongue. Her words stunned him.

"Pity Celia," he spat. "She has a man who loves her more than life. A man who tried to move heaven and earth to be worthy of her."

"A man who lies and manipulates her to get exactly what he wants." She tossed her head.

It was as though someone had doused his rage with a bucket of cold water, chilling him to the bone. He knew he should stop but could not make his tongue obey. "A man who fought to defend her." His voice turned hoarse. "A man who fought to win her."

"Through trickery and deceit?" Her eyes flashed with scorn. "I fear you have lost, sir." She turned her back on him.

Jack stared at those stiff shoulders, her rigid posture, and his heart keeled over. Plummeted like a severed jib to his feet. He hadn't any more fight left in him. "Then perhaps you need time to restore your life. To belong again. I regret I have made you unhappy. 'Twas never my intent." Although her back was to him, he bowed. "I will leave."

She said nothing.

And so he walked away.

****

Waves swelled higher and higher, and higher still, building to a magnificent crescendo before crashing against the rocks. Celia's heart beat in tune with the passions of the sea, her emotions swelling toward their own fateful plunge.

She wanted to be out there. To stand on the cliff with the wind and salt spray in her face. To imagine herself at sea, far away from pain and heartache.

To a world she understood.

Hurrying to her bedroom, she snatched up a shawl and bonnet and rushed back down the stairs, nearly colliding with Rianna at the bottom.

"Goodness, sister. Where are you off to in such a hurry?" Rianna held her hand and searched her face, frowning at whatever she saw. "Devil take the knave. You've been in a brown study since he arrived. I say good riddance, though we should be fortunate indeed were he to return from whence he came."

" 'Good riddance?' " Celia repeated. "Whatever do you mean?"

"Brett's uncle is sailing for London tomorrow. Did you not know?"

Her hand rose to cover her mouth and she dropped down on the step. He was leaving her. Again. As he said he would. This time 'twas her fault. She had pushed him away.

"Come now," Rianna chided. "'Tis for the best. We shall all be relieved once he is gone."

Their mother entered the foyer and spied them on the landing. Her gaze narrowed on her eldest and she frowned. "Celia? What is it, dear?"

"He is leaving me." Her voice was hardly able to scrape the words.

"Leaving?" Mama sat down next to her. "Where is he going?"

"To London," Rianna answered. "To visit his uncle and his estate."

Mama wrapped Celia in a hug. "'Tis understandable is it not? Surely you are not surprised he wishes to see his home."

"But he is sailing without me."

"Well, you've not been yourself lately, dear. Perhaps 'tis for the best."

For the best? How could they think it when her heart was shredding to pieces?

Why would they not, she admitted, when she'd been acting the shrew?

How could he leave her? How could he do it again?

She had been difficult, true, but no less than he deserved. He had manipulated her and hurt her and she wanted to punish him. To push him away so he would know how it felt to not matter enough. She had done a jolly good job of it, apparently. But she did not want Jack to leave. She could not bear losing him again.

"No."

"I beg your pardon, dear?" Mama looked startled. Celia had said it rather forcefully.

"'Tis not for the best."

"I must disagree," Rianna said predictably. "The man is a cad."

Celia jumped to her feet. "He has it all now, hasn't he? The *Bonny Lass*. A bleeding fortune in emeralds." She swiped the tears from her face. "My broken heart."

"It is not my doing," Rianna said quickly when their mother gasped at Celia's language. "She learned it from those tars she sailed with."

Fire scorched Celia's cheeks from the anger blazing through her. "By damned I'll not have it."

Mama shot Rianna a repressive glare.

She scowled at her sister. "Do behave, Celia. You are provoking Mama's ire with me when I've done naught to deserve it."

"Leave me, will he?" Celia turned to her mother and sister, arms crossed in defiance, toe tapping out a battle hymn. "We shall bloody well see about that."

Chapter Twenty-Six

Careening up the drive to Kensington Manor, Celia hung out the window of the landau, urging a harried Banes to hurry. The man drove as if he'd entered his dotage, for heaven's sake. Perhaps if she jumped on one of the horses she might whip them up faster.

They rounded the bend and Banes sawed on the reins, bringing the carriage to a teeth-jarring halt. She threw open the door and jumped down without aid of a step, slamming the door on her mother's moan.

Emily Kensington sailed out the front door of the gray stone manner before Celia reached it, trailing behind a footman carrying a large trunk.

"What is that?"

"Oh, just a few things my brother forgot." Mrs. Kensington marched down the steps of the portico in the footman's wake, leaving Celia to catch up. "He was a bit distraught when he left, dear," she added, gentling her voice.

Guilt stabbed at her. She looked away and encountered Brett bounding down the steps.

"I say, Mother. Isn't that my trunk?"

Emily turned a bright smile on her son. "Oh no, dear. However it does resemble yours." Although Celia could easily hear, she added sotto voce, "Marlena and I've packed a few gifts inside."

Gritting her teeth, she followed, impatient to be on

their way. "I do not know that it will fit, Mrs. Kensington. Mother packed an extra trunk as well."

"Oh, we shall make do," Emily assured her. "Clarence here is a wizard with trunks."

This hardly seemed necessary as time was of the essence. "Come, we must hurry," Celia urged. "Captain Taylor awaits."

Brett dropped the step on the landau and held out his arm, handing Celia and his mother in before stepping up behind them. Emily squeezed next to Rianna and Mama, leaving the seat opposite to Celia and Brett. Banes took care of the step and closed the door.

"What is he doing here?" her sister demanded petulantly.

"You cannot imagine I should miss this?" Brett chuckled. "Not even you are that cruel, Rianna."

She bristled, and Celia had an overwhelming desire to kick them both out of the carriage. She hadn't the patience, not when her heart was about to thrash right out of her chest. "Please. We must focus on our purpose."

Mama placed a quelling hand on Rianna's knee. "Of course, dear. This is your day."

Rianna threw herself back against the seat with a huff.

Celia shot her a look of gratitude, though she had not actually relented. She would simply bide her time.

Her sister sent her an arch look and a puckish smile. Brett shifted uncomfortably in the seat next to Celia and cleared his throat. Rianna's smile widened. Celia might have felt pity for him were she not thoroughly disgusted with men at present.

Particularly from his family.

They entered town and Banes predictably slowed the carriage. She leaned out the window to check their progress. “Papa must have the slowest horses in all of Christendom. I vow the smithy shod them with anchors instead of shoes.”

Ten minutes later they pulled up to the wharf where the *Bonny Lass*’s empty berth greeted them. All of Celia’s extremities froze and she could not breathe.

Rianna leapt to her feet and clasped Celia’s face in her hands. “Look at me, Ce. He sails to London, not the colonies. Calm yourself. He has not gone far.” Her brusque tone broke through the terror clogging Celia’s throat. She swallowed and nodded.

“There, you see?” Her sister released her and pointed out the window. “The *Nighthawk* is prepared to leave. Everything is just as you planned.”

Mama looked to where Rianna pointed and lifted a shaking hand to her throat. The carriage ride alone had bleached her complexion.

Mrs. Kensington leaned forward to clasp her hand. “Marlena, are you certain you wish to go? I should be happy to look after your girls for you.”

“Nonsense.” Mama pushed her shoulders back. “I shall be fine.” The group inside the carriage looked doubtful. “Quite fine,” she squeaked.

Brett jumped down and helped the women alight. Celia’s father left Charles Kensington and Reverend Baxendale at the dock and strode up to great them.

“Marlena, my dear, I must insist—”

“Save your breath, Robert.” Mama marched past him.

Papa shook his head in resignation and took each

of his daughters' arms. Brett followed with his mother.

Captain Taylor waved to them from the deck of the ship. "Ahoy, good friends. Come aboard and let us be off."

The trunks were unloaded from the carriage and hauled aboard. Emily and Charles started up the gangplank. Perspiration dotted the reverend's forehead, his face exceedingly pale. Celia shared an uneasy glance with Rianna. He looked ready to bolt.

Her sister rushed forward to take his arm. "Good day, Reverend. I've a story to share. Have you heard about the time young Timothy put a frog down his sister's back?" She waved her hand as she steered him along, further distracting him. "Faith, but it all went hurly-burly rather quickly." She glanced over her shoulder at Celia.

Thank you, Celia mouthed. Rianna winked and turned back, chatting gaily as she maneuvered the good reverend onto the *Nighthawk.*

Brett took her mother's elbow and escorted her up next, much to her father's dismay.

"She will regret this," Papa said gravely. "*I* will regret this."

Celia laid her head on his shoulder. "You needn't have come, Papa. I know what I'm about."

"Wouldn't miss it," her father echoed Brett. He held out his arm. "Shall we?"

They started up, but she stopped and ran back to the carriage. "Banes, the bags in the boot. We must have them."

Banes looked pained, but he called to a sailor and they hauled the heavy bags out and up the dock. Celia took her father's arm again.

"Come Papa. Let us teach that man the ropes."

****

Jack leaned against the helm and stared morosely at the coastline off to port. He pitied his crew. Though excited to be sailing to London where all manner of delights could be purchased, his black scowl had dampened their spirits. Try as he might, he could not lift his own. Not even for their benefit.

"Sail ho!" the lookout called from above.

Spinnakers lifted a glass as Jack had no interest in letting go of the wheel. The *Bonny Lass's* navigator left for a space then returned and nudged Jack aside, placing the glass in his hand.

"Ye ought to go have a look-see." He gestured with his chin over the stern. "We've a ship bearing down upon us."

"Aye?" Jack went to the starboard rail and lifted the glass. The ship was indeed coming on fast, every inch of her canvass spread. She looked oddly familiar. "Can you make her?" he called to the lookout.

"Mayhap she's the *Nighthawk*, Cap'n."

Odd. He spoke with Captain Taylor only yesterday. The man claimed he sailed for Liverpool three days hence. What the deuce was he doing out here in the English Channel? And with the whole nine yards up?

Celia. Uneasiness whispered through Jack's veins. What could be so tearingly urgent that Taylor would head east when he meant to sail west? His mind raced with all manner of morbid possibilities, his pulse rushing to keep pace.

"Ease off those port tacks!"

****

The *Nighthawk* fired a warning shot.

Unnecessary really, as the *Bonny Lass* had slowed sufficiently to overtake. Still, protocol ought to be maintained.

Celia settled at the bow, hands clammy, limbs wobbly, waiting for Jack to react. She lifted a glass borrowed from the helmsman.

His crew scrambled through the rigging. By degrees, the *Bonny Lass* slowed to a halt. Sunlight glinted from a spyglass on the other ship.

He watched her.

Swarms of butterflies took flight in her stomach. She glanced over her shoulder to her mother, who held the wheel while the helmsman stood alongside her. She still had a slight tinge of green to her, which was a vast improvement to her previous pallor. Captain Taylor had been correct when he suggested taking the wheel would help calm her stomach.

She actually appeared to be enjoying herself, surprisingly. Perhaps Mama would embark on a new career. Her father lounged with Charles Kensington a few feet away and watched over her mother with a scowl affixed to his face. Perhaps not.

Poor Reverend Baxendale had not fared so well. He leaned against the fo'c'sle, holding a bucket and his stomach in misery. Nothing had helped him, though the day could not be more perfect for sailing. Calm seas and frisky winds had carried them swiftly to the *Bonny Lass's* heels.

Papa would have to be very generous with the reverend.

The *Nighthawk* closed in, the helmsman taking over from Mama and bringing her port side dangerously close to the *Bonny Lass's* starboard as they came abreast of her.

Jack waited, his fist clamped tight in the ratline, brows drawn together with concern. Joy burst from Celia's heart, leaping boundlessly beneath her breast. She herded it back in its cage. She'd taken the wind out of his sails, aye. But now she meant to bring him up to scratch.

"Ahoy, Captain Beaumont," Captain Taylor called jovially, as he considered the entire endeavor a great lark. "We mean to board you, sir. Have we permission?"

"Aye. Make way," Jack called to his men. The *Nighthawk* dropped anchor and threw grappling hooks to the *Bonny Lass*.

****

Celia dropped to her knees beside the port rail and took up a sword from one of the bags Banes had brought in the carriage boot.

Rianna joined her. "I should prefer a pistol," she said as she selected a sword. "'Twould be ever so much easier to carry."

"Nay," Celia disagreed vehemently. "Pistols are far too dangerous. You've no idea when they'll go off. 'Tis how I shot Jenkins." The area around her grew silent. She looked up from her sword to encounter ten pairs of incredulous eyes focused on her.

"For heaven's sake, I did not kill him. I merely wounded him." Her mouth tilted up in a wry smile. "Jack killed him."

Her mother looked at her as if she'd born a stranger.

Rianna's eyes held new respect.

Her father grunted.

Celia addressed a young crewman with waves of strawberry hair and a host of freckles scattered over his face. "Would you be so kind as to carry my sword across for me, sir?"

He tugged a forelock. "'Twould be my pleasure, miss."

She took a deep, sustaining breath—for courage—and stepped up to select a rope. "Let us be about it, then." The crewman took her sword and helped her onto the bulwark before climbing up beside her.

Rianna chose a rope for herself and Brett one next to her.

"If you are determined to wield that cumbersome thing, at least allow me to carry it for you, Rianna."

"Absolutely not," she replied haughtily and waved him away. "I shall carry my own sword, thank you."

Celia pushed off and swung over to where Jack stood waiting to catch her. The young sailor landed at the rail beside her and jumped to the deck with her sword.

A high-pitched squeal came from behind, followed by a splash.

"Oh, good show, Rianna," Brett congratulated. "All the best swordsmen drop their weapons into the bleeding ocean when they head into battle. Much more sporting that way."

"A great pity, indeed," she returned snidely. "As I'd meant to skewer *you* with it."

Jack grabbed Celia by the waist and dropped her to her feet on the deck. His hands clasped her shoulders, and he searched her face. "What is the matter? Why are you all here?"

She shrugged out of his embrace, though God help

her, ’twas the most difficult thing she had ever done. She turned to the young seaman and took her sword from him.

Curious, the *Bonny Lass’s* crew circled a few feet behind their captain and looked on. Several nodded greetings to her.

“Hello,” she said brightly. “So good to see you all again.”

“Celia,” Jack prodded. His face looked haggard. ’Twas evident he had not slept well, if at all.

Well, neither had she.

She stood before him with her sword tip resting on the deck while the rest of her party swung over to join her, leaving only a few men behind to tend the *Nighthawk.* The newcomers lined up on either side of her, each brandishing some form of weaponry. All but Rianna, who’d donated hers to the sea. Then again, of all of them, she was the least likely to need one.

Jack’s men were unimpressed with the weapons they carried. She might have been gravely insulted if not for the fact that they all trusted her.

Pity them.

Jack was fast losing his patience. “Cel—”

She raised her sword and pointed it at his chest. Her cohorts flourished theirs as well.

His head went back and swiveled from side to side, taking in their arms. “What the deuce is going on?”

Daft man. Celia bristled. “I realize we are less violent than most commonplace pirates, but something must be said for orderliness. You will note we’ve not damaged your ship, sir, which renders us a more valuable prize.”

“What?” Jack shook his head, struggling to

comprehend.

"Heavens, Jack," Celia chided. "One would think you'd know a pirate attack when you see one. I am here for the emeralds. And the *Bonny Lass*."

Wide grins split across the faces of Jack's men. Celia could not help but smile back. They nudged one another, anticipating their captain's reaction.

He looked over her motley crew. Not the typical gang of ruffians one expected to be sure, but still.

"Have you all gone mad?" He rounded on Captain Taylor. "How on earth did she talk you into this?"

Taylor shrugged. "She offered me an enormous sum to bring her out here. Staggering really. Honestly, Beaumont, who could resist?" He chuckled and lifted a tankard to his lips, his sword held loosely at his flank.

Rianna gawked at him with undisguised admiration, but then Captain Taylor had swung over with both hands full and likely hadn't spilled a drop.

Jack scrubbed his hands over his face. "Celia, I comprehend you are angry with me, but you cannot sail out here and pirate us."

She rolled her eyes. Honestly, men could be so obtuse. "I just did."

"She has ye there, Cap'n." Rory snickered.

Jack shot him a nasty look. "Aye? Well, 'tis your emeralds she means to steal as well." He turned back to her. "Or am I mistaken?"

"Oh, no," she agreed hastily. "I shouldn't think it proper to pilfer only a portion. If one plans to be a pirate, it must be all or nothing."

" 'All or nothing.' " He sighed and massaged his forehead.

"I plan ta buy me a new suit of clothes with my

share, Miss Celia," Ollie said.

"Oh, how lovely, Ollie."

He beamed at her.

"'Tis not 'lovely, Ollie'," Jack snapped. "You cannot buy a new suit with empty pockets."

"Oh." Ollie looked chastened. "I should like to keep me share if ye'd be so kind, Miss. Ye're welcome to the Cap'n's, howbeit." A chorus of "ayes" and vigorous nods approved his suggestion.

Jack turned a black scowl on his men and stared until they dropped their heads and shuffled their feet in chagrin.

Celia took exception. She was the one in control here after all. "I suppose we might reach an accord. I shall need a crew to sail my ship for me. What say I take the captain's share and allow you men to keep yours if you promise to sail for me? We shall consider it a sign-on bonus."

"Oh, very good, Celia," Rianna approved. "One must be willing to negotiate to find an equitable solution for all parties concerned."

"Aye," her father agreed, proud of his youngest's insight. Jack shot him a peevish look. He laughed and nudged Charles in the ribs. "Your brother-in-law is as fusty as you are, old man."

"You'll not lay his sour temper at my door," Charles grumbled. "I'm saddled with him through marriage. Complain to my wife."

"He is having a trying day, dear," Emily defended predictably.

Celia watched Jack's face during their family's banter. He was not amused.

"What say you, men?" She addressed his crew.

"Are you with me?"

"I'm fond o' me emeralds," Rory said.

"She's a good sort," Deeds added.

"Aye," Crawley chimed in and snickered. "We shall spin a good yarn from this one."

Jack's face turned more thunderous with each man's words. Aye, she'd spiked his guns all right.

Spinnakers shrugged. "Ye'll do."

"Aye." Smitty stuck his pipe in his mouth.

His expression incredulous, Jack rounded on Smitty. "What the devil? Are ye daft, man?"

Celia waved her sword over his chest. "You'll not speak to my crew in such a fashion, sir."

"Do be careful, dear," her mother cautioned. "It looks rather sharp."

Emily lowered her sword to fuss with her bonnet. "I shouldn't wish to stitch up my brother so soon after he's arrived."

Charles snorted. "Ye'd faint dead away before ye stuck a needle in his hide."

Emily blanched. "Don't be vulgar, Charles."

"Where is your sword?" Jack demanded of Brett. "Do you not wish to duel with me for stealing your woman?"

"You stole nothing from me," Brett said, his gaze meeting Rianna's. She bristled, but quickly lost her aplomb and looked away.

Jack's attention returned to Celia. His gaze raked over her, ignoring the sword she pointed at him completely, the bounder.

"If you take my emeralds, how shall I restore my ancestral home?" His voice was soft, for her alone, and her heart greedily lapped it up. *Fool.*

She pushed the sword tip over his heart, but still he showed no reaction. His arms remained calmly at his sides. His eyes never left hers. Blasted man. “I shall be very generous with your pin money.”

Snickers from his crew and their families followed her pronouncement.

“My pin money?” Jack closed his eyes for a brief moment. Her sword lifted and lowered as he inhaled and exhaled gustily. “We’re to be married then?”

“Aye, you scoundrel. You’ll not slip the leash again.” She gestured to the helm where the *Nighthawk’s* crew had draped Reverend Baxendale over the wheel. The poor man looked as if he’d been placed in the stocks. “I’ve brought the reverend.”

Jack’s eyes widened and his startled gaze scanned the assemblage. *Ha!* She finally had the pleasure of shocking him. “Here? Now?”

“Aye,” she announced triumphantly. “Here. Now.”

Their eyes locked and his features softened in the face of her bravado. His arms rose and he made as if to step forward. “Celia, you needn’t—”

She shoved the tip of the sword more firmly against his chest. He looked down at the weapon piercing his waistcoat and scowled at her. “Blast it, woman, you are ripping my clothes again.”

“Again?” her mother murmured. “Oh, dear.”

Celia tossed her head. “This is how we shall proceed. The reverend will speak, and you and I shall answer.” He opened his mouth to argue, but she cut him off. “Those are the only responses required of you, else you will remain silent.”

She gave the sword another infinitesimal push. Not enough to injure him—she had plans for that magnificent body later—but sufficient to make her point clear.

His pewter eyes lit with a scalding glare.

Undaunted, hers flashed a warning back. "And if you value your precious clothing, Jackson, your answers had best be in the affirmative. Now, if you please, move. Slowly."

She forced him at sword-point to the helm in deference to the reverend's delicate condition. "He has a special license from Governor Glen of South Carolina, Reverend. His brother-in-law, Mr. Kensington, will give it to you when we are through here. You may proceed."

Reverend Baxendale looked to Jack for confirmation. He remained stubbornly silent. Apparently, she would have to slash a button or two off his waistcoat to force his compliance. The reverend nodded and cleared his throat.

Celia glanced between the two men. *What the devil had she missed?*

"Gather round," the reverend called, his voice threadbare. Everyone moved to stand behind her and Jack. "Take hands," he instructed.

Jack held out his hands.

Celia grew suspicious.

She rested the sword point over his heart and locked eyes with him. "He shall not touch me until the vows are spoken."

His eyes flashed silver at her words, but he remained silent. The ceremony proceeded, her mother and Emily sniffling into their handkerchiefs, Jack's crew blessedly silent for a change.

Though unnecessary, Celia prodded each of his

responses with a sight jab of her sword. She rather enjoyed being in control.

Jack's voice was calm and steady as he spoke his vows.

Her eyes blurred. Lord save her, this was her wedding, and she was *forcing* her groom to marry her. Surely, she'd have to serve a penance for her actions.

So be it, then. Jack was hers for the taking, and she was bleeding well taking.

Perhaps an additional penance for her language, though piracy rather demanded it of her. One could hardly be polite whilst pillaging.

The ceremony was mercifully short. A blessing as her sword had become deuced heavy. The reverend pronounced them husband and wife.

"You may…er, that is, if Miss Celia will allow…uh…"

Jack's hand shot out.

The sword clattered to the deck, and he yanked Celia into his arms, fusing his mouth to hers. An overwhelming sense of gratitude and relief assailed her, weakening her limbs. But then those beautiful, talented lips heated her flesh. The taste of his mouth invaded her starved senses, reviving her. She moaned and dug her hands into his hair, holding him to her.

The silence surrounding them registered and her eyes popped open. Rory, Crawley, and Ollie stood just beyond Jack's shoulder.

Crawley nudged Rory. "'E's gettin' better at it."

"Aye," Rory agreed. "Doubt she'll suffer any ill effects a'tall."

"'E must'a been practicin'." Ollie chuckled.

Jack ended the kiss, and before she could react,

tossed her over his shoulder. She squealed in protest and latched onto the back of his coat.

"Quiet." He swatted her backside. "Mr. Spinnakers. Mr. Oliver. Show our guests back to their ship. Mr. Smith, you have the *Lass*."

The men remained rooted where they stood.

Ollie scratched his whiskers. "Ah, beggin' yer pardon, Cap'n, er, Mr. Beaumont, but methinks the orders must come from Miss Celia now."

"Mrs. Beaumont," Jack corrected and spun around so quickly, Celia feared her stomach might drop to the deck next to her sword. She lifted her head, though her vision blurred from the blood pooling in her skull.

"Do carry on, gentlemen." She waved an airy hand. "I shall allow my husband to remain captain." He spun back around, and she clamped her lips together against the motion. Irritated, she added, "For the nonce."

Jack swatted her bottom again.

"Ladies." He bowed and the toes of Celia's slippers briefly brushed the deck. "Gentlemen. I thank you all for coming. If you will excuse us, I must take my wife below and give her a proper beating." He turned and nearly ran down the companionway with her draped over him like a damned toga. She heard the reverend's squawk of outrage behind them.

"Stow yer anger, Parson." Smitty's voice grew faint as Jack made for his cabin. "Cap'n would cut off his arm afore he'd harm that girl."

The door opened and closed behind them. Jack dropped her to her feet and his hands came up to loose the pins from her hair. "Quite a day's work for you, madam. You've pirated my ship, my emeralds, and my freedom."

Celia brushed her hand over the spot where she'd nicked his waistcoat and sighed. "Then I have failed miserably."

His eyes lit with humor. "You are not satisfied? Fie on you wife. What more could you possibly want of me?"

She raised on her tiptoes and wrapped her arms around his neck, pulling his head down to hers. "Why, your heart."

Epilogue

Quiet settled over the ship following Jack and Celia's abrupt exit. Gazes met and scattered as everyone knew what conjugal delights were happening below. Papa harrumphed while Charles Kensington laughed in his face.

Their wives dabbed at their eyes while they spoke with Jack's crew. Certainly, it had not been the wedding the two women had envisioned, but it had absolutely been incomparable. And though the Kensingtons had failed to gain a daughter-in-law, there was some comfort in acquiring a beloved sister-in-law.

The crew of the *Nighthawk* collected poor Reverend Baxendale, and as gingerly as possible, removed him to their ship.

Brett stared at Rianna but kept his thoughts to himself.

Rianna bristled, though if asked why, she would have difficulty answering the question. 'Twas simply that she did not know what to do with herself now that Celia had married her beast and left both Rianna and Brett at loose ends.

The trunks their mothers had packed were hauled aboard the *Bonny Lass* and taken below. Brett's gaze followed their progress with a frown on his face. The man frowned prodigiously these days. She hadn't seen a smile on his lips since…she could not recall.

"Beggin' yer pardon, miss," a tall, dark-skinned man drew her attention and removed his cap from his head. "Me name's Deeds, and I been asked to show ye and the gentleman below afore ye remove yerselves from the ship."

"Below?" Rianna said, her gaze skirting to where the trunks had disappeared.

"Aye," he said and hooked a thumb to the sailor at his side. "Me an' Rory here's supposed ta show ya where yer sister stayed while she sailed wit' us. 'Twill help ye…" His face scrunched and his eyes lifted as if trying to recall.

Rory nudged his arm. "Mend," he prompted.

Deeds' face cleared. "Aye, mend from the fright ye had when yer sister went a'missin'."

"Mend?" Rianna choked. Did her sister honestly think her—

"And ye, sir," Rory said to Brett. "She's asked ye ta escort the lady, if ye please."

"Why should you want him—" But Brett's furious look cut Rianna off. Very well, she would take this ridiculous tour so she could remove herself to the *Nighthawk* and sail back to Falmouth on whatever side of the ship *he* was not.

"Mother," she called, but her mother was preparing to depart the ship with a sailor's assistance.

She waved a handkerchief. "We shall see you shortly, dear," she called and off she went. Her father stepped up next and saluted Rianna before following his wife.

When Rianna turned back, Brett stood at her side. "Come along then, let us be about it."

Deeds bobbed his head and the four of them

crossed to the companionway, with Rory leading the way.

"My," Rianna said as they headed down the steps. "'Tis quite narrow."

Brett took her arm, and she allowed it, for she would hate to stumble arse over teakettle and make a cake of herself in front of these men.

"I am surprised they want us to join them," Brett ventured. "As they, er, seemed intent on escaping us."

"Aye," Rory snickered. "But ye're ta leave straightaway, so 'tisn't much of an inconvenience."

As they walked down the tight passageway, Rianna felt certain 'twas her new brother-in-law she heard laughing. Only they were heading away from the sound and deeper into the ship.

"Just ahead," Deeds assured them from behind when Brett looked over his shoulder.

Rory stopped before a narrow door and opened it. Brett stood aside to allow Rianna to enter before him. She was surprised to see the trunks their mother's had brought stacked up against the wall next to a narrow bunk. The room was so cramped there was little space for a body. Odd, when Celia had described her convalescence, she'd spoken of a bed and desk and even a dining table in her cabin.

Brett had to twist a bit to get his broad shoulders through the door. The two of them barely fit, leaving no room for their companions to join them.

"Sir," Rianna said, confused. "Are you certain my sister—"

The door slammed shut and a key turned in the lock. She and Brett shared a swift look before they both lunged for the door, which caused them to bounce off one another. Determined, Rianna shoved forward again, only to slam into Brett's back.

"What the devil?" Brett snarled, yanking on the handle. "What business is this?"

"Pound on the door," Rianna instructed and let out a yell. "Help! Help! We're locked in."

"Do stop shouting in my ear, Rianna."

"Then you shout."

"I doubt 'tis necessary," he said, running his fingers around the door's edge. "We shall obviously be missed."

"Whyever would they do such a thing?" Given Beaumont's crew was exceedingly fond of Celia, Rianna was unafraid. Of them at least. Brett was another matter entirely. One could hardly avoid a man, and therefore their reckoning, while locked inside a cabin with him. She shivered and rubbed her arms, though her trembling was not from the cold.

"You are chilled," Brett said, because he was exceedingly, annoyingly observant. He removed his coat and draped it over her shoulders. Then busied himself opening one of the trunks. "Aha. I knew this was my trunk. What the devil?"

"What is it?" Rianna moved closer.

"My clothes are inside." He pulled out a folded sheet of foolscap.

Rianna tried to take it from him, but he snatched it back. "What is it?"

"'Tis a letter. From my mother."

"Read it aloud." Though Rianna already knew she did not care for its contents.

"Dearest Children,

We've grown tired of waiting for the two of you to

come to your senses, thus we've taken matters into our own hands. We shall leave Falmouth by coach in a few days and meet you in London. We expect you to use this time wisely and settle your differences, for when we arrive, there will be a wedding. Post the bans immediately upon your arrival as it must occur within the month.

Do not squander this opportunity and disappoint us. Before either of you even thinks to feel outraged, do recall the night you spent alone together. 'Tis time to grow up, children. We prefer you do so before a grandchild is born.

Much love,

Your Mothers"

"Bloody hell," Rianna said with feeling.

Brett clamped a hand over his temples. "They'd have done better to take you out to a woodshed than involve me in this business."

"Of course, you would say that." Her reply had been scathing; though, she admitted to herself, his suggestion did have merit.

"Capital." He made himself comfortable on the bunk. "This shall prove a howling disaster. Imagine my uncle's reaction when he discovers *me* on his wedding trip."

"Bloody hell," Rianna said again and plopped down next to him.

Author's Note

Although this story is a work of fiction, some people and events are factual. Jack and Celia arrive in Charles Town on September 1, 1752. Two days later, *The Great Hurricane of 1752* struck in the evening of September 14th and continued into the afternoon of the next day. How is that possible? Great Britain switched from the Julian to the Gregorian calendar and 11 days had to be eliminated to correct the dates. Thus, September 2nd was followed by September 14th.

The hurricane of 1752 was devastating and extremely destructive to the city and its inhabitants. Most of my descriptions are accurate, including the ship poking out a balcony door and the drowning deaths of the Bedon family. (I have no idea if Mr. Bedon actually had a duck walk.) Given the storm's severity, it's amazing how many structures survived. And as truth is stranger than fiction, Charles Town did experience a second hurricane on September 30th, fortunately without the same flooding or damage as the earlier one.

Pirates were widely condoned in the Carolinas and New England as they provided banned or otherwise excessively taxed goods, though not as late in the century as this book takes place. I've taken a little artistic license here. South Carolina in particular cooled on the subject of pirates after Blackbeard formed a pirate alliance and blockaded the city of Charles Town in 1718.

For those who've been to Charleston, you'll recognize the names Pinckney and Drayton. Would Governor James Glen have tolerated Jack? Likely not, but it made for fun writing. Pink House on Chalmers

Street still exists today and indeed served as a tavern at the time. I chose Tradd Street for Jack's residence as it features some of the oldest homes in the city.

I'd like to thank the Charleston Historical Society for help with my research. There are many books and articles about *The Great Hurricane of 1752* available. If you love history and have never been, I highly recommend visiting Charleston. It's my favorite southern city to explore, and my husband and I have stayed there several times.

Thank you, reader, for spending time with Celia and Jack. I look forward to sharing her younger sister's story, for while Celia is stranded in the colonies, Rianna wreaks havoc in England and drives poor Brett to distraction.

A word about the author…

A love of history and happily-ever-afters lured Jeri Black from reading historical romances to writing her own. She earned a B.A. in Finance after working several years as a bartender. Spending countless nights with a variety of humanity has given her a unique perspective on the attitudes and exploits between the opposite sexes. Her lively, witty characters are a result. Jeri writes historical and contemporary romance. She lives on the west coast of Florida with her husband and forty-year-old box turtle rescue named Klide—who likes strawberries, chasing bunny rabbits, and chewing on her shoes.

JeriBlack.com

Thank you for purchasing
this publication of The Wild Rose Press, Inc.

For questions or more information
contact us at
info@thewildrosepress.com.

The Wild Rose Press, Inc.
www.thewildrosepress.com

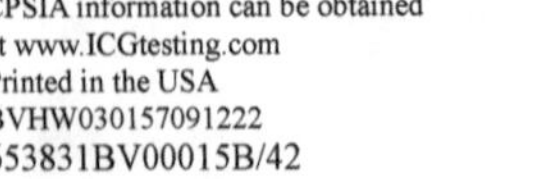
CPSIA information can be obtained
at www.ICGtesting.com
Printed in the USA
BVHW030157091222
653831BV00015B/42

9 781509 246328